EVOKE

a novel

JIM FREEMAN

B

Published by Barkley Press

ISBN: 1-937674-00-2
ISBN-13: 9781937674007

Copyright © 2010 Jim Freeman
Cover design and typesetting: Michaela Freeman
Photography credits:
Front cover *President*: © Sean Locke
Front cover *Computer Circuit Board*: © Pgiam
Front cover *Capitol*: © Alina555
Back cover author photo: © Jana Labutova

Printed in the United States of America

DEDICATION

To Susan and Jack

*"It is as easy to dream a book
as it is hard to write one."*
-Honore de Balzac

BOOKS BY JIM FREEMAN

Novels

EVOKE

Letters from Ceilia

The Island

Non-Fiction

Dick Cheney's Fingerprints

The Dark Side of the Moon
(a five-book series)

Poetry

The Smell of Tweed and Tobacco

Corner of My Mind

Broken Pieces

ONE

"Just because you do not take an interest in politics does not mean politics will not take an interest in you."
-Pericles, statesman (430 BCE)

"And he won't say what it's about?"

"Nope. Not mysterious exactly, Senator but close to the chest, like Romeri always is. Said he'd send his personal jet, dinner at his home, just the two of you and have you back in Washington by midnight."

"Well, I'm not flying halfway across the country not knowing what's on his mind, private jet or no. Can't we settle for dinner here in Washington?"

"At a restaurant?"

"Yeah. Private room upstairs at *LaFrance* if that'll do it."

"Personal dinner, personal jet and you're going to offer a *restaurant?*"

"That's a mite on the *instructive side,* Dan." Senator Fairweather shifted a bit behind the desk and fiddled with his fingers spread out across his lap, pressing the tips, un-pressing.

"That's why I'm your Chief Of Staff, Senator. Romeri's not a guy to piss off. That's why I didn't let him through to you or let Sally handle it. Thought we ought to talk this one out."

"You're right…" He sighed. "How about out at Fairacres? Think he'd settle for Fairacres?"

1

"I think that's what he's been angling for all along, to get an invitation to *your* private home. Make himself guest and you the host."

"Hmmm..." Bob leaned forward, elbows on the desk. "Well, set it up then. A Sunday evening, week from Sunday if he can make it. Otherwise it'll have to wait 'till the end of next month."

"Done."

"I still don't like it."

Robert Billings Fairweather sat the big bay thoroughbred comfortably, alone on the hillside above his hounds, attention riveted on the patch of woods, seeing with his ears as well as eyes. He shifted in the saddle and the bay's left foreleg trembled in anticipation, ears pricked in the direction of hounds.

"Easy, son. We'll be away in a moment."

He moved the coiled whip against the bay's neck, rubbing reassuringly and standing once more in the irons. Master of the Fairweather Hounds, third term Senator from Virginia, Bob Fairweather had history enough to sit easily in the saddle. Yet he was distracted this morning by events, things vaguely beyond his control.

Son of a Senator, grandson of a coal baron and great grandson of a Senator. Bob belonged in that august body not merely by wealth or the whim of politics, but in the only sense that mattered, the tradition of family. Since the Teddy Roosevelt administration there had been a Fairweather in the Senate, except for grandfather's years. Grandpa John built a dynasty from West Virginia coal, a vast empire that stretched into Pennsylvania, Illinois and finally Montana. A base of power and wealth that allowed his son and grandson access to the United States Senate, handing off that access from father to son like the smooth pass of a runner's baton, with never a break in stride.

He steadied the big horse. The days of handing off such power, along with the surety of family empire might well be passing. Probably was…there was trouble in the Senate. Hell there'd always been trouble in the Senate, but the threads of power were coming unstrung and the old steady alliances he'd almost taken for granted could no longer be counted upon. Strange times now, particularly in the EVOKE Committee, *his* committee. Bob was only chairman *EVOKE* had ever had during its ten year history and he'd watched it struggle from a tortured and divisive beginning to a phenomenon that worried him. Truth be known, the whole concept frightened him and he was a man unused to fear. Technology galloping full-out, gaining ground on them all and if hounds were loose in the Senate, he was an unwilling fox.

A horn sounded, his Huntsman's two quick notes, rolling up from the wispy partly obscuring the woods below, a pause, then two more blown on the short brass horn Jerrold kept handy, jammed between the front buttons of his pink coat. Jerrold MacCay had his own traditions and the horn he blew with seemingly casual skill came with him from Ireland, handed from father to son to grandson, three generations of hunt servants and huntsmen all. Endless stories belonged to that battered horn, each dent, crease or scratch in its polished brass a reminder of foxes that ran, hounds that found the line, faltered to lose the scent, found it again and chased off across Jerrold's dreams of Ireland. It was a rare man who handled foxhounds, a dying breed in a dying sport and Fairweather valued his huntsman, sending him off for a month every year to his beloved Ireland after the season ended in Virginia.

How many seasons left, before that final departure? For either of them, truth be told.

The pack broke from the edge of the woods, Ravage in front, noses down, tails furious with expectation. Their muffled cry broke into frustrated yelps until the seasoned old hound found the line once more. Honoring his deep voice they came together, spilling away down the edge of Bottom Creek. Jerrold burst from the woods on the gray horse he favored, his forearm raised against branches through which he plunged, hard on the heels of his hounds. A faded scarlet coat he'd refused to retire over the past ten seasons caught the early morning light as he galloped, coattails flying, blowing the long wavering call of "gone away." He glanced hurriedly up the hill at his Master, pointing in the direction of the streaming pack with coiled whip to let Bob know he'd viewed the fox.

Fairweather booted the big bay horse, cross angling down open meadow, sitting well back in the saddle as they finally slid and scrabbled their way to the creek. Bottom Creek wound around this section of woods and doubled back on itself, finally crossing the Middleburg Road at the old steel bridge. This fox was sure to cross it several times, throwing hounds off scent, but Bob doubted he'd cross the road. More likely to run up toward Miller's place. This early in the game Bob counted on him to hold tight to thick cover and the larger patches of woods.

It was a gamble but he was well behind his hounds now and he'd chance leaving the creek to skirt the edge of the woods, hoping to pick them up again near Miller's. Damn, he might better have stayed with Jerrold rather than climbing that hill, but it was a great vantage from which to watch his pack work. From the corner of an eye as he galloped, he spotted his Field Master jogging around the edge of the woodlot from which the pack had just come, thirty or forty Members in tow in a long uneven line of men in scarlet and women in black. They'd stay well behind the Huntsman and pack and they'd damned well stay clear of the line.

If he guessed wrong about Miller's he'd be all but out of the game and a hell of a way behind his hounds, should the fox make an early break for it and cross the Middleburg Road. Have to chance it he thought and spurred the bay again, the horse reluctant to turn from the voice of the pack. Galloping the west edge of the woods, standing now in the irons, he spoke softly to the horse and his thoughts fled back ten years in the Senate. It annoyed him, this scattering of focus on a hunting morning with hounds running, but there it was.

EVOKE occupied the irritated corner of his mind, a force to be reckoned with now and bargained over. Conceived in the early century technology that brought blinding multiplications of chip-power and in their wake corresponding breakthroughs in computer imaging. Born of that, there were astonishing advances in virtual reality, progress so stunning it boggled the mind. Hell, in most ways it *was* the mind and the implications were so widespread the FCC stepped in. Greasing bureaucratic wheels with uncharacteristic haste and absolute secrecy, they seized licensing, control and distribution, and dragged it kicking and screaming into Bob's Senate committee, slammed the door and walked away. It was almost like having a lock on the drug trade, though none but a few realized it at the time. Mistrustful of market forces, government had effectively snatched all power and control for itself, creating yet another bureaucracy. Irrevocably, that intervention changed Bob's steady and predictable life in the Senate.

The bay horse stumbled, recovered handily to gallop on and Bob's mind snapped back to the matter at hand, listening, aware, making instinctive decisions... then drifting.

True virtual-reality. The real deal, delivered to an implanted chip in the brain. Not some novel theater experience or quirky Internet fascination, the recorded human mind was now as deliverable as an e-book. The final barrier between one mind and another was now no further from access than that chip and a computer. Watching quarterbacks in replay was as passé as network news, as onliners *became* the quarterback, seeing through his eyes, thinking his thoughts, *being him* with an adrenaline rush exactly matching his. Recording as *they perform* and replayed directly into our own minds from a vast and building library of available experience, we *become* for that recorded period *another person*.

Demand was instantaneous and overwhelming, everyone clamoring for an invitation to this perpetual sensory banquet. The public demanded access and eventually they'd get it, he mused, for better or worse. There was of course a price to pay. Everything has its price. The entry-fee worried and wearied its way through endless congressional debate while the country waited, eager for the newest and best ... anxious to be part of that most American addiction, the thirst for whatever there is.

He pulled the big horse down to a trot, cut a corner of the woods and ducked branches that snagged his coat and breeches, taking in the heavy, decomposing scent of late fall. Finally a kind of lottery for access had been agreed, based on random selection of social security numbers. A million citizens came online the first year, nearly four million the second, popularizing the term *onliners* and the numbers were growing at a geometric rate. Everyone who cared to would be online, perhaps in another ten years. Perhaps not, it was hard to tell. There was a fairly simple surgical procedure involved, but an invasive procedure none the less and that's neither as quick nor simple as distributing software.

There were other complicated issues as well, among them the most controversial, morally distasteful and difficult had been the administration's insistence on voluntary male-sterilization as a condition of becoming an onliner. Controversial hell, that didn't half state the case for this science fiction trade-off and a predictable firestorm broke over it, with the Catholic Church and right-to-lifers in the front lines. Population was nudging four-hundred million and the reality of that growth, along with a declining manufacturing base, hard core unemployment and the runaway costs of entitlement programs finally broke the back of protest. Doing nothing, there'd be six-hundred million Americans within another forty years.

But it'd been a long, drawn out, exhausting and bitter struggle. Finally the President threatened to veto the entire legislative package without that all but un-swallowable amendment. Congress predictably sputtered and damn near choked, but finally swallowed. As a result of that power play, the first sitting president in memory failed to get his party's nomination for a second term.

As Chairman of *EVOKE* on the Senate side, Bob Fairweather had personally fought hard against that amendment. All religious considerations aside, in his heart it represented an intrusion into personal life that was way out of government's role, probably unconstitutional and far too basic a right to be ceded to politics. Constitution be damned, he'd lost that battle, as finally they all lost to the argument that the sterilization program was voluntary. And even then, sperm banks were available and access to those personal bank accounts was an option once certain requirements were met. A steady job and long-term relationship allowed a couple to conceive a single child. Four years of unchanged circumstances allowed another, the maximum.

Cries of racism were raised, along with unwarranted but always reliable references to Hitler's genocide. Neither held up under scrutiny and the package finally passed on a voice-vote. No senator or representative was willing to have his personal *aye* or *nay* penned in the record and in both houses barely enough legislators to secure a quorum even showed up for the vote. Nonetheless, it cost a good many lawmakers their seats in the coming off-year election. Then like much of American history, as violent the storm, so quick the calm and life went on, attentions diverted to other matters and the anxious wait began for individual lottery numbers to come up.

He pulled the bay to an abrupt halt, its flanks steaming with effort and excitement, snorting and stamping in anticipation, eager to be off again. Bob listened for the faint cry of his pack and then turned, quartering across the pasture. This was his land they hunted, just over eight thousand acres of rolling pasture, hardwood forest and patches of crop land. Secured for his family through past generations against the encroachment of developers and whatever else lay in wait outside the gates to this private world. The mansion, farm buildings, stables and kennel were known as 'Fairacres.'

Great grandfather built the main house in 1895 and grandfather added massively to it in 1921, four years before Bob's father was born here. After his death, Bob further remodeled and brought the old place up to date in 1990. Times changed and he changed with them, turning the servants' wing into several guest apartments, a more habitable layout for the downsized household help. There were only three live-in staff now, Charles the butler whose wife Amy was cook and a widowed chauffeur, Wilson. They occupied two apartments over the gabled red brick garages and the others needed to run the place were all day help, excepting Jerrold and his wife who lived in the cottage at the kennels. Grandfather kept twenty-one full time staff, but those days were gone forever and probably well gone. There were still twelve in the house or on the grounds every day, but you couldn't call it staff, not in any proper meaning of the word. Sufficient for the constant entertaining that was required of him and Maggie. Sufficient. A twenty-first century word for a nineteenth century property.

Tonight's dinner would be small, requiring only the cook, butler and two for serving. But they'd pull all the stops for Lonny Romeri and the agenda would be intense, something Bob preferred to keep in Washington, separate from Fairacres. Romeri was as tough and straight as a ten-penny nail, a self-made guy who seemed to live only for business. Shrewd as hell and not at all the type to push his way to your dinner table, yet he'd all but forced the invitation and Bob submitted grudgingly in his mind and graciously on the phone. What the devil could Romeri have to say that wouldn't more properly be discussed in Washington?

He pulled up the bay at the crest of a small rise and listened, then smiled. *Damn.* They were indeed headed for Miller's, he'd guessed right. If he and the big horse were quiet and careful they could get to the edge of Miller's woods and watch both fox and hounds break out. Unsnapping the cover of the leather flask case attached to the saddle, he slid the glass out, un-stopped the bottle and took a long sip of the liquor, nudging the bay north along the edge of woods he'd hunted for nearly fifty years.

Only the land is constant, he reflected and his entire life, with the exception of boarding school and Princeton, he'd spent here on this land. Fairweather owned for four generations and soon to be five. He'd walked every inch of it, knew the feel of every field and woods and creek bottom underfoot, looked across the marshland where he hunted ducks in every conceivable kind of light. He'd plowed and planted and harvested each cultivated field as a kid, helping the farm manager and keeping the careful records his father demanded. He knew its intimate smell and sound, the taste of what grew there in every season.

He smiled at the memory of courting Maggie here and the first time they'd made love, a spring Saturday afternoon after a picnic up in the north meadow. A warm, sunny day in mid-April and he remembered how she'd touched him with her eyes and her spirit as much as her physical presence. She still did. A quick afternoon thunderstorm caught them naked on the blanket, their minds only on each other and they'd dressed quickly, laughing in the rain on the way back, guessing they were being scolded by the storm and not giving half a damn.

Jerrold's long wavering "gone away" floated again across the top of the woods and he knew hounds were in full tongue now, hard on a fox that should break from the woods at any moment a little below and ahead of him. He squeezed the bay into a bold trot and headed for the crest of the open, sloping pasture above the north end of the woods.

Standing on the ridgeline, Bob listened to his pack. Working their way steadily through the woods below him, he imagined in his mind the ripple of brown and white, as crossbred English and American foxhounds surged across the forest floor. Jerrold was hunting thirty-two couple this morning, sixty-four well-muscled hounds, averaging sixty pounds apiece, forging their way after a fifteen pound fox. He smiled at the seeming imbalance of power, knowing that the game may be afoot but the odds were very strongly in favor of the fox. Bob grinned at the metaphor of foxhunting to politics. The bay horse trembled again under him, ears pricked and listening.

"There, *there* by God," he murmured. The fox broke from the edge of the woods a hundred yards below in a hot coppery streak, angling toward Beecher's a half mile away. Fairweather held his breath, standing again in the irons to watch the fox pause halfway up the knoll, look back and gauge his lead. Comfortable, he loped easily toward the woodlot. Damn, what a rare view.

He settled back in the saddle, completely contented and immodestly self-congratulatory at his tactic, proud to be in sight of his Huntsman when Jerrold broke from the woods and just the least bit chagrined over his pride. Anyway it felt good, made all the days when he'd guessed wrong worth it. Alonzo Romeri flashed to his mind and he shook off the thought, the intrusion unwelcome in a perfect moment on a near perfect morning.

Seconds later, the pack spilled from the feathered edge of woodlot in full cry, his Huntsman hot behind them. As Jerrold spotted him on the hillside, Bob stood in the stirrups and pointed his whip in the direction the fox had taken, calling the "Tally Ho" of a sighted fox. Jerrold nodded and Fairweather spurred the big bay horse across the meadow to intersect his line. Galloping alongside Jerrold's lathered gray gelding and standing in the irons, the two rode a carpet of hounds in full cry.

"Wonderful run, Jerrold. Sounded like they never really lost him."

"Aye, Master. They're doin' a hell of a job." His flushed face broke to a wide grin. "Hell of a job. That Ravage is a hound just made to find foxes."

"He'll go to earth in Beecher's, I believe. Looked back once, but I think he's had enough."

"Reckon we've all had near enough, Master. This horse's just about caved in. You made a hell of a judgment, comin' out on that hillside."

"Been on this place a lot of years Jerrold."

"Hell of a judgment, anyway."

They put the fox to earth in Beecher's just as expected and Bob decided to ride back the long way, just he and Jerrold and his hounds relishing again what had been a morning of sheer magic. How many more seasons, who could tell? Land was closing in, another big estate up for sale each year it seemed. Middleburg was less than fifty miles from Washington and there weren't but a couple dozen really large places left anymore.

Hunting took land, as well as the money to support a pack. More than that, it needed men and women to love the sport and keep it going, all of those factors in diminishing supply. Jerrold was fifty and in fifteen or so years when he retired to his beloved Ireland, Bob would be seventy-three. He reckoned that would be the end of hunting horns blowing across the early morning mists of Virginia. George Washington hunted his personal pack of English Foxhounds within a hundred miles of this very place, a continuity that spanned the life of the country, soon to be lost. What the hell, it was no longer a jolting two-day carriage ride into Washington anymore either. Bob shoved his leg forward in the saddle, reached down to catch the buckle, loosened the girth a notch or two to let the big bay horse breathe a little easier on the walk home. Hounds heads and tails were down, they were tired too.

Well, whatever Romeri had on his mind would wait, damned if he'd fret over it. A nap sometime in the afternoon would be just the thing to clear his thoughts and freshen his spirits before dinner. There seemed a hidden purpose in this man, not precisely on the square, a veiled agenda, something to be asked and given. Romeri always carried a trump card to play.

Whatever... it had been a grand morning, a hell of a morning.

Alonzo Romeri lay aside the weekly European Sales Forecast, slid half glasses off his nose and let them drop to his chest, gazing out the window. A cloud bank lay like a white down comforter sprawled across Pennsylvania beneath the World Star corporate jet. How different the world was above and below. One was serene, sun drenched and knowable, the other in turmoil and scattered thunderstorms, unknowable. Damn, he'd had an exciting life though and there was still a lot left of Lonny after fifty-one years, pulling the focus of scattered dreams and achievements into position for the next surge. This would be his most ambitious, maybe the final goal in a life of goals.

A self-made man, he reflected, if you can call starting out with the old man's five million self-made. Still trim and slight of build, he was unremarkable in appearance, with a slight hook to an otherwise straight nose framed by soft dark eyes that seldom blinked. Not someone to pick out of the yearbook, not by a long shot. If a movie were made of his life, a little known actor could play his part. He scarcely fit the image of a leading man, more the decent looking but unassuming bit player, who would prove to have a shiv up his sleeve.

He touched the intercom.

"Joe, how long to Dulles?"

"Thirty-five minutes, Mr. Romeri," the pilot answered.

"What's the weather?"

"Broken cloud cover, scattered showers moving through, fifty-six degrees."

A pain in the ass, arranging this damned hat-in-hand meeting with another Senator. Pompous sons of bitches these politicians, but it was the way Washington worked, talking around the subject at hand and feigning interest in side issues. Lay *'em down, I got aces Jack. Whatta you got to beat that?* That was his style and with any luck, he'd be back in Detroit by midnight, time enough to spend the night at the apartment. He swiveled the armchair, got up and walked over to the sofa, stretching out full length, fluffing the pillow under his head.

"Anything I can get you, Mr. Romeri?" The steward glanced back from the galley doorway.

"No, thanks Edward, I'm fine. Just gonna relax for twenty minutes."

He closed his eyes and the image of his father came to mind, sitting behind the wheel of his fearsomely polished Lincoln in the driveway of their big house in Shaker Heights. Honking impatiently, trying to get the family the hell out of the house and into the car, facing another in the endless string of Sunday afternoons that were always spent with Momma and Papa. Italian families. Sundays all over the world were the same in Italian families, spent with grandparents over steaming bowls of pasta. The food always the same, always too much, conversations always the same, always too much, the ritual of family stronger even than the ritual of church. Lonnie grew to despise those Sundays as he entered his teens.

Only now, separated by thirty-seven thousand feet and the thirty-seven years that faded the sepia tones of his youth, did he see those Sundays in a nostalgic wash of color. His grandfather's face was an unclear memory and only the old man's strong, enveloping embrace remained. A one word description of the Romeri family would be *touch.* They hugged, chucked under chins, pinched noses, pulled affectionately at ears, threw arms across shoulders, kissed the kiss that wasn't a kiss but a touch on each cheek, tackled and wrestled and threw each other down with their love. Romeris never shook hands, that was for strangers who weren't family, weren't Italian. He rolled over on his side, lulled by the soft whine of fan-jets.

Papa had made what seemed at the time a hell of a fortune with his Ford dealerships. First one, then another and finally a third, settling the Romeri family firmly into the upper middle class. But they were still Italians, always Italians. Elbows on the table, pass the pasta Italians and that meant you had to take what you wanted, no one was going to give it to you or even give you a straight shot at it.

The summer he turned seventeen, Lonny was top salesman at the Garfield Heights dealership for all three months of school vacation, embarrassing the hell out of the old pros on the showroom floor. That summer the vision formed, took shape in his mind and became a guiding force of what he needed to do. And what he needed to do didn't include college. Been a hard sell to Papa, but his continued success kept the vision alive and growing until finally the old man had a sense of it too and got off his case. He was grudgingly forgiven for turning his back on Ohio State.

The old pros knew a kid couldn't sell cars. Who the hell would buy a car from a kid, a snot-nosed teenager? Lonny was only there because he was the boss's son, to pick up a few pointers from the old pro's shined shoes, fast talk and juggled numbers. Then he'd move on to marry some local wop skirt, have a bunch of grease-ball kids and finally own the company. But they were careful around him, he was still the old man's kid. Still, the wariness was there, born of contempt for a punk who had it made and didn't need the job.

Lonny pulled records of customers who'd bought cars two years back, then three years and called them in the evening at their homes. He told them what their cars were worth on a new Ford or Lincoln and how small the payments would be to move up. He stopped by commuter stations on his way in to the dealership and slipped his card under windshield wipers, with cash offers for the Fords, Chevy's and Buicks on trade-in.

He didn't sell price, told his prospects flat-out they could buy a new Ford almost anywhere in the Cleveland area for his price. But only at Romeri Motors would someone come out to the house, pick up their car and drop off a loaner for regular servicing. Only Romeri Motors would return the car freshly washed, at no extra charge. It worked, worked so successfully that it became the advertised policy of Romeri Motors and led to two additional dealerships. The old pros sucked it up and took another look at the punk kid.

Free loaners and pickup was a hard sell on Papa too, but he convinced the old man the loaners would be mobile billboards and he knew his ability to see things others missed made him different. The difference brought him this plane, along with the chairmanship and controlling interest in World Star. He sat up and moved back to the swivel chair.

"Edward, please bring me a Coke."

"Right away, Mr. Romeri."

The tractor was the start of his real climb, the laughable little tractor.

During Lonny's senior year in high school, his World Affairs class included a semester of study on disadvantaged countries. He still saw images in his mind of horses and oxen pulling wooden plows and barefoot peasants bent over in rice paddies. Unable to conceive why these people had no mechanical equipment, he drove out one Saturday afternoon to the Ford Farm-Equipment dealer in Twinsburg and learned why. The low end, bottom of the line cheapest Ford tractor was nearly twenty-two thousand bucks. But he couldn't get all those Third World farmers out of his mind, behind horses and oxen, needing tractors, millions of tractors.

Lonny didn't know anything about tractors, nothing about nuts and bolts and assembly lines beyond a few obligatory tours of Ford assembly plants and didn't want to know. He knew there was a market in the

Third World and set out to build a tractor to meet that need. It would be, had to be a basic unit he could sell profitably for twenty-five hundred dollars. Twenty-eight hundred, tops.

The prototype took a year to develop and cost Papa two hundred seventeen thousand bucks. It was a grimly beautiful little machine, steel wheeled with no power options, two cylinder and capable of pulling a two-bottom plow. It ran on low grade kerosene, heating oil, low octane gasoline, LP gas and probably Jack Daniels. Lonnie insisted that every exterior nut, no matter the size of the bolt it tightened, be only one size. He then had a wrench of that size fastened under the seat. He drove the engineers crazy with simplification, but they began to see what he was after and he got his way. He demanded a tractor that could be fixed by an illiterate farmer in the field, with a repair manual in pictures. He got that too.

With another half million of Papa's money and their fingers crossed, the Romeri Tractor Company built a hundred units. Lonny set up a leasing program for lease-purchase contracts and a modest international dealership network. International dealership... he grinned at the thought of those early dealers in the cow pens and chicken coops of remote corners of the world. In five years, at age twenty-three, Lonny was manufacturing in nine countries. His neighborhood buddies were busy graduating from Ohio State, Stanford and Penn State, out looking for their first jobs.

Lonny stretched, took a sip of Coke and gazed out the window. Currency he knew would be a problem from the start, but solving that problem was the key reason he wasn't just a middling wealthy and still struggling manufacturer. In those days there was no way to convert zlotys and rubles and a slew of other minor currencies into the hard money that had international value, without currency conversion taking a huge chunk.

Lonnie saw that as another opportunity and Romeri Tractor bartered in local goods, like a peasant in the Saturday market. Train loads of Polish potatoes bought with zlotys from tractor sales, were shipped to Germany and France for marks and francs. The Russian ruble, worthless on the face of it, was spent in Russia, building oil tankers in Baltic shipyards. Tankers that Romeri leased to the Japanese for yen and the Saudis for riyals.

The profit from his willingness to barter, was ten times the margin on tractors. Lonny's network of leasing and import-export businesses grew exponentially from the sales of his little two cylinder tractors and took on a momentum of their own. The beginnings of an international business empire was born of the vision of a seventeen year old kid, who knew enough to bring a loaner to the house if he hoped to sell a car.

Lonny always kept himself operationally aloof, raiding executive talent like a pirate on the high seas and becoming a billionaire a dozen times over in the process. Money was an accidental side issue and he was surprised and vaguely disinterested in the ever growing numbers. He recognized only the power of those numbers, the power to fuel a dream, along with the money to see it through.

"Dulles in five minutes, Mr. Romeri," the pilot announced. "Be a good idea to belt up, there'll be a few bumps on the way through the cloud cover."

"Thank you, Joe. Drop her in lightly."

The Starlight 3000 Joe handled so deftly was simply another profitable appendage. A corporate flying-carpet that Lonny developed in a down aircraft market, another Romeri Tractor scenario covering a need that no one in the industry even recognized. Six years after he'd led the successful takeover of an over extended automobile manufacturer, World Star made a run at Beechcraft. They came up a winner with a loser aircraft manufacturer as the prize. The ups and downs of periodic recession had taken its toll on the corporate jet business and the builders of airframes fought for years over larger and larger pieces of a smaller and smaller market, decimating themselves in the process. Beech was a disaster when Lonny finally got his hands on it and the industry, just like the old pros at the dealership, thought he'd bought himself a pickle. A very expensive pickle was the word on Wall Street.

But he had the staying-power of enormous cash flow by that time and went to work on his concept of a corporate plane. A fan-jet, nearly as fast as a jet, but with better fuel economy, far cheaper maintenance, increased range and the ability to drop into small airports. Comfortable and plain, efficient and cheap by the standards of the day, it sold like hotcakes. Sold like two cylinder tractors and built worldwide markets where there had been none, staggering what little competition remained. Fourteen percent of World Star profits now came from the Starlight Aircraft Company, building corporate and cargo planes in four countries. UPS and Federal Express flew Starlights, as well as a majority of the Fortune 500 and even the major airlines, who found them a thrifty and sustainable solution to feeder routes. He felt the slight snuggling jolt of wheels touching down at Dulles and the plane rolled across the tarmac to the corporate terminal.

If tonight's dinner at Fairweather's estate in Middleburg went well, the flight would be time well spent. If not, there were other ways to get to the Senator. All deals were not winners, even Lonnie's deals. The talent was in turning loss into something that could be leveraged. Fairweather might be a loss as well, it was a ticklish business, but Alonzo Romeri was not a man to be refused access. As long as he had access, a United States Senator was just another potential problem to be levered into an opportunity or defused and shoved aside. He unsnapped his seat belt.

"What's the return schedule, Mr. Romeri?"

"Midnight, Joe. File a return flight-plan for midnight."

TWO

Seven hundred miles and one time zone west, Martin Greene suppressed a sense of excitement tinged with guilt, dread or whatever it was that he'd felt as a youngster slipping into an X-rated movie. Today he'd get the keys to an alternative world, after the negligible bother of a neat bit of surgery would bring him online to *EVOKE*. In his thirty-seven years, Marty'd never been a patient in a hospital, but he'd sure as hell haunted the halls visiting his mother as she slowly and methodically died of breast cancer. The chipped paint and over-waxed tile smell of the old Henrotin Hospital bravely tried to cover the sick and dying smell and never quite made the grade. Those memories left him a little shaky, but this was out-patient surgery and would be a piece of cake.

EVOKE, spinning its illusive numbers had finally caught up with Marty. Even the name was exciting. Evocative all right, fucking by computer and he smiled to himself, thinking what he'd be do when he got home this afternoon. Yesterday's installation of the *EVOKE* online setup excited him and he'd had a hard time falling asleep.

He pulled into Henrotin's parking lot and his stomach churned as he grabbed a ticket and waited for the gate to go up. When his name had finally come up on the *EVOKE* availability list, he'd been sent a form to fill out asking if he were interested and, if so, an appointment would be arranged to see one of the government agents assigned to explain the technology. *Interested?* Shit, he'd been living for the day. The whole country wanted on that list and so far maybe only twenty million made it. There were rumors some people got moved up by knowing someone with clout, but what the hell, rumors were rumors.

They told him what everyone already knew, droning along like he was a school-kid. The *EVOKE* chip implant was entirely voluntary, but not removable once it was done and there was a voluntary sterilization required at the time of surgery, a vasectomy. Truth be known, Marty was quietly relieved to opt out of parenting. He carefully marked 'No' in the sperm bank box. He and Jean fought over that and the fight probably wasn't over yet, but this would settle it for good. She'd just have to live with it.

"Mister Greene?" The nurse smiled up at him, took his admission slip and typed the number into her computer, bringing up his records. "Just have a seat and we'll be ready for you in a few minutes." Marty sat down and felt his stomach flip again and it made him need to pee.

"Excuse me, is there a men's room?" Jesus, he *really* needed to pee now.

"Second door on the left." She smiled again, pointing back down the hall. He came back relieved, but had hardly sat down when a nurse in operating room greens poked her head through the door, checked her clipboard and looked up to call his name. He followed her down a short hall with examining rooms on either side, opening the door to the third room on the left, asked him to strip and put on the gown that was folded on the examining table.

Marty felt suddenly very much alone and wished maybe he'd asked Jean to take the day off as she'd wanted to, to come with him and be there to drive him home. The gown only fastened down the back and as he boosted himself up on the examining table, the plastic was cold on his ass. A little dribble of sweat began under each armpit and trickled down the sides of his ribs. The doctor's pre exam was brief and businesslike, his stethoscope cold as ice and the trickle of sweat kept working its way down Marty's side. No complaints, no previous illness? Never been in a hospital overnight before? Haven't had anything by mouth since midnight? Yes, he understood about the vasectomy. Yes, he knew he wasn't to have sex for three days and to come back in a week for a sperm-count. Yes, he understood that didn't include *EVOKE* sex, as there was no actual orgasm involved in the programs. Yes, he knew neither operation was reversible. Yes, yes, yes and let's get it *over.*

Marty padded down the hall in paper slippers, clutching the back of the flapping gown, then climbed on the operating table in a small and brightly lit room, kicked off the slippers and put his feet in two elevated stainless steel stirrups. Air from the ventilation system blew up his suddenly bare ass. The nurse from the front desk came in, dressed now in scrubs and began to lather his scrotum. She looked over the tented portion of his gown at him and smiled.

"Find the men's room all right?"

Sweat puddled at his armpits and he forced a grin.

"I'm your barber today, at both ends," she smiled. "When I'm done here, I'm going to shave a little tiny place on your scalp. You'll hardly notice it and can comb your hair right over the spot."

He felt her fingers and felt the razor against his scrotum and told himself that everything gets over sooner or later. She wiped him with something that had a rough texture to it. The surgeon was more talkative than an airline pilot, explaining every step of the procedure and though the local anesthetic kept him from feeling pain, he was acutely aware of the cutting and fiercely wished the whole thing over. The doctor snipped and he felt the tug of forceps, heard the cut like gristle on a chicken leg. Marty gripped the table and thought he might faint. He felt stitches being made.

"All done and no need to worry. Just walk a little carefully for the rest of the day and don't lift anything heavy for a few days."

Marty gratefully took his feet out of the stirrups.

"Just lie there and relax a few minutes," the nurse told him, "and we'll take you down for part two. The next will be easier, but when you swing over the edge of the table, keep your legs together and just ease yourself down." He lay there and began to feel he might not faint and further embarrass himself in front of the slim, dark haired nurse.

She was back in ten minutes and helped him down, holding on to his left arm as they walked to the room next door. Still aware of the opening down the back of the gown and still dribbling sweat down his sides, he no longer gave a shit. She helped him up and onto another table, this one supporting a long sliding carriage and complicated padded clamp for his head. A tunnel at the far end would receive him like a corpse in the morgue or a cigar in a tube, performing a brain scan prior to the implant. The nurse talked to him steadily, smiling, adjusting clamps, telling him the scan would take about five minutes and not to worry, she'd be right there while the doctor read the imagery.

She slid him into the tube, the narrow table gliding on smooth bearings and he heard and felt the slight click of the mechanism locking into place. *Piece of cake, lotsa people go through this, be over in no time and drive home.* Marty was drowsily aware of a long series of gentle whirring noises that began at his neck and moved slowly toward the top of his head. Moving back and forth several times, the whirr nearly put him to sleep. There was a slight thud, the locking device un-clicked and Marty felt himself rolling back into a wash of light, blinking after the unsettling darkness of the tunnel. He looked up into the welcome face of the dark haired nurse looking down at him as she unclamped his head.

"When do you do the implant?" he asked, as soon as the chin-strap was removed.

"All done," she said. "That was the little thump you heard just before we brought you back out. Easy, huh?" She put her hand on his. "You can feel for it in just a minute. But for now, lie here and relax, we'll get you on your feet soon and you can go home."

He gingerly felt the top of his scalp and ran his fingers over an inserted chip the size of a fingernail, that raised the skin slightly about three inches above and behind his right ear. This very afternoon he'd slide a headset over this small bump and travel where he'd never been before. His heart pounded with excitement and he could feel its pulsing in his neck and groin, but the sweat was gone. In moments he had become one of the special people, an *onliner*. Still maybe a shipping supervisor at Clark & Anderson, but special, with something even Mr. Clark didn't have.

The nurse came back with release papers for Marty to sign and walked with him to the examining room. He dressed and began retracing steps, back through corridors, down elevators and out into the bright, cold sunshine of the parking lot. Reaching into a coat pocket for keys and parking stub, he glanced at his watch. Twelve-twenty.

By a quarter to one Marty was home and dumped his coat and scarf on the living room sofa to sit in front of the screen, keyboard and modem. He knew he should call Jean, that she'd be worried about him, but the waiting, the years of anticipation were too much to put off. She'd probably be at lunch anyway and the first run-through should only take about an hour. He'd call her after he'd been where he needed to go.

The headset slid easily into place even though his fingers shook a bit and he had to feel for the spot, brushing his hair back with one hand. Marty pressed the 'On' button, watched the screen bloom and the menu come up, just as it had in the practice session. *Welcome to EVOKE. Please make a selection from the pull down menu.*

Marty scrolled, right clicked the mouse and a menu bar appeared, offering selections from ten categories; Adventure, Food, History, Literature, Music, Science, Sex, Sports, Philosophy and Travel.

Marty highlighted *Sex* and the screen popped subsections; *Heterosexual, Homosexual, Bisexual, Lesbian.* Highlighting *Heterosexual,* and *Male-Female,* brought him a full range of further choices. The available selections for where offered hundreds of possibilities.

Marty highlighted *Apartment, High-rise, New York City, Night, Blonde, Blue eyes, Mildly aggressive* and *One hour, fifteen minutes.* He nearly selected *Three hours.* Later... no time for that now. Jean would be waiting for his call.

He felt the tightness of excitement in his upper chest and throat as he pressed *Select.* A rush of blood and heightened senses nearly overwhelmed him, the feeling of being caught in a lie or watching a girl begin to take off her clothes.

The screen sprang at him again in green background, with another message. *You have selected a program with an elapsed time of one hour fifteen minutes. Total time remaining, three hours forty-five minutes.*

Marty highlighted *Start Program,* pushed *Enter* and walked into Cathy's apartment, easing the door shut with his heel and tossing his jacket on a chair in the entry hall.

He'd always liked the formality of the entry. White columns at the door and again at the two steps down into the living room, a perfect contrast to the dark stained parquet floor. He heard the soft strains of Vivaldi washing through the spacious apartment and smiled. Cathy was partial to Vivaldi. The softly lit oil paintings were bold, yet sophisticated, her apartment elegant in the extreme, just as she was. Her sense of restrained style was one of the many things that made her so attractive.

"That you, hon?" Cathy called from the kitchen.

"Yeah, babe."

He walked through the living room, glanced at the lighted New York skyline beyond the floor to ceiling windows that showed it so well from the fifty-seventh floor. Settling on the soft black leather couch in front of the fire, he reached for a cigarette from the silver box he'd given her, his initials and hers sprawled in script across the cover.

"I'll be there in a sec, hon. Just pouring us a couple of scotches." She came into the room with two shorties of Dewar's over ice, wearing a long black wool shift, scoop necked with buttons down the front, a sash at the waist of scarlet and green silk. Setting drinks on the table, she slid onto the sofa. Facing him, she pulled her long legs up, wiggling her bare toes under his thigh. "Mmmmm... I've been waiting all evening, just for you to walk through that door."

He liked the way she styled her hair and dressed, casual, yet with a care for detail that set her apart from anyone he'd known. She looked at him now with eyes that crinkled at the corners, lips lightly touched with violet, catching the highlights in her eyes and deepening them. Anticipating their time together, she touched his glass with hers, taking a sip of the scotch, reaching over to set her glass on the coffee table. Her fingers were long and slender, the nails buffed and unpolished, a silver ring he'd given her catching light from the fire. She wore no other jewelry.

"Damn, you look good in that black dress." He set his drink next to hers on the table and reached down to curl his fingers around the instep of her foot, feeling the warmth.

"You always liked it." Her eyes were more serious now and her hand slid down her bare leg to cover his. "I always like what you like."

She pulled her feet back and swiveled on the couch, all in one fluid motion. Laying her head in his lap, she took his hand to brush his fingers across her lips, settling it under hers, across her throat. He could feel her pulse, watched the flicker of firelight highlight the streaks of luster in her dark blonde hair. He ran a finger along the line of her jaw, then back to lie at her throat.

Cathy looked up into his eyes and gently pulled his face down to hers. Her left hand played across the back of his neck, her long fingers stroking back under his collar. Her mouth opened against his, lips soft and just slightly wet, parting as her tongue flicked across his lips and then probed softly and wetly into his mouth. She pulled away, settling her head against his chest, a wash of silky blonde hair. Her finger traced his throat and chest at the open collar, playing with the top button of the silk shirt, slipping it out of the button-hole.

"You make me so hot, just being around you." She reached back, with her right hand to the coffee table, picking up her glass and the black wool stretched across her breasts as she tipped the glass against his lips. "Scrunch down here on the couch beside me, hon. Slide your legs up under me."

She shifted her body as he slipped out of his calfskin loafers, eased his feet up and stretched out on the butter-soft leather, aware of the mixed scent... a drift of leather and the musky fragrance of skin at her throat, warm and fresh from the shower. Cathy ran a hand through her hair, brushing it back from her face, her left arm under him. She looked into his eyes, probing him with the softness of her own deep blue eyes, green highlights playing at the corners. Cathy's were eyes to get lost in and he was ready to be lost, a wanderer among her smells and tastes, the feel of her slender body against him... enveloped in the music, not wanting to stay on the sofa, not able to leave.

Her mouth was eager, tasted of scotch, searched his, fingers gently unbuttoning his shirt, leg sliding over his. She took his hand and slid it inside the wool, cupping her breast with his fingers , then slipping the top buttons loose, urging his drifting fingers across her nipples, her mouth open now on his neck, his throat.

"Oh, babe ... "

They took a long while to explore the art of their lovemaking, sculpting a stylized form of rapture with long unhurried strokes, smoothing the lines to shapes custom crafted only for each other… polishing the edges of their delight in the moment, burnishing them with the care that makes a moment last, become a timeless thing. The soft light of the fire and lamps turned low, threw shadows across an outline of bare shoulder, the curve of a cheek, the delicate ripple of hair spilling over skin.

Much later, as they lay in one another's arms, she reached wordlessly to press her finger across his lips, slipped from the sofa and ran lightly from the room. He watched her slim body disappear through the doorway to the master suite and, moments later, heard water running. He reached over to the glass on the table and sipped his scotch.

Cathy reappeared in the doorway, naked in silhouette against the light from behind, then crossed the room to stand before the fire for a moment, warming herself, coming to take his hand. She led him across the wall of windows where New York lay in shimmering, winking sweep, then through the doorway and down the hall to her room, where the bed awaited, its great white, puffy down comforter thrown back. She stripped him and hand in his, took him past the bed into the master bath.

Her huge square tub was nearly filled, the polished faucet gushing into a cloud of bubbles. She'd lit candles, dozens of candles, short, fat candles of colored wax, tall, slim tapers of delicate flickering white, some along the edges of the tub, others on shelves or in niches, each playing off against the others in the wobbling, swaying shadows of the bath. She'd arranged two massive bowls of fresh cut lilacs, one at each end of the foaming tub and their heady fragrance filled the room. Vivaldi followed them, even there, and the muted strains of violins carried from the bedroom.

She stepped into the water and lowered herself, graceful body uncoiling into mounds of frothing bubbles, hair up in a quickly conceived French twist.

"C'mon, babe… it's lovely in here. Warm and luxurious and absolutely lovely." She held out a hand and he stepped in, feeling the snow of bubbles cling to his legs, then a warm surge of water as he eased his way into the tub, legs slithering between hers.

"Oh, Cath... God, this feels wonderful... even the water smells of lilac."

He leaned back, stretched his legs alongside hers, feeling warmth envelope his upper body, his hand on her calf, squeezing the ripple of muscle across her soapy leg. Her skin shown radiantly in the wavering candlelight as she scooped water in cupped hands, pouring it over her upturned face, luxuriating in the warm flow down and across her neck and shoulders. Chasing the bubbles, it left her skin pink from the heat, droplets of moisture clinging and catching the glow like oil.

She swung around as she had on the sofa, all in one smooth motion. The water swirled under her, knees pulled up, lying back against his chest. She turned her cheek to his, the fragrance of her hair and skin more pungent now from the warm bath.

"Better?" She wiggled against him and pulled his arms around her waist, her hands over his.

"Better... always better, always the best." He sighed against her smooth wet neck, condemned to her musky scent, fated to hold her, willingly sentenced and destined.

"Ummmm... I feel the stirrings of interest, my love." She wrapped her arms more tightly over his, snuggling against him. "Enough intermission? Are you ready for a second act?"

"Just a few more minutes." He slid his arms over hers. "I'm lost in you, Cathy, as I'm always lost. Let me have my lostness for a moment. Let me lie here with you in my arms in all this candlelight and warmth. Let me wonder if I ever want to be found." He closed his eyes and felt the music become part of them. Holding her, he opened his eyes again, just enough to watch the dance of shadows. Feelings of timelessness consumed his senses, illusive and indistinguishable, beyond his need to define... just out there floating, as he felt himself floating.

"Ummmm... now I feel my own stirrings." She turned her mouth to kiss him, starting at the edge of his jaw, working her way across his cheek to his mouth. "And my stirrings need to be answered, hon."

She broke gently away from him and stood, water and bubbles flooding down her, stepped lightly from the tub and held her hand to his, watching him as he followed. She turned and, not bothering to towel off, ran through the doorway to the waiting bed, leaping to the middle. She pulled her hair loose to tumble across her wet shoulders, holding her arms out to him.

"Come here, babe. Here to me now, all dripping and handsome and hard."

He came to her, giving himself over to the pleasure of the concept of timelessness.

Marty looked at the screen in front of him. *This program has an elapsed time of one hour, fifteen minutes.* He blinked, suddenly aware of where he was. *Total remaining program time available, three hours, forty five minutes.*

Jesus, that was it. One minute there, the next here. No easing back, no heavy breathing, no skin on fire, no sweating like he was with Jean, after they'd made love. Shit, not even the remnants of a hard-on if there had ever been one. Jesus, but the memory was incredible. He had actually *been* there with Cathy. It was fucking unbelievable.

Marty pushed back from the monitor and closed the program, saving it under the reference *Cathy* and the date, an option the menu offered that recorded all his experiential choices. If he went back, it would be the same program. They'd told him that in the counseling session. But he wouldn't realize when he was online that he'd done it all before. When he was *there*, inside her apartment, inside the experience, inside *her*, it was always new, always the first time.

He could elect to win the Grand Prix and know beforehand, when he selected the program that he would win. But once the program started, once he was actually behind the wheel of the car, he'd be racing to win, as the recorded driver had raced to win. His memory, his emotions, his *brain* carrying all the hyped emotions of burning rubber and whining gears, not knowing the victory was his until the exhilaration of the checkered flag. He could win the Grand Prix every fucking day and never diminish the thrill of that flag. Athletes winning events, gourmets dining out, men and women making love, all those experiences *were recorded during the actual event by participants wearing EVOKE chips* and their sensations became Marty's in all their unique character. He *was* those people, the golfers, jockeys, basketball stars and handsome guys on a beach or in Cathy's apartment.

Cathy stayed in his mind, as though they had actually made love. Her voice was still in his ears, the remembered details of her apartment clear in his mind. The feeling and smell of her body still in his senses, as if they had just left each other... as indeed they had.

He was wonderfully relaxed and at peace. A feeling of well-being enveloped him as he got up and walked into the living room, the throb of the vasectomy reminding him of this morning's surgery. Even that memory was no more real than what he had just experienced. It was a small price to pay, he thought.

The sex programs were available only once every twenty-four hours and now he understood why, understood exactly how he would have spent the remaining three hours, forty-five minutes, were he able.

At quarter past two Marty dialed Jean's work number from the kitchen phone. He felt flustered, like he'd just had an affair behind her back.

"Marty, I've been worried honey. I called a little while ago, but there was no answer. You okay?"

"Yeah, fine. I was here but I was messing with the modem and that cancels out everything else."

"Well, I wish I'd gone with you. I should have taken the day off. Haven't gotten anything done here anyway honey, wondering how you are and all that." She sounded unsure of herself and a little unsteady, jittery maybe and that wasn't like Jean. Jean was always in control, always had things thought out. She'd made Marty's life workable in the two years they'd been together, taking the chaos of his bachelor existence and turning it to order. A degree of comfort he'd come to depend on.

"I'll be home a little early hon. Taking off from here at three-thirty. Anything you want me to bring? I guess ice cream won't help where you hurt." She laughed but it was tentative and forced, looking to Marty for a clue.

"Nah, thanks babe, maybe some beer if you get a chance. We're down to four bottles. See you a little after four."

"Okay, I've got to run, lots to do before I can get out of here. I'm really glad you feel all right." She paused, then "Marty?"

"Yeah?"

"Did you do the sex program thing?"

"Yeah."

"Was it . . .?" She paused again, jittery voiced but determined. "Was it... was it good?"

"It was okay. We'll talk when you get home."

He hung up and opened the fridge, pulling a Bud off the shelf and sat down at the kitchen table. Marty took a long swallow, sitting with the bottle in his left hand, his right elbow on the Formica table top. Cupping his chin in his hand, he gazed at the notes and cartoons pinned to the refrigerator door with flowered magnets. The elation and excitement were gone now, washed out of him with his call to Jean. He felt suddenly lonely and abandoned, almost on the edge of tears.

That was nuts. Nothing to feel low about, this was *it*. This was the big day. It had been better than he'd hoped, better than he'd ever dreamed.

The notes on the fridge were in Jean's long, looping, confident hand. A memo to pick up laundry on Thursday, part of a grocery list and a couple of reminders to return telephone calls. There were four *Far Side* cartoons they'd chuckled over, one of them yellowing with age. He drained the beer, fumbled for a cigarette in his shirt pocket. Jean bought him this shirt for his birthday two years ago and it was soft and comfortable from all the washings, felt good against his skin. He liked the feel of it. Marty sighed, stood up and put the bottle in the sink, lit the cigarette and headed for the living room. He ached and needed to lie down for a while. There were no cartoons or notes on Cathy's refrigerator.

A nap would help, he'd be okay after a nap.

THREE

The limousine waited at Dulles, courtesy of the local World Star dealership, but the chauffeur was Lonny's, just as always. Flying up front in the crew quarters, he'd studied the maps to make sure he knew just where the boss wanted to go and how to get to Fairacres with the fewest problems. Checking the current state of road repairs and local traffic conditions, as he'd done for the last ten years, a great job for an unmarried man, even though the hours were crazy. But Frank Thompson had seen a lot of the world this way and though Romeri was demanding as hell, he was also generous and thoughtful. This would be a long one, a night flight back and probably another early run in the morning.

Lonny stepped off the Starlight 3000 stairway, a light topcoat folded over his arm, passed the wingtip's blinking red light and glanced instinctively at the sky. Cloudy, but no rain and warmish for November in the East. Frank had the car pulled up close to the high winged tail section.

"Car looks good, Frank. You know where we're going?"

"Yes sir, Mr. Romeri." Frank held the door and Lonny scrambled in, turning on the reading lamp, reaching for his half-glasses and opening a dark blue calfskin briefcase. "Fairacres is only about forty minutes this time of night. You're due at eight, we'll be a half hour early, you want to stop somewhere?"

"Get us there, Frank and then cruise around the back roads for a while. I want to get a feel for the country. This guy chases foxes with dogs, you know that, Frank?"

"No, sir. Everyone does his own thing, I guess." Frank smiled and slid behind the wheel.

"Damn strange thing to do in this day and age." Lonny pulled the sales reports for Eastern Europe and South America from the case as Frank turned west to Route 50, toward Middleburg.

Sunday evening in Middleburg, he mused. Dinner at eight at Fairacres, with Senator Robert Fairweather and his wife. What was her name? Margaret, yes that was it, Margaret. But Bob called her Maggie, it was all there in the notes. Met her once a couple of years ago in Washington. Good looking woman, strong looking woman, in control but with that certain charming manner that set everyone at ease. Hell of a broad, he guessed.

Might have been a mistake not to bring Carla, but she always looked like such a peasant around money. Christ, she'd been pretty enough when he married her. Twenty-five years and four kids had turned her into a dumpy likeness of her mother. Hell, Fairweather knew this dinner was business and Lonny didn't really belong in Middleburg with a guy who chases foxes with dogs. A dumpy wife wouldn't help, just make him feel all the more remarkably out of place. Not that he wasn't comfortable around big money, he *was* big money, but Fairweather was *old* money and that was somehow always different. Shit, he was worth a half-dozen Fairweathers and he'd sat down with barons and princes and even one king. He smiled to himself, musing about the consultant he'd hired. Couldn't even remember the woman's name who'd tutored him in etiquette. Taught him all the right forks to use, how the courses were served in different cultures. Which wines went in which glasses and the proper form and time to make a toast. Paid her a thousand a day and didn't even get laid in the bargain, but she was worth it. No, Lonny was sure enough of himself... he'd mastered that.

It was that indefinable difference between old money and the kind he had that sometimes threw him a little off stride. Old money, even when it was petering out, tattered and ragged from too many generations of idle use, still somehow found a way to look down its nose at the Alonzo Romeris of the world. Okay to deal with, even necessary and powerful to deal with, but not folks to tag along when you chased foxes with dogs. Fairweather dough wasn't petering out, it was very healthy. He forced his concentration back to the reports, then gave it up and tossed them aside, looking out the window at the passing lights of farmhouses too dark to see. It would be in full fall color out there, nearly a month behind Michigan's already barren landscape. Winding and hilly, not unlike some parts of Ohio, just more intense, with narrower roads, more hidden gates to unnamed homes, maybe some of them huge estates like Fairacres, hiding wealth and power. This close to Washington, careers and countries were bartered away over quiet dinners and fine wine, all that bullshit sequestered behind private gates and long drives. This meeting was damned important, he needed access, needed to keep to the schedule.

Lonny leaned back and closed his eyes, catching a twenty minute nap.

They passed Fairacres, the gates open wide and drove nearly four miles before passing another entry to a neighboring estate, its wrought iron gate closed. Frank turned the big limousine right at every opportunity, circling the estate and finally coming back to its entrance. Marked only by a rural postal box, the lettering *Fairweather* was almost worn away.

"Here we are, Mr. Romeri. Eight o'clock, on the nose."

"Thanks, Frank. Good job, as always. Should be about three hours."

"I'll be here."

The drive was gravel, long and winding as he remembered from the only other time he'd been here, almost two years ago. Bob Fairweather'd been fighting an unusually tough campaign then, against an upstart young attorney from Roanoke, a handsome and powerful speaker with a lot of good ideas, but Bob was the incumbent and that still counted. It'd been a quick trip, to pull together some big money at the last minute and Lonny hadn't paid much attention to the place. But he knew when he left that Bob Fairweather owed him and owed him big. More important, he knew that Fairweather understood the debt, remembering how close he'd come to being thrown out on his ass. The family legacy almost destroyed, by a nearly unknown young prick from Roanoke.

They passed some sort of pens and the dogs put up a hell of a racket, bringing a gray haired man to the window of the small cottage, holding back the curtain to watch the limousine roll by. A quarter mile further, the road gravel changed to a different color and straightened, now formal and tree lined, leading to the huge red brick main residence. Its walled-in entry court was big as half a football field. Frank pulled to the front entrance, wheels crunching on salmon pink gravel and, as he opened the door for Lonny, a butler appeared on the front steps. A flood of warm light washed from the opened door to the car.

"Mr. Romeri?"

"Yes."

"The Senator and Mrs. Fairweather are expecting you in the library. If you'll follow me, please."

Lonny, coatless in the evening chill, followed the butler into the entry hall. It was octagonal and slate-floored, with matched winding staircases to the second floor. They walked down three steps and through the living room, a low-ceilinged room clustered with comfortable chairs and sofas done in muted shades of reds and greens. The fireplace was dominated by an oil painting of an older man, probably Fairweather's father, in a scarlet coat, hunt-cap cradled under his arm. He held a coiled whip and was down on one knee, among several foxhounds. Must have been the only time in his life the old man knelt, Lonny thought. He'd make the son kneel, if he had to. The butler led him across the living room to a pair of massive carved oak doors, opening one.

"Mr. Romeri, Senator."

Lonny walked through the doorway and the butler softly closed the door behind him. The room was nearly twenty by thirty, oak paneled, with bookcases on three walls, the fourth entirely taken up by a sweeping bay window that overviewed an expanse of lawn, bordered by woods, softly floodlit against a darkened countryside. The books had the disturbed and shuffled look of having been read, paid attention to, taken down and put back in regular use. The furniture was overstuffed and comfortable country chintz and pillows, leather, polished tables full of magazines. An enormous Persian rug covered the floor, fire blazing in a stone hearth you could have walked a small pony into and another oil looked down from the mantel. This one was a likeness of the Senator, scarlet coat and all. Astride a massive bay horse, hounds milling at his feet. The Senator and his wife were seated in red leather wing-back chairs on either side of the fire. Bob Fairweather rose to greet him.

"Lonny, it's good to see you. So glad you could make it for dinner."

"Bob, you look well, but remember, I damned near invited myself." He leaned his briefcase against the chair, straightening to shake the Senator's hand.

"Yes, so you did." Fairweather chuckled, remembering that Lonny had very nearly done just that, apparently wanting to talk with him out of the glare of Washington. He'd invited him to Grosse Pointe, knowing Bob would demur and knowing the personal invitation to the Romeri home would require a similar response to a private dinner at the estate. "You remember my wife, Maggie?"

"Indeed I do." He held out his hand to Maggie, who remained seated, but smiled up at him and took his hand more firmly than most women. "You always look lovely and it's a pleasure to see you, even if I intrude on your Sunday evening."

"Nonsense, Mr. Romeri, we're very glad to have visitors in the country."

"Lonny, please."

"Lonny."

They sat by the fire making small talk, the requisite to any meeting of importance. Inquiries were made into family and mutual friends, the current state of foxhunting in Middleburg, golf and skeet shooting in Grosse Pointe. They discussed the difficulty of maintaining apartments in New York, Paris and London, the problems of finding reliable help in all of the capitols of the world where such apartments are kept by those who can afford good servants, or any servants at all for that matter and are often disappointed.

The butler reappeared noiselessly, asking Romeri's preference and bringing scotch for the men and a bourbon and soda for Maggie. The conversation changed course for a time in the direction of worldwide terrorism, skirting most of the issues that would have made the conversation stimulating. Stimulation might have detracted from the issue that brought two powerful men to this paneled library. Fairacres seemed a long way from the world of terrorism or for that matter, the world at all. Dinner was announced at nine.

"Shall we?" Bob rose from his chair.

"After you, Maggie." Lonny held out his arm in a gesture toward the door and followed them, three steps down and back through the living room. Three steps up to the stone floor, across the entry hall through arched and open doors into a blaze of candlelight, green damask, polished sideboards, crystal and silver.

The message wasn't lost on Lonny. Formality would be the note for this dinner, an occasion where the three of them would have been much more comfortable and intimate at a small table in the library or sun room. Not a black-tie affair, he'd had his secretary check that out, although with three or four more guests it probably would have been. The table was set for neither comfort nor intimacy, but rather to impress and acknowledge. A blazing dining room proclaimed that you are an important guest, there's something serious on your mind that we'll get to later, but you're on my turf now and I have power as well as you. Bob held a chair for Maggie. The dining table, easily capable of thirty, had been reduced to a more modest six feet long. Places for three were set at the far end and a fire in yet another fireplace lent the candles moral support. Polished silver and cut crystal mirrored and amplified the soft light.

An excellent mussel soup was served, with white wine and easy conversation about the increasing interest in International Sporting Clays, an outgrowth of skeet and trap-shooting. Lonny served as United States Chairman. A sliver of cold poached salmon followed and another white wine, the conversation turning to Maggie's interest in the U.S. Women's Ski Team, their home in Aspen and her work on the board of that organization. She would be in St. Moritz just after Christmas for the first of the Women's European Cup

Races and had high hopes for the young team. They enjoyed rare venison tenderloin, with a dry red wine and the discussion turned to the powers that ruled in the Senate, including Bob's chairmanship of the *EVOKE* Committee, his membership on Ways and Means and Defense, as well as a close friendship with the President. Bob downplayed any intimacy with the President, but Romeri knew they were long-time friends personally as well as politically. They talked of their mutual friend, Preston Alberts, the Senior Senator from Michigan and next in line of seniority for Bob's seat as Chairman of *EVOKE*. Finally, they were getting to the real meat, Romeri thought, catching Maggie's eyes and smiling.

Along with the chocolate soufflé, the conversation turned, as it so often does when issues are being avoided, to children. Bob and Maggie had a son, a partner at a law practice in Richmond and a daughter, who'd left Foxcroft abruptly to travel in Europe, accompanied by a man they scarcely approved of, a freelance photographer easily twenty years her senior. Finally, decaffeinated coffee for Bob and cappuccino for Maggie and Lonny, who advanced a mild and healing view of young people and how they were usually okay, despite all the parental fears.

"I've a rather early day tomorrow, if you gentlemen will excuse me?" Maggie rose from the chair, extending her hand to Lonny. Remarkably graceful, always warm and charming, he thought and his mind flashed for a moment to Carla, the contrast painfully obvious. Thankfully, he'd left her in Bloomfield Hills.

"Good night, dear," the Senator said. Bob and Lonny both rose.

"Maggie, you are, as always a marvelous hostess and I've enjoyed myself enormously. Good luck with the ski team. Be sure to call on me for a donation." Lonny held her hand and she offered her cheek for a quick brush of his lips.

"Do come see us again, Lonny and I will indeed chase you for money." She smiled warmly, the corners of her eyes crinkled. "Don't you boys stay up too late." Then she was gone.

"Brandy, Lonny?"

"That'd be fine." Thank God Bob hadn't sat back down. Lonny needed to get away from the stiffness and formality of the dining room. He edged a look at his wristwatch. Ten thirty. Damn, time to get down to cases. Enough of this bullshit chit-chat, time to get to why he was there and then get the hell out and back on the plane.

"We'll have brandy in the library, Charles."

"Yes, Senator." The butler moved off and the two of them strolled back towards the library, settling on either side of a refreshed fire.

"Well, what's up Lonny?" Bob raised an eyebrow in inquiry, smiling. "You didn't fly all the way down here to try my venison or talk about kids or skiing. What can I do for you?" He leaned back in the leather chair and crossed his legs, signaling the end of formality and the beginning of what they both knew was to come.

"Straight out?" Lonny was relieved that there'd been no extension of amiability. Friendly enough fellow, this Virginia gentleman, but he appreciated a man who could get down to business and Bob had put it right on the line.

"Straight is always best for whiskey and business. It's only politics that require soda and ice." Bob smiled again and leaned forward in his chair, elbows on knees and long fingers locked together, looking up at Lonny, who stood and moved to the fireplace. He clasped his arms behind his back, like a teacher in a lecture hall, warmed by the flame and the brandy.

"Bob, we need commercial access to *EVOKE*, we need it badly and we need it soon."

"You know that's not possible." There it was, the reason for all the secrecy and why Lonny had chosen Middleburg to make his pitch. A guest in the house, rather than a corporate chairman in his or Bob's office. "We've been over all this before, in one form or another. I've never had you pitch me personally, but God man, your lobbyists have been trying to run down this same rabbit for years." He paused. "Ever since the very beginning, *EVOKE* promised publicly that it wouldn't get mixed up in commercial activity. That was a founding principle, a public pledge." Bob leaned back in the chair, re-crossing his legs. His body language belied a confidence and ease he hardly felt.

"First of all, Bob, anything is possible and politics is said to be the art of the possible." Lonny squatted down now, taking the poker from the rack and shoving idly at the logs, showering sparks up the flue of the huge chimney. A slight smell of wood smoke drifted into the quiet library. "This is not some overlooked advertising opportunity we want to pursue."

"I've got to tell you, Lonny, it sounds a helluva lot like one." Bob sipped his brandy. He knew better. Chairmen of huge multinational corporations didn't make pitches like this unless something was seriously amiss.

"Sales in the automobile division at World Star have been steadily dropping... nearly half a point a month for a year now. It's not a recession, it's more structural than that. And don't blame Detroit, the Japs, Germans and Koreans are down an equal percentage in America. This country has had pretty good times for the last seven years, since your buddy got in the White House. Trucks, heavy equipment, computers, aircraft and all our leasing divisions are doing okay. It's just automobiles and it's just in the United States. European auto divisions are doing well."

Lonny crossed to the facing chair, sat down and picked up his brandy, swirling the amber liquid and taking a sip. "We've had a whole focus group that answers only to me chasing this one, Bob."

"And?" Fairweather straightened in the chair, picked up a letter opener from the side table, turning it over and over in his hands, feeling the weight. Maggie had given it to him, the handle a standing fox, in top hat and pink coat.

"The drop in sales figures corresponds almost exactly with the percentage of population coming on the *EVOKE* system. Too mirroring a percentage to be overlooked just aren't buying cars." He leaned forward, cradling the brandy glass in both hands, watching Fairweather. He let the words hang, then settle in. Romeri knew when to lay it out and when to shut the hell up.

"That's a pretty strong statement, Lonny. The implications are enormous."

"I know."

Bob sighed. "We knew we had a potential tiger by the tail when this whole system became available." He held the opener by the blade, slapping the fox against his palm, emphasizing his words. "That's why the government stepped in so quickly. We were afraid of it, Lonny. Some of us still are." Bob's mind flashed back to the endless warnings he'd given in committee about *EVOKE's* repercussions among consumer buying habits and its long-term impact on the economy. Now, here was Romeri, saying it had already happened and looking to the source for a cure.

"It's not only World Star, Bob, but I worry less about Coca Cola. I'm paid to worry about my company and my company is World Star and that's why I'm here." He looked up at the Senator's face, reading his concern and relaxing just a bit. This was going okay, he thought. Just two guys worrying over a solvable problem, away from the wary formality of a blazing candlelit dinner.

"When we saw the correlation, we turned our guys loose on other consumer goods. Seems like anything necessary, deliverable and convenient is up. Pizza and frozen dinner sales are off the wall. Tourism, automobiles, fashion, furniture, even clothing are all hard hit." He reached into his breast pocket for a cigarette. "Mind if I smoke?"

"No, please do."

"All the things you'd expect to be up and down when people are busy elsewhere fall right into the pattern. It's no accident. It's almost a textbook response." He lit the cigarette and inhaled deeply. "Probably *will* be a textbook before long. You're going to have a whole parade of guys in to see you, Bob, but I wanted to get here first. I want to let you see what I know to be the case and get some help before this thing gets out of hand and we find ourselves in a major and unstoppable depression." The words were forceful enough and he was quiet... waiting and quiet. He wouldn't press this issue into panic peddling and weaken his case. Bob seemed to want more, but he waited him out.

"What do you have in mind, Lonny, short of opening the gates to your advertising people?" He watched the smoke from Romeri's cigarette, drifting in slow spirals, until it caught the draft of the fireplace and was sucked up the chimney, illusive as words in a conversation. "I know you. You've thought this through and came here with a goal in mind, not just a general complaint."

Lonny let the silence hang for a few moments. Okay he thought, here it comes Senator, the case we're here to get down to. "I have in mind the same thing they've been doing in Hollywood for decades. Product in the background." He took another long drag on the cigarette, feeling the bite of the smoke in his lungs, stubbing out the butt in a heavy crystal ashtray. "Nothing heavy handed. When some guy gets laid on *EVOKE*, we want him driving to her apartment in our latest model roadster. We just want our product in the experience." He leaned forward. "*Only* our product." He glanced at Bob, looking for his reaction. He wasn't going to get *that* and he knew it. It was a concession for later.

"That's pretty much what I thought." Bob eased out of the chair, poked at the logs in the hearth, straightened and turned back to his guest. "That's a precedent that will open the floodgates and put Congress in the advertising business."

"It doesn't have to."

"How so? How are you going to stop a constant trail of supplicants just like World Star, all beating a trail to our doors? All asking for the same access, for the same good reasons and making the case for fairness as well."

"Congress doesn't make up these little ad campaigns that are so popular. They're done in studios. Congress just oversees the finished product through the FCC and approves or disapproves, like they should, like the public expects them to." He clasped his hands between his knees and leaned toward Bob, playing the teacher once more. "Let the whole thing happen at the creative level. Let market forces work as they've always worked when government leaves them alone." He glanced up. His last remark was pretty close to the edge, pretty close to stepping on the Virginian's toes and he knew it, but it needed to be said.

"You giving me a history lesson, Lonny?" The toes had been stepped on and pinched.

"Maybe." All right Senator, he thought, if that damned shoe fits, wear it and don't complain. Twenty-four percent of World Star's costs were tied one way or another to the expense of government regulation and much of it in his judgment was meaningless, not only meaningless but a cost foreign competition didn't have to bear.

"Lonny, I know your position and I must say in some ways I have a helluva a lot of sympathy for it. You've always felt that government was fighting business, that it was on the wrong side and ought to run itself more on the Japanese model." He fiddled with a paperweight on the mantel. "Mind if I try one of your cigarettes?"

"I didn't know you smoked." Lonny reached in his pocket and held out the pack.

"I don't very often. Seems this is a time to smoke."

"Well, Bob, I don't want to beat dead horses and I didn't come to bring up that issue. But the fact is, the Japanese are an old story and now the Koreans are kicking our butts, the Chinese right on their heels. The whole Pacific Rim is aflame with market innovations that we won't even recognize are there in the States." He lit Bob's cigarette and reached for another himself. "The Japs have their own version of *EVOKE* and some say it's ahead of ours. So do the Koreans and both of them are full of product." The lighter flared. "It's working for 'em, too. Their consumer goods sales are doing just fine in their home markets, even up a bit in most of the places ours are down."

"But look at the decades of scandals in their governments." Bob reached for the decanter of brandy, pouring an inch for Lonny, an inch for himself. The cigarette made him a little lightheaded. "When business gets too close to government, they both suffer."

"Bullshit, Bob. Washington is *run* by lobbies and always has been, as long as you and I've been around. Lobbies run on money, corporate money and so do elections for that matter, I shouldn't have to remind you of that. They're just the long arm of business and we both know it." He stood now, back to the fire, cigarette in one hand, the brandy glass in the other. "We're not asking for anything we haven't had before. No new precedent, just access to a growing part of the market." He took a sip of brandy.

"Sooner or later, the whole country is going to be wired, Bob. We better solve some of these problems while we can still fine tune them. While, I might add, we still *have* a market to fine tune."

Bob looked at Romeri and knew it was time to wind this thing up, that everything he'd come to say was said. "I don't want to say I'll think about it, Lonny, because that makes it sound trivial and it's not trivial." He tossed the last third of the cigarette into the fire. "You *know* I'll think about it and very seriously. It's a problem we have to deal with and it won't go away, but I've got a committee to handle and I'm only the chairman." He respected this slight, black haired Italian. He was a tough cookie, but it was a fair request and he'd put it fairly with no reminders of chips to be cashed in. "You have any figures for me from your focus group?"

"You know I do." Lonny reached for the slim, polished briefcase. "This isn't something I'd like seen by anyone but you Bob, but it's all here and I think you'll find some interesting reading." He handed the Senator an inch thick bound copy of a report, marked 'Confidential.' Bob sighed and slid the report on the coffee table.

"Lonny, give me about a week and let me look this over and make some inquiries on the Hill." The two of them walked to the front entrance, through rooms less brightly lit now. The butler appeared as if by arrangement to open the massive oak entry door.

"Your car is waiting, Mr. Romeri."

"It'd better be, Charles. Thank you." He turned to face his host.

"This is important Bob, maybe the most important conversation we've ever had."

"I know." They shook hands. "Call me a week from Monday, Lonny, or would you prefer I call you?"

"I'll call. My regards to Maggie." He walked down the broad steps to the car, where Frank held the door. It was just past midnight.

FOUR

"Marty?" Jean called from the front door and he heard her throw the keys on the kitchen table and set something down, probably beer and groceries.

"In here, babe. In the living room." He was cranked all the way back in the recliner, in the same shirt and faded blue slacks he'd worn to the hospital. She ran in, threw her coat on the couch and sat quickly on the arm of the recliner, taking his head in both her hands and kissing him wetly on the mouth. Her cheeks were still cold from the two-block walk home from the bus. But her lips were warm and he felt a bit overpowered, a bit too quickly smothered in concern.

"You okay, hon? God, I didn't get a damn thing done in there, today. Joe and Ed were both on my ass about some printouts for next month's sales projections and all I could think about was you getting that frigging operation and me not being there. Do you hurt? You want a beer? Tell me all about it." Jean looked at him with the same look as if he'd just hit his thumb with a hammer, words tumbling out in one long stream. Questions, with no time for answers before more questions and it made him grin.

A sudden spill of words was so like Jean, quiet most of the time but then the words came spilling, times when all the unsaid shit came like too much whiskey and she threw up the words, purging her mind. She drew back to look at him and ran fingers through his hair, but there was a hint of fear in the corners of her brown, nearly black eyes. Marty knew the fear, the same old fear they'd talked around the edges of ever since he'd gotten notice his name was up for *EVOKE*.

Jean was tall, nearly his height and if not a head-turner on the street, still someone he was proud to be with and probably a notch or two above what he'd ever expected from life. Still... there was the hint of mothering and he'd had a mother and he'd buried her. Jean wore medium length brown hair she helped along a little, highlighting it in streaks where she combed it back from her forehead. Her lips were still wet and glistened at the corners from the kiss. But now she bit her lower lip, holding it pensively in her teeth and Marty wondered, as he often wondered, why she was still here.

She worried about her shipping supervisor live-in boyfriend, with the dull throb between his legs and computer chip under his scalp. She brought home groceries, insisted on splitting the rent, did most of the cooking and all of the cleaning, took him to bed and made love often enough, sometimes over-often but shyly and predictably. Not like Cathy'd made love to him just hours ago, not with candlelight and music. Whose fault was that? He could buy a candle, slip on a CD. Maybe there were no whispered words and murmurings and urging from Jean, maybe no proudly showing him her body, but their love-life was pretty good even so and maybe good enough.

Pretty good for a shipping clerk. They called it *traffic supervisor* at the office, but they called garbage men *waste management technicians* these days and they were still garbage men. He put his arm around her waist and pulled her, carefully, down onto the recliner with him, against his hip, where it didn't hurt.

Jean was long-waisted and just a little pudgy in the middle, but at thirty-five her body still had a smooth tone that Marty seldom tired of running his fingers over. She blushed when he caught her naked coming out of the shower or in the morning if they'd made love and left their pajamas crumpled on the floor. She had good breasts, a little on the plump side too but that was okay for breasts, but he sometimes wished she wasn't so shy about her body, always making love to him in the same rhythm and sequence. Kissing and then letting him slip his hands up under her pajama top to feel her breasts, then letting him suck her breast, while she slipped both their pajama bottoms off. Spreading her legs as he adjusted himself over her, always underneath him.

Always in near silence, except for the *Oh, Marty*, as he entered her. Always pulling her bottoms up and her top down afterwards, except on the few occasions when Marty stripped her and held her away from the pajamas, making her sleep naked in his arms and blush at being naked in the morning light.

She seemed ambivalent about their lovemaking, never reaching for him in bed. Never suggesting in a whisper over dinner out, or at the end of a movie that they get home quickly and fuck. But she never turned him down. Jean settled against his hip and he worked his hand up under her sweater. She cut him off, closing an elbow against the wandering hand, reminding him he couldn't do that for three days after the operation. Shit, Marty thought, the doctor said no sex, not that he couldn't feel her up.

She rattled questions at him, then laid her head against his as he told her about the routine at the hospital, how he'd sat on the cold table wishing she'd been there. About the nurse, shaving his balls and the 'thunk' that drove the chip into his head without his even knowing it. He felt her fingers tighten against his leg when he told her that. He uncurled them and took her hand, running it lightly over the slightly raised spot on his scalp. She shivered as she touched it and asked him if it was sensitive. No, he said, it was just there.

Then they were quiet together, her arm around him and her head against his neck. They sat for a long while, not talking, until his hip began to hurt from the pressure of her body against it. He slid over in the chair, letting her butt settle. Then the mix of their positions got all wrong and he grunted her off the chair.

"How 'bout a couple of beers, babe? I'm still sore as hell and I don't think I want to get up for a while."

She went to the kitchen and he closed his eyes, hearing the refrigerator door open and close, bottles rattle against the counter top, cupboard door opening and the clink of glasses, door shutting again. Then, the predictable hiss of popped caps and the rattle as they dropped into the white garbage can with the flip lid that annoyed him when it wouldn't stay up. A pre-flight check list of asking for a beer.

Life was so fucking predictable. He knew every sound that would come from the kitchen before it came. Knew the precise rattle as Jean got TV trays out of the narrow cupboard next to the pots and pans. Then he heard it, anticipating the sound of one, then the other bottle, one, then the other glass set on the tray and Jean's steps down the hall. Metal capped low-heels clacked against the wood floor. It would be one of the black trays or one of the gray trays. He bet on black and won... and sighed.

"You okay?"

"Yeah, fine."

"You sure?"

"Yeah."

She set the tray on the coffee table. She'd pour his first, down the side of the glass, the way he liked it. Then she'd pour hers right down the middle, building half a glass of foam and getting rid of the bubbles that made her burp. Right again. He knew with the same certainty that before the night was over, they'd talk about kids and the damned vasectomy again.

The conversation drifted into silence and Marty flicked on the early news with the remote, while Jean got him another beer and settled down with a needlepoint she was trying to finish before Christmas. He watched with his eyes half closed, his thoughts wandering back to the New York apartment and Cathy. Jean started dinner. Stir-fry chicken. He liked stir-fry chicken.

After dinner Marty told her he thought he'd get on the computer for a while, trying to sound casual about it like he was going to take a shower or something. But his voice sounded strange to him from the inside of his head and he wondered if it sounded strange to Jean. She looked at him with fear in her eyes, like a wounded bird.

"The Country Music Awards are on tonight. You usually enjoy that. Don't you want to watch them with me first?" She cleared the plates, took them to the kitchen.

His mind raced. The awards show came on at eight and wouldn't be over until about eleven. He was nearly frantic to return to those other worlds that were just sitting there in the box, waiting for him. But they went to bed at ten-thirty on week nights, just after the news. He and Jean both got up at six and she'd be even more pissed if he went on computer at eleven. Particularly right there in the bedroom, off on what she was sure to think was some fuck trip while she lay in bed, not six feet away.

"Nah," he called to her in the kitchen, "I'll only be on a little while. I'll watch the last part with you." He hadn't told her about the lockout on the sex menu. Might as well keep some things to himself, look like he had an interest in other stuff. She came in from the kitchen and he eased out of the chair, still tender as hell between his legs and started down the hall.

"Marty?"

"Yeah?" He stopped at the door and glanced back.

"Get fucked."

She didn't look at him, staring intently instead at a blank television screen. There was no humor in her voice and she *never* used that word. In two years, he couldn't ever remember her using that word. His balls throbbed and he thought about coming back to be with her, but it was a no-win situation at this point. He knew her well enough to know he was already too late.

Fuck. He walked down the hall, hurting more than the doctor told him he would. Shuffling a little to ease the throb, he passed white painted walls with smiling photos of him and Jean, taken in Jamaica last winter. Their first real winter vacation, smiling at each other from the big porch of the Ocho Rios Inn. Wearing floppy straw hats, a native creation the hotel gave its guests to wear on the beach. Passing the kitchen, he glanced at the smear of multicolored magnets across the refrigerator door, dinner dishes still on the counter, the door ajar. Jean always washed the dishes right after dinner, unless she was pissed.

He stopped at the bathroom, reached into the mirrored cabinet to shake a couple of aspirin out of the bottle, washed them down with water cupped in his hand. He wiped his hands and mouth on her bath towel and noticed the wire that barely held the shower rod together. He'd promised to fix that last weekend. *Fuck.* He snapped off the light and turned down the hall toward the bedroom.

The modem sat on a small fake Queen Anne dressing table in the corner, its built in screen and keyboard promising what? *Everything* was what! Shit, didn't she realize that? The whole fucking country was trying to get at this system and she wanted him to watch the Country Music bullshit.

EVOKE crowded the table, sharing space with a framed picture of Marty and Jean at her brother's wedding, last summer. Him in a rented morning-suit and her in an almost electric blue bridesmaid's dress, with puffy short sleeves and a low neckline. Wearing pearls at her throat and a little bunch of flowers in her hand, she looked adoringly at Marty and slightly down at him from high heels as he gazed straight into the camera.

There were two other smaller framed photos from the wedding, one of her parents, her father looking self conscious in his formal wear, arm around her mother's waist and one of his dad. The old man looked sad, all by himself and sort of unstrung without his wife. Thirty-three years together, Marty thought. *Long time.*

The rest of the table was strewn with perfume bottles, though Jean seldom wore perfume and the big square glass ashtray that held all the crap Marty tossed from his pockets when he undressed.

Marty pulled down the *Save* menu and changed *Cathy* to *NYC-57*. Stupid to leave her name on the screen, even though it locked out when the lead wasn't plugged onto his head. Jean could always walk past when it was up and *Cathy* wouldn't make his life any simpler.

He knew from the training sessions that when he was online, his eyes were closed and the screen was blank, his body showing no sign of what was coursing through the chip in his head. Still, it was foolish and he knew that once Jean got over being pissed, she'd want to see the screen and the selections. Her Social Security number was in that grab bag as well.

Marty double clicked *NYC-57* and the message came immediately, *This Selection Is Locked Out Until 10-14 at 1315 Hours.*

He opened the full menu, double clicked *Sex* and got the same message. He looked over the rest of the selections and as he highlighted *Travel,* the screen brought up one hundred twenty countries and he chose

Mexico. Then *Cancun* and the menu gave him an unexpected choice of *Alone* or *Accompanied.*

He selected *Accompanied* and was given the same choices as earlier in the day. Shit, maybe he could get laid through a different program. He entered *Beach front cottage, Female, Blonde, Blue eyes* and wondered... hoped it would be the same Cathy. On the TV in the living room, he heard *"Live, from Nashville, the Country Music Awards ... "* and pressed *Start Program,* looking out across the vibrantly blue green Caribbean.

"Hey hon, I've got a couple of rum punches and they said we could take the glasses if we promised to bring them back." Vikki called to him, skipping lightly across the hot sand from the direction of a thatched beach bar, carrying two huge glasses of rum, orange juice and honey, shaken and poured over ice. Her beach sandals were clutched under one arm. She wore a white bikini, in stark and heart stopping contrast to her tanned body. Her long blonde hair was now in a pony tail, sunglasses shoved up across the top of her head.

"Thanks, babe." She held the glass out to him, stooping to drop her sandals on the beach blanket spread under their umbrella. "C'mon," he said, "let's walk the beach, like we always do before dinner."

She took his hand and walked to the edge of the water. She ran into the thin surf, still holding the glass, laughing and splashing her long tan legs, running back to throw an arm over his shoulder. Resting her head against him, they walked into the sun, low now in the sky but still throwing heat that worked its way through their skin directly to the marrow of the bone.

A mile down the beach, curving out into the Caribbean in the direction of Cozumel was the point of beach they usually walked. Sometimes they'd watch the sun drop behind the palms, turning the sky from white blue to deep blue, to shades of streaky purple blue. Then, in a last guttering wave goodbye, to blue-black and the first early stars. A languid wave crested and just before it broke, a school of flashing silver fish caught the sun, swimming right across the crest. His chest and arms were bronzed and warmed, as much by her as the wavering sun.

He set his glass carefully in the sand and ran into the water, diving shallowly into the third wave. He felt the saltiness in his nose and eyes and mouth, rolling to his back and watching Vikki follow him into the warm, buoyant, heavenly rolling water. She swam easily alongside him to the sand bar where they stood and laughed at their happiness. Splashing each other like youngsters, they swam together back in to the beach. Where they sat, watching a sixty or seventy foot ketch round the point, headed for an anchorage at Cancun. Its billowing spinnaker filled with the steady south wind, stripes of red, pink, purple and plum, followed by three white sails. They wondered what it would be like to sail around the world on a boat like that and felt sun drenched and giddy, watching it out of sight. Pulling her to her feet, they walked hand in hand back toward the palm roofed beach cottages. He sat on the cool tile porch, looking across the beach through a small island of palms while Vikki showered and changed for dinner.

She reappeared in sandals and a long flowered print dress, a clinging, off the shoulder dress, her hair swept back behind her ears and down her back. He quickly showered, changing to white slacks and a deep blue linen shirt.

Dinner was served on the broad, red tiled terrace of the dining room, overlooking the bay. Framed by coconut palms, a scene so typically Caribbean it was featured in the resort brochure. They both ordered fresh tuna steaks, elegantly served with rice, fresh pineapple and a chilled white wine. The rice had a local red sauce, piquant with spices he'd never tasted. Coffee was dark and rich, already heavily sweetened and served in demitasse.

A cruise boat lay at anchor a quarter mile from the resort pier, lights strung from bow to stacks to stern, rows of cabin lights dappled across the length of the hull. Midway through their second cognac, a full moon broke over the water, rising from the horizon like a huge copper disc, cutting a long, shimmering path to their table. They danced on the terrace in the moonlight.

59

"... the winner of this year's award for Best Direction of an Album by a Male Vocalist goes to ... "

Marty stared at the screen, distracted by the sound from the television in the living room. *This program has an elapsed time of one hour, twenty minutes. Total remaining program time available, two hours, twenty five minutes.*

It wasn't Cathy, but Vikki he realized. He'd been unable to get her back, but he hadn't gotten laid and hadn't even tried, even though she was a knockout in the bikini. *Of course not.* It wasn't in the frigging program, you dummy. These are actual experiences, you can't just program them to suit yourself. You want Cathy, you get her tomorrow.

He walked into the living room in bare feet and sat beside Jean on the couch. She looked at the screen, arms folded across her chest like it was the most interesting program she'd ever watched.

"Any of the big stuff been awarded yet?" He reached over and fiddled with the hair at the nape of her neck.

"Not yet." She squirmed her neck away, but he saw her legs relax just a little and she unfolded her arms. "You all through screwing around?" She still looked intently at the television, even though it was showing a beer commercial.

"C'mon, babe, ease up." His voice was soft and his fingers returned to the nape of her neck. "It was fun and sun in Cancun and no screwing around."

"*Sure.*"

There was sarcasm in her voice, but he got a glance this time and then she reached over and slipped her arm through his, leaning up against him.

"Oh, Marty, I'm so damned jealous of that machine and it's only just come into our lives." She was spilling words again. "I'm envious of you having that kind of access and I'm bitchy 'cause I don't have it and I'm scared to death you won't love me anymore. I'm terrified of all those perfect women and the things you do with them. Most of the time, I panic that you'll think I'm plain and dull and not worth it."

"C'mon, Jean." He slipped his fingers into hers. "Twenty million people have this thing and still love each other." He wanted desperately now to watch the Country Music Awards. No dice. She shut off the set with the remote. Here comes the vasectomy shit, he thought. She looked up at him, the wounded look in her eyes again.

"Marty, we've been together two years now. Really three, 'cause we dated for almost a whole year before I moved in." She picked at a thread that had loosened and stuck its head out of the seam in his pant leg.

"We've talked about us before Marty and I don't want to get into anything too heavy, what with your operation and the *EVOKE* system and all. But I'm thirty-five years old and not some kid who's still wet behind the ears. Thirty-five years old, Marty. If I live to be seventy, my life's half over." She yanked at the thread.

"Now I'm scared, because I see this machine you're in love with and I understand *why* Marty, I really do. But I look at the messages on the refrigerator door and my clothes hanging in the closet and I want to burst into tears, because I'm so scared and I don't even know what I'm scared of."

She sighed a long, trembling sigh and drew small circles with her finger on his pant leg, where the thread had been.

"What am I scared of, Marty? Where are *we* now? Where are *you* now?"

"We're where we've always been." He turned toward her. "We love each other." Oh God, he thought, he hated these goddamn conversations and he hated his stupid words. He never knew what to say to Jean or any other woman for that matter when conversations turned to stuff like this. Always felt behind, always felt like some kid trying to catch up. That sinking feeling that he was too far behind, like he might get lost before he got home, before things were normal again.

Women looked at life with some sort of mystic clarity that Marty never seemed to have. It was like being back in school, squirming while his mom or dad delivered some long sermon on what he was supposed to do with his life. What was expected, always what was expected. Something that he didn't want to understand, that made him want to run outside and shake it all out of his head until he could find one of his friends and go see a ball game.

It was so goddamn complicated, what they all wanted. So fucking mystic and unreachable and serious. Jesus, *always so serious*. Marty wanted to get seat covers for the fucking Honda and squeeze a raise out of old man Clark, stop for a beer on the way home and get back to the fifty-seventh floor for a while. What was so wrong with that? What was so wrong with the way they lived? He put his arm around her.

"You know I love you, babe." That was Marty's sign off, his resignation to just another conversation he couldn't handle. His floundering, out of depth way to get out of what they were talking about when he didn't know what to say. When he couldn't think about it anymore. It usually worked. Maybe it would work.

"Marty, are you going to marry me?"

There it was again, he thought. *Fuck*. His mind raced for an answer, some answer, any answer that would make all this go away for a while. It always goddamn came to this, sometimes sooner and sometimes later, but it always finally came to this. After you met some nice chick and flirted with her and she flirted back and then you took her out a few times and ended up in bed, everything easy and fun and good hearted. Just flying through life for a few weeks, or a few months or a few years and then it came to this.

They'd had this talk four or five times in the past year and he'd always been able to get around it somehow without pissing her off enough to leave. She'd be quiet for a few days maybe, but then everything finally came back around to normal. Damn, he wanted a couple more aspirin. His balls were on fire.

Marry Jean? Christ, he guessed probably so, but what was all the rush and what the hell would some certificate mean? It sure as hell hadn't made her brother Larry any happier with that hot piece of tail he'd married last summer. She'd sure cooled off and turned into a wife in a hurry. Now they had a house in Palatine they couldn't afford to put furniture in and she was knocked up. Larry could look down the road as far as he wanted and all he could see was mortgage payments and college tuition, the poor bastard.

Shit, he and Jean were comfortable, both of them working at pretty good jobs and they got along all right, okay in bed too. Sometimes a little predictable, but always there, someone to roll up against in the middle of the night and know was there. The apartment was okay too and they had a swell time in Jamaica last winter. Seat covers first, then maybe marriage. Why'd she want to fuck up what they had?

"I don't know, babe, we keep talking about getting married and I look at Larry and I mean, what's it done for Larry, except tie him up in knots? Shit, he's your brother. How happy are they now, with the big mortgage payment and no furniture and a kid on the way?"

"That's what life *is*, Marty." She drew bigger circles on his leg and he wished he had some aspirin. "Big mortgages and used furniture and kids in the backyard. That's why I need to know. What you've done to yourself, in return for that machine means we'll never have kids in the backyard. Unless we adopt or I go to a sperm bank and have someone else's kid to run around in the backyard." She looked directly at him, the way she did when she wasn't going to settle for sliding away.

"That's why this isn't the same old conversation, Marty. I need to know. I need to *know*, before my life is more than half over, if you want what I want. A big mortgage and no furniture and a life that means something *more* than a new car and a trip to Jamaica."

There it was again, he thought, her being pissed because he wanted a new suit or a car or a vacation. Jesus Christ, did they all have this mothering instinct? No wonder the vasectomy was part of the agreement. The goddamn world was just overflowing with people.

"I need an aspirin, babe. I'm really hurting now. Can we talk about this later?"

"Yeah. I'll get the aspirin. You want two?"

She got up and turned the awards show back on, tossing the remote control onto the sofa next to him where she had been sitting. Letting him know she wouldn't be back to the sofa and that he'd won again, but it wasn't over.

"Better get me four."

He turned up the sound to protect him, but he could hear her bare feet in the hall, hear the medicine cabinet opening, the water running into the glass, hear the door close and her feet in the hall again. Now standing in front of him, silently offering the bottle of aspirin and the water. He felt her mind saying, *take the whole fucking bottle of aspirin, Marty and take your fucking sterile body off to bed and stay on your own side.*

She never used those words, but he knew they were the words in her head. He popped the aspirin into his mouth and washed them down, wondering how long it would take to get back to normal.

Jean walked back to the bathroom and the fifty-seventh floor filled his mind until he heard her rattling pots in the kitchen.

FIVE

Bob watched Lonny Romeri's limousine pull out of the courtyard and turned back into the house.

"Will there be anything else tonight, Senator?"

"No Charles, that will do for this evening. I'm going to be in the library for a while, but I have everything I need."

"Good night, Senator."

"Good night, Charles."

Bob walked across the entry hall and down into the living room, his hands deep in his pockets, idly jingling change and he stopped in front of the oil of his father over the mantel. He looked up into the gray eyes that gazed out across the backs of his hounds. The old man's hand was on Wrangler's collar, the hound that sired the line that led to Ravage. Two great hounds, one for each lifetime and now it was all slowly drifting to an end, an era gone. A sport losing its heritage and there would probably never be another Wrangler or Ravage at Fairacres.

No one knew that the portrait was more a tribute to Wrangler than it was to his father. The aging Senator had insisted on the painting before the hound died, before his likeness would have to be taken from photograph or memory. *It was easier in your day Dad*, he said to himself, looking again into his father's eyes. World wars and power struggles were easier in simpler times, or so it seemed and simpler times are fading along with foxhunting, lost in the mists of forgotten woodlands, the voices of the hounds all but gone.

He turned and walked to the library, lifted the fireplace screen and set it aside, settling a fresh log into the dying embers and another on top of that. He pushed at them with the heavy poker until the flames licked and spread. Draining the last of the brandy into his glass, he rolled it around in the crystal bowl, easing into the chair facing the fire, sliding off the polished loafers, resting his feet on the old red leather ottoman. The same ottoman, he remembered, where young Bobby used to perch, asking unanswerable questions before bedtime. Now there were more unanswerable questions.

Lonny had a point and it was a good one. *Damn*, he thought, *the good ones were always so difficult to deal with*. Too much importance on both sides of an issue that had only one solution. He'd seen figures that hinted at unexpected blips in the economy, speculated on their connection to *EVOKE*. Markets that shouldn't be down in a slow-growing GNP and a few anomalies that were up, way beyond any rational explanation. Beyond explanation unless you pointed a finger at *EVOKE* and Lonny had not been the first, but certainly the most credible to point the finger.

It wouldn't go away. There would be more Lonnys and more fingers. The report lay on the coffee table and he knew it would be accurate. Romeri was many things, but he wasn't a speculator, not a man to speak without the facts.

A cigarette would be awfully good with this brandy right now. Bob got up and walked back through the house, toward the kitchen and the butler's pantry. Occasionally Charles had a smoke, outside the kitchen door, around by the service entry and the Senator thought he'd seen a carton of cigarettes in the pantry. In stocking feet and feeling a bit like a burglar in his own home, Bob switched on the lights and rummaged through the unfamiliar shelves, finding a carton of

Marlboros. Sliding one package out of the carton, he padded back to the library, switching off lights along the way.

The fire was crackling and the first puff felt fine, slipping down his throat and bringing a pleasant lightheadedness. *EVOKE*, he mused, was just another chapter in a book already written. Unstoppable as evolution, the last link so far in a long chain of electronic meddling started so innocuously. Begun with scratchy early radio broadcasts of ballroom dance music, then on to Jack Benny and baseball, the nation intrigued and innocent. Twenty years later television, with its first grainy black and white images, pulling everyone a little closer, clustered around a six-inch screen in a wood case and calling in the neighbors. TV put a face on the voices and changed the world, leaving innocence forever behind. He shifted his feet, took a sip of the amber cognac and another drag on the Marlboro.

Television tipped the war in Vietnam and Bob mused that he'd hoped that war might at last become no longer as saleable, now that folks at home had to sit down over dinner and witness the brutality, watch the filth, blood, body-bags and suffering that came to the table along with the pork chops. Vietnam had ended that way. Without a national draft and the bodies returning without coverage, Iraq and Afghanistan blundered on for more than a decade, but they ended as badly, the last three of the nation's wars ended with a whimper.

Clean war now, fought and died for by other people's kids, disinfected by a media that was as tired of smoldering babies as the country. A hundred-thousand dead by remote control, with smart-bombs and drones, but no need to see the faces. No need to have the images of flesh burned from living bones and the wail of widows and orphans to interfere with dinner at eight and Late Night crooning us to bed.

The loss of innocence was more than just new faces on different voices. Technology improved, then improved again and Johnny Carson morphing to Jay Leno was more real to a large part of the nation than family and friends. Husbands and wives merely nodded to each other on the way to the TV. They spent six or seven hours a day watching perfect people, comparing their lives with perfect lives and constantly falling short. The poor and the jobless grew up to think everyone but them lived a better, perfect life. Their anger, lying dormant for decades and even centuries, began to grow. Who could blame them for that?

All this boiling discontent spread like weeds into middle class lawns, as well as the dirty, bottle-strewn vacant lots of the poor. Multiplied, the seeds blew across the whole country, taking root and cracking the concrete of a complacent society. Despair flourished in those cracks, forced them wider apart, crumbling the complacency of Chicago, Detroit and Los Angeles. The logs in the fireplace shifted and settled, streaming a shower of sparks up the chimney.

Bob reached for another cigarette. *Hell, it would have happened anyway.* Scales too far out of balance always tip. But it might have come slower, might have been manageable, even soluble. Maybe. But perhaps this was just the inevitable brought blindingly up to date and thrown in our faces like cold water. Announcing to a world already boiling in crisis that there were other crises of over-population, joblessness and decline. That the age of innocence was over. Country's a damned long way from perfect, but anarchy won't put it right. Not in his mind. If not anarchy, then what? Circular thought, Bob... *circular thought...* everything drifting in circles and he couldn't seem to get a grip on answers. No advanced nation on earth allowed the seeds of discontent to blow and take root with such utter abandon. He poked the logs, stood in front of the fire and stretched his shoulders, hands at the small of his back, easing tightness in his neck.

Virginians voted for Senator Robert Billings Fairweather and then turned mindlessly to game shows, shopping malls and junk bonds. *His voters.* They'd allow the Senator occasional wars if they were served discreetly and humanely at dinner, won in a hurry and kept the economy cranked, but you couldn't hurry war, not any more. Virginians as well as Californians knew damned well we needed a military. The jails were over-crowded and the poor needed a handhold on the lowest rung or they'd start burning again. Now this incessant electronic intrusion into daily life hitched up its pants and took another stride into the unknown. But Jesus, *EVOKE* was such a mega leap. Who the hell could know where it would lead? And here was Romeri, blowing his damn bugle and insisting on a charge.

"Enjoying a little secret smoke?" Maggie leaned against the door.

"Yes, my love." He smiled up at her, glad to leave the thought." I'm getting to an age where I have so few vices left that I'm beginning to treasure each and every one of them."

"It's almost midnight. You coming up soon or do you want some company?" She wore her old white terry robe, with tatters on one sleeve and looked incredibly beautiful to him. Fresh from a long, hot bath and aglow from the warm water, without makeup. Maggie would be fifty in two years and still had a sensual grace that seemed more profound with each passing year of their marriage.

"Come sit by me." He settled another log on the fire and she knew he was troubled.

"You may as well slip me one of those cigarettes you filched from the butler's pantry." She pointed to the pack, lying on the table next to him.

"Maggie, you haven't smoked in years." He winked at her and tossed the pack, which she caught deftly in one hand, snatching it from mid-air.

"Oh, I have one every once in a long while, usually out in the garden while I'm wandering, trying to sort out some aspect of the world that I don't quite understand." She reached for the table lighter, her slender fingers unpolished, elegant.

"A secret smoker." He gazed at her and shifted his feet on the soft leather of the ottoman. "And now you've caught me too."

"You and I are like two house-dogs, love. We know each other so well, we have no secrets and each knows where the other can be found, digging in the garden or chasing a rabbit." She took a long drag and surprised him with the depth of her inhale. "You digging in the garden or chasing rabbits, tonight?"

"Got a rabbit chasing me, Maggie. Not really a rabbit, more like a foxhound and I don't know whether to keep the hunt going or duck down a hole." He swirled the last of the brandy.

"You've never been much for ducking down holes, Robert. Not your style." She looked at him and held his eyes. "Romeri?"

"Yep and this one won't go away, Maggie. This one just won't go away."

"Is this more brandy for us both, dear, or is this fresh coffee and another log?"

"Probably coffee, Mag. Let's go make a pot." They headed for the kitchen, Bob still in stocking feet, Maggie in slippers, trailing a thin line of smoke behind them.

———————————

As Maggie reached for coffee, forty miles northeast of Fairacres the wheels of Lonny's Starlight

3000 left the surface of Dulles Runway L-7 and the Virginia countryside fell sharply away below the fan-jet. Joe held steady in the departure pattern, fingers flipping switches, holding for two or three minutes. He checked with the control tower and got clearance, swinging the craft in a wide left turn to the flight plan filed to deliver Alonzo Romeri in Detroit at approximately 2:34am, Eastern Standard Time.

"Edward, please bring me a decaffeinated coffee and keep a pot going back there, will you?"

"Right away, Mr. Romeri."

Lonny released the intercom button and settled back in the seat. He'd napped in the limousine on the way to Dulles and hadn't yet reflected on his conversation with Fairweather. This ability to instantly shut things out of his mind, to will himself into catnaps, served him well over a lifetime of important meetings in strange cities and different time zones. Always appearing as though he'd stepped out of a shower, intent, immaculately dressed and piercingly sharp, no matter the circumstances. Always ready, intuitively ready to pursue the advantage, to see the abstract and bring it into the sharp definition of a focused mind.

He preferred important meetings be held early in the morning, very late at night or just after a sumptuous meal, when his adversary would be sluggish and off balance. It was time now to focus on this goddamn Senator, with his blue-blood attitude, still living in another century and chasing around the fucking woods with a bunch of dogs.

Fairweather was key to his plans and he had to be careful with him. The Senator was a shoo-in for two more terms or three, if he wanted them. As long as he was elected to the Senate and chaired the committee, no one else was going to sit in *that* seat. Preston Alberts was next in line seniority-wise and Lonny owned that stupid jerk, but there was no getting around Bob. Not yet, not right now. For the time being he had to smooth his way along and it was all 'Lonny' and 'Bob' and little chats in the boondocks of Virginia. But if it didn't work, if the schedule got too stretched, he'd bury Robert Billings Fairweather. Lonny was skilled at that.

On the plus side, the dinner meeting wasn't meant to get results. Just an opener and Lonny pretty much insisted on the privacy of Fairacres to give it an air of importance, something that couldn't be broached in Washington. He knew just how to handle Fairweather. The Senator didn't do business at Fairacres, not unless he had to. The President had been there a number of times, but they were old pals and after all, he was the President. Lonny smiled, setting the decaf on the coffee table and lighting a cigarette. Chairmen of huge multi-national corporations usually got what they wanted, but Presidents *always* got what they wanted.

He put his feet on the coffee table. Lonny was fifty and the President's second term was up in two years. There would certainly be another Republican win, if the militant blacks and Hispanics could be bought off again. Hell maybe even Fairweather might run, he was well positioned and well known, getting better known every day, thanks to *EVOKE*. Figuring two terms, if the incumbent didn't screw up and get caught in some petty but unforgivable flap, the office would be up for grabs again in ten years. That suited Lonny, he would be sixty. On the other hand, in two years he'd be fifty two. That suited him better and it could be done, if he made the right things happen.

The meeting went just as he'd expected. An earnest pitch, framed in the needs of the country, raising just a little threat of Japan's influence and the whole thing wrapped neatly in the flag. Hard facts and figures to back it up. The Senator had blinked. That was enough for Lonny. Oh, there was the usual jawboning about the influence of commercial interests, but it had to come. Lonny knew it had to come and so did the Senator, even though he didn't relish being the Chairman of the Committee when the crack opened and the ad agency boys slipped through. That was okay with him. Preston Alberts, with his manicures, thousand dollar suits and silver hair, would be pleased to sit in that chair. A smile made for television, along with his deep and resonant voice would make life a whole lot easier. Fairweather had to be moved out of the Senate.

"Edward, patch me in to Bill Wearley." He lifted his finger from the intercom and focused on the eight o'clock meeting with Ryan Walker at Interstate. Walker wasn't going for the merger and Lonny wanted to make sure the wheels were ready and greased. He didn't want to think about this one again.

"I have Mr. Wearley, Mr. Romeri."

"Thank you, Edward." He picked up the phone. "Hello, Bill?"

"Hello, Mr. Romeri. What can I do for you?" The voice sounded tired and Lonny smiled. Bill Wearley was used to this, but it always took him a moment to cut into the loop, remember where he was, if he was in his own bed or not and where the boss was, at least in which time zone.

"Bill, this guy Ryan's not going to buy our offer tomorrow, I just got a gut feel. He built that goddamn company and I got a hunch he's not going to want to sell it, no matter the price, you get me?" He fished in his shirt pocket for another cigarette.

"Yeah?"

"Well, I just want you to get Plan B organized, so I don't have to look back and spend a lot of time with this."

"Which way you want to go?" The voice was alert and Bill was in the loop.

"Same as we did with Pilot Industries. We'll give Ryan more business than he can handle. Let him get tooled up and build a couple new plants. We'll need the new plants anyway and this way he can hold the bag. Keep him loaded, keep him into the banks, give him so damned much he drops most of his other accounts and congratulates himself on how fucking smart he is. Just about the time he builds a second house and takes on a mistress, we'll cut him like the plague. Should be able to pick him up for about thirty cents on the dollar and the plants will already be built. May take eighteen months, but it'll save us a hundred million."

"Okay, get right on it, first thing in the morning."

"Get on it now, Bill."

"Mr. Romeri, it's almost two in the morning. You want me to call four Division Presidents and the Corporate Attorney at two in the morning?"

"Call 'em *now*, Bill. That's what I pay 'em for." He took a long drag on the cigarette and swallowed a mouthful of coffee over it.

"Yes sir!" Bill sounded like he'd enjoy rousting some of the corporate types on the boss's behalf. It wouldn't be the first time they'd heard his voice in the middle of the night and hated him for it. Lonny loved it, making him seem never to sleep, never to be unguarded, always out there somewhere, day or night. Kept people on their toes.

"And, Bill." He set the cup carefully, in the middle of the linen napkin with the World Star Logo.

"Yes, sir?"

"We're setting Ryan a fair deal in the morning. He'll come out with a hundred million in his pocket after taxes if he accepts and broke in a year and a half if he refuses. That's *important*, Bill. That's the message I always want out there. Lonny Romeri is always fair, but don't fuck with him. You hear me, Bill?"

"Yes, sir."

"Why you don't just tell her, Bobby and be done with it."

Webster Brooking rolled his legs over the side of the bed and set both feet on the floor. Reaching for a ripped package of Winston Lights, he spilled the change from the bedside table as he groped for the lighter, taking a long drag. He stared morosely out at the drizzle that collected on the window, forming droplets, the droplets edging together as though magnetically attracted and finally too heavy to maintain their footing on the glass, sliding down in jagged, meaningless patterns to the windowsill. "What the hell are you going to do, marry this girl and let your whole life turn into one long lie?"

"We've been over all this, Web. It would kill the old man, kill my job for sure, wreck the whole fucking world." Bobby Fairweather stretched and arched his back, the cool sheet draped across his long body and reached his arms overhead, linking fingers. He turned his palms up, continuing the stretch, feeling the muscles in his shoulders, along his arms and into his hands, tense with the pressure. He relaxed abruptly, flopping his arms on the bed and yawning. "I shouldn't even come here so often. It's dicey."

He slipped from the bed and dressed, silence between them. There was more to say, more that had to be said, but now was not the time. Now never seemed to be the time, because the arguments were thin and the truth was like a rock just beneath the surface and waiting, ready to shatter his life. As he closed the door behind him, Web still sat on the edge of the bed, watching the rain. The cigarette had gone out.

Bobby walked to the car, parked on a side street four blocks away and slid behind the wheel, glancing at his watch in the light of the street lamp. Quarter past twelve. Home by twelve thirty and six hours before the alarm went off. *Good enough*. Monday morning Partners Meeting at nine and the Walters Investment thing was pretty well in hand. Maybe should have worked on the prep for depositions over the weekend, but he could probably wangle an extra intern to catch up. Fake it 'till you make it, Bobby boy.

He turned the ignition key in the black Porsche roadster and the engine instantly throbbed to life. Bobby pulled quietly away from the curb, cautiously and unlike the way he normally gunned the supercharged car around Richmond. No need to call attention to being in this neighborhood. The car was his only aggression and he drove it with an almost sexual sense of power and daring. He felt it in his hands on the leather-wrapped wheel, the short throw of a close gearbox, pressure against the small of his back as he hit the gas. Felt it in the whine that's distinctively Porsche, winding down through the gears.

The roadster smelled like the inside of a saddle shop and fit him like skin. He kept all that power under control in Richmond, where there were too many cops and old ladies. Bobby let it run free, only on the winding country roads, kicking it in the ass like a point-to-point horse, galloping with ears pinned back, pounding the roads with its muscle.

"Good morning, Mr. Fairweather. How was your weekend?" Marcia smiled up at Bobby from the reception desk. The Monday morning flower arrangement, already delivered, held down a corner of burled walnut with its furious burst of summer daisies. Very chic, very out of season. The flowers told the world *this is Wayland, Roth and Barnes and we don't give a*

damn about the season, we get what we want and we'll get it for
you too.

"Fine, Marcia, a little drizzly, but okay. Anything in the box for me?"

He paused, noticing that Wayland had three messages. Good, the old man wasn't in yet and Bobby was ahead of the game. Roth was long retired to the ceremonial "of counsel" accorded doddering old men and Barnes didn't matter. No old Virginia name behind Barnes, even if his name was on the door. It was Wayland who had to be smoothed and buttered.

"Nothing but the Friday afternoon message from Mr. Walters, but you got that when you called in. Partner's Meeting in a half hour, as usual. Coffee?"

"Yes, thanks."

He walked through the arched entry, down a short hall past four senior partner's offices. Turning left, he passed the law library and conference room, left again to his own office, glancing at the brass plate on the door. Robert Billings Fairweather, III, Partner. Junior partner perhaps, but no law firm identified a partner as junior. There were only partners and senior partners on the letterhead. If you weren't there, you worked your butt off over the weekends and evenings, hoping to get there, struggling to get there. Bobby knew damned well that his name and family would draw him a senior ranking as soon as the firm politics allowed. Probably next year.

He left the door open, sitting down behind his big walnut desk with a sigh, fingering the message from Walters to drop it in the middle of the polished surface. Who really gave a shit, anyway? Certainly not Walters. That prick was chafing because he'd dropped out of Wayland's personal orbit, down to Bobby. His father would be pleased when he made senior partner, he guessed. Ginny would gush at another notch in his belt. Walters would pay more money for his advice and counsel, climbing back up the ladder and be a little more pleasant to deal with. But who really gave a shit?

He looked at the walnut paneled wall and the painting of his father, seated at his desk in the Senate, hands clasped, short gray hair framing a strong face. Only a corner of the desk showed in the painting, the Seal of the United States Senate and the ever present American flag. A forest of walnut trees had given their lives to Wayland, Roth and Barnes. Turned and polished, shaped and mitered, carved and stained, in arches, balustrades, coves, lintels, frames and panels. What the fuck did it all mean?

Prestige... that's what it meant to Wayland... prestige. All the dignity and prominence that could be mustered in a backwater city like Richmond. A couple hundred thousand residents, a third the size of Washington. Power, too... Bobby guessed they meant the woodwork to be kick-ass powerful, but renown wasn't in the graining of walnut. It was in the names on the doors and his name was the most powerful among them, junior partner or not. It was a name to be carried around, the three Roman numerals dragged behind like an anchor, an unwanted, unasked for legacy. He sighed again and fingered the message, hungering for the Porsche. It sat in quiet black elegance stabled under the building and throwing its head with impatience, champing the bit, longing to run the roads.

Bobby was only six when he learned the power of the Fairweather name. He was bored by a midday Hunt-Breakfast at Fairacres and he'd been chasing around the back terrace, begging goodies from the caterers. They'd set up white-clothed tables for a couple hundred Members, guests and followers, all of them milling about in Bobby's six year-old world. The men wore polished black boots, with brown tops and shiny silver spurs, soft white breeches, yellow vests over creamy starched stock ties, with gold pins stuck right through them and wonderful scarlet coats. Bobby heard them called pink coats, but they weren't pink, they were red.

Women Members had the same long polished boots, but the tops were black patent leather. Bobby could see his face in them when he bent down, which wasn't a very long bend for a six year old. Their breeches were pale yellow and they had the same yellow vests and stock ties. The coats, long and black and elegant, with pale green collars and gold piping, the colors of the Fairweather Hounds. *His father's hounds.* Their hair was always pulled back and they were the prettiest ladies Bobby had ever seen. Much prettier he thought, than the ones who wore dresses and those fur things, wrapped around their necks and constantly talked to him like he was a baby.

He remembered standing next to his father, holding his hand and needing to pee. There was much too much fun on the terrace to go into the house, so he was standing there, thinking about peeing and not wanting to. A gray-haired man who didn't even have riding clothes on, walked up to his father and shook his hand.

"This must be your son," the man said in a booming voice and squatted down, his face big and grinning, right in Bobby's face. He had a big head and Bobby could smell his breath in the closeness of the loud voice.

"Bobby, this is Governor Williams," his father said. "Shake hands with him, son."

"So *you're* Robert Billings Fairweather the third?" the big man with the big head said in his big voice, shaking Bobby's small hand. "With a name like that, young man, you're going to be a Senator from the State of Virginia." Bobby peed in his pants and ran into the house, crying.

"Partner's Meeting, Mr. Fairweather."

"Thank you Marcia, I'll be right there."

Ginny called about four-thirty, interrupting a minor flap over whether depositions in the Walter matter should be taken individually. Bobby was in sock feet, sitting on the floor of Ben Wilson's office, glad for the interruption, letting Ben and Ed Roberts fight over the details. He didn't care if they deposed the whole damned bunch in the town square, but there was a turf battle going on between Ben and Ed and it suited Bobby not to take sides. He took the call in his office, swinging his stocking feet up on the desk.

"Hey, Gin." He tried his 'upbeat, but in the middle of work,' voice.

"Darlin', you *didn't* forget about the Winslow's dinner at the country club tonight, did you?" He could tell it was her *it's okay, but why do you keep doing this to me* voice. It came through the phone like southern magnolia blossoms, gone a little by.

"No, honey, I never forget something as important as Harlow Winslow. He's one of our oldest clients and I hate his guts and think less of his country club. But I'll be with *you* honey, and that'll make it all worthwhile."

"Now, darlin'."

"Ginny, don't *now darlin'* me. I always know when you're pissed and covering it with all that charm." He glanced at his father, gazing down from the portrait and gave the old man a wink. "Sorry honey, I just got in the middle of a case preparation battle between two of my esteemed associates and didn't keep track of the time. Said I'd check with you about four. Only four-thirty now honey and they'll cocktail themselves to death before dinner."

"Just a little *nudge*, darlin'. You know, it takes us girls more'n just a little while to get ready." That was her 'southern belle' voice and it always charmed and irritated him at the same time.

"I know, but it's always worth it, Gin." He raised his eyebrows at his father.

"Well, darlin', cocktails are at seven and dinner at eight, so I think we should be there by seven-thirty, at the *very* latest. I'm wearin' teal darlin' an' it would be awful nice if you dug out that light gray suit of yours with the almost teal pinstripe." She paused, expectantly.

"You got it, gray with the pinstripe."

Ginny planned social occasions like Civil War campaigns, with too much time on her hands and too many scattered references to pull it all together, like his mother seemed easily to do. His father had no advice from his portrait on the wall.

"And, darlin'?"

"Yeah?"

"Don't be late. Pick me up at seven-fifteen *sharp*, like that wonderful darlin' you are."

He hung up and studied the toe in his black sock, wagging it from side to side, then from front to back, wondering how he had come to be engaged to someone who kept calling him darlin'. He winced every time she said it, but somehow never got around to telling her, knowing it was important, this pet name for him. Something with which to guard her turf, not unlike a leash. He hated it and began to question how long it would be, before he began to hate her for using it. The continuation of all the endless unraveling that began with being untrue to himself. He swung his legs off the desk.

The Porsche was explosive under him as he headed, properly pinstriped, for Ginny's apartment, picking up the phone and speed dialing her number so she'd meet him downstairs. It annoyed her when he wouldn't leave the car in front, ride the elevator to the top floor to be let in and announced by Ellie. Then she could make an entrance. Better than walking to a waiting car, the passenger door shoved open like she was a high-school date.

Virginia Claybourne Fentress was all the right background, rolled up in the wrong person. Old Virginia Blue-Book, daughter of Worthington Fentress and Sis Claybourne, breeders of four Virginia Cup winners. Houses on four continents, they laid claim to a shipping fortune and a willful daughter who called Bobby darlin'.

He'd first met her, when his sister Katherine brought her home for a weekend from Foxcroft. A weekend he'd gone home to sulk and think things out after one of his fights with Web. He was in a pissy mood, but she kept after him with a girlish-womanish banter that filled the gap between him and Web. She personified a sort of never-never land, that took him out of himself and kept him entertained. The next thing he knew, they were sort of dating. Then they *were* dating and she began to call him darlin' and he wore her on his arm like a badge of honor. Dishonorable as it was to use her that way, she wore him as well. Ginny was always somehow more happy to be seen with him than to be with him.

Mutual survival, perhaps. He gunned the Porsche through a changing light. It was what he had to do in order to live in a world he'd never asked to live in. That compulsory Roman numeral followed him like the tail on a dog, a constant reminder of who he was expected to be, who he *had* to be. Ginny was entertaining to be with, so long as things kept moving, so long as gaiety kept her in shallow water and away from any serious discussion. That was fine with Bobby, he didn't want to discuss life anyway at this point. Hell it was better than okay, it was what he needed to stay away from the apartment in Richmond and Gin made it easier.

Even screwing her was okay. He couldn't bring himself to call it making love, but she was surprisingly aggressive and took a kind of black delight in fucking. It was a dangerous, wicked thing for her and she didn't want or expect much of Bobby except to be there while she was being dangerous and wicked.

He was willing to be there, but he still saw Web.

Bobby allowed inertia to take over and their relationship took on a life of its own, almost independent of the two of them. Friends began to see them as a couple, always inviting them as a pair, welcoming them into a world that was becoming more and more paired. A world of shiny smiles, weddings, newborns and late-night intimate suppers. Bobby felt himself being swept away, not by love, but by events outside himself. There were the approving looks of friends and his father asked them to ride up front with him, the Master. His mother developed a casual intimacy with Ginny, beginning with their collective parents invitations back and forth for dinners. Ginny's father began to put his arm around Bobby. There was a widespread, all inclusive, uncompromising, never ending, overwhelming sense of affirmation in them all.

They were engaged in September at a big party at the farm. Awash in a sea of congratulation, Bobby now found himself with darlin' on the front of his name and those three Roman numerals on the back. He was a man in parentheses, unsure whether he was saved or doomed, but knowing at last he was surely approved.

Web had just looked at him, like a haunted man.

"Darlin', you know I like to be *called for*." She slid in and slammed the door, pouting, knowing he hated it when she pouted. Particularly when she slammed the door of the Porsche.

"Sorry, Gin. Afraid we'd be late and I wanted to show you off fully and completely, before dinner."

"Okay, darlin', but you know how I hate to walk out like some tramp." She brightened and brushed him with a quick kiss.

Cocktails were the usual bore and they drifted around the huge glassed-in terrace, smiling and shaking hands. Ginny carried on the small talk she was so good at, making him both proud and relieved to be with her. Taking him off the hook again. Dinner was called at quarter to nine and went well enough, but he felt vaguely anxious to have it over with. Harlow Winslow's wife, who he'd never met, was on his left, an honor that he'd be sure to drop on old man Wayland in a casual remark sometime tomorrow.

She was a touch on the plump side, early sixties, motherly looking, expensively but unfashionably dressed and utterly fascinating. They talked about the upcoming exhibition at the Richmond Institute and her knowledge of art and art-history brought them to a lively discussion of Picasso, who left a void they agreed, that no one seemed able to enter. They talked politics, always a risk, particularly with a Senator's son. But her political philosophy danced across incumbents and parties with nary a feather lifted, concentrating on the historical use and misuse of power. His opinion of warty old Winslow soared, upon meeting the woman with whom he had chosen to spend his life. Or was it the other way around? He smiled at the thought.

A small band began to play and he danced with Mrs. Winslow, but she was a popular lady and they were soon cut in upon, leaving him to search for Ginny. As he looked around, she danced past, tapped him lightly on the shoulder and gave him a pleading look over the shoulder of her partner. He cut in.

"Who was that?"

"*That*, darlin', was an old beau of mine and he started gettin' more than just a little out of line. I dearly needed rescuin'." She put her head on his shoulder and gently nipped at his ear.

"Ginny, this is a very public dance floor. Watch your manners."

"Just playin' darlin', just playin'."

"Ummm, well watch yourself. I just made a very big hit with Winslow's wife and I have to look the part of a serious and capable shylock lawyer."

"Know what we could *do*, darlin'?" She nuzzled him again.

"What?"

"We could duck outta here about eleven an' take that little bitty hot Porsche of yours up on top of the ridge an' do some *wild* things in it." She nipped at him again. "I'm feelin' a little bit wild, darlin'." Harvey Brenner cut in on them and Bobby made his way back to the table.

It was empty, a clutter of wineglasses and sequined handbags, as Bobby sat down and idly swirled the Cabernet in his glass. The wine slapped the edge of the glass, rippling back and he found himself thinking of the ripples on the duck pond at the farm, where he and Billy Waterman swam the summer he was fourteen.

Christ, he hadn't thought about Billy for a long time.

"Hey, Bobby." The two of them had swum out to the raft and were lying there in the sun, drying their cutoffs. Billy was home with him for the weekend, from boarding school.

"Yeah?"

"You ever go skinny dipping in this pond?"

"Yeah, sometimes."

"Let's go!" Billy ducked out of his cutoffs and dove in. "C'mon in, the waters really fine with no pants on." Bobby unbuckled his pants, sliding them and his shorts off, rolling into the pond and the two of them began to tread water, holding each other's shoulders. The water felt entirely different naked, cool and free. He felt Billy's hand between his legs, but it wasn't the 'grab your cock' of boys playing, but a long, slow caress, that kept him from backing off, allowing the hand to slowly stroke him into an erection. He reached for Billy underwater and found him already

hard and gently ran his hands between his legs. He looked at Billy, who returned his gaze directly and with no embarrassment.

"Race you to shore." Billy turned and swam toward the shore, reaching it and running out of the water, into the woods, Bobby close behind. They fell into a panting heap, in a small clearing, where deer had bedded, matting the grass down.

Billy reached for him again and he slid his body closer, heart pounding, sliding his hand over Billy's erection, welcoming the strange and deeply erotic feel of that hardness. The strange sensation of someone else's hand on his cock. They massaged each other and touched all the parts of their bodies together and just as he felt himself about to come, Billy gently covered his mouth with his own and he felt his tongue.

He'd only kissed a girl twice before and never put his tongue in her mouth. Kissing girls didn't seem as important to him as it was to the other boys and he guessed he was just a late starter. The sensation of Billy's tongue was nearly overwhelming and they stayed in the grass for a long time, just holding on to each other. They spent much of the summer together after that afternoon.

"Well, young man, I think I've had enough dancing for one evening." Mrs. Winslow laughed and he leapt out of his chair to seat her.

"Mrs. Winslow, you are as delightful in conversation as you are dancing. Please sit down and talk to me some more." He smiled at her with genuine affection.

"Dear boy."

SIX

Marty's first day back at work was endless, one of those days that seem to start in the middle and work both ways, when the clock is frozen. Most things went wrong if they went at all. At least the soreness was gone. He was grateful just to be able to walk normally and not think about the operation, just concentrate on the payoff. *EVOKE* wasn't out of his mind all day. Tonight he was going to take the long route through the pleasures of the modem and to hell with whether or not Jean decided to sulk.

He knew he ought to call her about midmorning. It was a usual thing their calls, but last night's blast about marriage was still ringing in his ears. Then the ten o'clock truck scheduled for Cincinnati got all balled up and his ass was in a jam. Two fork-lifts out of service and the backup units didn't have the capacity to reach the high stacks. Marty was short a man on the loading dock and with people scrambling everywhere, they screwed up the ten o'clock with a half load for Dubuque instead of Cincinnati. The whole goddamn truck had to be pulled apart and spread back out on the dock while two additional rigs were backed up waiting, their drivers sitting on the edge of the dock. Wouldn't fucking help, just sat there legs dangling, smoking cigarettes and giving him a running update on their fucked-up schedules. Everyone was pissed.

Well, let 'em wait. Tonight they'd be on the road drinking coffee and popping speed and he'd be on the fifty-seventh floor. Take a goddamn day off and the whole dock falls apart. Some asshole grabs a wrong ticket and Marty's boss looks at him like he was to blame. Hard to keep focused with Cathy drifting around in the back of his mind.

Marty pulled onto Oakley Boulevard about six, making the right turn from Division and immediately looking for a place to park. Today was a day from hell and getting home a half hour late didn't help. The side streets filled up early. He cruised to Augusta, back over to Western and down Thomas, looking for a spot, finally wedging the Honda between two junkers, the power steering screaming. This goddamn neighborhood was full of beaters, their hoods up on weekends, owners tinkering and sometimes the snow stayed on these wrecks for three weeks before they were moved. No sense thinking about a new car 'till he had a garage and didn't have to put up with this shit.

He locked the car and walked the couple of blocks to the apartment, trying to fix in his mind where he'd parked so it would come to him in the morning. More than once he'd forgot where the hell he put the car the night before and had to walk up and down the side streets, looking for his little blue wreck like it was a lost dog. Damn this early snow, the sidewalks were a mess. Winter's a bitch in Chicago and half the year is winter.

He kicked his rubbers off in the hallway and unlocked the door.

"Jean, I'm home, babe. What a hell of a day."

No answer.

Shit, she should be home by now but maybe she was still pissed and sulking from last night. Sometimes when they'd had one of these arguments she'd take herself out to dinner and catch an early movie, probably with Marian. Damn, he should have called. He knew he should have called and the disaster in shipping was only an excuse. Maybe she was tied up in traffic and would want to send out for pizza and not cook. Shit, maybe he should offer to take her out to dinner, but that would take time and Cathy waited, just down the hall. Shit.

"*Jean.*"

Nothing. He started down the hall, peeling off his jacket and scarf. Something was out of place, the apartment didn't look just right. Where the hell were the pictures in the hallway? Just nails in the walls. He walked into the living room and the stereo was gone, some other stuff too but he wasn't quite sure what. Fuck, had they been burgled? This goddamn neighborhood. No, that couldn't be right, the television was there. He walked into the kitchen and saw the note on the refrigerator door, held up by six magnets.

'*Marty--- If you decide to get your shit together, call me at Marian's. If I'm not there, she'll know where I am. Otherwise I hope EVOKE keeps you warm at night! I only took my stuff--- Jean.*' The message was scrawled in black marker.

Holy Christ. Marty sat down at the kitchen table and looked at the note again. Even from ten feet away the writing looked angry and he got up, opened the fridge, twisted the top off a Budweiser and tossed it in the sink. He drained half the Bud and walked back through the apartment, checking closets. No clothes. She took everything she owned, even the cross-country skis, her bike and the Stairmaster. Must've had a fucking truck, must've taken the day off from work. Must've been really pissed this time.

He walked into the bedroom and sat down at the modem. Maybe she'd call, once she had a chance to cool down. She always called. The screen popped in front of his face and he made the selections he knew he would. This time he changed the name to Valerie and the place to an East Bank flat in Paris, selecting the three-hour program and pressing *Start Program*, looking into Valerie's eyes.

"Baby, I'm so glad you're here. I've been waiting for you all afternoon and you know how hot I get, when I have to wait…"

At nine-thirty, Marty pushed back from the table and walked into the kitchen to get another Bud, tossing the cap into the sink with its mate. My God, this machine was absolutely unbelievable. He'd just spent three hours with Valerie in the bistros and bedrooms and narrow streets near the Place de la Concorde. And what a city Paris was. Somewhere to go when he had the bucks, maybe with Jean if they ever got things patched up. *Why*, he thought suddenly? Why the hell would a guy spend money to go to Paris, when he could go there any damn time he pleased? And why with Jean, when Cathy and Valerie and God-knows who else were available whenever he wanted them? No fucking notes on the refrigerator from Valerie or Cathy.

Marty was hungry and ordered a pizza with everything, cracking another beer to take with the half full bottle in his hand to the living room.

There were two hours left on the machine, but he'd have to settle for a trip somewhere or conducting the Chicago Symphony Orchestra. Have to settle? He smiled and dumped himself on the sofa, putting his feet on the coffee table the way Jean hated. Have to settle? Some settling. Everything in the world at his fingertips and he wondered what those 'other' people in the neighborhood or the state or the country were doing tonight, the people who weren't onliners. All those people just like Marty, only yesterday.

Christ, that seemed a long time ago. A long time since he'd thought about seat covers for the Honda, a long time since he'd been worked over by Jean. Even a long time since he'd come home and found her gone. Well fuck the Honda and its ripped seat, who the hell cared, when he could spend three hours in Paris? The hell with Jean too. Who needed her anyway, with her lights off fucking and her mortgage, backyard, kids and college loans?

The pizza guy rang the bell and Marty tipped him five bucks, knowing he hadn't been to Paris and had damn little chance of getting there anytime soon. He wolfed down half the pizza and the rest of the beer, remembering Valerie the whole time. Leaving the remainder in the opened box on the coffee table, he walked back to the bedroom, leaving the two Bud bottles as well. The pizza would be okay for breakfast or he could stick it in the microwave tomorrow night.

Marty thought he'd like to see Africa, someplace in Africa, where they had lions and maybe some half-naked natives...

At midnight, he slid the lead off his head and turned off the modem. Jesus, it was late and he was tired. Been a hell of a day. He kicked off his shoes on the way to the bathroom to take a leak. Dumping his suit on the chair, he stripped off his underwear, nudged it into the corner under the nightstand with his toe, scratched at his belly and opened the window an inch or so. Falling into bed he remembered Valerie, the beginnings of a hard on stirring between his legs.

Marty awoke in confusion, reaching for Jean who wasn't there to get him up and looking at the bedside clock. Eight twenty. *Holy shit*, he'd overslept. Christ, his shift had started without him twenty minutes ago and it was an hour's drive in morning traffic to Clark & Anderson. The Eisenhower Expressway would be one giant clog by now. He jumped out of bed, stubbed his toe on the radiator and hopped, naked and cursing to the dresser to grab at the neatly folded underwear. He left some of it strung across the open drawer and headed to the bathroom to pee, brush his teeth and splash water on his face. No time for a shave or shower.

Christ, how had he missed the six o'clock buzzer on the goddamn alarm? Should he call in or just slide into the office and hope nothing had gone wrong with today's shipment to Cincinnati? Fuck that, he couldn't call in. He grabbed a rumpled suit and checked the clock. It wasn't set. Damn, he'd forgotten to set the fucking clock. Call in and say what? That he'd been up too late in Africa and Jean had left him and he'd forgotten to set the goddamn alarm? And oh, by the way he hoped the Cincinnati shipment was going okay?

Old man Clark was pissed about yesterday's screw-up, even though it wasn't his fault. Everything on that goddamn dock was his baby and they didn't care how often it was on time, they cared how often it was screwed-up. Should he bluff it out and call in sick? Too damn late for that. If he was sick, he was supposed to call in by seven, so they could pull Ed James out of receiving to pinch hit. He wasn't supposed to call in anything short of a heart attack. Goddamn, it would be weeks now before he could take a shot at Clark for that raise.

Marty grabbed his coat off the sofa and stumbled out the front door, looking like shit and feeling worse. The car. It was on Thomas, he was sure it was parked on Thomas. Goddamn Jean anyway.

When Marty got home in the late afternoon, his ass was dragging and he looked like he'd been on a three-day bender. The shipments got off all right, thank God for that, but Clark himself had come by at eight-thirty to talk to Marty about yesterday's mess. Rita had to tell him Marty wasn't in yet, they didn't know where he was, he hadn't called. The old man didn't say anything in front of Rita, but she thought he was pretty steamed. Marty saw him twice during the afternoon and the son of a bitch wouldn't even look at him. Rita told him he'd better go into the locker room and shave. He'd had better days.

The pizza was still on the coffee table, droopy and glazed with congealed cheese, like something left over a weekend and he slid it into the microwave, forgetting the tinfoil. The pizza spat tomato sauce all over the microwave. He shoveled it onto a plate and cracked a beer, eating half of it and throwing the charred part into the sink. Time enough to clean up all that crap later. Right now he needed the modem and he needed it bad.

Marty slid back from *EVOKE* a little after ten, still in a state of suspended euphoria from his three hours with Amy. She'd welcomed him to a mansion overlooking Los Angeles, a swimming pool, a hot tub and a friend named Karen. He walked into the kitchen for another beer and the remains of the pizza stared up at him from the sink, a stinking mess of cheese and tomato. Scooping what was left into the garbage, he left a red smear across the sink and snatched Jean's message off the fridge door, crumpling it and tossing it in with the discarded pizza. Only two beers left. He'd have to stop on the way home tomorrow.

Goddammit, he thought she'd call by now and tell him she was willing to come back, if he'd promise this or promise that or promise some other goddamn thing. He sure wasn't going to call her. But he missed having her around to talk to. Missed the juggling routine of their sharing the bathroom in the morning and missed calling her at ten-thirty in the mornings, hearing her ask how his day was going, asking about hers. The place was starting to look like a wreck, too. Well, he'd get after that. He didn't need some woman around to keep his shit straightened up.

That was the only trouble with these *EVOKE* programs. They were great, better than great they were absolutely unbelievable, but he never had a real dialog in any of them. Oh sure, things were said and he said some of them and other people said some of them, but it was never really conversation about his life. It all happened somewhere else like a script that seemed to be already written. A script that couldn't be improved, no doubt about that, but not a *conversation*. He couldn't talk to Cathy or Valerie, Amy or Karen about old man Clark or anything else in his daily life.

Maybe he'd just watch a little of some talk show on TV before hitting the sheets. Suddenly he just wasn't up for another program on the modem, not after the last three hours in LA. A momentary stab of loneliness ran through him, but he shrugged it off and turned on the TV. He'd make damn sure he was at work a little early in the morning with a clean shave and a clean shirt. Let old man Clark see him busy when he came in. The old fart always liked to be among the first there, to say "good morning, Marty," with that damned self-satisfied look.

Tomorrow he'd "good morning" the old man and see how it went.

Sunday Service was scheduled for eleven, but they began to arrive as early as nine, because *He* was preaching today. Not the capital He of God, in whose church they met, but the He of Prentiss Washington Everett, godlike in this church, His church. He was the right color for their God. *Black*. If that was blasphemy, so be it.

They came in polished limousines, on foot, off the bus and in beaters, sun-faded and rust speckled from the streets, flaunting the clear, cold December day in their pastel and pin-striped Easter best. Fathers in quiet conversation, breaking into grins and laughter at a shared joke, mothers in animated clusters with an eye on the children, darting and tagging among the cable news and network vans. The early crowd washed across the steps of the Columbus Drive Baptist Church, a wave of anticipation and bright clothing that lapped against the edges of the curb.

Prentiss Everett was their preacher, although his national responsibilities kept him from the pulpit with any regularity. A *national figure*, their preacher, and they said it with pride, taking nothing away from Reverend Billy White, the associate pastor who carried the workload of the daily and weekly concerns of the congregation. There was a lot of concern to spraed around and need constantly overwhelmed resources. There were pockets of wealth in the community, no doubt about it, but too few and far between to iron out a broad fabric of poverty and joblessness.

But not today.

Today, everyone was rich with the prospect of His presence. Arched oak carved doors swung open at ten and sucked at the crowd like an opening in a levee, pouring inward and quickly flooding the twelve hundred seats. Those who lingered over a last cigarette or bit of conversation, found themselves standing along the walls or in the back, under stained glass disciples, saints and angels. At ten thirty, the organist began to play softly and at five to eleven, the full choir filed in from both sides. Serious for now, young men and women amidst a rustle of black choir-gowns, finding their places and casting eyes across the congregation, searching for friends and family. Eleven o'clock and ushers swung the heavy doors closed. Eleven o-five, a hushed crowd, glanced down pews or across shoulders to raise an eyebrow at a friend. Youngsters quiet, hands clasped and looking forward between shoulders, legs dangling among family. No matter it's December, women fan their faces, the smell of suspense and woolen winter coats begins to fill the church. Eleven o-nine and the Reverend Prentiss Washington Everett sweeps from the vestry, striding across the altar rail and up three steps to the pulpit.

His vestments are cream colored, a stark contrast to the sea of black choir gowns that sweep four ascending rows behind him and he reaches for the edges of the pulpit... waiting. Microphones have long since been checked for volume and balance. Lighting was adjusted yesterday to suit the requirements of news cameras. Twelve of his staff, men and women are scattered strategically throughout the congregation, his 'responders,' to lead the spontaneity of reply. Nothing left to chance. There *will* be reply. It will appear reflexive. it *will* be timed perfectly, as is the need of spontaneous reply.

He waits.

They wait upon him.

"*Brothers!*"

"Yeah, brother." A low rumble from the men.

"*Sisters!*"

"Yes, brother." Higher, women's voices, more musical and excited.

"The *slave traders* are among us, again." Reverend Everett raises one long, well manicured finger in the general direction of God and holds it.

"Tell it, brother." Scattered voices.

"They don't *come* this time with whips and chains!" The finger wags, but remains raised. The voice deepens, amplified and commanding.

"Better *not*, brother. Won't *take* no whips and chains." Dispersed voices, the twelve setting the pace of response, laying out the script.

"They *come* this time like Satan, driving steel into the black brothers' skulls!" The finger comes down. Strong hands grip the lectern, his head leaned forward, the response a roar.

"Noooooooooooooooo!" The howl comes back like a tide. He waits, bathes in it, times it and knowing instinctively, precisely, *exactly* to the split fragment of seconds, when to speak again. When he does, his voice is hushed almost to a whisper, an intimate, conspiratorial tone and they lean in to hear, the fans stilled.

"They put the black brother to sleep, with Satan's steel in his skull!"

"Tell it.. . .. tell it.. . .. ., tell it!" A chant, begun by the twelve, taken up in swelling repetition, over and over, the congregation beginning to sway.

He waits.

"They take away the black brother's power to *think!*" The long fingers fly from the lectern to both temples, pistols pointed, the cream white sleeves of his robe drape and frame the glistening visage of the Reverend.

"Noooooooooooo, ain't gonna take away our power!" The twelve, across the congregation, all in unison and the assemblage takes it up, repeating.

"They take away the black brother's power *to have children.*" A roar from the Reverend, amplified by a dozen speakers.

"Noooooooooooooooo, ain't gonna take away our power!" Power is the word now and a few follow it with 'to have children,' but are drowned in the chant and find the thread, find the common ground of the chant and the energy rises.

"They take away the black brother's power to *vote.*" The long fingers clench into fists and the fists crash down on the lectern.

"Ain't gonna take our power!" The chanting goes on for minutes, becoming a continual scripted, directed roar, the Reverend acknowledging the congregation with his outstretched arms. He is sweating. The congregation is sweating. A hundred people stand and several faint in the tide of sweat and chant.

He waits.

"*Why*, brothers and sisters?" The voice has dropped low. The pace changes.

"Why do they do this *now*? Why, after stealing us in chains from our homes, after buying and selling us at a price less than cattle, after buying and selling our children, beating and hanging and shooting our men, degrading our women… after four centuries… why *now*?" The voice is almost a whisper and fifteen hundred lean forward in silence.

"I'm going to tell you, why now. Because *now*, brothers and sisters, we are of no further *use* to them. *Now*, brothers and sisters, all the black work, all the dirty work, all the *servile* work is gone and there's only white work and not enough of that."

He waits. The Reverend Prentiss Washington Everett leans into the silence and waits.

"There *are* no more back doors through which we can slip, hat in hand to do the cleaning and the yard-work and the raising of white children. And they are *lovely* and they are *innocent*, those white children. They are as *almost* as lovely and *almost* as innocent as our black children."

He waits.

"They are not as *hungry* and not as *undereducated* and not as *forgotten*, but they are very nearly as lovely."

"But lovely as they may be, they are growing up and we know that. We are growing up and we know that too. They don't know *what to do with us*. Can you imagine that, brothers and sisters? For four hundred years, they knew well enough what to do with us. They used us like oil in a lamp, but now they don't know what to *do* with us. All six foot four, two hundred eighty pounds of the Reverend recover from the leaning intimacy of his whispered voice and stands erect, shoulders thrown back, towering over the congregation.

"Well, *WE* know what to do with *THEM!*" He thunders the words.

"We know… we know… we know," the twelve led the response and the congregation is glad for release, desperate for release. The quiet, whispered words of Everett, the amplified whisper, built a tension that unburdens itself in their chant. "We know… we know… we know."

He waits.

"And we're *doing* it, brothers and sisters." The voice a near whisper again, the assembly leaning. "Mayors in the major cities… not Little Rock and Waverly and Peoria… no, brothers and sisters, New York, Los Angeles, Detroit, Chicago… the great cities of this country." His voice rises along with his right arm, index finger spearing New York, stabbing Los Angeles, a needle through Detroit and Chicago. "They're *afraid*, brothers and sisters, afraid of that power, afraid of that political influence. We're not supposed to *have* that influence. But the white man doesn't need to be afraid. Doesn't *need* to worry about us poor black folk knocking on the front door. We don't want his door. We want OUR door and we're dangerously close to having it, brothers and sisters. *Dangerously close to having it.*"

He waits. He lets his words sink, the lure settling close to the bottom before the slow retrieve.

"So, brothers and sisters. So, how *does* the man slow us down after four hundred years in chains. Yes, brothers and sisters . . .*four hundred years*. We're *still* in chains, brothers and sisters… *exchanged* the slavery of the plantation. *Exchanged* that slavery for the slavery of welfare. *Exchanged* the slavery of the plantation for the slavery of worthless schools. *Exchanged* the slavery of the plantation for the slavery of drugs."

Now the slow retrieve.

"We black people are the world-champion *exchangers*. But they got a *new* slavery, brothers and sisters. Got a slavery this time, to slide into the black

man's head and the black woman's head. Chains around
the black man's ankle and wrist and pocketbook won't
do it anymore, brothers and sisters. This time, he's going
to chain your *mind* and take away your *children*."

A huge banner drops, behind the Reverend,
'*EVOKE* TAKES THE BLACK MAN's POWER!' in
slashing red letters across a bold splash of black on a
white background.

He waits.

The twelve begin. "Power... power... power."
They are standing now and their voices dominate,
exacerbate, reverberate, the very air nearly in flames
against those soaring vaulted walls.

The organ thunders the choir into a rousing
gospel song and the Reverend Prentiss Washington
Everett turns his back on the congregation, walking
quickly down wooden steps behind the lectern, a
stairwell directly into the basement of the Columbus
Drive Baptist Church and he disappears as if swallowed
by Satan himself or carried off by God. The drama of
his exit invites either interpretation.

Reverend Billy White, the Associate Minister, will
take over now and carry off the message of the evils of
EVOKE from a scripted sermon. Everett's done his
job, they're whipped up and Billy can do the legwork.
The press, the networks and cable were there as
promised. The media in Chicago always comes when
Prentiss Washington Everett whistles. Sunday is a slow
news day and barring a train wreck or a plane going
down, he can count on a minute and a half on network
evening and late news. Maybe two minutes, it had been
a pretty good show.

He was sweating still from the damn lights and
the energy and he tossed the robe to Willie, who follows
him down the corridor to offices across the back
courtyard. At the turn of the century, in the heyday of
the south side before it became a black ghetto, the

mansions along Columbus drive were owned by the city's elite. Fat cats, the merchants and brokers and manufacturers attended Sunday Service in the massive complex that was once their Episcopal Church.

This sanctified, stained glassed, soaring building of God was still massive and imposing, but the power had shifted along with the ownership. White flight brought a black Mayor, a mostly black City Council and an imposing domination of that power by Prentiss Everett.

He was National Chairman of *BURN*. Blacks United Rising Now grew like a prairie fire, sweeping across the country, feeding on the desperation of the nation's poor, mostly black and largely unemployed underclass and Prentiss Washington Everett was their leader. Fifty-two million black African-Americans knew his rhetoric and white America listened with concern and the grudging admiration born of four centuries of guilt. Everett was not a man to be ignored. *EVOKE* had him worried. It was an enemy and he didn't suffer enemies.

He slumped in his leather chair, behind a huge mahogany desk that overviewed the gardens through leaded glass windows. The desk fairly glowed from polishing its deep blue leather top, tooled at the edge with gold leaf matched the high backed chair. It was clear and uncluttered, with nothing but a personal computer and five channel videophone, with speed dialer. Direct channels to the Mayor, Police Commissioner, two Illinois Senators, five United States Representatives in Congress, the floor leaders of both parties in Springfield and several numbers that had only initials. The lamp that hung centered over all that highly polished mahogany was massive, its deep green glass shade washed the desk and the Reverend in a circle of light. Beyond that light, all was muted, creating a radiant circle of inclusion and exclusion.

He peeled off the sweat-soaked shirt and Willie brought a fresh one, heavily starched and gleaming white. Tucking it into his forty-four inch deep-blue pinstriped trousers, he turned up a seventeen inch collar, slipping on a conservative dark wool tie. The dimple was perfectly centered in the knot, a carefully crafted work of long slender fingers, the cufflinks heavy gold, B for *BURN* outlined in diamonds. Willie held his suit coat and Everett tugged French cuffs clear of the sleeves, sitting down again, elbows on the desk, hands clasped, gazing outward from the circle of light.

"Where's Flip?" His voice was even, unreadable.

"Waiting," replied a shadow from the broad leather couch by a wall of bookcases, where two of six round-the-clock bodyguards flipped through magazines in feigned and careful boredom. Willie eased into his customary slouch against the cases, inspecting his fingers in admiration of a fresh manicure.

"Get him. Then get out. Stay close... not too close... not *listening* close."

"Right."

The three filed out the side door, arms slack, fingers flipping nervously and a moment later a whisper-thin man in black Italian silk slipped through the door, pulled it closed behind him and strolled sulkily to one of the blue leather chairs facing the desk. He dropped into it, the scale of his slight body nearly swallowed by the chair, swinging one leg casually over the arm. Too casually, he gazed at Everett with a look that bordered insolence, from just outside the circle of light. Osmand 'Flip' Haskell was thirty-six years old and he'd been shot twice, his arrogance born of a man who doesn't expect to make his fortieth birthday and earned on the streets. Four of the six others, who'd been with him in those shoot-outs, never made it to their thirtieth year. There'd been no doubt Flip was the target when the bullets started to fly. Maybe he was just too skinny to hit.

For a day or two after the last hit, he'd felt bad about Dolores, but he'd gotten past it. Plenty of other chicks, but she'd been special somehow... all too briefly, special. High on coke, laughing and reaching for him one minute and splayed halfway out the door of the limo the next, her head and one arm spread across the filthy curb of 47th Street, a surprised look on her face as a sheet of her blood washed across her white silk blouse, draining away down the gutter. Those were the risks. You run with dogs, you get fleas. Everyone ran with Flip, everyone who wanted a piece of the life and Black Afrika *was* the life on the south side. Most of the west side too, up to Oak Park and Cicero, bordering the Italians. Sometimes Black Afrika pushed that edge. Sometimes the Mafia pushed back. Sometimes beautiful twenty-three year old women choked on their own blood in the gutters.

"Hiya, Rev."

"Hiya, Flip. What's on the streets?" Someday he'd have to break this impudent prick into pieces, if someone didn't beat him to it.

"Same. Black Afrika *owns* the streets, home boy and in Black Afrika, *I'm* the man." Flip let the lapel of his fifteen hundred dollar silk suit drift open, showing just a hint of leather.

"You carryin', Flip?" The voice from the circle of light was even. Low and even.

"I always carry, Reverend... *always.*" He laughed. "Don't worry about it, preacher, your boys got the piece." He swung his coat wide. "I just got the leather."

"Too much trouble on the streets lately, Mr. Black Afrika. You make it tough for me and I don't like things to be any tougher than they already are." Still low and even.

"That's the game, Reverend." He shrugged. "Little wheels turnin' make the big wheels roll. Sometimes the little wheels need grease."

"Deek's calling me a lot. Three times, this week."

"Deek's your man. The Police Commissioner is *your* baby, Rev." He sat forward, clasping his hands to point two fingers." You're supposed to be able to handle that, it's your part of the deal. The reason Black Afrika puts over a million a year in the *BURN* hat when you pass it, brother." His eyes were insolent.

"Flip, cut out all this jive shit. I don't put up with no jive shit and that's all I'm hearin' from you" His hands were clasped, voice still even, washed in light gleaming accross his broad black head, a clipped fringe of graying hair curving over his ears and around the back. A wreath, surrounding ebony baldness.

"Deek's gotta play the same game we all play, Flip. He's gotta keep the public thinking he's on top of all this. The white public, but the black public too and don't you forget that. You make it tough when you shoot up half the west side in some damned turf war." The Reverend's voice was level, but the intensity of it carried from the pool of light to the chair and the silk suit. "I don't *like* it tough."

"Cuttin' in on our business, brother. Can't allow no cuttin' in on our business, you know?" His fingers no longer pointed and Flip gathered his hands in his lap, legs crossed now, the ankle at the knee, long black silk stockings exposed and showing a run of gray diamond pattern up from the ankle.

"That's what Deek's for, to keep the competition from 'cuttin' in on your business,' as you put it." Everett was losing patience with this black sliver in Italian silk, who'd never lost his street bravado and the street muscle that went with it. One call to the Police Commissioner and Flip would be history. Not arrested and arraigned, but killed *unavoidably* in a police shootout and Deek would enjoy it as much as the Reverend. But they couldn't be sure who would emerge in the power struggle at Black Afrika. Flip was insolent and arrogant and occasionally uncontrollable, but he was a known quantity and sometimes a known powder keg is preferable to an unknown mine field.

"Deek makes thirty drug busts in this town every week and all but four or five are your competition. Those four or five raids you always know about ahead of time, so there's never any evidence. For Christ's sake, settle down." The voice was deeper now.

"Deek ain't hittin what *I* need hit." Flip was on his feet now, close to the circle. "I'm spreadin' green all over and I ain't gettin' what I *need* to get, where I *need* to get it."

"Flip, I'm only gonna say this once and then I don't ever want to have this conversation again." The Reverend's voice was all the emphasis needed, his hands still clasped, cufflinks gleaming in starched white, exactly two inches beyond the cuff. "You listening?"

"Yeah." Sulky. Sulky as hell, but listening.

"If you keep popping off, the Italians are going to break into a full-fledged drug war. This isn't some jive neighborhood where you hold the cards. You hold the cards because *I* hold the cards and there's heat from Springfield and starting to be Federal heat. I want this shit stopped. *Now.*" The voice allowed no leeway. "You hear me, brother?"

"Yeah."

"Okay. Now go do whatever the hell it is you do on Sunday."

"Say, Rev?" Flip stopped at the door, one hand on the knob.

"Yes?" Prentiss rose behind the polished desk, his head above the circle of light, a huge headless creature, the white shirt-front bathed in light.

"You ain't no motherfuckin' Martin Luther King." The slight man in black silk slipped through the door. Before it had closed, Willie and the two body guards slunk back into the room, the three of them taking their accustomed positions at the far end, picking up magazines.

The following morning, Reverend Everett lifted the receiver, shut off the video screen, speed dialed and leaned back in his chair. "Margaret, this is Prentiss Everett. Is the Commissioner available?" His broad smile radiated through the phone.

"He's in a meeting with the Mayor right now, Reverend Everett," the secretary replied. "Is there a message?"

"Ask him if he'll take my call please, Margaret."

"Yes, Reverend. Just a moment." There was a short pause.

"Commissioner Johnson."

"Deek, you don't have to tell me who you *are*." Everett's voice still held the smile. "I made the call, remember?"

"Sorry, Prentiss. Habit, I guess. In with the Mayor, you know … " His voice trailed off. "What can I do for you?"

"I had Flip in here yesterday. Things oughta quiet down a bit now." He enjoyed getting the Commissioner out of a meeting with the Mayor. Relished the power that let him to get done what the Chicago Police Department couldn't, savored being the power over the power. If he'd asked for a conference call, he'd have the Mayor on the line now too.

"He says you're not doing right by him."

There was a snort on the other end of the line. "That skinny black scumbag. One day he'll push me too far. I don't think he knows how close this city is to an explosion and he keeps running around with an open gas-can and a match in his hand."

"I know he's not reliable, Deek, but he's all we got right now." Everett carefully picked a loose thread from his pant leg and swiveled in the chair, dropping the thread in a big onyx ashtray on the credenza. Expensive suits weren't supposed to lose threads. "One of these days he might have an accident, but we gotta have someone in place."

"Slippery little cocksucker."

"Give my regards to the Mayor, Deek."

"Yeah… thanks, Prentiss. Maybe this'll get a little heat off, at least for a while."

He replaced the phone and swung his big frame around in the chair, propping long legs on the credenza, crossed at the ankles, his shoes polished to mirror-like perfection and gazed into the landscaped courtyard, long fingers pressed together at the tips. The opening salvo against *EVOKE* had gone all right, but it wasn't a battle he was going to win and Everett didn't like to lose. There was no profit in a loss and he particularly didn't like to start something he knew in advance he was going to lose. But he had to have some cards to play. The congregation didn't mean jack shit. Columbus Drive Baptist Church was his turf and they'd roar and moan and slather their support if he stood up there and called them all worthless niggers. Statistically, sixteen out of every hundred were already sitting out there with those goddamn spikes in their brains, nodding and swaying and roaring their dismay at the power of white suppression. But they *had* the implants. He didn't know of a black man or any man for that matter, who'd passed up a chance to get online once their number came up.

Who could blame them? Shit, they had nothing, nothing but fear and poverty. Along with street crime, rent coming due and a crying baby. What jobs there were, drying up and closing down, without enough heat in the winter. He knew. He remembered and he didn't need a long memory or even a good memory, it wasn't all that far in the past. He'd been just another shivering kid on those streets until he'd latched on to Jesse's coattails and hustled and muscled his way up through the ranks. Never saying no, always being there close to the power. Watching how it worked and who had it, seeing how they all used each other, learning the rhetoric and the rhythm.

Waiting.

Now Jesse's day was past, an elder statesman out to pasture, brought back and polished up for a convention speech or a talk show if the national audience was big enough. A handful of men held the power now and they were a little more polished and a lot more ruthless. At ease with the white power. Soft spoken for the most part, like trusted business partners, but comfortable with the money. The money was where it had always been, in drugs and prostitutes and political clout.

A handful, no longer possible to ignore, they had to be dealt with and Prentiss Washington Everett was among them. He tapped his forefingers together, uncrossed and re-crossed his ankles.

Fairweather had been ducking him. It was time to put some heat on the good Senators from Illinois. He reached over and lifted the receiver, hitting the speed dial and working his face into the smile he'd carry over the line to Washington.

SEVEN

Wilson waited with the car and Bob climbed into the back seat, already tired and the week not yet begun. Lonny Romeri's report lay buried in his briefcase and it was this as much as anything that wore him down. The face-up to something imponderable. He knew his calendar was chock full of meetings. God, they never stopped and now, with the Christmas break at hand, every lobbyist, every subcommittee meeting, every drink with a friend seemed to assume an added burden of time slipping away. He'd manage. He'd always managed.

"Morning, Senator." Wilson grinned back at him from the front seat, looking well rested as always. whatever the hour. "If I may say so Senator, you look a bit bushed, this morning."

"You may indeed say so, Wilson." He smiled, but the smile was thin. "Too much Sunday I'm afraid, to make Monday look as bright and shiny as it should."

He settled back for the ninety-minute ride into Washington, wishing for once the Buick sedan had a bit more leg-room. Maggie had a ten year-old Rolls that Wilson much preferred, but the Senator liked the low profile of this car and its anonymity. His only concession was the Senate license plate and of course the phone, the ever present, demanding, oppressive cellular telephone. He refused to carry one personally.

Too much Sunday for sure. He reflected on his waking at 5am to pull on boots and breeches, with just a quick egg and toast for a hurried breakfast. Coffee scalded down to meet Jerrold at six to reconnoiter the territory and lay out a plan among the most viable options. Scenting conditions were near perfect and it turned into one of the better hunts of the season, but they'd been out over four hours and it left him exhilarated, but drained. The Hunt-Breakfast at Howard Worthington's prevented a much needed nap and the business with Romeri had been a fencing match at best. He guessed it was nearly three, by the time he and Maggie finally got to bed. *Getting too old for this shit* and yet as he thought it, he rejected it as well. You are what you think you are.

Life would be empty indeed without Maggie. Middleburg, Washington, the entire world and all the couples in it appeared hell bent on coming apart and breaking up. Bob hardly knew a soul who hadn't been married more than once and the remarriages broke up as fast as the originals they so eagerly replaced. He'd never wanted anyone but her and it seemed, he thought with a smile, she loved him equally. The years just brought them closer. Last night wasn't at all unusual, just Maggie and her incredible sixth sense she had that he might need coffee and conversation.

They'd meant to take their coffee back to the library, but ended up just sitting in the kitchen. The brandy was put by and the two of them sipped decaf and talked out his concerns over $EVOKE$ and where it was taking the country.

Romeri wanted in and Bob wasn't surprised. He knew the pressure to open up access was coming and had been building a long time. Ultimately, he knew he couldn't hold the line. If not Lonny, someone else would press the case. Probably lucky it *was* Lonny. At least the man had some common sense and it was useful to deal at the top, useful to be direct.

Only a matter of time. His wry smile reflected in the side window, the countryside sliding past, thinking back to the committee chairmanship he'd taken. Ten years ago, most Senators thought *EVOKE* was a joke. They pretty much thrust the chair upon him and now it had become a power base he'd never wished for or expected. He was the only chairman they'd had through those ten years and last night he'd admitted to Maggie he was afraid to let go. Afraid of what would happen, when some airhead like Preston Alberts took over and gave up control to the highest bidder. She'd looked him square in the eye, slid her hand over his and squeezed it, saying everyone has to let go, sooner or later.

She was right. He knew she was right.

Mankind was hell bent on opening that box of Pandora's, needing to look inside, prying away at whatever lock held it shut for the moment, worrying at the hinges until the lid popped, unleashing forces like careless children at a party with no idea of the consequences. *We just can't keep our eyes off the horizon* he thought, it must be something inherent in the human condition. Our curse as well as our perfection. Nor should we or could we, he mused, smiling again at the debates he had with himself. These conversations, so like a Princeton bull session. Half the world gone nuclear and now this.

But the blinding speed and geometric growth of what we have the power to know leaves no time at all to think. Geometric leaps confounding an arithmetic calendar and then while we're still absorbed in today, not just tomorrow, but an entire next generation of the unknowable is on us like a rabid dog.

Wilson eased into Fairfax County and traffic began to build.

Romeri and his damnable, ever present, all important cars. An icon reflecting the twentieth century need for speed and independence, overwhelming us a century later. Two thousand years on horseback, two before that on donkeys and camels and in an eyewink, gagging on traffic. Impossible to imagine life without the automobile, but my God, in less than a century they'd essentially crippled the country as cities became almost unlivable and public transportation was just a cruel joke. The suburbs were merely continuous shopping strips, each family needing two cars and *everything* was a suburb now, from Fairacres to Washington. Every single stab in the direction of high-speed rail and urban tram systems was fought by the auto and airline industries and Lonny was at the front of every one of those fights. They fought them with PAC money, speaking honorariums and reelection-fund contributions, including his. Christ, money was another example of geometric growth in what was once a staid old institution. Congress was awash in money. Yeah well, in Abraham Lincoln's day a citizen could pop in off the street and actually talk to the President. Things change.

He wasn't all that squeaky-clean himself, taking Romeri's money along with the PAC contributions and lobbyist support. Couldn't sit on the big bay horse and look out over much moral high-ground, but that was the way it was. The way Washington functioned, the legacy of Jefferson only the power today was money instead of ideas.

Wilson pulled up to the curb anchoring a massive spill of steps to senate offices.

"Nine twenty-five, Senator. Pretty heavy traffic this morning." He opened the back door and Bob climbed out, legs cramped from the longer-than-usual drive. He envied Maggie the back seat of the Rolls, but it wasn't an image he wanted to or even could convey. Outside Virginia, foxhunting had cost him dearly, all those comparisons running back to Jackie Kennedy and suggesting the Senator was a throwback to forgotten times, an anachronism somehow out of step with the new century. Outside of Virginia mattered, but it wasn't what kept him in office. Christ, maybe he *was* out of step.

"Thank you, Wilson." Bob flexed the cramp in his left leg, draped a dark blue cashmere topcoat over his arm and hefted the briefcase that held Lonny's report. He was bareheaded, as always. "I'll be staying in town tonight, but I plan to hunt on Wednesday morning, if nothing comes up. Pick me up about seven tomorrow at the town house."

"Yes, Senator. Mrs. Fairweather asked me to remind you that your son and his lady are expected at dinner tomorrow evening."

"Make it six then, Wilson." Bob turned and climbed slowly up the steps he usually took two at a time, working the stiffness from his legs.

"Good morning, Senator. Nice weekend?" Julia looked up from the reception desk with a smile that was always there, no matter her mood. He wondered what her weekend was like. A party perhaps? Someone new in her life or the isolation of a town with too many parties and too few connections?

"Yes, thank you, Julia. Dan and Sally in my office?" She nodded and he walked into the staff hallway, smiling to a half dozen young faces that looked up from coffee cups, cluttered desks and computer terminals, with scattered 'good mornings.' The other hall to his office was austere and formal, the acknowledged pathway to the power and prestige due a Senior Senator from Virginia, but Bob seldom walked it without a guest at his side. He much preferred the shirt-sleeved energy of staff offices that led by a narrow and somewhat shabby hallway past Dan McCarthy's office, then on through his appointment secretary Sally Brentwood's office, adjoining his own.

Bob stopped at the makeshift kitchenette-lunchroom, dumping his topcoat and briefcase on a chair, pulled a white mug off the shelf and reached toward the coffee maker and its two steaming pots of fresh coffee. A couple of staffers leaned against the radiator under the window, sipping coffee and lost in conversation, glancing up to smile a greeting. Coffee never got stale in those pots, it was fuel for the machinery. Bob carried a small staff for a senior Senator and they put in long hours, loving the work and their proximity to action. They cared about and respected him, as they'd shown in countless ways, but it was a job that led to other jobs and the networking was intense. He was as likely to make fresh coffee as they, the job done by whoever poured the last cup.

"How's the draft of that speech coming, Mike?"

"Pretty well, Senator. Should be finished this afternoon."

"Terrific. Run it by Dan before I see it, will you?" He took his coat and briefcase in one hand, the steaming coffee in the other and walked down the hall, through Sally's office and into his own, bumping the door open with his butt. Dan and Sally sat on the couch, a jumble of papers and cups spread across his coffee table.

"Sorry to be late, traffic was awful and I got to bed too damn late for a man my age." He grinned at them, like a kid late for school. "Should know better, but there you are, my weaknesses exposed." Apologizing to staff for a minor inconvenience was typical of Bob, another of the personal courtesies that bought a lot of loyalty in a flagrantly disloyal town. "What's on the list, Sally?" She picked up a sheet from the smear of papers and sat back on the couch, pulling one leg under her. Dan McCarthy walked to the edge of the desk and sat on it, as Bob hung his coat in the side closet and eased into a chair across from the couch.

"Senator Rhodes from Illinois at ten. Said it was very important and your schedule's full until Thursday, so I penciled him in. Said he'd only need a few minutes." She reached for her coffee. "Hate to do that to you and then the regular subcommittee meeting's at ten-thirty, so we'll probably have to get back together over lunch to work out the rest of the week."

"What's Rhodes want?"

"Wouldn't say." She sipped and set the cup back on the table. Tall and slender with dark hair always pulled back from her face, Sally forswore prettiness for serene good looks. Her bright blue eyes seemed to belong in another woman, someone more frivolous and scattered. Mid-late twenties, Radcliffe, Sally was anything but frivolous and scattered.

Dan stirred from his corner of the desk. "When the Senior Senator from Illinois needs to see you and won't say why, it's got to be Prentiss Everett."

"Hmmm... I suppose you're right." Bob crossed his legs at the knee, rubbing his right ankle. "What's the Reverend got on his mind that he wants to see me bad enough to get Alf Rhodes up this early?"

"Won't know 'till you see him, I guess. But Everett's been pestering Sally for a month and now, apparently he's gotten hold of Rhodes to run interference for him." Dan settled back on the edge of the desk, shirt sleeved arms crossed, one toe pointed and stabbing at the carpet. He was too short and pudgy to look at ease on the corner of Bob's desk, but it was his preferred spot.

"You know I don't like that, it's just like getting cornered by Romeri. Nobody wants to say what the hell they want anymore and I don't like to have meetings with people when there's no agenda." Bob frowned and rubbed the ankle. "This fellow Everett is from Chicago and has a huge national following among blacks. What's he want from a Senator from Virginia?"

"Again, Senator, no one will say. He just wants a meeting and now it looks like he's putting on some heat."

"Can't we get a damned agenda?"

Dan gave up searching for the carpet with his toe and slid off the desk, leaning against the corner, brushing one hand through thinning blonde hair. "Nope."

"Well, let's get back together, after the subcommittee meeting and by then, I'll have met with my esteemed colleague from Illinois. Coffee, I guess, Sally. Don't have time for anything more. Don't really even have time for coffee."

"Right." She uncoiled from the couch and began to shuffle the piles of papers into neat bundles. Dan picked up both their cups, walking through the side door to his office, setting Sally's cup on her desk as he passed. She followed him out, an armload of work cradled, closing the door behind her. She'd been with Bob for four years, Dan going on six now and he didn't look forward to either of them leaving. But Washington was a town of other opportunities, a town of leaving. He knew it would happen and he'd wish them both well... he hoped not at the same time.

Bob walked to the closet and hung his London-tailored suit coat on a hanger. Italian suits were the in look these days, but he always felt more comfortable in Scottish wool crafted by his tailor in a style that hadn't changed much over the years. He'd meet the Senator from Illinois in shirtsleeves from behind the huge eighteenth century partners desk his father had sat behind, putting aside an obvious workload to take time out for Alf. Then they'd move to the more intimate leather chairs on either side of his small fireplace and that would show he was taking the interruption seriously. Dan understood these fine points and had seen to laying a comfortable log fire. Shirtsleeves would be appropriate for Rhodes.

"Senator Rhodes is here, Senator." Julia ducked her head into the office after knocking briefly.

"Thank you Julia, send him in." The door closed behind her. The endless opening and closing of doors was in the character of the office and the minor conspiracies that went on behind closed doors. Sometimes lofty but mostly frivolous events discussed in privacy and the sensitive opening and closing was as much a tribute to power as the formal hall down which Senator Rhodes trod. Sometimes Bob felt like nailing all the doors open. He counted and, as he got to five, the door opened again and Julia held it, allowing the Senator to brush past her, closing it carefully behind him.

"Bob, good to see you. Damnably short notice and I appreciate it." Senator Rhodes strode across the room in an Italian suit, his bald head gleaming. Near seventy and catlike in his movements, with small eyes behind bushy gray brows, he was otherwise hairless. He reached across the desk, for Senator Fairweather's outstretched hand.

"Alf, it's always a pleasure." Bob walked around the desk, gesturing toward the fire and the two chairs, facing one another, a gleaming mahogany butler's table between. "Julia said it was important and if it's important to you, it's important for me. Coffee?" The polished silver coffee service, creamer, sugar and two Meissen cups and saucers waited on the tray, a heavy crystal ash tray at the side. The Senator was a cigar smoker.

"Thank you." He poured himself coffee, settling in front of the fire. "Mind if I smoke?" already reaching for a cigar from the inside jacket pocket.

"Not at all." Bob was glad of the fire that would suck the cigar smoke up the chimney. Cigarettes were tolerable, a pipe rather pleasant if the tobacco was plain and of good quality, but cigars had somehow always put him off with their heavy stench.

"I'm sorry we don't have more time, Alf. Subcommittee meeting at ten thirty, I'm sure Julia mentioned it." He poured himself coffee, creamed heavily and sugared.

"Yes, yes. Lovely girl Julia, very efficient." He clipped the end from his cigar, with a silver cutter that hung on the end of a chain, like a Phi Beta Kappa key. "Well, I'll get right to the point." He frowned at the cigar, rolling it in his fingers. "Prentiss Everett wants to see you about something and it seems he's having a difficult time getting an appointment." Alf Rhodes tried not to look like an errand boy.

"What does he want, Alf?"

"About an hour of your time I gather, but he won't tell me what it's about." He lighted the cigar, rolling it around in his mouth, as he sucked against the flame.

"What would you do Alf, if one of the most powerful and controversial black leaders in the country wanted an hour of your time and wouldn't tell you what it was about?" Bob sipped his coffee, crossing his legs, repelled by the wet end of the cigar, wondering how that would taste at ten in the morning with coffee.

"Well hell, I'd see him I guess. But of course he represents a large part of my constituency. He's sure as hell not from Virginia, so you'll have to make a judgment on that, but he stands for a hell of a lot of people Bob, both inside and outside Illinois. Some of 'em in Virginia I suspect." He sucked on the cigar and blew a long, tapering blast at the ceiling. "Hell of a lot more constituents than you and I, for that matter."

"That's what worries me, Alf."

"Well, it worries me too, Bob." The cigar dangled in his hand and Senator Alfred Porter Rhodes, Senior Senator from the State of Illinois, looked into the fire, unwilling to meet Bob's gaze.

"You know I'm not here to plead his case. I don't even know what his goddamn case is. But he called me and put on the heat. I can feel the flames and they're not coming from this lovely fire." He rearranged himself in the chair, noticing that the cigar had gone out. "Or this cigar, apparently. I'm up for reelection in November Bob, same as you are and I'd like one more term in this club. You'd do me a big favor, seeing him."

"An hour, you say."

"An hour." Alf drained the last of his coffee. It was clear he didn't want to be Everett's messenger boy, but equally clear he was carrying the message.

"All right, I'll see him. But I'd like you to make it clear to him it's a favor to you." A fly fisherman's presentation is everything and Bob's words dropped lightly on the water, drifting toward Alf, as if there were no hook.

"Oh, you can be sure I'll take every opportunity to make it look as if there'd never have been a meeting without me." He glanced at his watch and stood.

"Thanks, Bob. I owe you one."

"Not at all Alf, always happy to help." They walked to the door, Bob's hand on the Senator's shoulder. "Give my regards to Missy."

"I surely will, Bob, I surely will. She'll be pleased you asked after her."

The Senator was gone out the door, walking the long hall by himself. Julia would help him with his coat and what was left of his pride.

Through December Marty lurched from encounter to encounter, with a fiery redhead from Atlanta, an exotic and long legged Asian girl in Singapore, a green-eyed strawberry blonde in Berlin and a legion of other beauties of all nationalities. He lived only for the modem. The rest of his world slid slowly into a blur of inattentiveness, sloth and increasing isolation.

Pizza boxes and Chinese takeout cartons piled up around the apartment, nestled among scattered groups and clusters of beer bottles, all of it overcast with a film that turned to fingerprinted dust. His shirts, suits and unpolished shoes lay scattered where he fell out of them at night, too exhausted and distracted to care what chair they were thrown at. Underwear was piled in corners, as often worn again as washed.

Jean had kept the place spotless, his clothes carefully folded and put away. But Jean was just a shadow compared to any of the girls in the voluptuous memory of the modem.

Sometimes… only sometimes, he yearned for her anyway. Someone he could talk to, a soul-mate who knew his heart, to hold as he fell asleep, the memory of Valerie or Cathy or whoever fading from his mind. Those were times when he fell into the rumpled dirty sheets and felt himself collapsing inside like a black hole, getting smaller and smaller. It was an almost physical sensation, as if he were falling down a long tunnel, the walls closing in, everything spinning. Falling away from himself, disconnected from his voice, calling something or someone he couldn't make out, the voice fading. Finally, after eternities of minutes turned into hours, he'd stumble into a restless, fitful sleep and wake the next morning feeling as if he'd had no sleep at all.

The apartment was a wreck, a mirrored image of his life and the inexorable need to be wired, online, elsewhere. He knew better, but of course knowing was a trick of the mind, something put down like a book and picked up later, if at all. He wanted better and the gap between wanting and reality pissed him off every time he walked in the door at night. The apartment began to smell, a heavy stale odor of cigarette smoke, windows too long shut and food gone bad. It was Jean's fault for leaving, goddamn her anyway.

Marty meant to clean it all up, meant to get it pulled together and keep it that way. But the pull of *EVOKE* became a torment of procrastination. Later would do, tomorrow or Saturday and between this moment and that undefined future time he needed another computerized fix. Resolve slid away toward the bedroom, inexorably toward the nightstand and the damnable, incredible box.

While the modem was there for him, it was all he needed, all he would ever need. When the five hours were gone, he sank into profound depression, with nothing worth doing except mindless bodily function until the incessant buzz of the alarm.

He'd do a laundry tomorrow, honest to God he would. Get rid of the stink, that awful body smell of clothes worn too long. He'd clean the apartment from end to end, honest to God he would. Vacuum, empty ashtrays, dust tables and bookcases, wash the thick scum off the bottom of the bathtub. He'd go through the mail, clean the gravy off the kitchen counter where it had run down the front of the drawers and throw out all the collected, overflowing garbage. Wash dishes and take back piles of bottles, begin to read the newspapers stacked in the hall or at least cancel the subscriptions. Hang some of his own pictures on the bare nails in the hall, buy another CD player and retrieve the half-package of doughnuts that lay behind the couch. He'd take his rumpled suits to the cleaners tomorrow, always tomorrow. Go shopping and lay in a supply of groceries, start to cook for himself again. But that would have to wait. At the moment, whatever moment it happened to be, he was just too turned-on or too turned-off. In the meantime, there were plenty of joints that would deliver beer and something to eat.

The days at Clark and Anderson, his working life, were a nightmare. His mind was anywhere than the paperwork and it took a conscious effort of will to bring his eyes to focus on shipping documents. Drivers became the enemy and he was short tempered and forgetful with guys he'd known ten years. They began to stay away from him, clustered out of hearing for a quick smoke and a glance in his direction.

Old man Clark had him in the office more than once over the past few weeks, for petty shit. Every little minor fuckup became a big deal. The second meeting was a bitch. Seventy gross of specially tempered band-saw blades had gone to Marietta, Georgia instead of Marietta, Maine. Jesus Christ, anybody could have screwed that up. The old man had closed the door, walked all the way over and closed it, like he was some kid in the principal's office. Then sat for a moment at his desk, fiddling with papers, pulling himself together and making Marty sweat before finally looking up.

"Marty, what the hell is going on with you?"

"Sir?" Part of his mind was still in Venice with three Italian models, still connected to last night. What the hell would the old man know about Italian models and how three of them could work him over at one time? Clark's wife was in her fifties and he bet the old man had never been laid outside his marriage. Particularly the way Marty was getting laid, every night. "What do you mean?"

"I'll tell you what I mean," the old man replied, his annoyance barely covered. "I mean in the last five weeks we've had a dozen misdirected shipments on your shift. I *mean* Marty, you come in here half the time looking like you've been out all night and slept in your clothes. I *mean*, Mr. Greene that most of the time you need a shave. I mean all of the time you need a clean shirt and your suit pressed." He looked at him squarely, bringing Marty's mind back into focus.

"You on drugs, Marty?"

"No, sir. Absolutely not, Mr. Clark."

"Well Marty, if you've got a problem with drugs or booze, Clark & Anderson is not a coldhearted firm. We'll go to bat for a long-time employee like you, take you all the way through a rehab program and pay for it too. We like to be known as a family kind of company, you know that. We say it often enough but a family has responsibilities on both sides. If you're just laying down on us and forgetting your responsibilities to the family, we won't stand for it. Not for a damn minute, you understand that?"

"Yes, sir." He just wanted to get the hell out of the old man's office.

"Marty, I want you to know that in my mind you're on probation around here. You understand me? You understand what that means?"

"Yes, sir." The old man started to shuffle the papers on his desk and Marty eagerly got up to leave.

"And, Marty ... " Clark looked up from his desk.

"Yes, sir?" He was halfway to the door.

"Shave tomorrow morning and get that goddamn suit pressed."

"Yes, sir."

The following week, Marty got a jolt that grabbed his attention big-time. He came home on Friday afternoon, dogged out from another endless and frustrating week on the dock, sitting gratefully down at the modem.

Nothing.

No screen, no menu, *nothing.* He flipped the switch again, then once more, fighting the urge to slam the box with his fist.

Jesus, what a time for the goddamn thing to fail. He fumbled through the drawer and found the manual, flipping through the pages for an 800 service number.

There it was. Thank God, a twenty-four hour number. Marty picked up the phone.

Dead. No dial tone.

Holy shit, *the phone bill.* It must be there somewhere in the pile of mail and bills he'd meant to get to. Frantically he flipped through bills, tossing the phone invoices into a pile, one from October, November, December and here, one postmarked last week. He ripped it open to find the red bannered *Final Notice Prior to Disconnection*, requiring two hundred ten dollars and twenty seven cents before reconnecting. A service charge of ten bucks as well, total bill to date, two hundred eighty four dollars, eleven cents. Son of a bitch.

There was a bill payment center on Damen near North Avenue and he thought they were open late on Friday nights. Jesus, he hoped so. Grabbing his checkbook and the Final Notice, he bolted out the door, car keys in hand. It would be hell finding a parking place when he got back, but that was a small price to pay… just get the modem working again.

Better get through those bills this weekend. If they shut off the lights, he'd be fucked all over again. More accurately not fucked, he thought grimly.

"I can't do it."

"You *can* do it and you *will* do it or I'll goddamn destroy you and your worthless children and that family of yours that I keep so comfortable on their fat wop asses." There was no anger in his voice, just the deadly power of a decision already made and Carla's lower lip began to quiver, the cigarette growing an ash that dropped into her lap.

"Oh, Lonny, what do you *want* from me?" They sat in the living room, fire blazing, two figures reflected in the light, dwarfed by the massive space and the insignificance of their once having loved each other an eternity ago. "I had your children. I live by myself in this mausoleum, knowing you're with other women. I'm here when you need me to entertain." A tear puddled in the corner of her eye, blurring her vision and hung there, then ran down her pudgy cheek. She hated herself for the tear. "Why this? Why *now*? I don't think I can do it."

There it was. She'd waffled and now he'd won. He always won.

"Because you've become a sack of garbage and I'm tired of looking at you." He watched her wince, surprised that she still had the capacity to be hurt. "You're the wife of Alonzo Romeri and you're going to start looking the part." He leaned forward and stubbed out his cigarette, grinding it out as he was grinding her, no more feeling for one than the other.

"You want specifications? I'll give you the fucking specifications. Carla Romeri, height five foot four, weight one hundred two pounds, hair black. *Black* again, goddamn it and lustrous. Fit body again instead of that sack you call skin. Fit enough to play a decent game of tennis and you'll *learn* to play a decent game before you goddamn come back."

He rose from the chair and paced in front of the fire, looking at her as if she were a part moving down one of his assembly lines.

"I don't even know what you weigh now. You look like a goddamn tugboat."

She bit her lip, fighting back more tears, *willing* the tears not to run. Not now, please God. Not until later, when he's gone and she's alone. She was alone most of the time in this huge house, this perfect house that had not a trace of her in it. Filled with antiques from England and France, hung with paintings of all the important periods by all the important painters and no evidence of Carla anywhere.

The children gone as well, except for young Tony. Busy with their own lives and glad of the escape, seldom home but for alternate Thanksgivings or Christmases. Command performances, when Lonny re-created the family gatherings he'd hated as a child. His legacy of discomfort passed along to the next generation. His rules of mutual embarrassment poured over them like sauce over pasta. Carla's days were spent in the garden, often in sudden and uncontrolled tears, on the phone with her mother or at lunch with a girlfriend. The lunches and drinks and loneliness fattened her thighs, thickened her body and stole the glow from her skin. Lonny was elsewhere, occupied with business or his blonde slut. Merely an occasional thunderstorm to be endured until the sun came out again. Now even the sun was growing cold.

"I never heard of this place." It was over and she'd given up. His will had taken over her life again without even asking. Another demand to be met. Well, she'd meet it and maybe someday she'd kill him. So much of her time in the garden was spent killing him, savoring the moment, exploring every detail of his death and watching, endlessly watching his life drain away.

"That's because it's not a goddamn society fat farm. It belongs to me, just like you belong to me and its only purpose is to turn you out according to my plans." He looked at her without feeling, taking momentary satisfaction from the look on her face, a total collapse of features.

"It's in the mountains of Idaho. Complete with trainer, dietitian, speech coach, hairdresser and tutors for etiquette. God knows, you could use some of that. You'll goddamn learn current events so you can hold up your end of what passes for conversation. Literature, art, music, all that crap. There's a pool, stables and tennis court, complete with instructors." He paused and turned on her.

"You think I'm going to have you lolling around some goddamn spa, getting your name and my name in the goddamn trash magazines? You're gonna be *buried*, until you're fixed, until I'm satisfied."

"*When*?" She was suddenly terrified.

"Monday. Joe's flying you out at two."

"When can I come home?" Oh, God, there would be no booze. She knew he'd see that there was no booze. She clutched the arms of the chair and tried to breathe. How could she make it, without a drink?

"That's up to you. When you're done, you're done and if it takes a goddamn year... I've *got* a goddamn year."

"Do I have to be alone, Lonny? Why do I have to be alone?" A year. Oh God, a year stuck away someplace at age forty-eight trying to become someone made over. Trying to live up to something Lonny had in his mind and no matter how well she did it, knowing it wouldn't be enough, it would never be enough.

"If the reports I get back are good, after a month you can have a friend or your mother up, one at a time, no longer than a week. If I ever see anything in print, if a goddamn *word* of this ever leaks out, it's over. No more visitors and you can rot up there for all I care, all by yourself."

He lit another cigarette and put his foot on the edge of her chair, leaning his arm across his knee. "I'd get rid of you, but divorce doesn't fit my plans."

"Oh, Lonny ... " The tear started again, her nose ran and she didn't have a Kleenex.

"So, you're gonna shape up until you *do* fit my plans." The ash grew and he flicked it into the ash tray on the side table, taking another drag, arm back across his knee.

"It's not all downside, Carla. You get to kick that booze habit that you don't think I know about. Get self-improved so you're no longer the dumb wop slut I married. And you get to keep access to your snot-nosed kids and this life style." He dropped his cigarette on the Persian rug and ground it out with his shoe.

"Get that rewoven, tomorrow. I don't want to see it when I come back."

She watched him stride from the room, knowing Frank waited with the limousine to take him to his blonde whore. As he left the house tears began to roll and her whole body wracked with sobs that grew into a soundless lack of breath. Nearly an hour later she rose hollow-eyed from the chair and walked from the living room across the glass-enclosed porch through the dining room into the kitchen. Once there, she reached for the bottle of vodka on the top shelf, behind the formal dinnerware.

It was gone.

EIGHT

Lonny walked slowly down the front steps, a gray vicuna topcoat thrown over his shoulders, to the door Frank held for him and slid into the warm leather interior. He felt good and savored the feeling like a brandy after dinner. Carla was way out of hand and he'd let it go too far because he didn't really give a shit and seldom saw her. The Fairweather dinner made him realize how much he'd need a wife on his arm and Carla was the only wife he'd had or ever would have. If she didn't fit his needs, he'd see to it that she was changed into someone who did fit, as nearly as that was physically possible anyway. The plan for a new Carla was in motion and it pleased him, just one more thing under control.

"Where to, Mr. Romeri?"

"The apartment, Frank."

"Yes, sir." Frank closed his door, walked around the car and eased into the driver's seat, pulling silently away from the enormous Georgian mansion, most of its windows dark. The servants had long retired to their televisions, leaving only Carla, alone now in the living room and Tony, long gone to bed at the back of the house. Lonny knew she'd head for the booze.

The limousine wound its way down the curving drive through nearly two acres of heavily landscaped front lawn, its groves of pin oak holding their winter-brown leaves until new buds would push them off in the spring. A half million dollars worth of pin oak, mature trees moved in place with enormous cranes. The work was completed during a week Lonny was in

France and he returned to a new and forested entry, dropped into his yard as if by God himself. Frank touched a button at the visor and the wrought iron entry gates rolled back. The car pulled through, paused at the street and turned north, a wisp of exhaust vapor riding the chill night air as the gates closed behind receding taillights.

Lonny stretched his legs to the facing seat and settled back in the soft leather, reflecting on the day. His morning meeting with Ryan Walker had gone okay... better than okay. At eight o'clock on the dot they'd met in the private dining room off Lonny's office over coffee, fresh-baked rolls, Icelandic salmon and scrambled eggs. Very private, very friendly, very soothing to Walker's ego. Breakfast with one of the most powerful men in the industrial world.

Ryan, his chief financial officer, Ed Tate and George Wilkins, the senior partner in a Toledo law firm with seven names were right on time. Lonny let them wait precisely six minutes in his reception room. Miss Everleigh apologized for the delay, but he was on the phone to Washington and this sometimes happened. She knew they would understand.

The six minutes was precisely arranged to break the momentum of their arrival. They'd be forced into meaningless small-talk in earshot of his personal receptionist and slowly absorbed into the aura of his power and turf. The thick carpet, hushed voices, polished metal and soft leather established his territory as accurately as if a dog had peed in each corner. A single photograph of Lonny and the President of the United States was casually framed like a family snapshot on a side table. The pair of them grinned at the camera, arms across one another's shoulders, custom made Italian over-and-under shotguns broken at the breech and cradled casually. The President wore a shooting cap emblazoned with Lonny's club logo.

Six minutes wasn't offensive in an office that was obviously running full tilt at 8am, serving the needs of a man who seldom seemed to sleep. It was just right, precise, *sufficient*.

"Ryan, it's so good to see you again."

Lonny burst through the door from his office, in shirtsleeves rolled at the cuff, reaching out to Walker, who struggled to get out of the deep leather chair designed for exactly that purpose. Shaking his hand and nearly lifting him from the chair, Lonny's eyes drilled the center of his slightly flustered face. "I apologize for the phone call, but some calls I have very little control over." He let the implication hang.

"Yes Lonny, no problem... no problem at all." Walker recovered, turning to his companions, both standing now. "I believe you've met my CFO, Ed Tate and this is George Wilkins, who handles our legal work." Hands were shaken all round, Lonny's eyes smiling and intent as drill-bits.

"Gentlemen, shall we?" He gestured toward the open door. "Miss Everleigh, no calls please, unless of course He calls again." There would be and had been no call from Washington, but even so, the pronoun was capitalized. Lonny was pleased to be outnumbered at breakfast. There would only be Bill Wearley on his side and Romeri always functioned best from the minority position. He preferred setting his own pace and agenda, entirely capable of outflanking without the bother of troops. Advisors merely stumbled over one another and slowed him down.

"I hope you gentlemen haven't had breakfast. I had a few things prepared and Stewart does an excellent job in his small kitchen." Lonny strode back through his office, Bill Wearley rising from a chair near the desk for introductions. He led them to the dining room where a round pedestal table was set for four, silver coffee and tea service steaming. "Stewart, another place for Mr.

Wilkins, please." Naming the odd man out, he nodded toward the chef standing quietly by a side door.

"Wonderful, Lonny, very thoughtful," said Ryan, as they found seats and the place settings were rearranged. Christ, the three of them had met at five for coffee and eggs in Ryan's room at the Wilshire. It was brought by a surly night porter and the eggs were cold, the toast unbuttered. It seemed already to be noon.

"Well Ryan, let's get right down to cases." Lonny creamed and sugared his coffee. "Interstate's a hell of a company, one of our best-regarded suppliers." He took a sip of coffee and smiled across the table. "I want it and I want to make you richer than you already are when I buy it."

World Star wasn't making the offer. It was never World Star. *Lonny* made the offer and when he talked of the huge conglomerate it was always in the first person singular. He *was* the company. World Star never hungered for acquisition, cornered markets, issued stock or forced unwilling mergers. It was always Alonzo Romeri who thirsted, whose personal appetite must be satisfied.

"That, of course, is always a possibility." George Wilkins's baritone voice answered for Ryan, whose mouth had just closed over a sliver of salmon. He now chewed furiously, trying to catch up with events he assumed would follow a leisurely exploratory breakfast. Wilkins could smell more than the salmon cooking. His law firm would earn in six months from a sale what Ryan paid them in ten years of boring but steady legal service. His was a boring and steady business, the law and George Wilkins was boring and steady as well, but he was no fool.

"Three hundred million, one third cash, the balance in World Star stock parceled out however it best suits your tax needs." Lonny looked across at Ryan, whose eyes widened a bit and then narrowed, looking at

Tate and Wilkins. Lonny carefully applied his knife to a rosy fillet of salmon, a curl of fresh onion and several capers, the knife against his plate the only noise. Bill Wearley tried not to smile, looking down at his eggs.

"Interstate is nearly my whole life, Lonny. Started in my brother in-law's garage twenty-five years ago ... " Ryan was stunned and tried not to look it. *Three hundred million.* The last twenty-five years had been a rush of growth, not well enough financed, never enough money, a race between growing market share and the agony of capital. Huge payrolls, inconceivable payrolls to be met and sometimes nearly not met. He'd always made it, but Jesus sometimes it was close. Plant expansion, trucking contracts and teamster strikes nearly put him under. Now, one of the world's top executives was sitting across from him, chewing salmon and offering three hundred million.

"... I guess this is every man's dream, to cash out ... " Most men's dream at any rate. The pot of gold, but Ryan had never looked at the end of the rainbow, always too busy, too absorbed in the wonderful, frightening roller coaster of Interstate. He was still seen and seen often on the polished floors of his massive production facilities, still knew a couple dozen of the foremen and an equal number of machine operators by name. Jesus, Research and Development had started in his *basement.* Ten feet by twelve feet that he walled off next to where Marge hung the laundry, because they couldn't afford a dryer. Ten by twelve feet where Ryan perfected a lamination process for the magnetic steel stampings used in nearly every automobile and truck and airplane and lawn mower in the world.

He hadn't invented the process, that would've taken genius and Ryan wasn't in that class. He was a toolmaker, good enough to make the lamination faultless. Not ninety-three percent of the time like the industry standard, but with a failure-rate so close to zero it defied measurement. A lamination that failed in a finished product cost consumer confidence, down time and call-backs. Interstate's laminations simply didn't fail and their refusal to accept a failure rate made Ryan Walker a wealthy man. Stamping machines ran three shifts a day on polished floors. R&D now took six thousand square feet of the main plant in Toledo. Cash out… Jesus, it was like selling his children, but he knew that was why he was here.

"Not many men go from their garage to three hundred million." Lonny held his fork at half mast, gazing across at Ryan like he might become the next bite. Lonny could tell Walker was waxing nostalgic on him. Nostalgia cost money and killed more deals than greed. "You've been cash-strapped all your life, Ryan. No kids to leave it to and you're almost sixty." His voice was understanding, almost fatherly. Though Lonny was the younger man, his voice was low enough to be personal, to show he was touched by the strain the toolmaker had endured and so intimate the others leaned forward to hear.

"I'm offering twelve million for every one of those twenty five years, a million a month."

Walker would either reach across the table, shake his hand and tell him it was a done deal or there would probably be no deal. He didn't reach.

"Your offer is very generous for a preliminary offer," Wilkins baritone broke the spell Lonny wove. It wasn't lost on him, that word 'preliminary.' "We anticipated the subject of this meeting and Ed Tate has put together some figures … "

Greedy son of a bitch, the lawyers always got greedy. Tate stirred in his chair uneasily, taking a last gulp of coffee. He wiped the corner of his small mouth with a linen napkin, its whiteness contrasting a four-thirty shave.

"We have some numbers ourselves," Lonny said and looked at Wearley. "Just a few things scratched out by our Financial Division. Suppose we adjourn to my office where we can spread out?" He slid his chair back and nodded to the chef still glued to the side door. "Stewart, that was excellent, as always. More coffee in my office, if you will."

"Yes, Mr. Romeri."

"Let's see what you've got, Ed." Bill Wearley took over now and herded them into Lonny's office, Romeri following as if he were distracted by more important issues. They settled into soft chairs around a low table, cigarettes coming out of shirt pockets and gold cases. Ed Tate was obviously nervous about what numbers the dreaded 'Financial Division' might have. How the hell would his compare? Was he likely to leave money on the table, or blow this thing out of the water? Almost either way, Walker would be all over his ass. The meeting droned on, 'till almost eleven, Lonny stepping in and out. George Wilkins self-servingly screwed up negotiations, playing upon Ryan Walker's foremost fear, the fear of selling his life work, no matter the number.

It was clear to Lonny within fifteen minutes that the deal would never be struck. He let Bill set the pace and played the cordial host and interested billionaire as the need arose. He engaged Ryan occasionally in private conversation as some mindless detail was described. Two entrepreneurs having a chat and well above discussions over detail. If the deal were done it would be done at a profit to both.

The deal was not done, unable to surmount the steady, insidious lawyering and accountancy.

"Well, Ryan, you've built yourself a wonderful firm. Hell, damn near an empire and I want you to know how much I respect that." Lonny had his arm across Walker's shoulders, strolling out to the receptionist's office. "Our boys have a lot more to discuss and I still have hopes." He paused and took Ryan's hand in both of his, the seldom used and almost conspiratorial double handed shake of close friends. "I just want you to know, Ryan, and I mean this in great sincerity, if we are unable to come to an agreement, Interstate has a long, uninterrupted and very profitable relationship in its future with World Star." Bill Wearley was busy with the others. Lonny aimed these words only at Walker. "Gentlemen." He waved at the others and turned back to his office, followed by Wearley, who softly closed the door.

"Plan B, Bill. I want the negotiations to be friendly, but fruitless. Bury him." Bill Wearley nodded.

Now the wheels of Plan B were underway, for Carla as well as Ryan Walker. The limousine pulled to the curb and Lonny stretched, looking forward to an evening ahead with Tanya in the discreet apartment he kept for her. He hated the name Tanya. It sounded like an exotic dancer, but of course that's what she was before she belonged to Lonny. He hadn't seen her for a week.

One in the morning, she might be a little sleepy by now, but she was sometimes better when she was a little sleepy.

"When do you want me, Mr. Romeri?" Frank opened the door.

"Seven, Frank. Seven will be fine, thanks."

An hour east of Detroit's time zone, Bob Fairweather took off his reading glasses and set them carefully on the coffee table. He pushed himself up from the sofa where he'd sat for four hours poring over Lonny's report, unable to put it down. Needing now to take a leak and get himself a brandy.

There were no servants at the townhouse they kept, his only residence without staff and they maintained it mostly for what necessary entertaining drew the powerful to Georgetown. Besides, his father had owned it and there was a degree of conservatorship in maintaining the place. Day staff was available when needed and Bob rather enjoyed doing for himself on the infrequent occasions he stayed in town. It gave him a chance to scramble eggs, should he feel like it and he often felt like it. He avoided the regular Washington hangouts and Georgetown restaurants, even the Senate dining room. His preference was well known for sandwiches at his desk or a bachelor's meal at the townhouse. He rummaged through cabinets, finding the brandy and pouring himself a generous drink. It must be a little after one, he mused and it seemed like an eternity since he'd had a good long full night's rest. He was bone tired. He'd been tired when he picked up the report about nine, hoping to give it a cursory look and turn in early. But Romeri's figures were dynamite and even more than the figures, their source troubled him. He wished Maggie was there, to share a drink and her unfailing wisdom.

Bob expected something much like a corporate Annual Report. Smoothing out a few figures with conjecture on future opportunities, mostly gloss and not much unmanaged fact. There wasn't any conjecture here. He would gladly trade what he'd laid on the sofa for so innocent a document.

A full five years of the purchasing history of five million American citizens was laid out in the report, all of them connected unequivocally to *EVOKE*. He sighed, walked over to the credenza and fished a Rachmaninoff CD from the stack, the Piano Concerto #2 and slipped it into the machine, waiting for the volume, then turning it low. There was no guesswork in Romeri's figures, no numbers pulled from averages of total consumer activity. This was all hard data ferreted out of the records of five million onliners. They'd all been on the system for at least four years in order to establish trends. Those names were supposed to be inviolate, unknown, protected. It was the law.

Only a company the size of World Star had the capacity to put something like this together and even then only with some sort of pipeline to the Social Security Administration's *EVOKE Division* records. There was simply no other way and those records were protected by laws worked out in Bob's own committee. There had to be a leak, a serious leak and a hell of a lot of money must have changed hands. Even the Senate Committee couldn't get such records. They'd tried and been denied access by the very law they themselves had written. Bob picked up the report, hefting it, feeling the weight of its spiral bound content, wondering at the arrogance that ordered it done and, even more so, the absolute assurance of the man who delivered it.

Lonny had balls, no way around that. The music rose and receded, thundered, then faded to an almost excruciating delicacy. This report could put people in jail. There were even implications for his own knowledge of the information in it. It must have taken the better part of a corporate division to run this thing down. Hundreds of thousands of hours of computer time, tens of millions of dollars, to casually dump in Bob's lap. Dropped after dinner, with the offhand comment that he would 'rather no one but Bob see it.' Balls, the son of a bitch had balls.

World Star had developed computer software that provided access to a vast network of consumer credit reporting and sold or leased it world-wide, that division accounting for a very healthy share of overall corporate profit. They regularly took Social Security numbers and ran credit checks, the detail of the information reported determining the fee. But it was possible to *legally* access personal bank account balances and activity, mortgages, car loans, credit card purchases and payment history. Everything from buying a pair of socks to a country club application left a paper trail. That was all legal and available to anyone with the patience and expertise to track it down. Expensive as hell, but legal. The cost of tracing the purchasing records of five million *EVOKE* users and then cross-referencing the data was beyond the capability of any private data collection, certainly when there was no profit motive.

All that to back up a point made over dinner.

What was glaringly, flagrantly, egregiously *illegal*, was the source of those specially selected Social Security numbers. Matching federally protected *EVOKE* subscribers with such unerring accuracy pointed directly to a source inside the Social Security Administration. Dynamite was too mild a term. Rachmaninoff agreed with crashing clarity.

Bob would seek his own legal counsel tomorrow, before sharing this information with Dan McCarthy. Beyond the legal implications, the study left little doubt of what was happening in the marketplace. A steady slackening off of almost all financial activity among *EVOKE* subscribers, beginning within a couple of months of subscription. It became more apparent over the first year, then leveled off at a continued and substantially reduced rate.

Enough angst! Bob picked the report off the table, slipped it into his briefcase and drained the last of the brandy. He switched off the CD and headed for the bedroom, flipping off the master wall switch. He badly needed sleep, wondering if he'd be able to turn his mind off sufficiently to find it.

Lonny turned his key in Tanya's apartment door, opened it and walked into the smallish entry. He dumped his coat and briefcase onto a chair.

"That you, Lon?" Her voice came from the kitchen.

"Better be me. Who the hell else would you expect?" He moved into the living room, shrugged off his suit coat, loosened his tie and unbuttoned the collar. A room to be comfortable in, a man's room all in shades of gray, but with a woman's touch that brought it to life. Fresh flowers. Always fresh flowers and tonight gardenias floated in a low bowl. The scent was heady, reminding Lonny of Mexico and swimming pools floating gardenias. Damn, when he dove into those pools he could smell them underwater.

"Hi, Mr. Sweetness." Tanya walked in wearing a dressing gown he'd given her for some long forgotten occasion. A bottle of J&B dangled from one hand, two highball glasses in the other and she wrinkled her nose at him. "You sound like you had a rough day and I might have a rough night."

Nothing subtle about Tanya. She could give as good as she took and pushed Lonny, sometimes too close to the edge. But she was dead straight level with him in a world where few people were and he needed that. He needed her and sometimes that was hard to admit and made him vaguely uncomfortable. It wasn't Lonny's style to need anyone and never, *ever* did he presume he would need a woman.

"Hi, kid." He grinned at her. "Naw, I'm okay, just a little busy as usual and it takes me a couple minutes to unwind." He slumped onto the sofa, kicking off his shoes, stretching his legs to rest on the low, plate-glass coffee table. "Pour me a good hit of that stuff, kid."

"Here, unwind around this," she set the bottle and the glasses on the table, easing onto the sofa, her body across his, a hand around his neck.

"Whoa, hang on for a minute." He shoved her away from him, not roughly, but nearly so. "Pour me that drink and let me catch my fucking breath."

"Okay, sweetness. You catch it and I'll take it away when you're ready." She pulled her legs under her and coiled at the other end of the sofa, pouring two scotches neat, no ice, no water.

Winifred Eversly had lovely long legs to coil. A tall, dancer's body with a chorus-line figure rather than the bump and grind shapes that filled the cheap joints on the fringes of Detroit. Her hair was a dark golden blonde, full and swept from the forehead with the nearly invisible eyebrows and brilliant blue eyes of Nordic heritage from both parents. She had sexual confidence, as it only develops in a woman nearing thirty. Bright and well read, she had the intellectual curiosity of a girl who'd missed college, but never the pleasure of learning. Her given name was Winifred and no one knew, so far as she was aware. Tanya Evers had been her name since she'd legally changed it ten years ago at eighteen, lawfully able to leave Winifred behind in a courtroom in Great Bend. Tanya Evers gratefully abandoned Barton County Kansas and the hook in the Arkansas River that gave Great Bend its name. Left it behind, along with a husband and baby and in the intervening ten years she'd heard from neither of them. They were smoke, lying across the horizon of another life, long blown away by a storm of her own creation. She'd slipped away under cover of thunder and lightning, running from a life that held nothing for her.

Tanya watched Lonny in profile, hair black as coal, graying slightly at the temple. Long delicate ears just under that brushed back hair and a handsome Roman nose that made him look like he should wear a toga instead of a business suit. Not a Greek god, but very much a Roman Emperor.

"Better, sweetness?" He was winding down and she watched the process she'd come to know so well, a physical thing with Lonny like watching a horse at the track after a race, walking out under a cooler. Head high, ears pricked, sweating and taking those long strides left over from the race. Then the head dropped, the strides shortened as all the fear and noise and adrenaline washed out of the bloodstream and a pounding heart slowed to normal. She smiled to herself. They rubbed down horses too, after a hard race.

"Yeah, better. I'm going to get out of this damned suit." He got up and reached for the scotch, taking it with him to the bedroom where he kept closets full of suits and shirts and ties. He held the glass loosely in one hand, suit coat slung over his shoulder.

"Need help?"

"Later, kid, but probably not too much later." He disappeared into the hallway and she heard him begin to hum, his unwinding begun.

It was foolish to love him. Exotic dancers dreamed of marrying men like Lonny and she knew at best she'd grow old being his mistress, listening to him call her 'kid,' when her youth was long gone. They'd been together five years, four and a half longer than she'd given it to last when they first met in Vegas. Tanya was a setup for Lonny, just another courtesy of the hotel in which he held a majority interest, a one-night stand, like so many others before her and simply part of the job, the part she hated most. But he'd asked to see her again and they spent the week together. Then he was gone on his private jet and she figured that was that. Out of the blue, two months later when she'd all but forgotten this intense, dark man with the soft hands and the rough tongue, Bill Wearley called and asked her to come to New York.

They spent three days together and Lonny, not Wearley this time but Lonny, asked her to come to

143

Detroit. He set her up running Club Lago and bought her the apartment. It was a business deal and Tanya knew the business. She was there when he called, dressing as he wished in the clothes he bought for her, learning his moods, beginning to understand what was expected. Occasionally she threw him off balance with passion that turned wild and was deeply felt. Then receding, she retreated for weeks and sometimes months to what he wanted and needed, what quieted him. It wasn't supposed to last and she didn't want ever to be in love again. But here she was, five years older and breaking all the rules.

"Put on some music, kid." Lonny's voice came from the bedroom, followed by the man himself, still humming and wearing an old robe over khakis and a tee shirt, barefoot. "Some of that old jazz, nice and low." When she'd set the CD and came back to pick up her scotch, he settled onto the couch, reaching for her. "What was it you were saying, something about me wrapping myself around something . . .?"

"Mmmmmm . . ." She pulled him down and settled his head in her lap, his body stretched out, bare feet on the armrest. She stroked his hair, running fingers behind the long ears, gently massaging his temple, his arm across her bare leg, rubbing her as gently. The rubbing slowed, his fingers relaxed and he was asleep.

Lonny rolled over and felt for her, her warmth soft against the sheets, turned on her side, back to him. He pulled himself across the bed, sliding an arm under her neck, the other across her waist, snuggling against the warm flesh of her butt, like two spoons nested. She stirred in her sleep, then began to wake, rolling full into his arms, eyes fluttering. A murmured 'Lon?' and she drifted back, sliding a leg between his, their arms around each other.

Lonny had other women in other cities. He also had the chip just under his scalp he sometimes used when a flight was long and boring and the paperwork was done. *EVOKE* was fun, like looking at a skin magazine when he was a kid, but that was all. He preferred the real thing. He preferred Tanya, the only one among many that meant anything.

He lifted his head carefully, not wanting to disturb the wash of blonde hair across the sheet, straining to see the bedside clock. Five-twenty, he sank back to the luxury of half sleep. He'd drifted off last night on the sofa, then wakened to find her stroking his hair, Charlie Parker playing softly in the background.

Dan McCarthy poured another cup of coffee and nudged it toward Sally.

"He's late getting in again this morning and that's not like him. Two days in a row."

"I know." She took the coffee, wishing she'd learned to like it with sugar and cream. Maybe that would take the edge off the caffeine. "Give the guy a break, will you? He's not a machine." She sipped her coffee and checked the schedule. He'd be late all day now and probably have lunch on the run. "This is his third term and politics makes old men out of young men in a hurry, if they give a damn, anyway. He's doing pretty well, I'd say."

"Yeah, shit. He was born to be here." Dan fiddled with a stack of legislative recommendations and considered the irony of the remark. "It's me that's getting burned out. Don't know how much longer I can stick." He looked at his watch and idly twisted a class ring, his only jewelry. It would be hard to leave Bob Fairweather, burned out or not. Dan had maneuvered relentlessly to become the Senator's choice for the vacancy in his office. A graduate of Harvard Law with a Masters in Political Science, his credentials were made for a spot like this. Now he was here, the place he struggled for and began to second guess the choice. Nothing in his college career prepared him for the day in, day out drudgery and difficulty of each minor accomplishment in the Senate. The power and prestige he'd expected in the office of a three-term senior Senator was constantly drained off, bled away in compromise over the simplest issues. Political office of his own was the dream, the goal he'd set for thirty-five, forty at the latest. Now he wasn't sure. The Senator was at the top. The most exclusive club in the world, they called it. It was a struggle at the top, as he'd had more than enough opportunity to witness and he'd begin at the bottom.

"Who else gets the opportunities we do?" Sally looked at him straight on. "Small staff and access to the whole ball game. Right in the pocket of a senior Senator."

"Yeah ... "

"Dan, I need to see you in my office." Bob strode into Sally's office, startling them, a cup of coffee already in one hand, coat and briefcase in the other. He looked like he hadn't slept well, maybe not at all. "Sorry, Sally, we'll just be a couple of minutes."

"Sure."

She shot Dan a what's-up? glance as the two of them disappeared into Bob's office, Dan returning a how-the-hell-should-I-know? raising his eyebrows and closing the door behind him.

"Sit down." Bob set his coffee on the desk and hung his topcoat and suit coat in the closet, waving Dan to a side chair.

Something serious was up, something out of the ordinary. Fairweather looked grim and Dan sensed something unpleasant, remembering that he'd left the list of legislative recommendations in Sally's office. Jesus, he hoped it wasn't a woman-thing.

"I'm late, because I've been on the phone with Emerson Wayland. He's my personal attorney in Richmond. Emerson tells me that what I'm going to show you is privileged by my position in the Senate and my staff is covered by those same exemptions. I don't want to find myself out on a limb and I sure as hell don't want you on one." Bob pushed the bound report across the desk.

"Sounds pretty serious." Dan reached for the report.

"It is." Bob leaned back in the chair, thought better of it and put his elbows on the desk, chin resting on folded hands, looking across to his senior aide. "Kept me up most of last night and what little sleep I had wasn't worth a damn."

"You want to tell me what it is generally, or want me to read it now?" It wasn't like the Senator to swear, even the relatively harmless 'damn' had an unusual emphasis coming from him.

"It'll explain itself, Dan." His chin was still on his hands. "I don't want to prejudice your reading with my opinion, but it'll take about three or four hours for you to go through and then I need to know what you think." He paused. "*Today*. I need to know what you think *today*."

He paused again and Dan felt the blood begin to pulse in his neck. "I'd like you to drop everything else for half a day and see me here about two. Take notes as you need, but nothing in the margins This's likely to be the only copy we'll get and it is *not* to be reproduced on our own copier, nor is anyone else to see it. Don't leave it on your desk. If you go for even so much as a cup of coffee, take it with you and don't leave the building with it." He stood up. "Understood?"

"Yes, sir," Dan rose as well, his cheeks slightly flushed. Whatever it was that was on the Senator's mind and screwing up his schedules, McCarthy held in his hand.

"I appreciate it, Dan. Sally will just have to work around the schedules. Won't be the first time she's had to do that. Send her in on your way out, will you?"

"Yes, sir," he headed for the door, leaving it open and rolling his eyes at Sally on the way through her office. He reached down to pick up the staff reports and silently thumbed at the Senator's office, mouthing to words *wants you.*

"Senator?" She stood at the door, schedule in hand.

"Come in, Sally, I'm afraid we're going to have to do some rearranging." He smiled now and walked around the desk to sit in the chair across from where she sat during their regular scheduling meetings. "I know that causes you difficulties and there'll probably be some calls to make with the usual apologies, but it can't be helped."

"No problem, we can do that." He looks awfully tired, she thought.

"Good, I need particularly to clear the afternoon, from about two, until Wilson shows up at six to drag me off home." He smiled again. Home seemed a long way off. "Anything on there we can't budge?" He nodded at the schedule.

"Senator Watkins at two, something about a vote expected Friday, but we have some room for him tomorrow. A meeting with a couple of lobbyists I've already put off twice, but they're used to that. Nothing that can't be moved." She was scratching lines through names.

"That's fine. Tell Watkins I'm really sorry."

"Oh, that meeting with Reverend Everett. I set it up as you asked, lunch here in the office on Tuesday. Menu A or menu B?"

"Menu A, Sally. We'll give him a decent show, but I don't like going in blind like this and I want you to make sure we have only an hour. If I wave you off and I doubt I will, hour and a half, tops."

At ten o'clock, Lonny turned away from the window at Corporate Headquarters and reached for the intercom. *May as well get this moving, been thinking about it too long.* If it was stuck in his mind, he might just as well get it out and on someone else's mind. "Vicky, get hold of Bill Wearley and ask him to come in here, please."

"Right away, Mr. Romeri." She picked up a schedule and ran her finger down the list of names to see where Wearley was supposed to be at this hour. Sometimes she was lucky, but sometimes it took a while and he was always pissed when she used his pager as a last resort. Ego. Seemed the biggest part of her job involved smoothing over egos, protecting one from another like kids on the playground. She dialed Ed Walker's office.

"Jean, is Bill there? Romeri wants him right away."

Ten minutes later, Vicky announced him and Wearley walked into the Chairman's suite of offices, wondering what was on the boss' mind. Bill Wearley's official title was 'Assistant to the Chairman' and it was the ambiguous aspect of that title that was the source of his power. His call would bring the CEO of World Star to a meeting of his choosing, no questions asked. It was power he used sparingly but it was there and created an aura around Bill second only to Romeri's. He knew where his access came from and he knew where a lot of the boss's bodies were buried. It was a dream job that had cost him two wives and almost all that was left of his private life, but there were no regrets.

"Bill, sit down." Lonny waved toward a chair and came around from behind the desk to join him. The first November snowfall began to collect across the landscaped courtyard of the Executive Office Building and it was dirty before it even hit the ground. "I need you to ferret out some information." He threw a leg over the arm of the chair. "Very *sensitive* information."

"Shoot."

That was Bill's specialty, finding out what had to be known with no one the wiser. That and its counterpart, Romeri's security. Bodyguards were someone else's chore, but Wearley had charge of a full-time staff who constantly swept Lonny's homes and offices, both here and abroad for bugs and listening devices. That included cars, planes, boats, hotel rooms and even Tanya's apartment. The office they sat in had been swept at 5am, as it was every day of the week.

"You know the *EVOKE* system?" Lonny poured coffee from the steaming carafe. "You want coffee?"

"No thanks." He watched Romeri pour, his hands steady. "Yes, I know the system, most everybody does."

"I don't mean that. I mean, do you know the system *internally*? How it operates, the nuts and bolts?"

"Pretty much." He reached for the carafe. "Maybe I will have a cup." He poured and his hands were not as steady as Romeri's. It annoyed him and he poured quickly. "Got into it pretty deeply when we were researching product access, but they keep it under wraps as much as possible."

"Theoretically, Bill. Strictly *theoretically*, could someone get killed using *EVOKE*?" Lonny reached for a cigarette.

"I don't know." Jesus, what did the boss have in mind? "You mean accidentally?"

"Yeah… accidentally." Lonny flicked the lighter, held the flame to the end of the cigarette and took a long drag.

"Well, of course there's a stainless steel wire and chip, both of which are pretty good conductors, right into the goddamn brain and it is an electrical gadget, the modem runs on house current, but it's only a transmitter." He paused, watching Romeri slip the gold lighter into his pocket. "No direct connection other than headphones and those are damn well covered by surge protectors, I would imagine. Probably not much danger. Never heard of a problem."

"Never heard of one?"

"No."

"But there *could* have been problems?" Romeri was still gazing into the fire. "Probably well firewalled from the press, wouldn't want the public to know."

"I guess." Wearley sipped his coffee. It was scalding hot.

"How tough would it be to find out, Bill? To find out how many people, out of twenty million had died online?" Lonny waggled a toe, still looking into the fire, exhaling a long plume of smoke into the draft of the chimney. "And what they died of, heart attack, short circuit, whatever . . .?"

"Tough. Not impossible, but tough. Take a little time, the records may not even exist." Romeri didn't like the word 'impossible' and Bill never remembered having used it. What Lonny wanted he got or he found someone who *would* get it.

"As tough as access to Social Security records?" Romeri swung his eyes away from the fire and looked directly at Bill.

"Well, that was a different matter. At least those records exist." He returned the gaze. "These records may not exist."

"But they could be extrapolated?'

"Sure... take a while, I don't know exactly?"

"Of course you don't, Bill. This is dealing with unknowns and making knowns out of them and no one

151

knows what's involved in that. Rumsfeld covered his ass decades ago with just that very term." He sipped his coffee. "Pure research, the most difficult kind." The cup clinked cleanly into the saucer, without a rattle. "But, I'd like you to pull some people together Bill and make this a priority. Very quiet, but a priority and keep me posted, let's say twice a week. Whatever resources you need."

"Yes, Mr. Romeri." Wearley drained his coffee preparing to leave, his throat on fire.

"One other thing, Bill."

"Yes?"

"Put some people on this *theoretical* point of mine. "I'd like to know, exactly and specifically, under what circumstances *EVOKE* might be dangerous. Even... deadly."

NINE

The vulnerability of his online life so snugly cradled in the arms of Illinois Bell Telephone sobered Marty and brought him back down to earth. It shook him to recognize his life had become that dependent on outside influences, things entirely beyond his control. Okay, so paying the fucking bill wasn't beyond control, but the phone cutoff made him think about the electric bill, his credit card payments and whatever else was piled under a pizza box. It was what it was and he better look into it.

He dedicated the weekend, except for evenings, to getting his life in some kind of order, promised himself yet again he would stay on track and get back to normal, live like he used to live. Jesus, he felt like an alcoholic coming off a bender and making promises. Gotta watch yourself, Marty. Keep it together. Grabbing armloads of disheveled clothing, he piled it in the Honda and stopped off at the cleaners and laundry. Even bought a couple of new white shirts to tide him over until Wednesday, when he could pick up freshly cleaned clothes.

He waded through the apartment, gathering bottles and cans, wrappers and papers and even warming to the task as he saw some semblance of order and humanity return to the rooms he'd shared with Jean. Cleaned the toilet and bathtub, washed all the dishes and actually put them away. Found the vacuum cleaner in the back hall closet and dusted and washed and vacuumed and changed the wrinkled and crusty sheets on the bed. Restacked his records, tapes and CDs that were scattered across the living room and found the extra set of keys he thought he'd lost in the street. He paid the bills. *All* of them. That part was easy, Christ, he was spending hardly any money at all, compared to his old life. No more nights out with the boys, cruising from disco to disco, dropping twenty here and forty there. All the expensive dinners, movies and three-day ski trips to Colorado at a thousand bucks a clip now lay in his past. There wouldn't *be* another Jamaica in mid-winter this year. No need for any of it, the modem was his life now and it only cost a hundred bucks a month. Chicken feed. A small price to pay.

He'd drop out of golf with the Saturday morning guys next spring. After ten years of rain or shine fanatic commitment to their regular 7am starting time, this year's trip to Biloxi killed it. Their regular winter trip week of grab-ass and thirty-six holes a day on the Gulf, a getaway for just the guys. Five days of eighteen holes in the morning, lunch and beers, another eighteen in the afternoon and a tour of the local bars every night. The trip they talked about all through the regular season, but it was dead as a deer by the side of the road now.

This year, all Biloxi did was piss him off. After he'd won the Masters and the U.S. Open and the PGA on the modem, it took all the pleasure out of shooting 106 in the morning and a hundred, if he was lucky in the afternoon, more likely a hundred twenty. Made him frustrated and irritable, a regular pain in the ass to Mort and Frank and Cliff, who'd kidded him out of his ups and downs for ten years. Christ, winning the tournaments was so real for Marty that he was surprised the next morning not being recognized on the street. The letdown somehow ruined him for golf.

When he played the Masters, his name was on the leader board at Augusta National. No matter that it listed Tiger Woods, six under at the sixty seventh hole and leading by two. He *was* Woods, because he inhabited his body, emotions and spectacular talent. For five incredible hours, he *understood* the drive to win and the unparalleled talent Woods brought to the game.

He played the final round with Davis Love, two strokes back and trying to put together a charge. Steady, deadly Davis, with two birdies on the closing four holes. Yeah, Marty was in the lead, but two strokes was razor thin and the five finishing holes had buried many a two stroke lead. He was pumped, but worried about being too pumped. As he walked to the eighteenth tee, Love had crept to within a stroke. Marty looked down the final fairway. Five hundred five yards away from the fabled green jacket of Masters winners and he pulled out the driver, instead of a more conservative three-wood. It was a bold move and he knew countless tournaments had been lost by bold moves on the final holes. Always termed foolish in the Monday sports columns by sportswriters who couldn't break a hundred on their home course. Tailing just a bit, the shot took a bad bounce, ending up in an almost impossible lie, just inside the heavy rough off the left side of the fairway. The tee shot left him a hundred seventy yards to the pin and it was all carry to a fiercely bunkered green.

Love, just a shot behind, nailed his drive and landed comfortably in the middle of the fairway, a hundred fifty yards out, hitching his pants with a grin as he strode off the tee. He had a straight shot at the flag and few tour players were more deadly with short irons.

Marty settled over the shot twice, changing from a seven iron to a six and then back to a seven, as forty million people world-wide held their breath. His heart moved several inches up in his chest and he felt the pulse at his neck as he looked at the ball, only half visible and nestled deep in the long-cut rough. He took two deep breaths, lush breaths full of cut grass and azalea and walked a small circle back to his caddy. The most important shot of his career and he was unsettled.

"What do you think, Steve?"

"Hell, Tiger, I think it's a six." A six is always your club at a hundred seventy. If you don't get there, those bunkers won't give you enough room to the flag and you'll never get up and down."

"I'm pumped though, Steve. This one's got to come out high and drift in and bite. There's nothing behind the green but gallery and TV cables."

"You're the boss, Tiger. All I do is follow you around, picking up money." Steve grinned at him and he knew a seven was right. He could make the shot.

His swing was textbook and the ball came out high and clean, landing eight feet behind the pin, with so much backspin, that it almost hit the flag on its way back down the glassy green, settling in the fringe forty feet below the hole. A roar came up from the crowd in the bleachers surrounding the eighteenth hole. Marty was lightheaded and grinning, handing the seven iron to Steve, who winked at him and slammed it into the bag.

That should settle Davis. He'd need a birdie to tie.

As they walked down the fairway to the green, there'd been the traditional standing ovation and Marty could still feel it washing over him. Davis made an absolutely faultless approach shot and lay seven feet from the hole and the birdie that would tie, setting off another roar.

Forty feet was too far out to try and hole the putt, not with a one stroke lead. Marty lined up the putt and considered the alternatives, squatting on his heels and squinting across the green. Love could easily make a seven-footer, but this was one he *had* to make. The pressure was all on Davis. Unless Marty did something foolish and trying to sink the shot was foolish. Lag it up for a tap in and keep the pressure on Davis. The greens were slick as glass and if he tried for the hole he could slip past by ten feet, putting all the pressure on himself. Just cool it. Lag it up for a tap-in.

He stroked the ball confidently and it slid up the left side of the green, curling with the break and came to rest about eighteen inches out, dead flat level to the hole. Steve grinned and took the putter as Marty strolled over to the edge of the green to watch Love's putt. God damn, his heart was pounding. Relax, he told himself, just try to get a grip on it and finish. Let's not take this to a playoff.

Only seven feet, but there was left to right break in it and the touch would be the ball game. If Davis had the right speed, the break wouldn't be a problem. He lined it up from both sides, stepped up, then stepped away, squatting down to once more plumb his putter against the break. He settled over the putt, touched it and Marty watched, along with forty million others as the ball curved through the break, caught the edge of the hole, rimmed it and settled an inch away. The gallery sighed a collective sigh as Love tapped in for par.

Marty's heart continued to race as he walked to the putt and he took several deep breaths. Eighteen inches from another green jacket. There was nothing tentative about his stroke, the rattle of the ball in the cup lost in a wild and nearly endless cheer from the gallery. Love shook his hand, Steve Williams gave him a hug that lifted him off the ground. Tiger's moment was his now and if he needed another reminder, there was always the program to play again.

At any rate he felt silly at Pine Meadows, taking constant double and triple bogeys and his heart wasn't in it anymore. Joe Hogarth would play in Marty's spot next spring. Matter of fact, Marty wasn't seeing much of anyone anymore. It was all business during the workday and the bull sessions of the guys on the dock and in the warehouse went on in clusters and bunches that no longer interested him. A kind of wariness developed between them that had never been there before.

Old man Clark scared the shit out of Marty about two weeks after their sweaty meeting in his office. Told him straight out, if he didn't get back on the ball he was scheduled to be let go as of January 31st. That stung him personally, got his attention and bought into focus a world increasingly blurred.

Fired, after almost ten years with a firm like Clark & Anderson? Jesus, that would make it nearly impossible for him to find another job. Not without taking a hell of a cut in pay and seniority and most of all, the profit sharing pension trust. Too much at stake to fuck around with the old man, way *way* too much and Marty forced himself to concentrate. He didn't win the Masters by losing his concentration. He forced himself back into the routine of checking every detail, every ticket, every load and made sure he was there fifteen minutes before his shift to take over from the night-man as smoothly as passing a baton, handing it off easily to the late shift at four. The guys stopped coming to Marty with personal problems or the joke they heard last night at the bowling alley or just to bullshit while trucks were loading. It was all business. Sometimes he missed the old days, the cluster of guys around his desk, smoking and drinking coffee and being easy with one another. That was okay, things change. Good stuff comes, other good stuff goes.

Even so, *EVOKE* was closing Marty down and he was so *willing* that sometimes it scared him to death. Not often and not for long, but sometimes. The chill that ran through him on those occasional introspections was like coming to the end of a long Christian life and finding there was no God.

He had a recurring nightmare. It woke him sweating, heart pounding and dry-mouthed, unsure whether or not he'd screamed, but he felt like he screamed and no one heard--a Marty no longer audible, no longer visible. In the dream he was an observer of others, others who could be heard and seen and felt. In his nightmare Marty opened the program and was getting laid, right on the green leather couch in old man Clark's big corner office. She was on top of him and he was powerless, unable to stop, to run, to do anything except the fucking. All the while Clark was at his desk going over papers and answering the phone. How could he not notice Marty, the blonde and the wild, sexual racket they were making?

Clark and one of the vice presidents talked about how sorry they were that Marty was gone. Gone? Shit, he wasn't gone, he kept trying to tell them he wasn't gone but all he could do was keep fucking. Then in the dream, his mind blossomed in an explosion of green just like the modem screen and he was locked between the legs of a brunette, in his own apartment. They were in his bed and Jean sat on the edge of the bed, talking on the phone to Marian and crying, telling her how deeply she had always loved Marty and how difficult it was to realize he was really gone. Marty tried to scream that he *wasn't* gone, he was still here, still in love with her. All that came from his mouth were the animal noises of his orgasm. Then his whole head exploded into another blooming greenness and he woke up, sweating. He was still screaming, or at the end of screaming or maybe it was just the echo of his screams from the nightmare, but the sweat was real. He ran with sweat and his whole body shook.

Marty hadn't had nightmares since he was a little kid. The dream of being gone, disengaged, uncoupled and unable to be heard or seen, terrified him. Maybe it would go away, but he began to fear sleeping and slept badly when he finally dropped off, the threat of the nightmare covering him like his blanket. He moved away from everything and everyone, turning inside himself and just going through the motions of his life. He knew the clinical definition of paranoia and understood the rationalized delusion of persecution, but he was powerless. If fear was inside, he'd have to stay outside. Plugged in and tuned out, he was okay. Plugged in and tuned out, he could survive.

It was meaningless and a waste of time to talk to those mindless creatures at work, when he could talk philosophy or politics with the world's finest minds whenever he decided. Of course he'd never *chosen* to talk with any of them, but that wasn't the point. They were there for him and only him, anytime he wanted to call them into the chip in his head.

What was the purpose of hitting on some babe in a bar when the most beautiful, provocative and most willing women the world had ever known were his for the asking. He asked often, he asked endlessly and it was great. Wasn't it great? Wasn't it a small price to pay for access to the best?

Eating whatever the delivery boy brought around was okay. It was okay forever, so long as Marty could dine at will in the world's finest restaurants, seated at the best tables, hovered over and fawned upon by legions of waiters and wine stewards. Wasn't that what it was all about in this world? Getting the finest, getting the best, getting the most?

Golf was a drudge, when you were a twenty handicap, but could win the British Open on command. Skiing was expensive, when for nothing you could plunge down the giant slalom at St. Moritz in record time. Going to a movie, a nightclub, ball game or out with the guys was a waste of time, when anything in the world was possible on the modem.

Except for that one thing, the opportunity to share his thoughts. There was no way to search inside the mind of another human, no way to share what was really going on inside him. *EVOKE* should be all he needed. For Christ sake, almost everything possible had been or was about to be recorded for the absolutely perfect experience. They *were* perfect, weren't they? God damn it, *weren't* they?

There were times when Marty realized just how much he missed the imperfections of his life with someone else. But Jesus, it was swimming against such a strong current to want Jean. What was it she'd said about life being mortgages and backyards and kids? How could Marty live with that, when he had the choices of the modem? It was hard to talk to Jean sometimes and so easy to be perfect with a Cathy or Vanessa. He hated those moments of longing and tried to drive them out of his consciousness before they grew. They simply wouldn't go away, not for long. Never for very long.

He could only *be* with Cathy or Vanessa or whoever. Never lie in their arms and question what was going on in his life, never talk about old man Clark and his problems on the dock. Clarke didn't *exist* in those borrowed minds. Never wake in the morning to stretch and roll over and ask them what they planned for an unplanned day. Never understand with them, the imperfections that make two people perfect. Marty shook it off, buried it, put it where he wouldn't have to look, wouldn't have to think. He'd be okay. The nightmares were probably just a passing thing and he'd get over them. It would be all right and he was one of the truly lucky people in the world, one out of thousands who wished they were him. *Wasn't* he? *Weren't* they? He sat down at the modem.

"… . *ohhhhhhhh, baby. Have I ever been waiting for you.*"

He missed four Bulls games in a row and gave away his playoff tickets for the first time in fifteen years. They were night games and Marty had other things to do at night.

Jean called on his birthday near the end of January and he was startled by the call, somehow thrown off balance by the unexpected sound of her voice. It stirred an uneasiness so deep inside him that he couldn't even comprehend what it was. He'd entirely forgotten about his thirty-eighth birthday. Her voice nearly knocked him down, left him flustered and at a loss for words, unable to talk easily with someone he'd lived with for nearly three years. The girl he'd always assumed someday he'd marry. Their conversation was stiff and unreal to Marty and he felt he'd said all the wrong things. She'd reached out to him, made the first move. But the feelings she aroused were feelings he wanted left alone, even though part of him cried out. Just like in his nightmare, *Here I am, please hear me, please come back into my life and save me, save me before I'm gone and can't be saved.*

She wished him a happy birthday, said she missed him and maybe she'd call again sometime. If he wanted to call her, she could be reached at her new apartment and gave him the number but he hadn't written it down. After she hung up he thought of all the things he wished he'd said. Jean's voice came back to mind for weeks and he choked it back, held it down, pushed it aside. He couldn't live with them both. Jean wouldn't settle for that and the modem was too strong. He couldn't undo the implant or the vasectomy, although the program had an option to send back the subscription and could be stopped. Stopped, if Marty had the strength to give up the world.

Marty didn't even have the strength to quit smoking.

He got a card from his dad in Phoenix, wishing him a happy birthday and asking him to call. The old man wrote that he tried to call him in the evenings, but no one ever answered the phone and it was lonely in Phoenix since Mom was gone. He hoped Marty was okay and wasn't working too hard. Please call him collect whenever he had a chance. Maybe he'd better call his dad this weekend Marty thought and sat down at the modem.

The Blackhawks opener against Detroit in Stanley Cup playoffs was close as hell, a real scrambler won in the last four seconds by Detroit, five to four. The crowd in their new stadium was so wound up there'd been brawls in the parking lot and the guys on the dock talked about it all week, speculating on the first rematch.

Marty had season tickets. His seat was empty.

"I've been over this thing twice, Senator, some of it three times and there's just no place it could come from but Social Security." Dan McCarthy dropped the report on the table between them and looked at his boss. "A serious leak at SS."

"Yeah… been racking my brain to try and understand where Romeri got all this stuff and came to the same conclusion, Dan." Bob leaned back in the leather chair and crossed one leg over the other, fiddling with a shoelace. "You know what they say, it never rains in Washington, just leaks enough to keep things growing." He smiled wryly and uncrossed his legs. "What else?" Dan had earned Bob's respect over the past five years. The pudgy body held a quick legal mind with sure political instincts. He'd make a fine Congressman someday if he stuck with it. A fine Senator, eventually.

"I don't think it's a payoff, although that's possible. God knows enough money floats around this town." He looked at scribbled notes. "Romeri gave this thing to you casually, like it was some ordinary backup piece for a lobbying effort." He tapped the report with a finger. "This thing's illegal, at least the basis for it is… illegal as hell."

"I know."

"That makes me think he didn't just bribe some staff guy for numbers." He tapped the report again and picked it up. "On the face of it, even though it doesn't have any corporate markings or signatures, this is an indictable document. And it points right to World Star."

"Not only that. It wasn't delivered through some ambiguous back channel. Romeri handed it to me himself." Bob looked at Dan's eyes for reaction.

"Well, that's careless and Romeri isn't a careless guy. Tends to confirm what I'm thinking."

"Which is?" Bob stirred in the seat and tried to keep exasperation out of his voice. Every so often, Dan played this game of wanting to be drawn out. He was never sure whether it was a matter of deference or a move toward more equal footing. But occasionally it annoyed him. Like now. He was tired, too tired to play games.

"I'm still fresh to this, still turning some of it over. Looks to me like Romeri knows this won't ever be pressed. Thinks it won't, anyway." He dropped the report back on the table. "That means to me that his access comes from high enough up he's not worried about disclosure."

"Hmmmmm." The Senator shifted again. "He's got a hell of a lot of money and power, Dan. Guess I don't have to tell you that, but the point is he could find a loose thread almost anywhere in the Social Security Administration and pull it. With enough money and someone to spread the money he could find what he needs. Looks like he's found it."

"There's nearly a thousand people in the *EVOKE* Division now," Dan replied, twisting his college ring. "That's a lot of places for loose threads, but there aren't twenty of them who could lay their hands on the source

EVOKE

information in this report. They keep it that way as you know Senator, because of all the regulations that came out of your own Committee. The whole idea is to protect confidentiality."

"Well, the protection isn't very effective." He glanced up at Dan. "Twenty people shouldn't be hard to check."

"An investigation?"

"Well, I don't know, Dan." Bob got up, walked around the back of his chair and leaned on it. "Certainly a possibility, God knows the document warrants it." He leaned across the back of the chair, hands clasped, his eyes on Dan. "It troubles me greatly where this whole *EVOKE* program is going. We're not supposed to be out of control and yet I feel the controls slipping. What are the problems with an investigation? Run me past the downside."

"For one thing, I don't know any quiet way to do it. Who's going to investigate, the FBI, the Justice Department? Hard to keep that quiet and everyone would run like hell for cover. You'd need authorization from the Committee."

"I could get that." Now Dan was giving him what he needed, a sounding board against which to bounce alternatives.

"I know you could, but you'd have to disclose this." He picked up the report. "Lay it out to the Committee and we," he corrected himself, "*you'd* want to think that through, pretty carefully. Senator Alberts is a virtual hotline to Romeri."

"That might be just what we need." Bob sat down again and leaned forward. "Use Preston Alberts to warn him off, head him in."

"It might work."

"But you don't think so. Whenever you say something might work, I know you think it won't work."

165

"I think Romeri and World Star are hard to head off... maybe even dangerous to head off." Dan turned his attention back to his ring, looking at it, twisting. He glanced up at the Senator, knowing it was thin ice to talk danger.

"The Committee is a part of the United States Senate ... " Bob's words trailed off and he clasped his hands. Dan understood why he looked so tired. Knew that he'd probably wanted to call last night when he'd finished the report and found it impossible to sleep.

"Senator Fairweather, the fact is we've got an extremely wealthy and powerful man with a major international corporation behind him and a Senator on your Committee in his pocket. He's just voluntarily given you a document that would send any ordinary man to jail. Romeri is an aggressive businessman," Dan smiled at his own understatement. "But he's also an ambitious man politically and I don't think he'll roll over on this one."

"What then?"

"What does he want? If you'll forgive me, he didn't give you this for bedtime reading."

"He claims to want limited commercial access to EVOKE, much like what they do in the movies, showcasing his product, woven into plot lines."

"Claims to?"

"Well damn, that's where the whole thing comes unraveled in my mind, Dan." Bob lifted the heel of his left foot to rest on the coffee table. "Commercial access is possible without abuse, maybe even desirable." He waggled the foot. "Probably inevitable, given our worship of the marketplace . . ." He lapsed, seeming lost in his own thoughts.

"But?" Dan prompted softly.

"It's where it *comes* from." His voice was low, coming from his thoughts and Dan leaned forward to hear. "It's Lonny Romeri. And I hate to make it personal... shouldn't make it personal in my position, but it *is* personal. If George Waring at Pepsi or Walter Manfeld at Coca Cola had come to me with this, it'd be a different ball game. They're not so ruthlessly politically ambitious." He smiled to himself and then at Dan.

"God knows they're politically aware and big lobbyists, but I mean they're not personally ambitious beyond their corporate position. I don't know anyone but Romeri with balls enough to drop a report like this, a glaringly illegal document, compiled from equally illegal sources, on the desk of a United States Senator and think he could get away with it." Bob's foot waggled again. "He didn't even think he could get away with it, he seemed to *know* he could get away with it."

"Will he?"

"He will if you and I don't figure a way around it. This is pretty much an ultimatum." He touched the report with the heel of the shoe. "This is pretty much *fight me here and now or I'll have my way.*"

"Well, the other alternative is an internal Senate investigation, but it's not a particularly good route." Dan looked at the waggling foot, like a metronome holding his attention.

"What's the downside?" Bob already knew the downside.

"Investigation by a political organization, against a guy with unlimited," he caught himself, "almost unlimited political clout. A lot of chits to call in if he needs them."

"Hmmmm."

"Senate investigations historically are more to cover than uncover."

"Hmmmmm. So it's FBI, Justice Department or nothing, in your view."

"Pretty much." He may as well spell it out, Dan thought. "Or . . ."

"Or?. . . or, what?" Bob looked at him, both eyebrows raised.

"Or, give him what he wants. Try to control what comes later." Dan thought they'd probably both arrived independently at the only viable solution. Romeri knew it all along, counted on just such a meeting to look over all the alternatives. He knew there were none to be found, none that could be lived with.

"Yeah . . ., well, that may be what I have to do. But I wish I knew how far his wires ran in this administration, where the heat was coming from." Bob lifted his foot from the table and crossed it over his knee, fiddling with the shoelace again. "What about Representative Baker? Think I ought to talk with him?"

"May as well. He's your counterpart on the House side and Romeri's got to have been pressuring the *EVOKE* Committee over there." Dan tapped the report again. "Wouldn't show him this, though. If he already has it, he'll be pretty damned cagey."

"Ask Sally to set something up with him, maybe tomorrow if he's available."

"Here?"

"No, over there on his own turf. Representatives always like it when Senators come over to see them, hat in hand." He sighed, "This is still all a game of egos, Dan. I need him to feel in the driver's seat if I'm going to learn anything worthwhile." The Senator struggled out of his chair.

"Okay, Senator. I'll see if Sally can catch him in the office right now." Dan got up, the meeting over.

"And, Dan."

"Yes, sir?"

"This goes a hell of a lot deeper than the commercial access thing. Romeri's got some personal agenda and I'm not sure what it is. You better keep this in the safe for the time being." He tossed the report to his senior aide.

Late that evening, Maggie sat at the glass-topped table in her dressing room. She brushed her hair and looked at her reflected image in the mirror. Holding her hair back, over her ear on the right side, she thought the look too youthful and brushed again. It was a good ear, but not all that good.

Dinner had gone well and they were overdue to see Bobby and Ginny again. It was like fresh flowers in the house to have young people around, but Bob had looked so tired. He'd given her a quick hug, waved good night to the kids and headed for bed at ten, looking more exhausted than she'd seen him in years. Foxhunting in the morning he'd said, as though she didn't know the Wednesday, Friday and Sunday schedule after all these years.

That damned Romeri fellow. She tried her hair pulled back. That was more like it, maybe she'd wear it back for a while.

Even Bobby noticed, asking her casually after dinner if there was something wrong with Dad. It was good Bobby was hunting with him in the morning. The two of them were spending more and more time apart, as Bobby's responsibilities in Richmond grew. Changing the brush to her left hand, she wondered sometimes about Ginny and whether the two of them were really right for each other. Mothers always wondered, she guessed and it was an idle and too motherly exercise. But sometimes Bobby seemed so distant, so detached somehow from the planning for their wedding, a world away as if it were all planned and happening to someone else.

Men. She reached for face cream. Bob had his own partnership in the firm when they were engaged, but his eye was always on politics.

She'd loved him with a schoolgirl crush, since she was seventeen. Bob was just home from Princeton, a law degree in hand and his eye set toward Washington. She peered into the mirror, studying the lines at her eyes, gently pulling the skin back in erasure, relaxing the skin and liking the lines. My God, he was handsome then. Handsome now... good looking men just got better with age. Lucky men, taking on a depth in their eyes and character in the lines on their faces, the lines that traced their lives.

She was so young back then and worried that he'd never wait for her to catch up, that some pretty debutante would take him before she grew up. Maggie smiled at her reflection, remembering how she stood before her mirror at seventeen, willing her breasts to grow, discouraged at the minimal differences between waistline and hipline, *hurrying* herself for Bob Fairweather. She practiced her signature... Margaret Fairweather, Maggie Fairweather, Mrs. Robert Billings Fairweather, II.

He'd waited, though. Somehow he'd waited, not knowing of course that it was Maggie for whom he was waiting, but he waited all the same. Her father wasn't rich but he ran a small pack, hunting his own hounds, insistent that a professional Huntsman took a man away from his hounds, away from the sport. Love of foxhunting brought the two families together often, often enough for the waiting. Bob whipped-in to his father's pack in those days and Maggie stretched a thin interest in riding to a furious intensity toward the sport. She was finally allowed to whip-in to her own dad, although she thought he knew why she'd taken such a sudden interest. No matter, she and Bob shared a sport. He teased her unmercifully when on occasion she rode sidesaddle to impress him.

Maggie unscrewed the lid of the jar, dipping her finger and working the soft unscented cream into her face, beginning at the right eye and working around the corners and edges, across the cheekbone. Bob loved to talk politics and hunting and Maggie was a good listener on the long walks they took across Fairacres, always asking a key question that would take them further when she felt Bob was about to turn back. They were good questions. She learned and worked at politics because it was Bob's life and she'd determined that Bob's life was going to be her life.

At some point, the roles reversed and Bob began to ask her about things that troubled *him*. The constant struggle for power in the party and the small chips in his own father's ethics that his dad traded away for other advantage. He worried if the exchange was an even one, whether those sorts of exchanges were ever justified if they pulled at a man's conscience. They sat on logs and leaned against trees, chewed blades of grass and threw pebbles in the pond. They learned about each other through a third person named politics.

Maggie wasn't surprised that he'd talked at such length about the ethics of politics, but it warmed her and made the love deeper to find that he had compassion to balance the degree of his ambition. Bob thought politics was man's highest achievement, when it was elevated by knowledge and compassion. It made her smile to hear him sound so much like Kennedy. Now, in his third term in the Senate, there were times when he found more despair and disillusionment than ethics, but he still believed in the process.

She reached into the jar and dabbed her other cheek. The day of the picnic in the north pasture, their first lovemaking seemed to overwhelm Bob, but she'd known it was coming, planned for it and known it would happen in this wooded country. Knew it would happen in the out of doors, where they knew each other best. She blushed even now at her partly creamed face in the mirror, to think how they came together in a slow unbuttoning that became a rush. Their hands frantic for each other's bodies, rolling nearly off the blanket in a need to touch, to feel, to breathe each other. Then Bob inside her, filling her body with his, filling her life with his life. She'd been a virgin, not by design or religion or some romantic notion of saving herself for him, but just because she was. Because there hadn't been anyone else she'd ever wanted. Were there still virgins today, who knew who it was they wanted? She wondered.

Maggie switched off the light and walked to the bedroom door, moonlight flooding through the window. She gazed at Bob stretched out in bed, never having moved or rolled over or so much as twitched since he'd lain down. Over tired, almost drugged from lack of sleep. Maybe there'd be a chance to talk this weekend. Only the Sunday Hunt would intervene, no other plans on the calendar and she'd see there were none. Charles had laid out his hunting clothes and she looked at the polished boots, gleaming in the night-light from his dressing room.

She walked to the window and pulled the old white terry robe around her, gazing out across the lawn, to the woods beyond. The woods where old foxes silently moved among the trees and younger foxes paused at the edge of marked territory, trembling at their boldness, a sort of Senate of the forest. Metaphor. That was all right, it was an analogy that fit.

What of Bobby and Ginny? Did they know each other in the Porsche, as Bob and Maggie came to know each other on those long walks? Had they thrown pebbles in ponds, learned each other's mind? Had they chewed grass and sat on logs, knowing the heart that lay beyond each other's eyes? She made a mental note to call Sis Fentress and touch base on the wedding, dropping the terry robe on the chair and slipping into bed naked, as they always slept. Her hand moved carefully against Bob's leg, not to wake him, just to feel the warmth.

––––––––––––––––

"Mr. Baker, Senator Fairweather is here." His receptionist's voice broke into Wilson Baker's thoughts and he shook them off, swinging back to the desk in the high backed chair and punching the intercom button.

"Thanks, Ellen. Tell him I'll be right with him." He smiled to himself. It wouldn't hurt to let the Senator wait just a few moments. They all thought they were just a lucky break away from being President up there in the Senate. That Congressmen went to Washington only to bow to the Senate, but they did the tough and grinding work of initiating legislation, all too often just to watch the Senate quash it. Bob Fairweather had chaired the Senate *EVOKE* Committee nearly twice as long as Wil had *been* in Congress, but his district in Florida didn't send him here to bow to anyone. A couple of minutes in the reception room would make that message clear. *EVOKE* was his baby on the House side.

He turned himself back toward the window and wondered if it would snow this afternoon and screw up the drive home to Arlington. Damn, Fairweather wouldn't be here without a purpose. Romeri must be on his ass and he was probably beginning to sweat, coming over to feel out the House side, a little chairman-to-chairman chat. Romeri wanted access and he was going to goddamn get it, or move things around until he did. Well, Wil Baker wasn't going to need to be moved around. He hadn't just fallen of off the potato truck, he knew where the power lay and had sense enough to run with it. Fairweather might have a lock on that cushy Virginia Senate seat of his, but a seat on his side was a constant cat-fight. A man had to choose his backers with the long term view. Who the hell could tell, someday Romeri might help him win his own seat in those hallowed halls the Senior Senator from Virginia walked with such authority. Have to be careful with him though, Fairweather was powerful. He swiveled the chair and pressed the intercom. Damn, the snow was starting. Damn the north anyway.

"Send him in, Ellen."

He slipped on his jacket and checked the knot in his tie with his fingers, walking around the desk as the door opened and the Senator walked in, Ellen quietly closing it behind him.

"Bob, how are you? Not often I get to see you over here." He gave the Senator a warm handshake behind cool eyes.

"Wil, not often enough, I'm afraid. You're good to see me on such short notice, I know how hectic things get with schedules and I appreciate the courtesy." The two men faced each other, smiling and for a moment Bob wondered if Baker was going to sit at his desk, leaving him the straight backed chair. The moment passed.

"Let's sit over here, away from all my clutter," Baker waved to two comfortably upholstered chairs and low table. No fireplace in Congressional offices, except at the very top. "We'll be more comfortable. Coffee?"

"That would be nice, if it's no trouble." Bob sat in the chair with the window behind him, as Baker asked Ellen to have coffee sent in.

"Well Bob, what can I do for you?" Baker settled into the other chair, leaning back and smiling. Ever the gracious host, ready as always to help the Senate in time of need.

"Wil, we're getting a lot of pressure to open *EVOKE* to commercial uses." Bob disliked this hat in hand business and if the truth be known, he guessed he disliked Wilson Baker as well. The air in Baker's office was heavy with insincerity and he meant to get to the point and get out.

"It's always been there, the constant lobbying to put a Coke can or a pizza box into the experiences. But it's getting more serious now and I've seen some figures that make me wonder just how long we can hold out or even… if we should hold out." Ellen slipped in and out again, setting a tray and carafe of coffee between them. "I know you boys are getting the same pressures, unless things have changed very much in the way lobbying is done. I need to hear your thoughts, need your counsel to help me think this thing through." Bob reached for coffee, looking earnestly at Will Baker and playing the very distasteful part of supplicant.

"Yes . . , we've seen a steady increase in lobbying pressure too." Baker reached for a cigar from his inside coat pocket, offering one to Bob, which he waved away. "Frankly, this fellow Romeri from World Star seems to be leading the pack and he makes a pretty good case." Wil bit off the end of the cigar, dropping it into the ashtray and sniffing the panatela. "I've thought for a long time now we ought to get some kind of pilot program going. Something to test the waters and see how to handle this thing as more people come on line." He lit the cigar.

"It worries me, Wil." Bob dropped one teaspoon of sugar in the coffee and reached for the cream. "Always has, although I guess I've known we'd have to deal with it sooner or later." So Romeri had made himself felt on the House side as well. Baker sounded pretty much won over.

"How so?" Wil blew a stream of smoke at the ceiling. Best to let Fairweather get it all out on the table.

"Where does it start, where does it stop? Who makes the decisions? Once that door opens, it's open and very hard to close again. This is a big country Wil, with a lot of commercial interests. Who do we let in and how are the rules laid out? Every Senator and Congressman is going to be expected to deliver for the home vote. The whole issue of fairness bothers me a great deal, as well as the more important issue of consumer protection." Bob sipped his coffee, finding it lukewarm and too long in the pot, setting the cup back in the saucer.

"I don't know if decisions really have to be made, Bob. We have oversight. That's what the House and Senate Committees are supposed to do, provide oversight." Baker sat back in his seat and pulled on the cigar, rolling it in his fingers, lecturing the Senator on the duties of his Committee and enjoying the role. He smiled, "This is a market-driven economy. Why don't we just let the market work and see that nothing too abusive gets into the programs?"

"Sounds simple, but I wonder." They were Romeri's words, even down to the phrasing, Bob thought. "Sounds easy to do and maybe you're right, maybe we just let the market set the pace. But the thorny issue for me, the problem that I can't seem to settle in my mind has to do with the enormity of that concentrated market. Wil, we've got over twenty million on line and it won't be thirty years before the entire nation is hooked up." He paused and reached for the coffee, more from habit than desire. "That's just a few years out and we're not talking about television or the movies. You know the power... you're hooked up, I'm hooked up. Have you ever known any experience so forceful as *EVOKE*?" He sipped.

"Well Bob, it's a pretty good show, no doubt about that. But I don't think it has the power to make me run out and buy one of Romeri's hot sports cars." Baker smiled again and leaned back, crossing his legs. Damned if he was going to let himself be lectured on morality. There was money and power in chairing the Committee and money and power was the engine that moved Washington, moved careers. It would move his career if he played it right, to who knew what heights? "We still have to keep the GNP moving in this country, or we'll all end up watching while the rest of the world takes it away from us. The Chinese are already doing a pretty good job. That's business. That's always been business"

"Hmmmmm. Wish I could be that circumspect." Not much point in taking this any further with Baker. Most likely the push would come from the House side on this issue and Wil would lead the pack. Romeri was just warming Bob up for what was to come. Damn, this battle was being fought on the wrong issue, cloaked in the flag and obscured in seemingly harmless commercial issues.

"Well Wil, I needed to hear your views. I do appreciate your taking the time from your schedule to hear me out and let me know your thoughts." Bob drained the last of his coffee, looking forward to getting away from the cigar and the easy answers to complicated questions. He rose and Baker struggled to his feet, clamping the cigar between his teeth and using both hands to launch himself from the chair.

"Not at all, Bob, not at all." He shook the Senator's hand. "Let's stay close on these issues as they come up." Baker put the other hand on Bob's shoulder and gave it a squeeze, like a father, who had just soothed a son's concerns. Bob walked slowly to the door, forcing the small talk of mutual concerns, wanting to flee the Congressman's office. There'd be no help from Wilson Baker's side of the hill, but at least he had confirmed that in his own mind.

The currency of the Congress was in knowing who opposed.

TEN

Web tapped his fingers on the table, then began to fiddle idly with the ashtray. He pressed the heavy glass edge, tipping it and then letting go to watch the drumming circles it made, settling back against the table top like a spun quarter. He raised his eyes to the door from the corner booth at the back of the long and narrow pine paneled dining room that opened out on the bar, where he'd sat for twenty minutes. Glancing again at his watch, he wondered how much of his life he'd spent waiting for Bobby. At restaurants, bars, the health club or apartment.

Webster Brooking was a waiter. Not with dark jacket, black bow tie and napkin over his sleeve, that would be too easy and make the waiting somehow purposeful. Instead, he waited as wives wait for husbands out on the town, not knowing what to expect, as children wait for parents to stop fighting while they lie curled and clenched in bed, hoping it'll be all right if they can only fall asleep. The way hopeless romantics wait for love and the elderly wait for death. He waited the wait of the entirely dependent.

Web slipped a pack of Winston Lights out of his pocket and laid it on the table. Bobby wasn't happy about his smoking and reminded him more than he liked. He was right of course, just another self-destructive habit like the waiting. He pulled the strip of cellophane, opened the top of the box, tore away the front slip of silver-foiled paper and carefully peeled back the remainder. Catching the edge of a filter carefully in his teeth, he worked out a single cigarette, sliding it cleanly away from its nineteen companions.

Perfectly made, a miracle of the machine age and absolutely cylindrical, tobacco neatly formed and clipped at the lower end, each filter unerringly attached to the upper and unequivocal in its sameness to the remainder. Tobacco, the dreaded addiction and foundation of Virginia wealth. He sighed and lit up, leaving the pack on the table, his thin gold lighter quartered across the box, catching light from the heavy green glass shade of the side lamp. Not many places you could smoke anymore, he reflected.

The hand that held the Winston was strong, fingers long and slender, the nails well manicured. Part of the easy care Web gave to every aspect of his appearance, from his well tailored Harris Tweed jacket to cuffless, perfectly creased light wool gabardine slacks and polished chukka boots. The details of the man as flawless as the cigarette, all carefully thought through and sometimes too tightly packed.

Glancing up yet again, he caught sight of Bobby coming through the door, coatless and wearing an Irish tweed cap he favored from October to March, a scarf thrown back over one shoulder. He waved at the bartender and stopped for a moment, apparently telling a brief joke to two friends at the bar. Laughing and slapping their backs, he worked his way back to the booth and dropped into the seat across from Web.

"Late… again… sorry." Bobby's eyebrows rose in mock despair and he dropped the cap on the upholstered bench next to him, unwinding the scarf. "Last minute call from George Benson at Wilgate Electronics. They always know they can catch me, just before lunch." He smiled. "How ya doin'?"

"Okay." Web felt himself relax, his tension washing away as though resentment had just gotten up and left the table. "Got an assignment from the paper to write a Sunday Supplement thing on the spring race meetings. Maryland Hunt Cup, Virginia Gold Cup, the whole bit." Web ground out the cigarette and Bobby waved away the smoke. "May have to interview Ginny's parents, them being such famous breeders and all." He grinned.

"Great." Bobby reached for the menu, "That'll take time from the book, though."

"Guy's got to eat, you know. Books don't pay the rent, at least not for now." He picked up his own menu, knowing it from top to bottom, glancing at the penciled daily special, deciding as he usually did on pasta primavera and a glass of house-red. "Speaking of which, the old rental apartment hasn't seen much of you lately."

"I know. What are you having, same old thing?" He glanced up and Web nodded, but Bobby wouldn't hold his eyes and looked away. "Been up to my ears in this case and Ginny's got us on a social schedule that seems to be the main focus of her life. Hasn't made me happy either, Web." He shot a quick pleading glance across the table, then away.

"We breaking up, Bobby?" There it was, direct as he could make it. A question that had to be answered. The waiter paused at the table and they ordered primavera, crab cakes and two house-reds.

"No." He paused. "I don't know." Another pause and Bobby studied the salt shaker as if he'd never seen it before and it was the most interesting of salt shakers. Picked it up and turned it in his hands, screwed and unscrewed the cap, tested the fit and found it adequate for the purpose. He sighed.

"What do we do, Web? I'm going to marry Ginny, you know that." He screwed and unscrewed. "I have to do that or it all comes apart... the whole direction of my life comes apart and I don't think I'm strong enough to tear it all down." He set the shaker down and looked at his hands. "She's as good as anyone for what I need... better than most, I guess."

"You being fair to her?"

"No, not really. How much of life is fair?"

"You being fair to you?"

"C'mon, Web." He studied his hands, flattening them on the table. "We all do what we *have* to do and I don't control very much of my life… never have." The hands pressed, fingertips touching, a place for his eyes that was not Web's eyes. "This is about obligation, the things I was born into." His voice was so low it was nearly lost in his framing of the thought. "Things over which there's no control… stuff that's expected, that just has to be done. It doesn't really matter how I feel about them."

"Yeah … "

The waiter arrived and hurriedly set plates on the wrong sides. They switched. Web took a gulp of wine. "So, when's the big day?" He forced a tone one might use with a co-worker, trying to bring the conversation up a notch so it wouldn't turn into a lover's quarrel. So it wouldn't drive them further apart, leaving Web waiting without end.

"Third Saturday in August." Bobby wolfed the crab cakes. "Probably be hotter'n a bitch, wedding at Fairacres under tents and reception there too."

"Am I invited?"

"Of course, can't get married without the person I love there." Bobby grinned across the table and Web grinned back, a grin that fought desperately against a heaviness in his chest, wondering how life would go on in any really meaningful way after August. There wasn't anything he could do. August would come, August would go. Life would continue and something would happen… something always happened, didn't it? But the heaviness remained and made it difficult to swallow.

They talked about Bobby's current caseload and about World Star. There'd been a preliminary discussion about Wayland, Roth and Barnes representing World

Star in the southeastern territory, perhaps the entire east coast. Feelers came to Bobby, not Wayland and it sounded big but there'd been no meetings yet. They talked about the book and Web's freelance work. Coffee came and they talked about all the things lovers talk about when they can't face a break in their love and need to turn instead to other subjects.

"Can you take off and dump the rest of the afternoon?" Web's question was casual and he knew the answer would be no, yet could not bring himself not to ask.

"I can't, Web. Goddammit, I wish I could, you know I wish I could. I've got a deposition at two-thirty and some other stuff that just can't be left."

"Yeah."

"What about Thursday night?" Bobby looked across at him, wiped the last of the coffee from his lips, rumpled the white napkin, then folded and smoothed it on the table. "Would have to be late, though, sometime between one and two. Ginny's got us committed again, but I could drop by after."

"I'll be there... I'm always there."

"Reverend Everett is here, Senator." Bob pressed the intercom.

"I'll be right out, Julia. Will you have Dan come into my office, please?"

Bob walked to his closet and slipped his suit coat off the hanger, absently nudged the door closed and pulled on the tailored wool herringbone, wondering again what on earth brought the National Director of *BURN* to his Senate office. The prep notes Dan gave him told more of what he already knew from the newspapers. Everett was a street-smart black, nationally prominent and spokesman for an enormous voting bloc. By far the most outspoken and popular of the half-dozen black leaders in the country.

But again, why the focus on Bob whose leadership had little to do with traditional black issues? Yet Everett had pushed for the meeting and pushed hard, unwilling to name the focus of his interest. It just wasn't the way things were done and he was damned if he'd see him alone under such circumstances.

Dan knocked once and came through the side door, raising his eyebrows in question and Bob nodded, waving him toward a chair at the desk. Better to keep this somewhat formal, at least for the time being. He opened the door and walked into Julie's reception area, smiling but not broadly.

"Reverend Everett," he reached to shake hands with the tall and heavily built black man, who stood with one hand casually in a pocket, studying the books on the shelves. "I'm Bob Fairweather and I'm glad to meet you. Your name and work are well known."

"Senator, you're very kind to see me." Everett's voice was low and well modulated, ignoring the offer of first names, his handshake firm. He looked him directly in the eyes. "Not much on these shelves of black history or current African-American politics."

"Those things are more easily found in my private library, Reverend." He smiled at the attempt to throw him on the defensive, but it seemed easily enough said and Everett smiled broadly as he said it. Probably not more than an ice-breaker, a reminder of his constituency. "I don't like to use the reception room as a display case for my political views. I'm afraid it's an overflow of things not needed elsewhere." They faced each other, a draw in the first round. "You alone?"

"Yes, Senator, I'd like to have our first meeting as informal as possible." The reference to a first meeting wasn't lost on Bob. "Just a friendly chat between men with common interests. The interests of the people each of us represent."

"I understand, Reverend. My constituency in Virginia, as you well know includes a large number of African-Americans. Yours, if I understand your focus, is more entirely black." He shoved both hands into the pockets of his trousers, leaning back slightly to look up into the broad face. Everett was only a couple inches taller than Fairweather's six feet, but he seemed massive, perhaps fifty pounds above Bob's weight and none of it gone to fat.

"On the contrary, Senator." Everett flashed the broad grin again and Bob began to feel this might be an interesting lunch, with an interesting man. "I have a great sense of kinship with the white community. We are after all, just people."

"Since you're alone, I hope you won't mind that I've asked my senior aide, Dan McCarthy to join us." Bob waved toward his office, gesturing Everett ahead of him. "All my work eventually involves Dan and sometimes the translation of a conversation leads to ambiguity."

"That will be fine, Senator." They walked through the doorway and Everett flashed the smile again. "I shall try not to feel outnumbered."

Introductions made, hands shaken, smiles smiled in all three directions and they adjourned to Bob's small dining room. Bob instantly regretted the appearance of a black Senate waiter who would serve the luncheon. He should have thought of that. It would have been more gracious to avoid the inference, as the Senate wait staff was about equally black and white. They settled into chairs, as a chilled white wine and escarole with strips of salmon and a Dijon-vinaigrette was served.

"Reverend Everett, I'll be frank." Bob sipped his wine. "It's not often I'm asked to host a meeting with an undeclared agenda. There's been a good deal of pressure to have this one, part of it from my good friend and colleague, Senator Rhodes." He set the glass down and cut a small piece of salmon. "I'm intrigued, as I'm sure is Dan. Tell me what brings you to the Senate and," he smiled, "more specifically, to my office."

"The road to your office, Senator, began in Selma more than a half century ago." Everett laid down his fork and looked intently across the table, first to Bob's eyes, then to Dan's. "I don't mean to lecture either of you on black politics," half a smile flitted across the broad face, "because you're undoubtedly well read." He paused. "From your private library."

Prentiss Everett reached for wine, took a sip, held it in his mouth, then swallowed. "You see, the movement of blacks in our society... your society, but perhaps one day our society, took a great leap forward under Dr. King. When he was assassinated the forward movement died, the *momentum* if you will was assassinated with him." He sliced a portion of salmon. The waiter stood frozen at attention in the doorway. "Our horse was shot out from under us and we found ourselves on foot. Found ourselves heeding the call of too many leaders. Found ourselves disheartened and disparaged by a loss of the irreplaceable. His death set us back a half century... maybe more. We are not yet moving as we moved then."

Dan shifted in his chair.

"We are burning, but we are not moving." Everett's eyes narrowed, then relaxed. "It is no accident, that the acronym for our organization is *BURN*. It was once *PUSH*, but that merely got us shoved back. Even so, when the neighborhoods burned, in an agony of repression and suppression, the smoke bit only into black lungs and the dead on the streets were not white."

He paused, took up his fork, sliced another piece of salmon and chewed thoughtfully. "I *do not like* the acronym *BURN*." Everett paused again and looked from one to the other. It was his show and he knew the pauses well. "Does that surprise you?"

"Not particularly," Bob replied. "It's too much of a call to arms, from what I know of your philosophy."

"Ex-act-ly," the word broken down into all three syllables. "You have identified me Senator, as one who wishes to burn no society, black or white. Rather, one who wishes to join in the *re-con-struc-tion* of that society in a way that is meaningful to all its members. If I were free to select an acronym appropriate to me for our direction, it would be *VOTE*. And vote we will Senator, vote we will."

"And vote you have, Reverend." Bob smiled across the table. "Two thirds of our major cities have black mayors, we have four black Governors, fifty-seven Congressmen and eleven Senators. As I recall, you have even elected a black President in recent times"

"And there will not be another for fifty years, perhaps a hundred. But you know something of us, Senator." He raised his glass in toast. "I honor that. Yes, there is progress at the top, progress on the political side and there will be more." The black waiter reverently removed the plates, bringing a main course of rare roast beef and red wine.

"Unfortunately," and Everett glanced at the retiring waiter, "too little progress on the streets. Still too large a proportion of unemployed and under-employed, uneducated and under-educated, but that will come later. Benefits always accrue to political power and we can wait. We are good at waiting, although there are those who think we've waited far too long and far too patiently. Perhaps even, far too *sub-ser-vi-ent-ly*." The Reverend knew when to stretch a word to each of its syllables and Bob found it at first annoying and then intrigued by the presentation, wondering how far downstream the hook was floating.

"Unemployment is no longer a cyclical thing in this country, Reverend." Bob sliced a piece of beef, hoping to turn a lecture into a discussion, looking for the thread that would make the general more specific. "For thirty years, we've had a more or less permanent underclass. Black, but white and Hispanic as well and government seems unable to find any credible answers."

"Unwilling?"

"No, I think not. I think unable is the accurate word." Bob looked evenly across the table. "Administrations of both parties, even one with a black president and quite wide power swings in the House and Senate, haven't been able to make much progress. With all due respect, *BURN* seems as unable as government."

"You are absolutely right, Senator. *Absolutely right.* BURN has no answers either." He wiped the corners of his mouth with white linen. "The sole purpose of *BURN* is to get twenty-one percent of what is there. Twenty-one percent of what is *a-vail-a-ble*. Merely a reflection of the black proportion of the population so that we can share, not unfairly, the burden of poverty."

Dan's eyes leapt from his plate and Bob sipped his wine. They were drifting downstream.

"It is our *dis-pro-por-tion* that is troublesome, Senator. We blacks represent twenty-one percent of the national population. We blacks shoulder a burden of fifty-three percent of the unemployment." His long finger wagged emphasis. "*That* is what we expect to change as we establish a further participation in the political process."

"Are you planning to move to Virginia, Reverend and run for my seat in the Senate?"

"Not at all, Senator." The broad face flashed another smile and he chuckled. "Although, I suspect Virginia will have a black Senator one day."

"I don't doubt it." Bob did doubt it, but *one day* was pretty open ended and all things happened, if one lived long enough.

"It is precisely the matter of continued political participation that brings me to your office. Brings me here, all these years and all these miles from Selma."

"Tell me more, Reverend." Bob finished his last slice of beef, touched the napkin to his lips and sat back in his chair. "My duties and rather limited influence in the Senate don't have much to do in any direct sense to the expansion of franchise."

"*Ex-act-ly*, again, Senator." Everett leaned forward. "The franchise has been expanding at its own rate for a number of years. We blacks are now fifty four million. Your official duties here in that august body we call the Senate have a very direct bearing on the *con-trac-tion* of that franchise." He paused over his coffee. "It is *that* matter that brings me to this very excellent lunch."

Dan's eyes took another leap and he and Bob each looked at the complacent features of their guest. Had they had missed some salient point in the discussion?

"I don't believe I follow you, Reverend," Bob replied. Dan watched his boss, alert now to every tone and inflection. There was a challenge here, but what possible motive for a challenge? "In what way do my actions, either in the Senate or personally, restrict or as you put it, contract anyone's franchise?"

"*EVOKE*, Senator."

"I beg your pardon?" Bob looked at the placid face. "How on earth does *EVOKE* have any effect on the franchise of citizens, black or white?"

"By its process of *avail-a-bility*, Senator Fairweather. *By the very method by which it is obtained.*" Plates were cleared, more coffee served and Bob paused, waiting to reply until the waiter left the room.

"Reverend, the process, well known by everyone is a lottery based on Social Security numbers. What do you find in that, possibly connected to disenfranchisement?" Bob was puzzled. The hook was here somewhere, lurking below the surface and the reverend held the rod.

"In that case, twenty-one percent of the *EVOKE* availability should be going to blacks."

"Generally." Bob sugared and creamed his coffee. "It is, of course a lottery, but we have tens of millions on line so far. In that large a group, the percentages should very closely reflect percentages of ethnic background."

"What if I were to tell you that nearly forty-four percent of those that you euphemistically call online, are black?"

"I would say I didn't believe those figures." Bob looked directly into Everett's eyes. "Nothing personal, Reverend, but I think you're misinformed."

"I am not *mis-in-formed*." The voice was quiet, steady, believable.

"Where do you get your figures?"

"From their source." Dan stirred in his seat and Bob's brows rose.

"That source is not available." Bob looked steadily at the broad black face. Everett's eyes didn't blink or move away. "By *law*... that source is not available... even to *me*."

"Am I committing a felony then, by coming here to speak to you?"

"Not yet." Bob poured more coffee from the silver service.

"If I were to give you such figures?"

"You would have to trust me to a very great degree, Reverend. In my position in the Senate, I have protection for what I learn from you." He stirred the coffee. "You do not necessarily have the same protections from me."

"I do trust you, Senator." He drained the last of his coffee and reached for the silver pot. "If we can't trust our elected officials," the smile was there again, "whom can we trust?"

"Presuming you have such figures, Reverend, may I ask where you got access to them?"

"Ah well, Senator, that's another question. Another question *altogether*." He sipped hot coffee. "Let's just say I have my sources, as so many others do in a free society. Those sources are not really the issue. The *num-bers* are the issue, Senator. And I think you'll find them quite credible, by whatever means you choose to have them authenticated." The hook.

"I would very much like to see what you have, Reverend. Those are pretty serious allegations. Frankly, if they prove to be true, they trouble me greatly. And the purposes of such a skewing of *EVOKE* availability isn't clear to me." Bob leaned back in the chair, draped an arm over the back and ran the fingers of his other hand through his short gray hair. "It seems to be clear to you, however. I would value your views."

"My people are being put to sleep, Senator." Everett leaned his forearms on the white linen tablecloth, clasping his hands, the diamond cufflinks blazing.

"*Dis-en-fran-chised* is the polite word, genocide is the more accurate term and this *gen-o-cide* serves a political purpose that makes me angry. Very angry. Genocide is an angry thing." His voice was low and controlled. "This *gen-o-cide* seeks to set us back, not merely another fifty years. It seeks to enslave us once again to the white majority."

"Those are explosive terms, Reverend and I must say I find them personally abhorrent." His arm came off the back of the chair and Bob mirrored Everett's posture, hands clasped on the table, like two men seeking mystical guidance, lacking only a Ouija board. "I don't know you personally, but your reputation has been, at times... how shall I phrase it... explosive." He paused, looking at his clasped hands, searching for the key to this complicated black man with the shocking allegation of genocide. He looked directly into the unwavering eyes across the table.

"Our conversation here today leads me to think you are not only honestly concerned... that is too moderate a term... but deeply worried. And as you say, angry. But I know that you save your more explosive aspects for the public forum. I need to know more, Reverend." He paused. "I am not your enemy."

"Senator, the enemy of the black man is not the Ku Klux Klan, or even those who shoot down our leaders. The enemy of the black man is the white man who acquiesces. The enemy of the black man is content to leave the face of history unchanged. The enemy of the black man is committed to *make sure* the face of history remains unchanged." Bob felt blood rising to his face. "Whether or not you are my enemy, has little to do with the fact that you do not attack me. It has everything to do with how you hear my persuasion."

"Go on."

"The black man in America, as you have so accurately pointed out in your earlier remarks, has come to a level of political prominence unthinkable fifty years ago. How has he done this?" His hands remained clasped, but the brows arched. "By sheer numbers. The black man has multiplied at twice the national average and he has become politically aware and politically powerful. Black political power stands at the very threshold of real change in this country." He paused. "*EVOKE* has risen at those very gates of entry, to take back that power."

"How?"

"The requirement of sterilization is nothing more than a thin disguise for genocide. Beyond that, the power of *EVOKE* is its easy access to everything the mind of man can imagine. When all the things men strive for are at hand, *they cease to strive*. They are willingly managed by the controllers of access to the box that makes it all possible."

Bob replied as evenly as the flush in his face allowed. "The requirements Reverend, are the same for all citizens, black or white. How can the benefits a society turns willingly on its entire population, possibly be construed as genocide?"

"Through the numbers, Senator, the *numbers*. White society already has the lowest birthrate in four generations. A welcome trend, some would say in an overpopulated world that threatens geometrically to destroy itself by the burden of population." He unclasped his hands and sat back in the chair, Dan's eyes riveted to his face and words.

"Numbers are the black man's *hope*. His *only* hope, history would seem to teach us. The day will come when the black man joins this lowering of birthrate, but that day is not yet here. *EVOKE* has been made available, *by a two to one ratio*, black to white. It seeks to *force* that decision upon us." He paused, letting the words sink, like stones to the bottom of a pool, like drowning men. "The white man would keep hold of this country and *his* weapon is *your* weapon."

"Reverend, you spoke of figures… numbers from your source." Bob looked at Dan, who seemed mesmerized by the implications, then at Everett. "Are you prepared to leave those in my confidential care?"

"I am."

"I would very much appreciate that. Those of us in public office are used to telling our constituents that their information will receive our earnest consideration." He rose, as Everett opened his briefcase and withdrew a thin sheaf of papers, rising also and reaching across the table. "In this case, you may be assured of that fact in the most literal sense. I don't know exactly what will come of this and where we'll have to look for verification, the time-schedule and all. But we *will* look and we *will* find out. You have figures that are not available to me and that troubles me greatly. Perhaps more than you would realize."

They walked back through Bob's office, pausing at the door and shaking hands. "You will hear from me, Reverend and I want you to feel free to call should you sense a lack of progress. I assure you, we will progress as rapidly as possible. I'll instruct Julia to put your calls through to me directly and without delay."

The Senator and his aide stood in the doorway, watching the tall, broad black man stride down the hallway. They turned back to the office, closing the door.

"*Jesus…* ," Dan let a long breath carry the words.

"Maybe not Jesus, Dan, but a second coming of some kind. At least if what he says is true and I don't expect to find otherwise." Bob headed to the closet, shrugging out of the suit coat, dropping the papers on his desk.

"Did you see the waiter?" Dan dropped into the chair, opposite the desk. "He'd have given a year's wages to stay in that room. This guy Everett is a god to him."

"Hmmm, yeah. I can understand why. This is a very articulate man, who could hold his own… more than hold his own… become a national hero in front of cameras in a Senate Committee hearing. He'd love that opportunity. Already a national hero to tens of millions of people and well enough known to the rest." He sank into his chair and, uncharacteristically, threw a leg up on one corner.

"So, what do you want from me?"

"Two things, I think. First of all, get hold of Alan Longwell at Social Security. I need the Commissioner of *EVOKE* down here to my office to answer some hard questions. Set it up for next week, I need to think this through over the weekend. Second, read through what Everett gave us and let me know in the morning if what I suspect is true, that these numbers are another leak from the Social Security Administration."

He pulled, thoughtfully at his nose and looked past Dan, speaking almost to himself. "This thing is getting well out of control and I feel like I'm the last one to know what's really going on. Too much is being revealed in small pieces. There's a bigger picture out there and I want to see it.

By early February, Marty knew life as he had been leading it was running him into a black and hopeless swamp, drowning him, pulling him under with less and less power to resist. His only choice, if there still were choices, was to have the courage to try to come back into the real world. Or hurry-on the drowning, welcome blackness as a friend and get it over.

He'd spent the better part of Saturday night and well into Sunday's early hours looking at the pistol on his coffee table, picking it up, holding it, putting it back down and sinking into his recliner, staring into space. The apartment was clean. Meticulously clean. His suits were pressed and stood at the ready in the closet. His record at Clark & Anderson was spotless for the past two months, the kitchen reasonably picked up. His life was coming apart even as the reflection of that life, the visible image pulled itself together. Inside, he was flat as mirror glass.

He picked up the gun again and held it in his hand. Turning it over, he studied the engraving on the side of the barrel, *Browning .380 Automatic*. Its machined parts were sleek, well-oiled and smooth to the touch. It warmed in his hand, giving back his body-heat like a friend, alive and comforting. It would be so goddamn easy. One last wonderful, unbelievable, sensational, glorious, spectacular and mind boggling fuck online *and then do it*. Do it while he was still high from Cathy, his mind still saturated with that enveloping feeling of belonging. Do it while everything was still open and possible, quickly and before it all began to shut down. Before the turn-on turned off, became unreachable, slipping away and not worth the agony and isolation of clawing his way back yet one more time.

He wondered what death would be like. Not only death, but the actual process begun by pulling the trigger. Would there be a flash in his disintegrating brain? Would there be an instant of pain or just blackness, just nothingness? Was there a heaven? Was there someplace else to go after he pulled the trigger? He thought not, but how the hell could he know. How the hell did anyone ever know? Did there need to be, or was it enough just to end his life, to back away and get out? After all, that was the last great question of life, wasn't it? Death was the last adventure, *the last first time* in a life where firsts slowly diminished until they disappeared entirely.

Would he even know? Would he at last find out what was at the end of life or would everything just blink out like a turned off light? Would he be deprived of even that, the final knowledge? He turned the pistol over in his hand and rubbed his fingers accross the checkering on the shiny black inlaid plastic of the grip. He thought it was plastic, but it was a pretty damned expensive gun. Maybe it was something more exotic than plastic. The grip was smooth and perfectly machined, or was it stamped when it was still soft or maybe poured from a mold? Fascinating. So perfectly done.

What would Jean say or think? Would she care? No, that was silly and presumptuous and self-pitying, of course she'd care, *that* wasn't the point. He didn't want to hurt her, didn't want to hurt anyone... didn't want to hurt his father the most of all. God, the old man would take it hard, personalize it and think he should have somehow intervened.

They say suicides are people trying to get even with the world or lashing out to hurt someone. *They.* Who the hell made up the *theys* of the world, those who always seemed to know? *They* didn't know shit. Marty wasn't trying to hurt anyone, especially not Jean or his father. He loved them. At least he thought he did, tried to, wanted to. It was all so fuzzy now, so hard to get a grip on what was real and what was make-believe. Definition. Yeah, that was it, no fucking definition in his life anymore. What would they say at the dock? What would old man Clark think about Marty blowing his brains and an oh-so-desired computer chip all over the ceiling?

Would the bullet go through him and maybe hurt someone else? He wouldn't want to hurt someone else. And what about the mess? Jesus, it would probably make a hell of a mess and someone would have to clean it all up. Pack off what remained of Marty and scrub him out of the rug, repaint, re-plaster... whatever. The city had people to do that. They must. He turned the gun over again and ran his fingers down the slide and across the ejector. That was where the empty shell would fly out, still hot and smoking from the explosion. The bullet erasing all the places he'd been, the girls he'd fucked, the meals he'd eaten, the sporting events he'd won. Tiger Woods wouldn't care, because Tiger Woods didn't remember... only Marty remembered. Tiger Woods wasn't even there... only Marty was there. He slid the tips of his fingers around the smooth machining at the end of the barrel. That was where the bullet would come blazing out, a bright flash of exploding gas behind it. Couldn't take long to travel the ten inches or so into his head. Wouldn't matter how fast, it would be fast.

He slid the safety off and then slid it back on again, as he had two dozen times before. The click was equally satisfying in both directions, perfectly honed and fitted. He sighed . . a long, tired, melancholy sigh and laid the gun back on the coffee table and looked at it. He'd never fired it. He'd only bought it to fire once. Marty didn't like guns. Actually they frightened him a bit and he was never comfortable during the bloodier scenes of movies. That was all stage stuff, made up and phony, but he nearly always averted his eyes, glancing away to the back of the seat in front of him until it was over, slightly sickened if his eyes caught a glimpse the screen before everything was cleaned up. Still… this pistol was handsome and very well made. Such careful workmanship and so efficient, the way everything clicked into place.

Why, he wondered, had he put all seven bullets in the magazine. Only one would be fired, but it seemed right, a certain logic to it. The magazine was made for seven bullets and Marty had carefully shoved them in, one by one. Making sure they were all seated properly and amazed at how perfectly everything clicked. The Browning Company surely knew what they were doing…

He'd taken a week vacation at the end of December because his hiring year was coming up at the time and he had either to take or lose it. Old man Clark was a stickler for everyone taking their vacation time. God, what a week. Seemed it would never end. Money was no problem, shit he could have gone anywhere he wanted to go. But he could *already* go anywhere he wanted. And if he really left, physically left, he'd have to leave the modem behind, go somewhere and be lonely, a little overweight shipping clerk trying to get lucky, trying to get laid, trying to tell himself he was having a good time. Eating alone in some expensive strip hotel in Las Vegas. Not Marty.

Shit, he'd starred in Vegas two or three times. He sure as hell wasn't going to put up with lousy service and not being recognized when he'd been a star. Set a damn record at the Desert Inn for Christ sake, standing ovations at every show.

He drove the Honda down to the North Avenue beach and took long walks through Lincoln Park, as far north as Hollywood Boulevard and that was okay, no matter the cold. At least it took up some time. But it all seemed pretty pale compared to the Italian Riviera. He watched a couple of guys fishing off the Lawrence Avenue pier, not catching anything, just bullshitting around a can of charcoal, warming their hands and he had to walk away, swamped in envy of their easy friendship. It was easy to have friends, so long as you hadn't been anywhere, hadn't seen anything. So long as you hadn't tasted or smelled or touched or fucked anything really great. Once you'd done that, it wasn't so easy anymore to sit on a winter pier and not catch perch *and not care*, just having a good time being there.

He'd nearly called Jean in the middle of that week. Then two days later, he did call her and hung up when she answered, in a sudden panic over what the hell to say. What he wanted to say, what he didn't want to say. He went to a couple of movies and walked out halfway through both of them, bored with the plot and lonely by himself. When you've starred in a few movies, it's hard to sit in the audience, unrecognized and unknown. Hurting every time someone glances into your eyes and then looks away, not understanding what it's like to be Him, the star up there on the screen. To be the leading man. It turned into a lost week for Marty, too full of comparisons between life as it was and as it could be. He dreaded the fact that his seniority gave him three weeks in the coming year to try and get through. He drank too much, resenting the headaches he never got on *EVOKE*. He let the apartment get ragged, just to see the shit pile up and then cleaned it all on the weekend, grateful for something to do.

Now here he was with a fucking pistol in his hand, thinking about escape from what everyone else wanted. He pushed the button on the side of the handle and watched the clip slide out and fall onto the coffee table. Pulling the slide back, he watched the bullet jump from the chamber, where a smoking shell casing would have ejected. He slid each of the bullets out of the magazine and carefully fitted them back into their box, head to toe, neatly, as they were when he bought them. He laid the pistol carefully into the drawer in the cabinet under the TV and set the box of bullets beside it. A weekend with the gun and all the thought and questions and guilt was enough.

Marty Greene doubted he'd ever open that drawer again.

ELEVEN

"Jerrold will have the bay horse and your mare ready at two." Bob hung up the phone and looked across the table at Maggie. It was set for late breakfast and fragrant with morning smells of bacon, warm eggs, coffee and slightly burned toast. "How long has it been since we've just the two of us taken a long ride through this place?"

"Too long." She smiled at him, "We going to get all booted and breeched, sweetheart, or just throw some chaps over jeans?"

"Chaps over jeans," he grinned, "just us, slipping through the country. Nearly all the leaves are down and it's going to be a lovely afternoon." He glanced up at her from midway into a sip of coffee, catching her in profile at just the right moment as she looked out across the sweep of lawn. He was about to say something but lost the train of thought in how beautiful she was, how lucky he was to live with her, know her, listen to her. Able to measure off a part of his worth by the gift of her love, a gift she continued to give even though he hadn't the slightest understanding of why. He knew these feelings spilling over him were somehow outdated, didn't fit the current style of what passed for relationships, all the more a treasure for their rarity. Comfort maybe. Too stodgy a word for envelopment. Yeah, *rarity* would do for now, until something more accurate came to mind and he was too comfortable to chase another word.

"You don't ride with me much anymore." He broke her reverie and Maggie's eyes came back to his and crinkled.

"Oh Bob, hunting is almost all you have time for these days and it's time alone for you, just you and the pack. There's so little left just for you anymore and I know how you savor that time. You know how I am, how I hate all that formality. I sneak out on the mare sometimes when you're in Washington. Just to idle my way through the woods and remember who I am… that I belong to the earth and not the Rolls Royce." Her eyes crinkled again. "Sometimes I forget that… sometimes, I think we all forget that."

"I need to remember that, Maggie." His hand covered hers.

"I know … "

About two, they walked down to the stables, in scruffy old Barbour jackets and well-worn chaps. The big bay stood cross-tied in the aisle, the mare behind, one of the stable boys giving her a last wipe down. The boy slipped Maggie's Pariani saddle on the mare, high at the withers and then moved it back to smooth the hair, reaching under for the martingale strap. He buckled the girth and waited for the mare to exhale, so he could tighten it an extra notch. The smell of the stable was warm and heady, a friendly mix of clean shavings, old timber, horses and leather. An odor mixed of Neatsfoot oil, fresh hay and liniment, cotton swabs and harness. An aroma uniquely belonging to a stable and found in no other farm building.

The aisle was a hundred twenty feet long, a well swept brick laid herringbone pattern with sliding double doors at either end, standing open and streaming sun this early afternoon. Ten stalls on the south side, all deeply varnished oak to shoulder height, wrought iron bars from there to the ten foot paneled ceiling, the hay loft above. The bars were painted red years ago, but age and constant cleaning had turned them a deeper color, nearly maroon.

A tack room was centered on the opposite side of the aisle, one oiled and pine paneled wall given over to blanket racks. Gauzy summer fly-sheets, light tan and used to walk horses out once they'd been hosed-down and the sweat scraped away from glistening bodies. Summer coolers of light wool and deep colors, used not so much in summer as the chilly nights of early fall, when a blanket was too warm. Racks of heavy blankets, thick wool and cotton overlaid in diamond stitching, smelling of body heat and used now that nights were apt to bring frost. The back wall was given over to bridles, row on row of gleaming oiled leather, the bits polished, each to their use. Soft and heavy-mouthed snaffles for well broke and friendly guest horses. Rubber pelhams with standing martingales, full bridles, egg-butt twisted snaffles and the double twisted wire artillery-bit, with its running martingale that Bob preferred for the big bay. A third wall was saddle racks top to bottom. English Smith-Worthingtons, two of Maggie's French made sidesaddles, several Argentinean jumping saddles, fine German show saddlery and the Italian saddles by Pariani, in a variety of sizes that kept pace with the growth of several generations of Fairweathers. All well used, clean and deeply polished. His father's saddle hung there as well, still regularly cleaned and oiled. The south wall, in addition to claiming the doorway, was lined with framed photographs of the hunt and children smiling over the ears of clever ponies. Racks of brushes, hoof-picks, liniments, cotton rolls and bandages for legs rubbed down with those liniments, bars of saddle soap smelling of glycerine and a variety of miscellaneous stuff that collects in tack rooms, from leather-punches to bits of strapping and brass rivets. Two saddle-cleaning stands in good repair, but showing their age and a hook suspended from the ceiling for cleaning bridles completed the more immediate impression. It was a place for work, as well as the only allowable place in the stable to catch a smoke, a room soaked in soap and oil and conversation.

Adjoining to the east was a feed room. Five gallon pails of sweet molasses, bins of oats, another for cracked corn, bags of feed-supplement, bran mashes and pelletized feed for a couple of the old horses whose lungs could no longer tolerate the chaff of hay.

Next to that a wash-rack, stall sized and concrete floored. The center drain caught cool water in summer and warm in winter, a cleansing flood of soapy water followed by a rinse and then the banded scraper, sheeting excess clinging water from bays and chestnuts, blacks and roans, grays and occasional spotted ponies. Here were performed minor veterinary tasks, from running cold water on a swollen tendon to the minor surgery and suturings common to a working stable.

The remainder of the north side of the aisle allowed six more stalls, knee deep in bedding straw and flooded with daylight. Jerrold had insisted on resizing all the windows and ordering new protective bars, muttering all the while about stables never having enough light for creatures that were meant to live outdoors.

The bay pricked his ears at Bob and nickered, pawing at the stable floor. "He knows it's not a hunting morning and thinks I'm dressed badly," Bob chuckled. He felt the soft nose, prickly with clipped whiskers and the bay nudged him, nickering again.

Jerrold walked the mare out into the stable yard, the boy bringing the bay. He held her at the mounting block, as Maggie pulled down stirrups, took the reins and swung into the saddle, the mare starting a bit, under her. Bob climbed aboard his big horse, shoving his leg forward, fingers reaching under the saddle skirt to check the girth buckles.

"You'll be wanting the gray in the morning then, Senator?" Jerrold asked the question out of courtesy. He'd already decided the Master shouldn't be riding the bay on an off-day like this. The gray would set things right in his mind. The Master was none too fond of the gray horse.

"The gray will be fine, Jerrold."

"Will the Senator and Mrs. Fairweather be out long?" Another question of Jerrold's, obliquely aimed and meaning the stable crew would like to get out by four. They'd be back soon enough, at 4am to prepare for the hunt at six.

"Hard to tell Jerrold, what time a man may return when he's off on a horse with a beautiful woman." He grinned at the Huntsman, who couldn't help but smile. "We'll take off the tack and turn them back in their stalls. Feed and water, Jerrold and send the crew home. We'll be fine."

"Aye, Senator, have a good ride." It was a mitigating thing to work for a man who understood schedules. The crew would be happily off at three and tomorrow morning would be the easier for it.

Maggie nudged the mare and they moved out of the stable yard, Bob a half-length behind, the horses walking easily down the drive toward the entry-gate. February sun was warm against their faces, uncommon for this time of year, but it promised to be an uncommon day. Bob wondered if there'd be frost before the morning hunt and expected there would, another complication to make scenting difficult.

A half-mile down, Maggie turned the mare north, stepping lightly across the band of grass at the road edge and slipping onto a deer-trail that wandered its way through mostly hickory woods. The forest floor was heavy with leaves, ferns having long closed their fans to curled brown, squirrels busy in the trees with the business of squirrels, chattering down at them, intruders on their own land. Bob followed the mare and watched Maggie's long back, easy in the saddle. Her legs were close to the mare, hair brushed her collar as she looked left and right up into the trees, clucking at the squirrels and laughing at their chattered reply.

They broke from the woods into a large meadow and quartered across, Bob jogging up alongside her, their horses easy together, reins slack, heads down and nodding as they edged toward the creek. Not a time for talk, watching the sun spill across the rippling meadow to dance among the trees of the far wood-line. Red oak, holding their leaves through the winter caught the sun, each leaf an encouragement of reflected gold-brown curl, some still tinged in red. Two woodpeckers hammered, paused, then one hammered again, the other taking up the work. A pair of carpenters lost in the trees. Bob reached for Maggie's hand and they let the horses find the way, dropping down through the meadow, hand in hand, throwing long afternoon shadows.

They crossed the creek, letting the horses reach down for a drink, reins sliding through fingers. Then clambered up the muddy bank to wind back through Nichol's Woods, each lost in their thoughts and the wonder of this forested patch of Fairacres. Aware of being together, being alone and yet together, relaxed in the saddle, relaxed in the warmth of togetherness. They passed through shafts of sun, dappled with the patchiness of winter branches, secluded among those sleeves of light.

They left the woods at the north edge and the horses instinctively sought the high ground, chest high in winter-brown grass, stealing a mouthful from time to time with a sweep of the head, as though brushing away a fly. The mare paused at the top of the hill. Their hill. The old north meadow hill.

Bob dismounted, slipping irons up the leathers, sliding the reins over the head of the bay, crooking them over his left arm, as he loosened the girth a few notches. He took the mare from Maggie and walked the two horses to the edge of the trees, tying each high enough not to foul the reins, far enough apart to avoid swinging into each other. Walking back, he sat next to Maggie, who looked out across the valley, knees up and arms wrapped around her legs, chin on her knee.

"Lovely valley, lovely girl." He picked a blade of grass and chewed on the end.

"Hmmmmm… too lovely a valley for just two people. Too good a life, maybe. Sometimes I don't think we deserve such a life … "

"It's not meant to be deserved." He looked out across the sun and shadow, the trees behind them throwing long wavering stilts of black across the rolling grass, waves of grass on a gently rolling sea. "It's what we have… with very little control or credit for the having."

"Mmmmmm… you're troubled Bob. When are you going to decide to talk about it?" She turned toward him, swinging to put an arm around his legs, chin resting on his knee. "What's troubling you so much, these days? Same thing we talked about?"

Yeah, Mag."

He touched her hair with his fingers, so gently she barely felt it. "It's getting worse, this whole matter of people connected to computers. The access to modems becoming more real than their lives. More compelling, anyway and I guess that's what worries me, what makes me wonder about this meadow and where the world is going." He smiled at the concern on her upturned face. "All the things that have frightened all the men who think, for all the centuries of humankind and still no answers... never any answers... just tomorrow and tomorrow and tomorrow."

"Talk to me, Bob. Don't slip away in tomorrows, talk to me."

He told her about Romeri's report, the detail of it that could come from only one source, a source closed to him. He leaned down on one elbow and sucked at another blade of grass, going on to tell her of Everett's visit to the office and the almost incredible accusations of racial misapplication. And, as the sun kept slanting lower in the sky, he finally talked to her about his fear, not even acknowledging it to himself until it had been told. How fearful he was of the invasive technology and access to that technology.

"You never wanted *EVOKE*, Maggie. I could have gotten it for you, but you never wanted it." He glanced up and searched her eyes. "Tell me why."

"I don't want to live in dreams." She glanced away, then turned her face back to him, looking up his leg from where her head cradled in the bend of her arm across his legs. Her right hand on his chaps, just above his knee, twirling a stalk of long grass between her fingers. "I have everything I need, all the pleasure and all the pain." She looked back at the grass in her hand, rolling it between her fingers. "I don't need warm sun on my face or rain across my window from a computer, don't want to live a scripted life. I need the knife to slip and cut my finger, spilling real blood, my blood. And I guess I need there to be a scar the next day, a reminder of the slip, a memory of the pain." She looked up to him, "Does that make any sense to you?"

"Hmmmmm... absolute sense. Too much sense for the world as it seems determined to be. Too much sense for its often directionless direction." He touched her finger. "As usual my love, you've nailed it. But you may be among the last to understand, to really know how valuable it is to keep touch with reality, cut fingers and all." He shifted. His legs were stiff from her weight and the left one was nearly asleep. He drew his legs up and moved sideways, lying back in the grass to cradle her head on his stomach. "But you never said a word when I got the implant... how come? Wouldn't share your wisdom with me?"

"You know better than that." She reached up and held his knee. "You're the chairman of that committee that oversees it all and the country doesn't know how lucky they are that you're sitting there. But you can't chair what you don't know and you have to have that thing in your head, though it makes me shiver sometimes to know it's there."

"You're never jealous?"

"Jealous?" She squeezed the knee. "Jealous of what, my love?"

"That I might be having sex on it. That I might be in some exotic land, you've never seen."

"You not only might be having sex on it, you *are* having sex on it and I know that. You're so funny sometimes, maybe it's a common trait in all men." She slid her hand down his thigh, grabbing a handful of flesh and pinching. "All needing to have a peek in the skin-magazine, looking at some babe on the street and wondering how it would be."

"That doesn't bother you?"

"That's the way it *is,* sweetheart." The hand worked its way back up his thigh to the knee. "Yeah, I guess it bothers me in the abstract, of course it bothers me, but there's nothing I can do about it or really would want do about it. As long as you come home to me... by God, Mr. Fairweather, you've even learned some pretty interesting stuff that I *hope* came from *EVOKE.*" She raised up from his stomach and turned toward him, leaning on her left elbow.

"I don't know Bob, maybe fidelity isn't even as important as we've been led to believe, if it doesn't carry any feelings of self-worth. Maybe someone's sold us all a bill of goods, with all this endless neediness and togetherness. Sometimes I think too many people lose themselves entirely, I mean their deep down soul-selves, when they spend their lives constantly trying to please. Hoping to come up every time with a new rabbit out of the same old hat. I love you and I want you with me, but I don't *need* you in the sense that my life would fall apart if you left me for some hot young thing with good legs."

"You've got good legs."

"Don't patronize me, old man." She grinned at him, poking at the collar of his coat. "You know damn well what I mean... I can't be everything for you and you can't be everything for me... not all of the time. That's too much of a reflection for either of us to find in the other's eyes." She worked the corner of his collar between her fingers, kneading the fabric, picking at the edge of the zipper with her finger. "What do my eyes reflect, right now?" She looked up into his.

"Love."

"Yeah, well... yours too, but it's not always there and it's not supposed to be always there. I'll tell you something else that may shock you, as long as we're having this shocking conversation."

"What's that?"

"It's sometimes there in other eyes." She took the tab of the zipper in her fingers and ran it a third of the way down, back up, then down again, watching it to avoid looking at him. "There are other people I love. Not that I would sleep with perhaps, but maybe even that if the circumstances all fell together. And yet, I don't love you any the less. It's hard... this being expected to love only one person. It's hard even, to be expected to sleep with only one person and I don't want you to misunderstand that, or draw something from it that's not there. But... it's hard."

JIM FREEMAN

"I know." He didn't know, not if he was really honest with himself. But somehow he thought he knew, or wanted to know at least enough to realize that Maggie was sharing something with him that few people shared. The mare snorted and stamped her foot, the bay nickering back.

"So, what are you going to do with Mr. Romeri, Senator?"

"I was going to ask you, Maggie. What should I do?"

"I don't know, I'm not that smart." She swung around to a sitting position, facing him, knees drawn up again.

"Yes you are."

"Yeah, you're right, I probably am." She looked at him, watching him chew on the corner of his thumb, arms locked across his knees, thumbs pressed against his lip, fingers linked. "That wasn't very bright of me, but I'm not the chairman of the committee and you've told me a lot, but I don't know the currents that are drifting up and down the corridors of that strange place you work. I think your decision has to weigh updrafts against downdrafts." She folded one knee against the ground and pulled at the strap of a spur. "Is there an answer or are we technologically locked in and have to settle for wherever the ride takes us?"

"I think we're locked in and the best we can do is try to stay a little ahead." He looked over at the horses, then back. "It's like the bomb... we were never able to put that thing back in the box and now the terrorist world has its own junior versions." He unclasped his hands and leaned back on his palms. "All the bomb could do is kill people. This damned thing is so controlling and before long, everyone will be hooked up. How are we going to balance the powers that exercise that control? Mr. Jefferson never had to deal with that one. Old Tom and that wonderful document of his, never anticipated a world like this."

"So... what, then?"

"So, the Senior Senator from Virginia can either cave in or hold out. Cave in to what, I don't know and hold out for what, I don't really know either." He crossed his legs at the ankles, locking a spur against one boot and watching the top third of the edge of the woods turn orange, against a setting sun. "Romeri's building pressure over on the House side and Preston Alberts is just salivating for my chair. . . probably get it, too, but not as long as I'm in the Senate."

He sighed. "Seniority is great when it's on your side and a huge impediment when it's not. Crazy system we've got Mag, but we always seem to struggle through and I guess when Alberts gets his Chairmanship, it'll all still go on. In the meantime, I'm the impediment for as long as I can impede."

"So, who's on your side?"

"Not many... not enough and fewer every day by the feel of it." He stood up and stretched, glancing again at the horses. "But a chairman is a powerful animal and I still sit there."

They walked to the horses, who spooked as though they'd never seen humans and hadn't noticed them sitting in the grass, twenty yards away for nearly an hour. The mare had managed to loop a rein across her eyes and over one ear. She shifted a panicked eye at their approach until Maggie laid a quieting hand on her rump and she settled at her touch. Bob chuckled and unbuckled the reins, threading them through a mass of branches to disentangle the mare. He tightened the girth, pulling down the stirrups and holding her while Maggie swung aboard in one long, fluid, graceful sweep of leg over saddle. The bay stood quietly and it took only a moment for Bob to join Maggie as they headed toward home, the sun half an orange disc to the west.

"Remember that thunderstorm, Maggie?" He reached for her hand. "It was a long walk home. Easier now on a horse."

"It was easy then and it's easy now, sweetheart." She squeezed his hand, holding it, not letting it drop. "It's *all* been easy."

———————————

Bill Wearley poured his third cup of coffee for the morning and regretted it. Coffee made him jumpy and he already had a boss who more than likely would add to his nerves. But de-caf was like drinking dishwater and the coffee in Romeri's office was Italian espresso, made in full pots and rich as chocolate. Since that's where the hell he was, might as well take advantage.

7am. He'd been out of bed since five, when Joe had called from the plane. It was still snowing at Metro and flights were stacked up, the corporate jet among them until they got a second runway plowed and open. Joe and the boss would keep circling, expecting about another twenty minutes delay, but he'd get back to him if it was longer. Overnight from London after two full days of conferences with the guys from the European divisions and Bill knew that Romeri would stride into the office looking like he'd just had a long vacation. He'd be rested and alert and looking for answers.

Bill had some of the answers in front of him, but who knew what the hell Romeri had dreamed up in the three days since he'd left for London? That was the adrenaline rush of this job... hell it wasn't a job, it was something that defied description. An alter ego, a complicated second skin made up of part axe-man, diplomat, private detective, bag-man and Judas goat. Performing in the shadow of a man so complex, ruthless, focused and occasionally inexplicably simple, that Wearley knew he'd never really figure him out.

He'd long since given up the effort, happy to be along for the ride and wondering sometimes where the hell they were going, where and how it would all end.

He picked up the coffee and walked over to the windows, touching a button to open sheer under-drapes and watched snow pile up in the executive courtyard. He'd stood at that same window seven years ago, selling out his former boss and the company within which he'd spent his corporate life. Selling out the company he'd always expected to head. To Romeri. He'd switched horses in the middle of the race, for money and power and never looked back since last seeing Walton Cummings, a very pale and very shaken Walton Cummings. Arrogance and power drained from Cumming's face, as he sat at the head of a massive conference table, watching his company pulled out from under him. Romeri pulled the rug, but Bill gave him the grip, the power and handed him the edge to hold in his hands.

International Sea Container sailed the world's largest ocean fleet, an impregnable giant that virtually set the rules for competitors. Cummings was Chairman, grooming and trusting William Wearley to take over his seat when he moved up from CEO. But the dates kept changing and Wearley was too ambitious, too hungry and Romeri could smell ambition and hunger like steak sizzling on a grill.

He *wanted* ISC. Another link in Romeri's vision, although he was a newcomer in the business, hardly taken seriously with a fleet of twenty-five tankers, all of them leased and none carrying his flag. Bill smiled out at swirling snow. It was a mistake not to take Alonzo Romeri seriously, a mistake rarely repeated and sometimes regretted for a lifetime.

The offer to Bill had been so outrageous, so unexpected. He'd come to this very office at Romeri's request, to discuss a deal whereby ISC would pick up those twenty-five leases. A deal Wearley was only mildly interested in and only if the price was right. Romeri didn't waste time, it just was not in his nature to waste time.

"Mr. Wearley, I want to take over ISC and I want to make you a very rich man when I do." They'd hardly begun lunch in the private dining room. It was an approach Bill would hear many times from that dining table.

"ISC isn't for sale, Mr. Romeri." Bill had caught his breath and almost laughed. "I came here to discuss buying your leases and I'm not even terribly interested in that."

"I know. You shouldn't be. They don't really fit into your long-range plans." Romeri smiled, but the smile had no humor. His smiling eyes were intense, a look that Bill also came to know, over and over again in the years since.

"Then, it seems we're just having a pleasant lunch and I've come a very long way to have lunch."

"It'll be worth it."

Soup was removed, wine glasses topped and two medium rare sirloins served. Romeri had attacked his steak, eating in the European manner, fork turned over in the left hand.

"I want you to sell out the man who's brought you along in the company, used your smarts to build his business and won't give you the reins for at least another ten years." He glanced up, between bites, as if he were making an ordinary and reasonable request of a subordinate. "I'll make you Chairman the day after the deal is done, at a salary of a million a year and a piece of the action... a generous piece."

"What makes you think a million will do it?" Romeri's offer was unthinkable, but Wearley enjoyed the brash offer. He admired the balls of the man and cut into his steak, intrigued by his boldness, flattered in spite of the knowledge that he was being deliberately flattered.

"Money won't do it, I know that." Romeri chewed, swallowed and washed down the steak with a sip of Valpolicella. "Even though you're getting two hundred eighty thousand now, with a bonus and stock options. Last year those options made you another hundred and eighty-six thousand." He sliced a piece of sirloin.

"You have an apartment in New York, worth three hundred grand, with a two hundred twenty thousand dollar mortgage. A house in White Plains, worth a half million, with a three hundred ten thousand dollar mortgage and a fifty thousand dollar second mortgage. Two kids in private schools at twenty grand a piece, a Jeep Cherokee and a Jaguar, neither of them paid off and a very expensive wife." He looked directly at Bill.

"No, money won't do it, but money won't hurt. And more importantly, you want what Cummings won't give you and what I will."

"You've done a lot of homework." Christ, Romeri knew more about his finances than Wearley did and he was right on the numbers. Probably knew about Alicia too, although a reference to her would smack of blackmail. He was interested. They'd not yet finished their steaks and he'd gone from mild amusement to interest... real interest. But would Romeri deliver?

"There's five million on the front end." Romeri watched Bill's eyes as the younger man held a fork-full of steak midway to his mouth, seeming to forget it was there.

Lonny never negotiated, never sweetened the pot, never left the advantage to an opponent. Make the deal, make it generous beyond what it took and then own the man for life or break him. Never second chances, never another look. Only do it, do it now and join the team for the rush to glory or get run over and left behind. Forgotten, often ruined and left to struggle away at life with all the losers. Romeri knew who the losers were. They were the ones not with him.

"ISC's not for sale and I don't have any control over that." Bill knew that he'd been bought and the price of his life, his dreams, his frustrations and hopes had been set in ten minutes, between soup and dessert. Set by a man he'd only met twice before in his life.

"I didn't say I wanted to buy it."

"What then . . .?"

"I said I wanted to take it over. As you well know, that implies using ISC to buy ISC and that is why, Mr. Wearley, you and I are having this lunch. That is why I have proposed and you have accepted, although you haven't said so yet. I'm asking you to sell the company with which you have been so closely and intimately associated, down the river ... "

Romeri pushed his plate aside, nodding at the waiter and the plates were removed. He touched the corners of his mouth with the napkin. "Have I mistaken your resolve? Are we as one on this?"

"We are."

Romeri made Bill Wearley one of his acquisitions. Not a partner or colleague, but an acquired item, bought and paid for. He had accepted the designation, knowing full well that their relationship would be forever based on that interpretation of man and dog, governor and governed.

The coffee had gone cold and Bill reset the drapery as it had been, buzzing Vicki to have a fire laid, pouring another cup... to hell with the caffeine.

Romeri was a remarkable man and, with Wearley's help and knowledge of the strengths and weaknesses of ISC, they'd set a strategy of Machiavellian complexity that had driven the firm to the wall and into Lonny's lap, within eighteen months.

Walton Cummings was a broken man, thanking Wearley for his support in the fight to save the company. There were tears in his eyes as he acknowledged that Bill would no longer have his chance at the Chairmanship and the place in the sun he so well deserved.

But Bill was named immediate Chairman of the newly formed ISC-Romeri and the old man called to congratulate him, never understanding who wielded the knife that had so neatly cut his throat. Bill paid off his debts, divorced his wife, married Alicia and just a year later answered Romeri's call to become what he was now, however one defined that position. The job came with an extra half million a year, the use of all Romeri's homes, planes and yachts when they were unoccupied by the boss. It also came with that nebulous power that emanates from proximity to power.

It was a head-trip and it quickly cost him Alicia. Two marriages lost now to his work, but he never once looked back, never once asked himself if it was worth it. It *was*. It *is*. It would always be.

"Jesus, I hate the weather in this town." Lonny fairly burst through the door, tossing his topcoat in the general direction of a chair near his closet. "Joe set that sucker in like a feather on a silk sheet and two thirds of the commercial boys are headed right now for Toledo or Chicago." He chuckled, "Hell of a pilot, but then I pay him to be a hell of a pilot and that's a hell of an airplane. Like a fucking feather... you got that stuff together on the *EVOKE* system?"

"Right here," Bill waved at the table by the fire and retrieved Romeri's coat, hanging it in the closet. "There are no government figures on how many have croaked while they're on the system, but we didn't think there would be."

"So?" Lonny poured coffee and sat down, looking fresh and relaxed.

"So, we had to interpolate from five years of coroner reports in twenty six cities and it's a crap-shoot. I don't like reporting crap-shoots to you. I like hard numbers, but none of the reports show *EVOKE* as a cause of death, just an activity during which death occurred."

He sat in the chair opposite and picked up the report. "This thing probably isn't worth your time to look through, but it's already cost a bundle and if we try to look deeper, it's going to take an awful lot of computer time. We figure the chances of kicking off on *EVOKE* are about the same as watching television. Fourteen deaths by equipment malfunction... electrocution in all fourteen cases... surge protector failure."

"Surge protector?"

"Yeah, anybody with a computer, who doesn't want to lose the data in a power surge, attaches a gadget that shuts it down in case there's a surge that might blow all the memory. Power surges are not all that uncommon, sometimes when substations are switched or a lightning strike or even a squirrel getting fried in a power-box. All the *EVOKE* systems have built in surge protection, because of this thing being stuck right into the brain, you can imagine the possible consequences."

"So?"

"So, it's possible, but pretty unrealistic for accidental death."

"But, there have been fourteen."

"Yeah, fourteen out of twenty million, like I say, unrealistic."

"But it *has* happened... fourteen times."

"Yeah ... " What the hell was he looking for? He wouldn't leave this alone.

"So, let's get hypothetical again." Lonny crossed his legs, smoothing the crease in a pinstriped pant-leg with his fingers. "Hypothetically, let's say someone wants to knock off some guy while he's on the system. What would have to happen?"

"Well first of all, they'd have to know he was online. That's easy, a phone tap would tell when he was connected by modem to the national lines for *EVOKE*. Second, they'd have to monkey with the guy's modem and cause a malfunction in the surge protection." He cleared his throat and plowed on. "That's not so easy, involves breaking and entering and opportunity and all that stuff, but I suppose it's not really any harder than getting into a guy's place and setting up a bug. The third part is creating the power surge and that's iffy."

"Why, what's so tough about juicing up a line?"

"Well, it's not impossible, just problematic." Christ, Bill had talked over a hell of a lot of Plan B's with Romeri, but this one was a serious discussion of murder. Who the hell did he have in mind? Most of the big shots in the country had *EVOKE*, because it was hard to get. Easily given by lottery, but hard to get on demand. Things that were hard to get had to be gotten as a matter of pride, a symbol of big-shot power. Bill had it, Romeri had it, probably Tanya and probably Romeri's wife, among a hell of a lot of others. Fairweather, for sure, had it. Who the hell was the target, if there was a target? Plan B wasn't always used, but Jesus, this was a hell of a Plan B. The first time they'd ever ventured into this kind of a conversation. The word 'accomplice' kept running through Wearley's mind and he shook it off, but it refused to go away.

"It would have to be the power for just the target residence and the boost would have to be enough to kill, but not blow out everything in the place."

"Why? Why not blow out everything?" Romeri seemed intrigued by the crease in his pants, not looking at Bill, running his fingers up and down the crease. "Why wouldn't it look more like the real thing, if the whole neighborhood went out?... easier too. If everything else had this surge protection you're talking about, nothing would be in danger, except for a few televisions and toasters."

"I guess … "

"So, what you're saying is, it's possible."

"Yes… it's possible."

"Thanks, Bill, I don't need to see that report. Matter of fact, you may find it useful to get rid of any hard copy and purge the computers, as well." He got up and walked to the desk, looking through the messages and mail.

"There's one other thing." Wearley was half out of his chair. "A sort of adjacent possibility came up."

"Yeah?" Lonny laid down the mail. "What *adjacent possibility?*"

"Well, it's a little complicated, but if a guy looped into someone's personal computer, there's the possibility of post-hypnotic suggestion. *EVOKE* would set up pretty well for that."

"Go on."

"You know what computer viruses are?"

"Vaguely, go on." Lonny sat on a corner of the desk.

"Well, they're commands that are buried in the computer memory, usually by unauthorized insertion through a modem. They just lie there, undetected for whatever period of time. When an ordinary computer command is given that they're programmed for, they go into action. Usually destructive action and they keep wiping stuff from the memory or disfiguring data. The last thing they wipe out is themselves, without a trace."

"Without a trace … " Lonny swung his leg idly from the desk. "That's very interesting. You say someone could be hypnotized? Go on with that."

"In theory, an *EVOKE* user could be put into a state of hypnotism while he or she was in one of the programs. The result would be post-hypnotic. The

EVOKE experience remains as a remembered event, so it fits. The guy would theoretically shut down the machine and go jump from a thirtieth floor window or whatever, whatever the suggestion was. The virus would disappear."

"I always thought a person wouldn't do anything under hypnosis that they wouldn't do normally."

"I'm told that's bullshit."

"That's very interesting stuff, Bill. All very hypothetical, as I'm sure you understand, but very interesting."

"That all for now?"

"Yeah Bill, that's all for right now. We need to get together after lunch and go over the London meetings. You free?"

"I'll get free."

"Thanks and good job on this stuff, it's all I need to know right now." He sat down at the desk and reached for the intercom to Vicki, as Wearley picked up the report.

"Oh, and Bill?"

"Yeah?"

"Anyone talked to the kid yet?"

"Couple of weeks, they're still trying to set it up."

TWELVE

Two huge Daimler-Benz diesels, silently and without the usual throb of engines underway, slipped World Sea from the port of Naples. All two hundred fourteen feet of her and a crew of twenty, underway and focused for the pleasure of two people. Cruising up the Italian coast, Lonny and Tanya would enjoy a leisurely and very rare four days at sea, headed for Monaco.

There are less costly ways to travel the approximate three hundred nautical miles, far less costly, but few to match the luxury of this particular yacht. It was seldom that she sailed with fewer than fifty aboard.

She stepped from the shower into a spacious and mirrored dressing room. Toweling down, Tanya took a quick and critical, then longer and more appreciative look at her body in the angles and variances the mirrors produced in reflections of reflections. Walking naked into the stateroom, its walls lacquered in descending shades of dusty rose, where Lonny sat in a comfortably upholstered arm chair, she let him admire her body as she reached for the silk-print sheath on the bed. Her languid reach, her long stretch over the bed insisted that he look, demanded that he admire.

So of course he did. It wasn't all that hard.

She straightened, raising her arms to drop the slithering silk over her head and it fell like water washing across her shoulders, down over her breasts. Splashing over a slender belly, it caught for a heartbeat at her hips, dropping to the ankle, two thin straps over her tan shoulders. No underwear, just silk between her body and the breeze off the sea.

"You never change," he said.

He looked at her, not glanced but looked this time, as if he were appraising a piece of art he might buy. Studying the brush-work, an eye for color and the bold hand of the artist. "How is it, in this world where everything seems to go to hell, you never change? Only become more beautiful and make me fall more in love with you?"

"You don't use that word as often as I'd like," Tanya sat on the arm of the chair and brushed fingers across his cheek. "I wasn't sure you remembered how to spell it, much less the pronunciation."

"Love?"

"Yes, love. Whatever it is and whatever it means. Something different to each of us, I guess."

"Too cheaply said and too abused for you and me."

He put his hand on her thigh, silk the texture of mercury, the slipperiness of nothing. "Love is on every bottle of spray deodorant, every pair of designer jeans, every condom and every World Star roadster. It's come to mean nothing, just like fuck no longer means anything. Some word so overused we're not even shocked when someone says it at the dinner table. Maybe that's why I don't use the word very often. It doesn't say what I feel for you in any of the ways I want it to."

She swung around on the arm of the chair and dropped across his lap, her left arm draped across the back of the chair, head against his shoulder.

"Have I said I love you often enough, Lon?"

"Not very often."

"Maybe I'm still afraid... after five years, still afraid that if I name it, it'll go away. That you'll disappear." She ran her fingers across the back of his neck, hardly brushing the hair with the tips. "You ever want to disappear, Lon?"

"No."

He watched her breathe, watched her breasts rise and fall against the silk, a tightening and slack in fabric that was hardly fabric at all, a steady rhythm of whispered breath. He felt her breathe, air warm from her lungs against his ear. Her breath rose and fell with his when they were time zones apart, when they were sweating with lust in each other's arms, when they were lost in other things and unaware of the way each breath rose and fell in the other.

He nuzzled her gently at a place on her neck taut from the rise of her arm across the chair. A long muscle across her shoulder that shaped a graceful indentation above her collar bone, just at her throat and found himself unable to resist. She shifted slightly, her arm dropping and withdrawn, to rearrange itself behind him across the small of his back. Her head still settled against his shoulder, he drifted in her scent, the odor a new-washed fragrance, slightly musky and only hers, a fingerprint of smell.

"But I've always gone away, not disappeared, but gone away. It's my nature." He could have gone to sleep right here and right now in this chair, lost in quiet, lost in fragrance and warmth and the feel of her in his lap. "I won't disappear from you."

"Four days together." She took his hand and held it in her lap, feeling his fingers against hers, measuring them against her own, tracing the back of his hand. "Am I really to have four days of you alone, without sixteen meetings and four fancy dinners? Without all the sharing we do with everyone who wants bits and pieces of you?"

"Dinners aboard World Sea are pretty fancy affairs too, kid." He grinned at her. "Two chefs and three stewards, just for us."

"You know what I mean." She adjusted her head against him. "I don't think I've ever been on World Sea with just you. Is it going to last, or is that helicopter going to fly away and bring back strangers?"

"It's going to last. March isn't exactly the height of the yachting season along the coast, everyone still lingering in the islands." He moved his hand on top of hers. "World Sea leaves too, when we get off at Monaco. She heads for Alexandria to pick up a charter and then on to Crete." He grinned at her again. "Everyone and everything in my organization works for a living, including you and this yacht. Let's go back and have a drink and watch the sun go down."

They walked from the main stateroom, through arched rosewood doors and down three steps into the main salon, an immense room with teak flooring, covered by a half dozen nearly priceless Persian carpets. When Lonny entertained, each was the center of a cluster of chairs and sofas, arranged informally to accommodate six or eight in each group. Breaking the usual list of guests into manageable proportion, the carpeted groupings allowed their host to divide his attentions intimately. He drifted in and out of conversations as was his habit, shining the light of his interest on one set, then another, in an order and rank known only to himself.

Tonight, the space was softly lit and as they crossed the center, he stopped and pulled her to him. His need to hold her was so sudden, so strong in him that the embrace was more intimate than nakedness. He was more open to her now than any words could express and so they held each other wordlessly, then turned and walked up three steps and through another arch that opened onto a gallery. Paintings, mostly abstract, diffused the pattern of doors to sixteen double staterooms. There were eight suites port, eight starboard, sixteen more one deck below.

At the end of the gallery, the deck opened full width and they walked along portside windows to watch the setting sun. Shafts of orange and pink blazed the underside of the few clouds suspended above the horizon, where Sardinia would have been if Sardinia could be seen. Behind them, the sky deepened across low hills of the coast, layered in shades and intensities of blue, as the sun guttered out like a sizzling coal. Coastal villages began to wink their scattered lights of evening.

A pair of sliding-glass doors opened to a solarium, spanning the full width of the yacht, its rolling roof closed against the chill. A suddenly revealed jungle of tropical plants and trickling water, caged birds and meandering pathways of slate and marble and polished granite. The humid air pushed against them as if entering an Amazon jungle, heavy and heady with the pungent smell of green plants, black earth and growing things.

Toward the stern, they ducked into another starboard side passageway, open to views of small towns scattered among the hillsides north of Naples. They walked hand in hand past a galley and formal dining salon to the glass enclosed top deck lounge where a table for two was set against the deepening blue of night. Candlelight in a dozen directions amplified the crackle of logs in a corner fireplace. The Tyrrhenian Sea, between Naples and Sardinia had only a slight chop and good weather had been promised all the way up the coast.

It seemed to Tanya that World Sea *was* an island and the coast of Italy a moving ship, passing in the night. All the moment required was a moon and as she thought the thought, a cloud slipped away to reveal the face of a three-quarter moon. A streaming path of shimmering light shown like a roadway to the yacht, from which they could never escape.

"Do you ever get used to this, Lon?" She reached for his hand and touched just the fingertips. "I mean really used to it, so complacent that the magic disappears?"

"Yeah… it's a strange thing Tanya, how life conspires to take away the awe and make things commonplace." He pulled out the chair for her and slid it under her as she sat.

"I remember when Dad had a twenty-eight foot fishing boat. I was a kid then and we used to go out on Lake Erie for walleye and smallmouth, just the two of us. I remember thinking that was just about the biggest, neatest boat I'd ever want to see." He looked across at her. "There aren't a dozen yachts in the world like this and this is the seventh I've owned, each of them longer and more grand and powerful than the last." He tapped a finger on the tablecloth. "But none of them ever made me feel as excited as that fishing boat."

"I think that's somehow sad."

"That's what's lost, when you stop being a kid, all that sense of wonder that's so powerful it stays with you the rest of your life. Nothing stays with me anymore. No more sense of wonder." He covered her hand, running his finger back and forth.

"The first few deals I put together when I was starting out and under the gun, are just as clear to me now as when they happened. They were tough and made me sweat. If any of them had failed, I'd have been ruined, but they were all memorable and I can see every face that sat across the table. I made a buyout a year ago, over three billion dollars and I can't even bring a picture to mind of the guy on the other end of the deal … " His finger circled her third knuckle, the ring-finger knuckle. "Does that seem strange to you?"

"No… we all lose our wonder, except in bed and wilderness and sometimes even there."

The steward served scotch, Black Label on the rocks for Lonny, with a splash for Tanya and then Lonny waved him off, saying he'd ring when they wanted dinner. He took her by the hand, rose and opened the door to the deck where a soft but slightly chill breeze flattened the silk against the outline of Tanya's body. She shivered and turned away, walking to the sofa where he joined her. Lonny sat at the opposite end, a knee pulled up flat on the cushion, foot hooked under his left leg, facing her. He raised his glass in a silent toast and they both sipped. Tanya smiled at him as he looked away.

"How come you never told me about Winifred and the husband and the baby?" He said it as though he'd just had the car washed and noticed an unfamiliar dent, wanting an explanation.

"Oh, Lon."

Her heart caught and she suddenly felt her skin magnified, every pore opening and closing, the nerves exposed and vulnerable. The small blond hairs on her arm and across the back of her neck, were each a straining individual, aware of her skin, as though it was separate from the rest of her. How could someone suddenly become *aware* of their skin? God, why this? Four days to be together and he was at last the unguarded self, the man she so seldom saw and loved so much. Why this unanswerable question to smash it all in pieces? Why now, dear God, why now at this most perfect moment?

"Why do you have to know everything about everything?" She felt heavy, too heavy to stand, too heavy to run if there had been a place to run. "Is it the *power to know*? All those people you have who can find out anything?" She felt her breath leaving, wondering abstractly if she'd take another and then her body decided for her and she took another. "Why Lon, after five years, *why*?"

"I didn't ask just to hurt you or to prove I could find out." He'd known for almost all the time he'd known Tanya, but it never seemed important enough to bring up and he didn't really care and so, he hadn't. Now, he needed to get it behind them. "I wondered why you never said anything."

"Do you have me followed now, Lon?"

"No."

"Do you know what I do and where I go and how I spend my time? Do you get a report on where I ate last Tuesday at lunch and with whom?" She looked at him levelly. "Do you know who I sleep with?"

"No." He lied. He did know. She slept with no one but him.

"Do you care?"

"Who you sleep with?"

"Yes, who I sleep with, who I have lunch with, who I was married to in a life that seems so far behind me I can hardly remember."

"Yes... I love you... of course I care, but I don't check."

"Who do you sleep with, Lon? Perhaps you'd like to tell me that." Her skin still belonged to someone else, but it was beginning to be her own again. It began to flush just a little, slowly beginning to come back to cover her body, layering all those myriad nerves stripped raw. She knew she'd breathe again without having to think about it.

"That's not the point ... " That *was* the point and he became aware of it, just as he spoke the words. The realization caught him somewhere just below mid gut, where he never let anyone reach.

In a lifetime of analysis, a thousand meetings that depended on reading his opponent in truths and half-truths, lies and half lies, Lonny had prevailed. Always able to tell himself the protective half-truths that keep most people sane. Now Tanya had blindsided him, proved it didn't matter. He could lie without a trace, instinctively and malevolently. Be false on the spur of the moment and hold her eyes without a flicker... but not to himself, no longer to himself.

"Well, that *is* the point, Lon. That really *is* the point and I don't care if I lose you, if you're not the man I thought you were." Her voice was low and level and she wondered if he'd dismissed the servants to be alone with her or just to have something out that was stuck in him. "What do you want to know, that you don't already know? I'm sure you've seen every court record and birth record in Great Bend. I was sixteen and scared to death of my father, who used to drink too much and try to get my pants off." She paused and fought against tears. Please, God, this was not a time for tears. "Sometimes he did get them off. I hated him, but I don't even feel that anymore." She sipped her scotch and took a deep breath. "Then Billy Eversly got me pregnant our senior year in high school. You want to know where? You want to know how, every heavy breath and drop of sweat?"

"No."

"I didn't want a baby, didn't want to be a housewife or a mother and was too damned corn-silk green and scared to know what to do about it. We were married. That's what you do in Great Bend, when you're sixteen and pregnant, you get married. It lasted two years. Billy wanted the baby real bad and he wanted me real bad too, but I couldn't do it. I knew she'd be all right with him. He loved her... loved us both, but he was just a kid too. I told him and he cried and I cried and I asked him never to try to find me and he said he wouldn't." She took another breath. "I believed him. He was a good guy, Billy and he deserved something better than a wife who would grow to hate him."

"He's married and has two more kids." That's right Lonny, he thought, show the power you show off by knowing everything about everyone. When you don't know what the fuck else to do, hide behind the power.

"Well, I glad and I don't want to know anything more, all right?"

"All right."

"Why, Lon? You still haven't answered why now, why tonight, when the moon is trying to make this perfect and I feel closer to you than I've felt in a year?"

"Because I need to get some fences down that stand between us and your past stands between us as long as we haven't talked about it. I need to know if you're willing to go with me from here, the way I need to go." He touched a fingertip to hers, to see if she'd draw back, but she didn't. Her hand was still and lifeless.

"I lied to you. Lied to you just a minute ago… not about knowing where you lunch." He would tell a half truth and make it work. "But about you and Billy. I've known since we first met. It's the way I used to be… maybe still am in some ways." He looked into her eyes, trying to read the feelings hidden there and see how much damage he'd done, see if it was permanent.

"I've had the Club Largo put in your name and the apartment."

"Why?"

"Because I need to feel that you're with me because you want to be and not because of the job and the money and the apartment."

"And you think that'll do it?" She felt empty. It had finally come down to ownership, something she'd shoved off into corners, now thrown at her on a yacht in a perfect sea. She was another acquisition and he had to name the terms. She wondered if there was a pilot on board, if the helicopter would take her to a plane, if she could leave by herself before dinner.

"If I think what will do it?"

"Giving me this stuff. You think that'll make a difference?" Her fingers withdrew but her voice wasn't angry and reading her eyes wasn't working for Lonny for the first time in memory. "Well, maybe you're right. Maybe it's best, Lon if we just set the price and shake hands like business partners. What's Club Largo worth, a million?"

"Million and a half… the apartment maybe another half."

"Terrific, I'm a rich lady." She got up and stood in front of him. "I suppose I should at least thank you. Was it worth it, Lon? Did you get your money's worth or do I need to strip?" She slipped a finger under the thin strap at her shoulder.

"Tanya … "

"No, I mean it. Thank you, thank you very much … " She walked to the windows, walked to the path of the moonlight and looked out across the water. Turned away from him, tears rolled now and she fought them off, but her shoulders began to shake with quiet sobs. She wanted desperately for him to stay in his seat, for him to *not* come over, to *not* put his arms around her. But then she felt him at her waist, his hands at her hips, then circling her waist and she wanted to stiffen and couldn't.

"I'm doing this badly, Tanya." The voice was at her ear and she agreed. Whatever he was doing to her, he was doing very badly.

"And it may get worse," his voice continued and she tried to focus but he was talking about something getting worse and there was no worse than this. "Because I don't know how to get this all across without being clumsy, but I love you, in all the mismanagement of that word. I want to marry you and the part that's worse is that I can't marry you." His hands moved up her waist, just under her breasts. "And that's what I need to know, if you can make this work between us, if we can make this work between us for a long time. Without ever being married."

"You can make the moon go away or make this boat sink. You can make the world wake up tomorrow and think it's Sunday instead of Saturday. I've never heard you say you can't."

"Well, I can't... not and be President."

"President? You mean of the United States?" Her voice was flat.

"Yes."

"Why is it, even that doesn't surprise me?" Her body relaxed a little. At least there were reasons and she didn't doubt for a minute that he was serious. If he were serious, he would most certainly become President.

"Let's have another try at a drink." She took a deep breath and held it.

"You okay?" He poured scotch and sat next to her.

"Yeah, Lonny, I'm okay. It's just been a very long time since we sat down on that sofa and I haven't got very much left to give right now." She put her hand along the side of his leg, needing to touch. "Does she know?"

"Who?"

"Your wife?"

"She doesn't do much except drink, have children and spend money." He reached for the tray of seafood. "Have we had this conversation? No. Does she care about staying married to me? I don't know, probably not. But a divorce from a wife of twenty-five years, with three kids and one of them still home, won't work. A divorce and remarriage to a twenty-eight year old exotic dancer isn't possible." He looked at her and she didn't even flinch. "I'm sorry, but that's what the papers would say."

"Hey, that's what I am... ex-dancer and for the last ten minutes owner of Club Largo, but it's all the same." She felt her life coming back. Tanya never expected to marry him. God, he probably didn't even know that. After all the misunderstanding of what he was driving at, she was warmed by the love he must have for her. Lonny wasn't buying her off, but trying to fight through a problem that didn't exist. Of course she would love him. Nothing had changed, except that there had been a minor shift in the power between them and her skin belonged entirely to herself once again. "So, who else knows about this decision to be President?"

"Just you and Bill Wearley, for now. A lot of people probably suspect and speculate."

"That's a pretty small group. I guess I'm surprised you'd tell me."

"I love you."

"I know you do." She picked up her glass from the table and took a slow sip, looking at him over the rim of the glass.

"Why do you want it?"

"It's the top job." He looked at her levelly and then his eyes crinkled, just at the corners. I don't have a political philosophy that will save the world. But I can do the job probably better than the last four or five, because I'm richer than almost anyone and don't have to listen to their shit. Ross Perot had a shot at it, twenty-five years ago and he chickened out and fell apart when he probably could have had it."

He pushed away the scotch, reaching for wine and pouring a glass. "Red wine?" She shook her head. "That was a time that proved what no one ever thought was true. That the American people will let the Presidency be bought if the man doing the buying has something to offer. There's been no one rich enough or interested enough to take a run at it since then. Until me." He took a long drink of wine.

"I want it, I can damned well afford it and I'm going to have it."

"When?"

"I think twenty-one months from now, kid. But certainly within ten years."

The blue sedan's windows were darkened, protective as a pair of dark glasses and Everett used it when he wanted to travel anonymously. Chauffeured occasionally to any one of a half-dozen girls. Driven at other times and other places like now, to meet on the quiet in the back room of Samson's World Famous Ribs.

"Hey Reverend, good to see you." A huge aproned shape gave way in the narrow hallway by the kitchen, allowing two big men to pass, each renowned for their work. They shook hands and Everett nodded toward the rear.

"Hey, Samson. He back there?"

"Yeah, lookin' all sweaty and eatin' ribs. You want a slab?"

"Yeah Samson, extra hot like always an' see nobody bothers us." He grinned and the three hundred pound owner and cook shuffled back into the kitchen, barbecue smoke hanging like a low cloud against the ceiling. The sweet smell of Samson's caught on the air for two or three blocks in any direction and if the building were torn down and carted away, no one doubted that the smell of slow-cooked ribs would remain, a beacon to the hungry on the south side.

He walked down the long hallway toward the washrooms, the walls a mosaic of signed celebrity pictures, high fivin' Samson or with their arm around the shoulder of a man they wouldn't let in their living room. Smiling and lookin' cool, lookin' hip, a lot of white faces lookin' like they wished the brothers well. Smiling for the camera, before they caught a personal plane to LA or New York and locked themselves behind secure doors.

He passed a bunch of young brothers, laughing and handing around small folded papers. The talk died and the papers disappeared, their eyes drifting vacantly toward the walls, flattening, as this big man in the dark glasses turned sideways to squeeze past. A community of exhaled breath and renewed chatter resumed as he continued down the hall, walking through a door marked 'Employees Only.'

Deek sat at a table in the corner, wearing running shoes and black khakis. His Saturday morning black and green plaid flannel shirt worn outside his pants and covering a service revolver, a Bulls warm-up jacket thrown over the back of his chair. He was sweating, but maybe it was the hot-sauce.

"Hey, Deek."

"Hey, Reverend. Someday the Feds are gonna wire this back room and half the south side's gonna end up in Joliet." He grinned and nudged a chair for Prentiss with his foot, broad face glistening. "We oughta be janitors, my boys sweep this place so often. What's up?"

"Flip. Flip's up and he keeps on pushin'. That skinny nigger don't listen to no one, but he keeps on pushin' an' I'm gettin' tired of that sorry black ass of his, not payin' attention." Prentiss eased into the chair.

"I know. I been hearin' from the west side, from Cicero and Oak Park. There's gonna be some major stuff hit the streets if he don't ease up."

"How you plan on makin' that dumb fuck ease up?"

"Maybe you should talk to him again. Maybe he needs to hear it one more once. I thought he was beginnin' to listen after that last time you had him in."

Deek had his doubts. There was plenty of reason to doubt Flip and the longer this went on, the more arrogant and out of control he became. Control was the issue. Without it there was nothing. He knew why Prentiss was sitting across from him, but he wasn't going to say the word. Let the Reverend say the word, he was the Man and he could say it.

"Fuck talkin' to that skinny-ass, I want him gone. You know, Deek... *gone*." The flat of Everett's hand hit the table and Deek's ribs jumped.

Flip was new generation and it was time to go back to the old ways, the way things were when the Panthers ran the streets. With muscle and fear and guns and enough power to know their limits. Flip Haskell didn't know the limits, was too fucking smart for his own good... for Everett's good and Deek's and the Italians.

Those Mafia sonsabitches still remembered when they ran it all and the blacks were just users and runners. *BURN* didn't get shit from the Italians and Deek would get it either way, so it was up to him to say the word. Now was not the time to have the Italians remember, meeting in basements and back rooms in Cicero. Remember how it used to be, how it could be again, talking about the old days.

Flip's power came from keeping everyone off balance, changing the alliances, everyone guessing which pod covered the pea in a deadly shell-game. He had quick hands, too quick to get caught but too greedy to listen to reason. Well, to hell with that, it would be like it was with the Panthers once he was gone. Big men with big mouths, who knew when to shut those mouths. Knew when to go into the streets, Deek's streets.

"I know you want him gone. So who's comin' up when he goes down?" The same old question, but Prentiss was tired of waiting for an answer. The only way Flip stayed number one, was to make sure there *wasn't* a number two.

"I dunno." Samson knocked once and then came in to set a double order of ribs, extra hot in front of Everett, closing the door softly as his huge bulk edged back out. "We'll let 'em fight it out in the streets an' when someone takes over, I'll bring 'em in for a little chat."

There was no *way* to know and trying to set someone up in advance was too risky. The whole thing could fall apart. It might anyway and then they'd have to start over. Everett didn't want to start over, it had taken too damned long to get where they were.

"It'll be busy on the streets for a few weeks. Then it should be over and we'll know. I don't know any other way to do it, Deek, an' Flip's got to go."

"Okay."

Putting the pistol away was a turning-point for Marty, at least he thought it was. Something had lifted off him anyway, he felt like a person again and his mind cleared for a while. He began re-stringing the hours that lay scattered like so many beads, carefully adding one behind another into a day, the day to a week. A week was jewelry enough for the moment and he began to think there was some hope for his life beyond the extravagant pleasures that dominated his every evening. If he could clean up the house and keep himself in fresh laundry, he could do the same with people. Beads, just beads on a string. He'd train himself to listen, to reply and to keep his mind on what was being said. And if he could manage all that and keep at it, like he'd kept at his job, maybe he would learn to give a shit. More beads.

He edged back into the coffee breaks on the dock and listened to Fred Alcott talk about Friday night's game between the Bulls and the Pistons. The game went to double overtime, tied ninety-six, ninety-six and tied again one eleven, one eleven, the stadium rocking. Won by the Pistons on a foolishly early jumper from mid-court that took all the fight out of the Bulls and lost them their fourth in a row. A rookie play, that made no sense with ten seconds left, but the Bulls panicked and fell apart with a careless pass, a stolen ball and that was that. There was always next season. Chicago was a next-season town except for the all too brief years of Ditka and Jordan and they were history… ancient history.

Marty fought to keep his attention with Fred and the story, but the memory of how he'd taken the court for the Celtics in the final game of the Championship got in the way. He scored thirty-six points in the second half, firing the Celtics to a come-from-behind victory. Fighting off the memory, he tried to keep in the bullshit about the Bulls game, to keep reality and fantasy separate in his mind, tried to care.

He had his annual review with old man Clark and it went okay. The raise he'd looked forward to finally came through, but Marty didn't really need it now and came out of the old man's office a little depressed, wondering why. Another endless stretch of a year ahead of him, more beads to string and for what? More beads and twenty years yet to go before early retirement. Money was the least of his worries. *EVOKE* took him everywhere he cared to go and the money just piled up in his bank account. The old Honda was good enough, now that he'd driven the Grand Prix.

The old man was pleased with Marty's coming around to the detail of his job and the near faultless work he'd been doing the past few months, not understanding Marty didn't really give a shit. He just hung on to the detail of work to keep from losing his weakening grip on reality, the last thing left to keep him away from the drawer and the pistol.

Marty fought to keep focused even as the old man smiled and bobbed his head approvingly and nattered on about how important Marty was to Clark & Anderson. To keep up the fine work, he certainly had a good future with the company, finally standing to indicate the end of the ordeal and shaking Marty's hand warmly. Fuck Clark and fuck his company.

No, that wasn't fair. They'd been good to him. Clark was a pretty nice old guy, totally immersed in the little world of Clark & Anderson and proud of his son, who'd just graduated from Yale. The kid was climbing that secure and well-braced ladder of founder's sons, starting out in the marketing department, on his way up through all the important positions to someday take over the presidency from a proud father. The old man's age kept him from ever having a shot at *EVOKE* and a tiny corner of Marty's brain envied his naiveté. He wondered what would happen, if the ladder would shake a bit when his son came up on the lottery. Sure as hell *he'd* come up. He was only twenty three.

Struggling with contact and friendship was hard work for Marty and as he realized that no one in his circle of acquaintance shared any of his experiences, the effort seemed less and less worthwhile. Predictably and effortlessly, Marty relapsed into the old pattern, closing himself off again one by one from all his human contacts.

He needed Jean more and more as he blended into the colorless reality of himself, his job and the modem. She was the one who always had the time to listen to what was in his heart, the only one who knew him. He realized she was the only one who could reach him, the sole survivor who remembered his color in a world gone gray. He might still be able to have *EVOKE*, find some compromise, but he'd have to put it all in some sort of perspective so it didn't come between them and surely she'd understand. It was a small price to pay.

Tuesday, about seven, he called and Jean picked up the phone.

"Hello?"

"Hi, babe. It's me… Marty." His heart pounded and his voice sounded distant and too high from somewhere inside his head.

"Oh… it's been a long time. How are you, Marty?"

"Fine… no, Jean… babe, that's not true. I'm *not* fine." He took a deep breath and plowed on. "Jesus, I miss you and it's been so damned long and I've been such a damned fool and I'm scared as hell to call after so long." Another breath. "And the minute you picked up the phone and I heard your voice, my heart started pounding so hard, that I thought you'd hear it."

The words all ran together in a torrent and Marty just kept talking.

"You know, babe, this whole moving out thing has really been hard on me and made me realize just how important you are to my life." Breathe, goddammit. "And all the things I want for us and always wanted for us. It's been awful without you, Jean." Breath. "I *know* I've screwed up the having children, but Jesus, babe, the mortgage and the backyard and the college tuition look awfully good and we can still find a way to have a family." Breath. Breathe Marty, goddammit *breathe*.

"Marty, this isn't a very good time for me … "

"Someone *there* with you? You want me to call back later?"

"Not exactly… it just isn't a very good time."

"Well, hang on and listen to me for a minute. This is important. Jesus, babe, it's *important*." Take a breath Marty, get hold of your brain. "You know, all the time we were together, we talked about stuff that was important to both of us, stuff about our lives and how we wanted to live them and who we wanted to live them with and all our innermost thoughts and we really seemed to get inside each other." Oh shit, it isn't working, it's like talking to a dead phone.

"I mean, I know, I wasn't always into some of the long-term family stuff and I know I wasn't fair about your brother and what he was doing with his life, but that was before I *knew*. Before I knew what life really *was*." Slow it down. Keep cool, just slow it down and goddamm breathe. "Jean, you were right. You taught me what life really was and I was too stupid and wrapped up in myself to see it."

"Marty ... "

"*Wait* a minute. Hear me out." Scratching lines now, Marty was scratching long lines through the notes on the telephone pad. Heavy lines, crossed lines, dark and deeply impressed on the page. "I'm *not* now babe, *not* stupid and confused. I know what I want now and it's the same things you want." Silence. Breath. Heavy lines. "The same things we always talked about. I just needed to step back a little and see it. Jean... babe, I love you and I've always loved you and I know it now. I want us to get back together, not just to try again or some bullshit like that, but to stay together." Furious lines now, underscoring each other.

"To help each other get through and *be* there for each other and have the family and the mortgage and the whole thing. Together... just us, just the two of us muddling our way through, but together. It's what my life is all about. It's what makes it all worth while and I know that now."

"Marty?"

"Yeah?"

"Marty, I just got back from the hospital and this is just not a very good time to talk. Maybe in a couple of days, maybe Thursday or Friday?"

"Jesus babe, you all right?" The pencil was stuck to the page. "What the hell *is* it, you sick? You hurt? I'll come right over if you need me, you know that." He suddenly realized he didn't even know where she lived.

"No... Marty... this is a little hard for me."

"God, Jean... babe, I'm *here* for you now." Oh God, she couldn't be pregnant. Please god, don't let her be pregnant. "I've really always been here for you. Tell me what I can do and I'll do it. You *know* that."

"Marty, I'm not sick and I'm not hurt and there's nothing you can really do." There was a gap, a two-beat gap of silence on the line and Marty felt his life pouring away, sliding out of sight and the point on the pencil snapped against the phone pad.

"I've just had the *EVOKE* implant and I really need to get plugged into the modem ... "

THIRTEEN

A lan Longwell was commissioner for *EVOKE* over at Social Security and he'd held that position through two administrations. Civil Service rank made Alan bulletproof, a dug-in bureaucrat, experienced in trench warfare, who would watch many more administrations come and go, his pension and retirement secure. He didn't appreciate being called down to the Senate like some errand boy. He glanced at his watch and sighed, a barely perceptible sigh. That was the deal. They summoned, you came. The way the game was played.

He sat in Senator Fairweather's reception area and looked at his watch again, wondering whether he'd have to miss lunch at Renaldo's. The lunches were regular now on Tuesdays and Thursdays and he was hooked on Elizabeth, four Civil Service grades below him and ambitious to climb around on Longwell's ladder. He knew she was using him, but her grasp would hold firm on his rung until he kicked her fingers loose. Merely another way the game was played in this town. Besides, her long legs drove him nuts and she knew it. They were climber's legs. His mind wandered to her flat belly and small firm breasts, a tattoo of a small butterfly on the left, just above the nipple... the lunch he could miss, fuck the lunch. But if he missed her at Renaldo's, there would be no after-lunch.

Maybe he could get this over quickly, there was still two hours and Fairweather was usually pretty busy and got right to the point. Unusual though, to be called into his office instead of appearing before the Committee. The Committee was a regular thing and this was irregular as hell. Something on the Senator's mind. He might be getting numbers back, stuff he couldn't justify from public records or even some of the not so public things discussed in rare closed meetings.

Well fuck it, he could brush it away, say he'd look into it and get back to him. Thousands of goddamn employees, he couldn't be expected to be on top of every frigging event, responsible for every number. But he *was* responsible and he knew it and Fairweather knew it and it made his palms sweat. Probably couldn't get away with stone-walling, Fairweather could be tough when he was pissed. He'd have to duck and dive a bit, but he smiled to himself. Ducking and diving was how he'd outlasted two administrations. He was good at that.

He was good at Elizabeth too, if only this goddamn meeting would start, so it could end and he could spend his afternoon with the butterfly.

"Alan, I'm sorry to keep you. A subcommittee meeting that ran too long, I'm afraid, as they so often do." Fairweather was at his office door. Must have slipped in through the back, but at least he was there and they could get on with it.

"Not at all, Senator." He stood and almost offered his hand, but the Senator kept his hands at his sides, so he fumbled with the briefcase and cleared his throat. "Always glad to be available to the Committee or its Chairman." This meeting was going to be a bitch. Just a feeling, but the feeling wouldn't go away and there was something about Fairweather's eyes that made him feel like a shoplifter.

"Come in, come in," Bob waved toward his office. "This shouldn't take long, I've just a few questions I want to get clear in my mind, without taking up valuable Committee time."

Longwell walked into the office and realized that in the eight years of his directorship, it was only the second or third time he'd been there. Didn't matter who they were, and Fairweather was one of the less pompous, these frigging Senators wanted to get you on their turf and sit behind those big polished desks. State and Federal flags on either side, rubbing your nose in their power, letting you know what a little bureaucrat shit you are. The desks and walls always full of photographs of themselves with the President, smiling or signing things. They made you sit in a smaller chair, across the desk on the powerless side.

Well, Alan knew all about power and Fairweather might be able to order him down here like a flunky, but Senators came and went. The top Civil Service rankings were there forever, to withhold or dispense their prerogatives and authority to the highest bidder. He might be a little balding and knew the heavy glasses gave him a slightly nearsighted look, but the dark suit was pinstriped and there would always be another Senator and another Elizabeth who needed him to get where they wanted to go. Washington didn't run without the Alan Longwells.

"Alan, I'll get right to the point, because I know you have a lot of things on your mind and running your commission is no small job." He smiled and Longwell hated the smile.

"Since its very inception, *EVOKE* has been committed… publicly committed… to the protections of anonymity in all of its operations. As you know, that extends even to me, both as a Senator and as Chairman of the *EVOKE* Committee. There are things I don't know, can't get my hands on to find out and shouldn't be able to know without the very highest authority. Sometimes, not even then. That's a pledge to our citizens." Fairweather smiled again and Longwell shifted in his chair, glancing away from the Senator's eyes and concentrating on the polished millwork trim across the back of the desk. Shit. He *knew*. Someone had talked.

Bob leaned back in his chair, taking a reminiscent tone halfway between college professor and and a father who knew his son had hotwired the car.

"I remember four or five years back, there was a woman over at the Justice Department, who was selling documents from sealed files. She'd been doing it for years, doing it for so long that it didn't even seem wrong anymore. Nothing foreign-agent about it, thievery for sure, but just a way she paid the bills and sent the kids to college." He paused and looked off across the room, as though he were talking about a disconnected issue, just musing over an old war story.

"She's doing time now and of course that's always a tragedy. Especially with kids and all, but the real damage wasn't in the selling, it was in the failure of public trust. Sealed documents are sealed to protect the people whose lives are rolled up in those documents." He paused and looked at Longwell.

"They have a right to expect that sealing means just that... sealed, protected, *inviolate*."

"Yes, well people are just people, Senator. Some good and some bad I expect, even in Washington." Longwell shifted again in the chair and tried to read Fairweather's eyes. "Tragedy, as you say, when the public trust is broken... "

"Yes, of course it is, Alan. But we know it happens. You know it happens, I know it happens. I suppose it will always happen to some degree. But we have to be on our guard and always look for the problems." Bob leaned back in his chair again and cocked his right elbow against the arm, resting his head on a splay of fingers across his chin and up the side of his face, reflecting. Gazing at Alan Longwell. "Vigilant, Alan. An overused word and one that has begun to lose its meaning. But a correct word, nevertheless."

"Are you suggesting a problem at Social Security?" Longwell glanced from the Senator's face to the flag of Virginia. "A problem within my division?" Take it head on. Take it head on and then slide off into other issues, that was the way to handle it.

"Alan, two events have come to my attention over the past weeks and they are both entirely unrelated to each other. Well... perhaps that's not absolutely accurate, they both *appear* to involve a leak of information from the records of *EVOKE*." He kept his hand at his face, holding the moment with his posture.

"They each involve disclosures of protected information." He paused. "They are each, in themselves, indictable offenses."

Longwell's palms began to sweat again. Civil Service protected him from almost every conceivable angle of attack. Except indictment. Even Presidents, as the record so shamefully showed, were subject to criminal indictment. "That's a very strong accusation, Senator. Do you have something you want to show me, some sort of evidence of indictable offense?"

"No."

He watched Longwell's face, looking for a clue, finding in its place that long, slow retreat behind bureaucratic eyes. He'd seen it before, seen it often enough to know that Alan knew all about what he described and the evidence, such as it was, would be buried. Buried, perhaps along with a career or two thrown in, but buried all the same.

"I have the information and I will continue to hold it private. Dan McCarthy will give you a briefing on your way out, if you'd be so good as to stop by his office."

"I'll look into it, of course."

"I want more than that, Alan." Bob's posture remained unchanged and there was a heavy sense of just how seriously he took this issue, in the interminably splayed fingers.

"I want a full report on my desk, just as soon as one can be prepared. I need to see that report *before* I make a decision to turn what I have over to the FBI or Justice Department."

"Yes, Senator." Fuck, he wasn't rolling over. This could get complicated, but it wasn't going to get complicated until after lunch and an afternoon with Elizabeth.

"Thank you, Alan."

The hand finally came away from the face and the Senator stood, this time extending his hand and Longwell regretted the moistness of his palm. "We've always had such excellent work from you and I know that will continue. Your support is very important to the Committee." He walked them to the side door and opened it.

"I'm very serious, Alan. I want that report, without delay. Shall we say a week?"

"I'll do my best, Senator."

"I'm sure you will, Alan, sure you will."

He smiled again and Longwell returned the smile, hoping it had a reassuring glow he didn't feel. "Sally, would you show Mr. Longwell to Dan McCarthy's office?"

Bob walked back to his desk and sat down, swiveling his chair to face the windows, wondering at the events that had swirled across this city in the two hundred fifty years or so of the Nation. He walked his bookcase and selected the well-worn and dog eared volume on Jefferson's life, laying it on his desk. It fell open automatically, by constant reference to the quotation he'd read so often:

"It can never be too often repeated, that the time for fixing every essential right on a legal basis is while our rulers are honest, and ourselves united. From the conclusion of this war we shall be going down hill. It will not then be necessary to resort every

moment to the people for support. They will be forgotten, therefore, and their rights disregarded. They will forget themselves, but in the sole faculty of making money, and will never think of uniting to effect a due respect for their rights. The shackles, therefore, which shall not be knocked off at the conclusion of this war, will remain on us long, will be made heavier and heavier, till our rights shall revive or expire in convulsion."

He closed the book and placed it carefully back on the shelf. His fellow Virginian had an enormity of foresight, even though one could hardly know the immense changes that would transform those struggling colonials into a most powerful nation.

"Forget themselves, but in the sole faculty of making money." God help us, Thomas Jefferson, you anticipated us in the full-plumage of our adulthood and knew we would fall short. *"Expire in convulsion"*... or in a life lived dreamlike, Bob thought to himself. He sat at the desk again, his chair turned to the windows.

Four days into the following week, Alonzo Romeri returned from Italy and sat in Bill Wearley's office. An unusual place for him to be, a place he came when the news was bad, as though it would infect his own office to disclose anything negative inside those walls.

"So, Fairweather flat out stiffed us?" Wearley sat against the edge of his desk. He never felt comfortable, sitting behind it in the high-backed leather chair, when the boss was in the room.

"Well, not in so many words but that was the story, all the same." Romeri paced. He'd sat down twice already, only to get up and walk. "Said he was disinclined, that was the word he used, *disinclined* to make a decision on commercial access right now."

Romeri paused and frowned, "Can you imagine that pompous fuck, telling me he's fucking *disinclined*. I'll disincline his ass, before this thing's over."

"What else?" Wearley was afraid for the first time since he'd taken this job. Afraid of Plan B and exhilarated at the same time, waiting to see how far Romeri would go. How close actual push would come to actual shove.

"Oh, he was very cagey about the report. Talked about illegal sources and indictable cause, but all in the vaguest of terms. Pompous prick just wants me to know that report's illegal, as if I was too fucking stupid to know it myself."

He literally tore a cigarette out of the pack and lit it, ignoring the fact that it bothered the hell out of Bill to have people smoke in his office. Wearley slid the second drawer of his desk open to produce a polished ashtray.

"I talked to him about ten this morning and I'm still so pissed I want to throw things and that's not my style. But I can't buy the sonofabitch, he's already got too much money and I tried the reasonable man-to-man approach and he's not buying it." He took a long drag. "I've got to get him out of that chair at the head of the Committee and get that prick, Preston Alberts in. Alberts is a dumb shit and more pompous than Fairweather in most ways, but I own him and he'll do what I fucking tell him." Romeri stubbed out the cigarette, only half smoked and immediately lit another.

"A run at the Presidency means I have to get my hands inside *EVOKE*. And the only way to do that is get commercial access and then *control* the commercial access."

"You been watching Prentiss Everett, lately?" Maybe the boss would cool down, if he could steer the subject away for a few minutes.

"No, I've been in Italy, remember? Everett's big news here, but so far he hasn't exactly got an international reputation." Romeri sat down again. "What's he up to this time?"

"Making a lot of noise about *EVOKE* and how it's just another tool of the white man to enslave the black man. Getting coverage, too. Particularly in all the black papers, left-wing talk shows and liberal big city sheets. Claims the black population is getting a disproportionate access, out of skew with the census. Says it's a conspiracy, a sort of electronic genocide."

"He's right, I've seen the numbers." He looked like he might stay in the chair for more than thirty seconds and Bill relaxed a bit, boosting himself to sit on the desk, legs dangling. "If he wasn't getting his fair share, he'd be hollering about that, too. Goddamn niggers are never happy." He paused and looked at Bill. "I wonder where in the hell he got hold of those numbers?"

"Well, no one ever got to be President ignoring the black vote," Bill said, ignoring the last, swinging his legs and looking at the toes of his shoes. "There's over forty million of 'em and we're going to have to come up with a way to nail down that vote. We were counting on *EVOKE* for a good big part of that black vote. It doesn't help to have Everett running around making waves, not helpful at all."

"Yeah, so what's your point? My mind's on Fairweather right now."

"My point is, that I don't think we can allow the Reverend to end up on the other side of the issue." He slid off the desk and began pacing, knowing it would hold Romeri in his chair.

"Over forty million blacks and forty percent of them wired and we got this loose cannon walking around, raising hell. Pointing fingers and indignant as hell, when we want all of 'em wired. Everybody for that matter, but sure as hell all the blacks." He paused, knowing it was never wise to lecture Romeri. "What do you want to do?"

"Take him out. You're right, we need to take him out, before he gets out of control."

"How?" Bill tensed again. Romeri wanted the Presidency and he always got what he wanted, often using Wearley to get him there. But the research on killing was never far from Bill's mind and he wasn't up for that. He didn't *think* he was up for that.

"Same way we always have." Romeri was concentrated now and the flare over Fairweather seemed to be settling. "Buy him. Find out what his price is and buy him. Shit, he should be easy. There aren't many black politicians that can't be bought and Everett's more crooked than most."

"Preacher."

"Preacher, politician, what the hell's the difference, black or white? All that Reverend stuff doesn't mean shit. He's got a price and we'll meet it." Romeri sat forward in the chair. "I need the black vote and I need it solid. Find out what the price is."

"Right."

"And get me everything we've got on Fairweather in one package."

"He's awfully clean." Wearley leaned against the edge of the desk again, not anxious to start another tirade. "The file's pretty thin, but I'll boil down what we've got."

"Yeah, well his son's a closet gay. And his daughter's off fucking her way around Europe with some long-hair we don't know enough about. Find out about him and her too. Name's Katherine, twenty-six or seven years old and probably gives the old man fits." Romeri reached for yet another cigarette and Bill tried not to care that the carpet would stink for a week.

"There's an angle somewhere, there's always an angle and I need to get both of these guys the hell out of my way."

––––––––––––––––––––

"Of course you understand, all of this is just preliminary."

"Of course."

Bobby sat in the same booth at Lanagan's where he and Web often had lunch and looked across at Rawley Edwards. Rawley's eyebrows shot up in the obligatory facial expression that said 'don't hold me to this,' while he continued to forage his way through the menu.

A serious eater, one born to the job of expense-account power lunches, as well as the Chief Corporate Counsel at World Star International. Bobby wondered once again, why such a huge hammer had been sent to drive such a small nail into Richmond. Wayland Roth and Barnes was the target of all this culinary activity. More specifically, Bobby seemed to be the mark, the one for whom each Maryland crab cake was a sacrifice. His mind wandered from the subject at hand, fascinated at the game itself, all this playing out and reeling in. He wondered if the point to the whole meeting lay hidden under some neglected potato. If so, it would soon be revealed.

They'd been at it since noon and glancing at the clock over the bar, he realized it was just after two in the afternoon. He was still unsure of what Edwards was driving at and they seemed no closer now than earlier, just better-fed. Rawley's droning voice broke his reverie, "... but the figures, as you well know, could be substantial."

"Rawley?"

"Yes, Bobby?" There was a rhythm to the way Rawley ate, a sort of stroke not at all unlike a well-trained crew, sculling their way up the Potomac towards dessert. Incredibly, his conversation never interrupted the beat and food flowed in, conversation out of Rawley's mouth, quite without disturbing one another. It was hypnotic.

"Why are we here? More specifically, why are *you* here? The biggest gun in the World Star legal department come to little old Richmond, waving the promise of potentially huge fees in front of the junior partner in an only fairly well connected law firm?" Enough of this, it was time to call for the conversational check. "I'm not flattered Rawley, I'm waiting to know why we're doing this."

The chewing stopped. "That's pretty abrupt, Bobby."

"No… it would have been abrupt two hours ago. Two hours ago, when it first became apparent this was a fishing expedition. Rawley, I'm the son of a very powerful United States Senator, grandson to another, great great-grandson to a third." He leaned forward, elbows on the tablecloth, fingers splayed and pressed together.

"I suppose you'll excuse me if, under those circumstances, I've learned that my name and family are attractive. What do you want, Rawley? If it's just legal representation in the southeastern area, you ought to be talking to Emerson Wayland. As it is, he'll be pissed you went so far under his head." He fiddled with the saucer of the coffee cup.

"If it's something else, and I happen to think it's something else, let's get to it."

"Okay, let's get it on the table. We want what we always want, Bobby. We want access." Rawley broke the last roll in the basket and, unbuttered, popped half in his mouth. "No doubt, you're going to be the next

Fairweather Senator from Virginia and we want to get to know you and have you get to know us. The legal work's a good framework for that and you know goddamn well there's nothing preliminary about any of this. The whole east coast is yours, if you want it." He brushed away crumbs on the tablecloth.

"I'm down here, instead of some shirt-waist Vice President, so you'll know we're serious." The other half-roll ran for cover, but was snagged and eaten. "Emerson Wayland was your father's partner. Emerson hired you and he knows enough not to get his feelings get hurt when a lightning rod draws lightning."

"Dad's a young man and a long way from retirement."

"Well, he's close to sixty and there's been some talk... nothing definitive, but we're used to looking a long way down the road... "

"I'm not sure I want it... and not sure any longer if I *did* want it, whether I could be elected. Virginia's changed, just like the rest of the country. There are no dynasties anymore, no more Kennedys or Bushes and not enough people who remember or care about tradition. Probably a good thing... I'm not sure the Senate would be a good place, or even a possible place for me." Bobby signaled the waiter for more coffee and Rawley reached for the dessert menu. "But I'm glad we're talking straight. You guys at World Star may be looking down the wrong road."

"We get along by looking down a whole lot of roads, Bobby. I suppose if the American consumer ever realized just how much of the price he pays went toward looking down those roads, there'd be some kind of national scandal. But that's the system, the way it's always been. And the only other option here in Virginia, is that young attorney from Roanoake. He almost whipped your dad's ass in the last primary and frankly, World Star saved his seat." He let the words sink in. If

Bobby Fairweather wanted hardball, he'd give him hardball.

"We can make it happen either way and be just as happy with the result. That's why we look down more than one road. We don't know this kid in Roanoke very well, but we're getting to know him." Rawley creamed and sugared his third cup of coffee.

"But we'd rather see another Fairweather carrying on that tradition. And, for what it's worth, I've never personally visited Roanoke and don't expect to. But you can bet that one of my shirt-waist vice presidents has been there. That's what this lobbying thing, if that's what you want to call it, is all about these days. Nobody owns anyone anymore in the government. That stuff went out generations ago. What we're all after these days is access, the ability to sit down with the people who count when the issue is important and get ourselves heard. The price of what we euphemistically call free-speech is campaign contribution"

"And that's not buying your way in?"

Bobby looked across at Rawley Edwards, a man twenty-five years his senior. A man comfortable with buying and selling access, an expert in the commodity of governance. In Rawley Edwards' world, nods and glances settled future conditions, speculation in the soybean and hog-belly markets of politics.

"Sure it is. What the hell else can you call it?" Rawley looked particularly pleased with the new turn of conversation. This was meat and Rawley was an epicure when it came to the smell or taste of meat.

"But, it's somehow not unethical?"

"Well Bobby, it's all language, all definition. If World Star goes out and buys all the color pink in the country, we'd have a tremendous investment in pink. A huge profit motive in seeing that everything was pink." Rawley's eyes darted around the table, as if looking for anything that might have remained un-eaten, settling for another sip of coffee. "Instead of buying one color, we invest in as much of every color as we can afford. That doesn't give us a chance to paint anything all pink or all red or all green. But when the mixing is over and done with, we may have had some influence on the shade of the final color."

"Pretty nice word-picture, Rawley. Lots of good visuals. Sounds like you've explained this whole thing, more than once on a color-wheel."

"When the influence is *everywhere*, it's no longer influence, just access. I see no ethical problems whatever in access." He grinned, "That's what we're doing right now, Bobby, having a conversation that can only be had with access. I'm important enough… a big enough big-shot, that you've not only agreed to see me today, but let me bullshit around for two hours before we got down to cases, got to the point." He grinned again. It was a pretty good job he'd done and he knew it.

Rawley's explanation of power had made him rich as well as well-fed and he often wondered why there was no course at Harvard Law, called 'sincerity 101.' With a course like that, Rawley Haywood Edwards could have achieved everything he had today, without the bother of law school.

"What's wrong with that, Bobby?"

"Not a thing, Rawley. Except that the next election is seven months away. And my father is going to be the candidate for the Senate from the State of Virginia."

"And, if he's not?"

"And if he's not, I'll be very much surprised."

Rawley chuckled. "It's all well and good for you to be very much surprised, Bobby. But they pay me an obscene amount of money to make sure that World Star is *never* very much surprised. Let me get down to the hypothetical, Bobby. Assuming your father, for whatever reason, was not a candidate next time around. Would you be willing to run?"

"I don't know."

"But, you've thought about it. Surely in a family such as yours, it would be impossible for you not to have thought about it."

"Sure, I've thought about it." Bobby stretched his long frame into a corner of the booth. "But always in the abstract, always as something twenty or so years in the future. And now you're down here, making me look at it and asking me what I want to do." He picked at a spot of gravy, dried to the tablecloth. "What I *want* to do, is see my father continue to be the senior Senator from Virginia. To continue to hold the thought of my following him as an abstraction, something I don't have to deal with."

"Another thing that intrigues me Rawley, is you're suggesting all I have to do is make up my mind and it's mine to have. You talk as though there were no electorate. As though there were no process… just the deciding."

"That's pretty much true in your case. Well what about it, Bobby? For starters, are you going to represent World Star in the Southeastern United States?"

"Probably. But I've got to sit down with Emerson Wayland and talk this thing through with him. You're right I suppose, he won't be all that surprised, just figure it's about time his investment in me paid off. There'll be a senior partnership in it for me and that's fine. It was coming anyway. But it'll look good with the other junior guys to bring in World Star." He grinned across the table. "Funny world, Rawley. I walk into my office and get congratulated for bringing in World Star and you walk into your office and get congratulated for bringing in Bobby Fairweather. I guess everybody wins. But I have to run it all by Wayland. He expects that, in fact he demands it and he's the guy whose name is on the door."

"Nothing wrong with both of us being heroes, Bobby."

"I'll get back to you, probably sometime next week. But I guess the answer is yes and I guess I'm flattered that such a big gun came down to buy me lunch."

Bobby stood and shook hands with Rawley, then turned for the door as Edwards flagged the waiter over for dessert.

He met with Emerson Wayland at four that afternoon.

"Well Bobby, what's he offering for access to my hottest young property?"

"Jesus Emerson, you make me sound like a yearling at the winter sales in Lexington."

"Not a bad analogy, not all that much different." Wayland sat back in the tall-backed black leather chair. He occupied the chair his grandfather had shipped from England when the firm was founded a hundred years earlier. The chair Emerson refused to have recovered, even though the leather had begun to crack slightly at the nail-heads. There was continuity in the chair, a metaphor for the endurance and persistence of the law. It represented a continuum of Wayland Roth and Barnes through the dismemberment of politicians and vagaries of power structures. These forces ebbed and flowed and changed, while the firm remained steady, un-cracked at the nail-heads.

Everything about Emerson Wayland lent credence to that surety of purpose. If an actor had tested for the part, it could only be he, of middling height with a high forehead and a long thin nose that bisected his countenance like an axe-head stuck deeply into an aging log. His conservative suits draped easily across a frame made for suiting, with never a seam or crease or turn of fabric that didn't fall as if made for that very moment. Bald through the center of his head, his nose seemed to clear a path for thought, his silver hair swept back at the sides. That hair curled dangerously close to the shoulder for a man of his age. Shaggy dark eyebrows framed eyes that were meant to hold a jury or a client or a grandchild breathless and had often done just that.

His office boasted no polished desk and never had. Instead, an assemblage of low tables, clustered with chairs, where the work of the moment could be laid out, untouched and undisturbed, waiting for his attention. When he felt the need to be away from the work, there was a stand up writing table at the bookshelves, an addition whose design he'd directed and that he fancied an improvement on the similar piece at Chartwell, conceived and worn smooth by Winston Churchill. He admired Churchill and a very short list of others.

Now here was the second Fairweather that had sat opposite him, soon to be a partner in the firm like the other. And yet this one differed from the father and he found the difference somehow unsettling. Wayland had always respected the father and the grandfather, but this young man he *liked*. It was a chancy thing and slightly discomfiting to like a member of the firm. As for respect, there was still some work to be done before that definition could be fully applied.

"When I told Rawley that he was making his pitch too low in the firm and that you'd be sensitive to that, he said you knew I was a lightning rod. Said you wouldn't be surprised or upset unless the lightning failed to strike… words to that effect, anyway." Self deprecation wasn't Bobby's style, but his grin came close. "He danced around it for over two hours, Emerson. But the entire Southeastern Region legal work for World Star is ours, to take for the asking. I told him I'd talk to you."

"What's he want in return?"

"Access to me, is what he says. Hedging bets, putting World Star money on all the numbers. Seems to think Dad is getting ready to retire and that his Senate seat is mine for the asking."

His grin was gone and Bobby put the proposal in front of Wayland as clearly as he saw it. "This fellow thinks everything is for sale and the term 'mine for the asking' was framed pretty heavily in the promise of massive support from World Star. Dad never gave me any indication that he was thinking about getting out. He ever lead you to believe that?"

"No Bobby, that's news to me. I must say I find it somewhat surprising, if there's any truth in it at all. Everyone has their own network of information in political matters and I wouldn't dismiss Rawley Edwards' view. But of course I have my own sources and one of them obviously is your father. The information doesn't equate, but that doesn't mean a hell of a lot in Washington."

"Well regardless of the motivation, that's the deal. Southeastern Region, if we want it." He looked at the man who knew his father, probably much better than he. "Do we want it?"

"I want to sit on it for a few days and lay it out in my mind. But yes, we probably want it." Wayland ran a finger along the bridge of his long nose. "This firm has always been sought out by men like Rawley Edwards, to keep their oar in the water where they feel their interests can be served. It will take some staffing up and we'll have to bring on a number of strong litigators to support you, as partner in charge of the account. You know of course there'll be a partnership in it."

"Yes, I expected there would."

"Well, no matter, there would have been a partnership anyway. This just brings it into focus and makes it easier for me. The thing I have to realize and you have to realize along with me, is that accounts given can be taken away. I don't want the firm hurt too badly, when this one leaves." He smoothed a seam in a jacket already flawless.

"They *all* leave sooner or later. I want to make sure we have enough of the legwork on this account factored off to other firms, so we don't get killed when it goes. Rawley will have to agree to that, but I don't expect he cares one way or the other. He just wants his access and he shall have it. You comfortable with that?"

"Access is one thing... control is another."

"Well they go hand in hand, Bobby. Access is what he's asked for and there's no harm in access, no harm in an ear to hear. On the other hand, they're no doubt willing to support and bankroll a large portion of your Senatorial career, should you choose to have one. That's where you have to balance support and money against control. World Star has always been generous to your father and he's been able to remain very much his own man. Hasn't always been easy, but he's managed it."

"Everyone assumes that I want to be a Senator."

"Do you?"

"I've been born to it I suppose, as much as anyone can be born to it. Always out there, always expected. It's taken a huge part of my father's life, maybe his whole life. I'm not sure I'm willing to give over my whole life to something that's been expected, something over which I've really never had any control or choice." Bobby looked at the powerful face across from him and it seemed for the moment that his entire existence had been one of facing powerful men and powerful women. Men, and women who all had expectations.

"I don't know, Emerson, I always presumed that the choice would be somewhere in the future. Somewhere distant, where I wouldn't have to deal with it. Not until I'd looked a little further into myself and seen what was there, seen what was possible on my own terms. Now, Rawley Edwards has confronted me with the fact. The fact is, there are no real choices and I'm a little afraid of that. Does that sound terribly insecure?"

"No Bobby, that sounds to me like good judgment." Wayland felt the first stirrings of respect for the young man he liked so well.

There were twelve permanent members of the *EVOKE* Committee, six Democrats and six Republicans. At first it was by tradition and more recently by a change in the bylaws, an even handedness that left Preston Alberts most of his potential problems on the Republican side. As its only Chairman, Robert Fairweather had an amalgam of support that seemed to have no weakness. But Romeri demanded that a weakness be found and if it could not be found, it must be created. Unhappily, creativity wasn't Alberts' strength, although he was devious and disingenuous enough to make up for the shortcoming.

His strength, if the word properly applied to such surface issues, was his Senatorial look and his deep and resonate voice. A voice that thundered without any need for a gathering storm of ethical concern. Alberts' darkened brow could be conjured out of the clearest of skies. As the southern saying goes, he was all hat and no cattle. Still, his voice and countenance were made for amplification, a big-screen smile that carried an expression of interest and concern where none existed. This was his common currency. This, along with absolute dedication to his sponsor and the senior Senator from Michigan knew that name as well and maybe even better than his own.

Preston Alberts' weaknesses were many. But in them was a strength of sorts, the sinew wrought from being the unambitious implement of another's power. He was addicted to entourage and the perks of Senatorial junketing. The Senate Record showed him to be one of the most traveled and most sparingly balloted Senators in that august group of one hundred. Enjoying the convenience of a wife who remained in alcoholic seclusion in Michigan, he womanized on a truly grand scale and knew these pleasures were entirely dependent upon his sponsor.

Leadership made him sweat, but Alonzo Romeri asked him to lead. No... more than that, Romeri *demanded* he find a way to subvert or outright destroy the delicate balance of Fairweather's control. Un-impede the sole impediment that prevented commercial access to *EVOKE*.

There was little doubt that his comfortable ass was in a jam, that there could easily be another Senator from Michigan. An actor in a play that could close at any moment with a single bad review, Alberts had better learn his lines. Failing that, there would be a conference in Romeri's office and another player would appear, fresh from wardrobe. Another deep voice and heroic profile to assume the role, travel the world and pose for photo-shoots. Interchangeable, as willing as he to entertain this year's crop of beautiful young civil servants, all of them eager to be seen in the company of a senior member of the club. Preston Alberts was not keen to be sent home to his wife, a failure in his greatest and probably last starring role.

Seniority put him next in line for Chairman. Once there, his continuing value to Romeri would make him unassailable. The stakes were high for a two dollar bettor and his hand trembled slightly, drawing for an inside-straight.

Warren, Francosi, Stimwell, Jacobs and Sackman could be counted upon to pull behind his move against Fairweather. Still, Sackman had given Bob steady support on all the major issues, including commercial access. That was okay, Vern Sackman had his own needs and Alberts knew he could swap support for his irrigation project in Idaho. Besides, he was a fellow Democrat and the party chafed under too many years of Fairweather and the Republican domination of *EVOKE.*

Little matter that Romeri was a Republican and probable Presidential candidate. Alberts, in the thin atmosphere of his own mind was a man to be relied upon, whatever the need.

That left Essex, Stevens, Stewart, Godwin and James on the wish-list and Godwin seemed the most logical place to begin. Alex Godwin wavered on the commercial access issue, always coming over to Fairweather's side in the voting, but there wasn't much doubt that he didn't like the Chairman personally. Alex was first generation, self-made. Hard-driving and a fellow immediately drawn to the commercial side of almost any argument. He had little use for the foxhunting Virginian, with a hundred years of family behind his Senatorial seat. He'd start with Godwin. Alex had been pestering him for support of a bill aimed at combining aircraft weaponry research among the three services. He reached for the phone.

"Alex, Pres Alberts here. Fine thank you, just fine." The broad smile carried across the telephone line and the voice dropped to a level of non-partisan sincerity. "Alex, I was having lunch with Wilson Baker the other day and the subject of this commercial access thing came up again. You know it looks like they're going to get pretty strongly behind it over on the House side and it seems to me … "

FOURTEEN

Senator, Emerson Wayland is on line two.

"Thank you, Julia." Bob shoved the papers into a neat pile, took his reading glasses off and laid them carefully on the pile. He rubbed his nose with the fingers of both hands where the glasses pinched, relieving the indentation, then swung his chair around, propped sock feet on the credenza and reached for the phone. "Morning, Emerson. What's got you calling me so early on a Thursday? Thought Thursday was your tennis morning."

"Bob, you thinking about retiring?"

"I'm *always* thinking about retiring, Emerson. Have been ever since I first got here." He rubbed one socked toe against the other and gazed out the window, grinning at Wayland's directness. "What rumors have you heard lately, my trusted old barrister?"

"I'm serious, Bob. Something going on you haven't talked about?"

"No… nothing more than my usual grumbling."

He was suddenly tired, feeling a wash of weakness rolling from raised ankles to his hips, an undefined feeling of loss, as though he'd just learned of a good friend's death. He rubbed his nose with his right hand, cradling the phone with his shoulder, wishing he were home in bed. A corner of his mind wondered why he wanted so badly just to lie back in crisp white sheets and feel sun streaming in the window. It was gray outside this window and the weather was only partly to blame.

"What's cooking, Emerson? You sound serious."

"I am, Bob. I don't feel this is out of school, because I'm the Senior Partner at this goddamn law firm and your son works for me. But a legal-eagle landed here yesterday from Romeri's company and he had a big fish in his claws. Wants us to take over their legal work in the southeast. But that's all fluff. What they really want is to back Bobby for your Senate seat."

"Ummm ... "

"Ummm, hell. This guy was all very cordial about it and couched all his phrasing in terms of 'when and if your father decides to retire,' but there are things moving out there, Bob. I need to know where you stand so I can give you the backing I always have. Jesus, friend, sometimes you're so complacent you make me angry."

"You gonna take the work?"

"Sure, I guess." He paused. "You know any reason why we shouldn't?"

"No."

"Well I don't either, not at this point. Bobby's a good lawyer but he's not a great lawyer and we both know he's a honey-pot, here to draw flies. He knows it too, all the more to his credit. That's what you did when you were here and everyone profited."

Emerson Wayland's voice softened, glad he was into the conversation, glad the preliminaries had been broken. He chuckled. "Did a damn good job of it too, Bob. Lots of flies hummed around this old office when you had your shingle out. But this guy came in here like a whole swarm and that makes me nervous. Made Bobby nervous too, I might add. Nervous as hell."

"What did he say?"

"Well, he told this guy Edwards that he was not aware you had any plans to retire. Listened to him, though. The guy was here or at lunch with Bobby for nearly four hours, blathering away and shoving feelers in every direction. You know Bobby, he finally had to ask point blank what World Star was after. Turns out they're after *him* a hell of a lot more than the firm. He came directly in to see me and we talked it over. Caught me off base... Bobby too, I would guess. Surprised he hasn't called you"

"Julia said he called this morning, but I was in a subcommittee meeting. We're having dinner tonight."

"Well that's good. Sometimes I don't think you two get together enough anymore."

Bob sagged a bit in the chair and felt another wave of fatigue. "Fathering is an impossible job, Emerson. None of us seem to be able to do it right."

"Bob ... "

"Yeah?"

"The inference Bobby got from this guy Edwards, was that if you don't decide to move over and let him take a run at it, Romeri is going to back that young hothead from Roanoke into a really stiff campaign. That worries Bobby. Worries me too."

"Yeah, well Romeri doesn't give a damn about me or Bobby or our friend from Roanoke. He wants my chairmanship of the committee. If I don't run for re-election, that prick Preston Alberts is next in the line of seniority and he *owns* him. That's what this is really all about, Emerson."

"Ah... what's he want from the committee?"

"Well, that's a long story, Emerson. One that I'll be glad to spill out in all its devious and wrong-headed detail, sometime when we've got an afternoon at the farm to catch up on our lives. Bobby isn't the only one that's not gotten much from me lately. You and Maggie are on that list too, but it's too long a story for the phone. I'm not even sure I've got it all straight in my mind. Working on it though and none of this comes as too much of a shock. Feels to me like it's just another piece, falling into place."

"Well, you know I'm here for whatever you need."

"Yeah, thanks Emerson. That means a lot."

"Hang in there, Bob."

"Yeah... we'll talk later, Emerson. I promise we will... bye."

He hung up and gazed out the window, unfocused and turning interconnections over in his mind, feeling wearily as though every thought was uphill. Bob was about to swing back to the desk, when there was a quick knock on the side door and his aide came in.

"What is it Dan? I've got to go over this stuff you gave me for the meeting this afternoon." His voice edged irritability. Damn, he didn't seem to be out in front of anything anymore.

"Someone called from Social Security. Says he needs to talk with you."

"Who?"

"Wouldn't say who. Says he could lose his job if it ever got out that he talked with you. But there are things he needs to get off his chest."

"So, what's he want?"

"Wants to meet with you, somewhere quiet. I said no dice without me. He said okay."

"You think he's just some kind of malcontent?"

"No, I don't think so. Says it has to do with the *EVOKE* numbers and the selection process. I'd be willing to guess we've got someone here who may give us more than Alan Longwell and it's probably worth a bet. I tried to get him to see me, but he won't without you along."

"Well, see what Sally's got open on my schedule and set it up. I've wasted time on dumber things than this. Maybe he's got something we need to know."

They were both naked and she sat propped against the headboard of the bed, a satin sheet across her like a curtain, suspended from the tips of her fingers. Large eyes bright with cocaine, she smiled at him and raised and lowered the sheet, teasing.

Flip was on his hands and knees, straddling her legs stretched under the sheet, reaching the tip of one finger to the satin, slowly lowering it.

"Hey, baby… " He was hard, his voice a little slurry. Flip knew the drugs that kept him hard, the drugs that didn't.

Her skin was medium light, the color of coffee with just a touch of cream in it. Beauty is subjective, but hers were the finely drawn features of an Asian mother and African father and surpassed nearly any standard. Hair long and black, her eyes slightly almond shaped. Cheekbones, nose and neck proudly African. Delicate across the shoulders, with firm small breasts, nipples erect and blue-black against smooth skin. Long-waisted, narrow-hipped and, as Flip slid the sheet from between them, she giggled and raised her left leg over his shoulder.

"Baby, this is gonna feel *so* good … " He leaned forward and tasted her opened mouth. He felt her tongue, as she slid down the satin, under him, fingers closing around him.

"Uhnnnn… *now*, Flip. I gotta have you *now*, inside me baby … " Her fingers working, stroking, guiding him…

The crash of the door breaking in came with such force that splinters and plaster drenched the bed. The room simply exploded in a screech of wood, fiber tearing loose from fiber, hinge against hinge-pin against screws, lock against bolt and jamb. A violent eruption, the top coming off the world, slinging plaster, paint, hardware and shattered millwork.

The two who burst through the space that had been the door, worked fast and efficiently, adrenaline pumping. The two on the bed experienced their brief moments in slow motion, a speeding of mind that nature provides only once or twice in a life and then only to save it.

Not this time. The striving was there, the desperate *need* to be saved, a frantic, millisecond reach toward salvation. Two minds striving for options and seeing none, looking for compromise. Looking for a way to live and seeing none, settling for a mad, blazing, frenzy of hatred.

In that first blinding millisecond, Flip was inside her. Hard against her writhing wetness, his mind lost in her whimpering as she thrust her body, damp with perspiration against him, arching her back. It was a bad time to need all of his brain and finding it busy elsewhere with such a basic animal need. Feeling himself in the first stage of orgasm, about to pour himself into her, heart pumping, his brow wet with the sweat of primal activity. Mind and legs momentarily weak and trembling with the exertion of following her young body as it tore at him.

It was a bad time to switch mental gears from creation to survival to death. But Flip had always survived and with the crashing, splintering roar of plaster, instinct took over. He pulled himself from her in one fluid, slow-motion reach for the gun on the chair, beside the bed.

Milliseconds, divide to fractions of milliseconds.

In the instants that followed, the men at the gaping hole in the wall crouched as men crouch who know the work of killing and leveled twelve-gauge sawed off riot-guns, concentrating on targets. The girl was not a target. She meant nothing except as a distraction of the moment, a lithe and luxurious body. Only Flip was a target.

What followed was all one excruciatingly long, incredibly short continuum of sound. The crashing of wall and door still echoed within the confines of sweat and lust in the room, as a finger closed over the trigger of the shotgun, swinging, following the fluid rip of Flip's naked body. Following his lunge toward the chair, as though he were a bird in flight, leading and arriving just ahead of him.

Milliseconds.

The squeezed trigger unlatched a spring-loaded firing pin within the riot gun. It plunged with mechanical precision into a silvered primer cap encased in brass at the end of the three-inch magnum shell, itself encased within the smooth bore of the barrel. The mini explosion of primer ignited an ounce and a quarter of smokeless black-powder, exploding it with fifty-eight hundred foot-pounds of force against plastic wadding. This intricately honeycombed, cushioning plastic slammed against ball bearing size buckshot, now whistling down the barrel at thirty-two hundred feet per second.

Milliseconds . . .Flip was a mere twelve feet from the swinging end of the barrel.

The roar enveloped the room. Waves of explosive force, confined, bounced off walls and ceiling, fluttered the sheet that dropped away from Flip's reaching lunge toward the chair. Deflecting the glass in the window almost to breaking, the waves folded back upon themselves. Twelve ball-bearing sized buckshot arrived just a fraction ahead of target, the gunner surging with adrenalin and swinging a bit too fast. They caught his right shoulder, but mostly his outstretched right arm, as it reached for the nine millimeter automatic pistol on the chair. Flip's shoulder disintegrated in an eruption of tissue and bone fragment, the arm gone. The force of the blast opened a hole in the wall behind him, turning his body, fully facing the gunner, his expression a frozen mask of disbelief.

Milliseconds.

With the smooth efficiency of technological perfection, the riot gun ejected the spent shell, flipping it from the ejection port in a spinning arc across the bedroom. Still smoking from the explosion, bathing the room in the acrid smell of cordite, it effortlessly slammed a fresh shell into firing position. Un-caring of its target, unimpressed by the morality of the issue, faultless in mechanical function.

The second roar was almost a continuation of the first. All twelve buckshot caught Flip full in the face and neck, canceling his anger forever. His arrogance and fury altered in an instant from threat to no-threat, from mind and thought and face and passion to foaming pink mist of bone and tissue, splattered against a dirty wall, soaking into blasted plaster, blood pooling at the floor where his body had been flung like a rag. A very naked, very dead, human rag. His left leg twitched just once against the chair. The pistol tipped, settled back, nearly came to rest and then skittered off the chair and fell to the floor.

Both men were in the room now, both still crouched, as though in a jungle. Riot gun barrels swinging at unknown enemies, dark blue flak-jackets heavy against quick breath. Their breath noisy and harsh in the sudden silence, a two-fold gasping, grunting of breath, cordite smoke layering across the air.

She was against the headboard. Her hips raised, body almost halfway up the wall, sheet pulled across her again, not teasing now. Eyes blind with fright, the sheet pulled up to hold them off, hold the guns away. There was no sound, just the wide eyes. Her head slowly moved from side to side in a wordless plea... no, please no... I hardly knew him and I want to live... we were only fucking. The eyes, the sheet, those wordless eyes.

"Seems a shame… " The second man spoke in a voice out of place in that voiceless room.

"We both need to be in this," the first man said. He edged around the bed to the pile of human rags. "She's yours… "

The sheet rose and trembled. Torn from her hands by another mindless, heedless, mechanical progression of explosive energy, the twelve lead balls sprayed across her breasts.

Milliseconds.

There are still places across the city where the sound of gunfire will bring residents to the halls, with shouts of alarm or fear and frantic calls to the police.

Not here. Not this place in this city.

Here, such sounds are heard from behind doors already double or triple bolted. Here residents drop to the floor, covering small children and if they chance to move at all, it's to a bathtub for the safety of cast iron. No one moves to hallways. No one moves to windows, especially windows. No one moves to telephones. There is time in places like these and the time belongs to everyone. No need to rush, no need to hurry before discovery, because there will be no discovery. Just that turning-away of heads, the covering of children.

It wasn't a pleasant scene and the work brought no pleasure or revenge of scores finally settled. The first man picked up the nine-millimeter pistol with a gloved hand. He wore disposable surgical gloves, a protection from fingerprints and powder burns, too light to impede what might have been a surgeon's work. He found Flip's severed right arm, curled the dead fingers around the trigger and fired two shots randomly in the direction of the doorway. He dropped arm and gun, to fall as they may. He produced a small caliber automatic pistol and faced his partner.

"You ready?"

The other man nodded, turned toward him and grimaced, holding his breath as the shot was fired at his vest, slightly bruising a rib from about twelve feet away. Walking to her body, he wrapped her hand around the gun and fired an additional shot into the mattress, then one to the ceiling.

"Let's get outta here."

They picked up the two riot guns, standard Chicago Police Department issue, and left.

No one saw. No one heard.

Bobby was already waiting at the bar when Bob walked in at eight, nodding to the maitre d' who hovered, menus under his arm. The father and son gave each other a quick hug, then followed to a reserved table in a back corner of the restaurant. Anthony's had been too long in Georgetown to be an 'in' place to be seen. It prided itself after almost a hundred years of careful attention to good food, as a place for the socially secure to come and enjoy eating and drinking among friends. The *Pasta Chesapeake* was a near legendary dish of fresh bay clams, butter, herbs and garlic. A wine order given, Bob glanced at the struggle in Bobby's eyes between tension and composure.

"You know, you wouldn't make the worst Senator in the State's history, despite your worries about me." He grinned at Bobby and saw his eyes relax a bit, the look still serious.

"You've been talking to Emerson. Jesus I'm glad, I wish he'd told *me*. I've been trying to figure out what to say, on the drive up." Bobby circled the ashtray with his fingers, cradling the heavy glass and looking into it as though a future might be found in the depths of its plain surfaces.

"What the hell's going on, Dad? Emerson's just as confused as I am. He probably told you about my three hour sit down with this honcho from World Star. Pretty damned unnerving to hear from a third party that someone's gunning for your father." The words were spilling like a son's confession, not waiting for answers.

"Why are they after you, *if* they're after you? And why turn all the attention toward me? Think they'd know I'm not interested in unseating my own father." He paused for breath.

"Whoa, Bobby. Back up a little and let me put some background in for you." He grinned. "I'm still trying to catch up a bit myself. But the whole thing is over how I've run my chairmanship of the *EVOKE* Committee. And of course, it's tied up in what Washington's always tied up in, money and power and who's got the money and who wants the power." He reached to squeeze Bobby's arm.

"It's so complicated that it's simple. If they can get me out of that chair, the next guy in line is Preston Alberts and they *own* Preston Alberts. I won't resign, they know that. So they need to get me out, willingly or unwillingly." He watched his son watch him.

"If I'm unwilling, they'll throw all their support and money behind that squirt from Roanoke. He came damned close to beating me last time, *without* their help. So they figure I'll be willing, under those circumstances, to step aside for you and continue the family dynasty, for whatever the hell that's worth nowadays. They're probably right. I don't have a lot of choices at this point. The one option I *do* have as present Chairman, is to shine one hell of a powerful national spotlight on what they plan to do with the *EVOKE* system."

He paused, tasted the offered wine, nodded approval and glasses were filled. Father and son touched their glasses, sipping, resuming.

"Damned trouble is, I'm not entirely sure *what* they have in mind. But the bits and pieces that fall into place, along with their willingness to go to any length to get me out, make it clear the stakes are pretty high and I may be on the outside looking in before it all comes together. At least that's what they seem to hope. There will go my opportunity to shine that spotlight and they damn well know it."

He watched Bobby, realizing that all this was coming as news, something for which he had no background. They'd never talked much about Bob's Senate work, it was always merely a given.

"Also… and I know this is a prideful thing to say… it must be something they know I'd never be part of. Otherwise they'd just roll it all out in the open and negotiate."

"You keep talking about *they*. You mean Romeri and World Star?"

"Seems like it. World Star is just the excuse, as near as I can tell. This thing smells of Lonny Romeri's personal ambition, Bobby. He was out to the farm for dinner and gave me a pretty strong pitch for commercial access to *EVOKE*. Made some sense, but he knows I've always been very cautious about opening that door and I can't help but think there's something much deeper and more sinister behind his proposal."

"Such as?"

"Bobby, ten years ago when this whole *EVOKE* system was made available to the public, a lot of people didn't take it very seriously. The Senate didn't take it very seriously, either." Bob opened and closed the menu and then reached for the wine.

"I did. I maneuvered my way into the chairmanship because the whole thing scared me to death, this taking power over of people's reproductive and fantasy lives. Linking them together in a system that says, 'if you want this, you'll damned well give up that.' I was afraid it would be successful and if it *was* successful, I was doubly afraid of what uses such remote-control power might find."

"It *has* been successful, Bobby, pretty much beyond anyone's most generous expectations. And the public has shown itself willing to give up potential parenthood for unlimited access to fantasy. I guess that shouldn't be a surprise, but this isn't a game-show."

"But, … " Bob held up his hand, holding Bobby off.

"Wait a minute, let me just finish this thought. It's not all bad, this giving up having so many babies and besides, there are all kinds of exceptions. We're not giving up the species. Parenthood, intelligent parenthood is still available for those who really want to raise a family. But they have to show themselves to be responsible potential parents."

"That's the way it was sold to the Congress in the first place and it was a hell of a hard sell and a close vote. But the population control people won out with a last gasp show of strength from the unions. Too damned many people in the world. Here as well, in the good old United States. Jesus Bobby, half the people *who have ever been born*, since the dawn of mankind, are *alive today*. That's a very scary statistic. Shrinking numbers of jobs have faced off against growing numbers of job seekers for decades and we're stuck now with a permanent unemployed underclass. The Social Security system tipped over ten years ago and had to be given mouth-to-mouth resuscitation. As welfare rolls expanded and cities began to fall apart, the problems of homelessness, mental health, police protection, education and failed opportunity became more than anyone could bear."

"We didn't do jack-shit in the Congress, except sit on our hands. Wasn't really our fault, at least that's what we told ourselves. We quite plainly didn't know what to do and the resources continued to slide out from under us. Fewer and fewer jobs breeding more and more joblessness."

"*EVOKE* was an answer, maybe the only one left. Voluntary, pleasurable, distracting, it seemed like a sure way to buy some time. A way to create space for a period of civil peace, a chance to get control over runaway population and try to pick up the reins of fiscally and morally responsible government. A breather... another chance."

"The last four Presidents have been so busy dodging bullets, Bobby, there was never time to create a battle plan. Congress became meaningless. Sometimes, I think we should all be stood up at public execution. Your father has been just as neglectful as the rest. We used to solve problems in this country, but for fifty years we've traded that for buying time and electioneering." Bob waved the waiter away, not yet ready to order.

"Special interests, through their enormous lobbying power, have become a shadow government. Every four years we go through the motions of our high school civics lessons, to democratically elect leaders who are for the most part self-serving, industry-serving and meaningless. We're badly out of control, Bobby and no one has been steering for decades. Now, for better or worse, *EVOKE* has come along to provide a potential rudder and I'm worried about who wants to push me aside and take over the wheel. I guess before I step down, I'd like to have some confidence in the direction."

"You talk as though it were already an accomplished fact."

"There's an overwhelming truth in Washington, Bobby. The less powerful you are, the more options you have, the more opportunity there is to hang on. I seem to be sitting on a power base lots of people want to get their hands on, people whose motives will justify any means to control that source. They have almost unlimited finances. They understand the leverage of influence and the trading of influence."

"I still have some options but they're pretty narrow. One of them is to lie down and roll over to save my Senate seat. It doesn't mean enough to me to do that. Another is to step down from the chairmanship and go about my other duties in the Senate. Let Pres Alberts do the dirty work I won't do. That's a possibility, but not a very palatable one and it smacks of selling out. I've never been very good at selling out and it's caused me some problems before in the Senate, but I've always been able to handle them. It's probably cost Virginia some good legislation, too. But that's the way it goes and Virginians sent me up here to do the best I could, not to be perfect."

"The third option is to blow the whistle, while I still have some breath and a whistle to blow. Problem with that is what I said earlier. I'm not entirely sure what Romeri wants and I'm not even sure it's all that sinister. But it smells bad and the more I find out, the worse it seems to smell. So there you have it. You seem to be scheduled to be the next Senator from Virginia, if you want it."

Bob sipped his wine and looked at his son. He was a grown man, a very capable man at that. A thoughtful man and that gave Bob a great, swelling feeling of pride. A feeling that rose unexpectedly in him from time to time and almost brought tears to his eyes. They were talking man to man, equal to equal, yet somehow the father would always be the father, the son always the son. The way it was, he guessed, a sort of universal truth that would always keep fathers and sons from considering each other entirely man to man. Bob's intellect accepted the fact, but his heart regretted it and he wondered if such things would ever change in the world of fathers and sons.

"You want me to run for your seat?"

"I want you to do what you need to do."

"What I need to do... " Bobby shifted in his seat and his hands went back to the ashtray, turning it slowly on the table linen.

"What you need to do for *you*, Bobby. Not for the family, not for Ginny, not for the preservation of the line of Fairweathers in the Senate. Just *you*... it's come down to that."

He looked at his father and their eyes held for a moment, then Bobby looked away, back to the ashtray. "What if I wasn't *able* to run?"

"Wasn't *able*?"

"What if there was something about me that got in the way... something maybe I couldn't even tell you?" His eyes were boring holes in the ashtray, the fingers turning the glass, quarter turn, quarter turn, quarter turn.

"I already know."

Bobby's eyes shot to his father's and this time they held. "Already know what?"

"About Web."

"*What* do you know about Web?" Bobby's eyes were searching his father's.

"That he's your lover."

Bobby held his father's gaze for another moment, pleading for a clue as to what all this meant. Looking for some sort of understanding and fearing it, but wanting it so badly, wanting to throw his arms around his father. To be held like a child, back on the farm in the sunshine with his dad's arm around his shoulders.

He dropped his eyes and a long broken sigh escaped him. A catching sigh, that slid from him almost like a hiccup and he leaned back against the chair, the ashtray still in his hands. Legs stretched, he felt in his chest like all his organs were slipping down to his stomach.

"Oh, shit." It was an escape of two short words, drawn long in relief and fear of the relief. "How long have you known about Web?"

"He came to see me at my office about six months ago." The waiter appeared for their order and Bob waved him away again, touching their glasses and indicating two more glasses of wine.

"Why?"

"He said he was worried about you. Worried about your reasons for getting so close to Ginny. Whether it was a terrible mistake and whether he had the right to interfere or even the right to talk with me about it."

"Said he had no one else to talk to and that he loved you. Loved you enough to try to do the right thing, whatever the right thing was. Told me that so few people knew about the two of you, he had no place else to go. Knew no one else who loved you enough to help him." Bob acknowledged the refilling of their glasses, asking the waiter to hold off for a while on their dinner order.

"It didn't come as the absolute shock that you might think, Bobby. I was very touched by Web's concern, as well as his love for you. He wasn't frantic or desperate or out of control. Just looking for guidance from another man, someone to help him. We didn't discuss it, but I got the impression he can't talk to his own father. We found we both had a lot in common. He's a very thoughtful and compassionate man, Bobby, but you already know that. We both love you very much."

Bobby felt like he'd been holding his breath, but there was release in all of this, an opening of locked doors, but doors he'd hoped to open on his own terms.

Now that was no longer possible. They'd been kicked in.

"I wish he hadn't come to you."

"Why?"

"I don't know… it takes away my power somehow. Takes away my options, sort of like how you were talking about your options being taken away. It all comes down to honesty and I don't feel like his talking to you left me in control of my integrity. That's important to me. That's all there is, when I look at my life and try to make sense of it. I know I'm wandering, but does that make some kind of sense to you?"

"Yes, it makes sense to me."

"Does Mom know?"

"No."

"Why? How come you didn't tell her?"

"It's not my place to tell her, Bobby. You may be right that Web shouldn't have come to me, but he did. That's as far as I was willing to take it."

"What did you tell him?"

"Maybe you should ask Web. I'm not sure you should be hearing his thoughts filtered through me. I guess you and Web need to talk. Do you love him?"

"Yes."

"It would be presumptuous and needless for me to say that's okay, Bobby. It is what it is. And you need to deal with it in the best way you can."

"What should I do?"

"About Web? I don't know, Bobby." Bob chuckled and there was warmth and love and as much understanding in it as is possible, for a life he was still trying to understand. "I've never been very good at advice on matters of the heart. I don't understand your sister and I guess I don't understand you and Web." He looked at Bobby and felt energy flowing both ways across the table.

"I'm not even sure I understand your mother and me. I've looked for what holds us so closely to each other and wondered many times, what makes us different. Why so many of our friends drift away into divorce. But I've never been able to put a name to it. Sometimes, I think it's just a lightning strike, something that happens randomly and without any preparation or lessons to be drawn... just an unusual event."

"What about Ginny? What the hell do I do about Ginny?"

"Be fair with her, Bobby. That's all that can be asked of anyone. More importantly, be fair with *yourself*. I hope above all else, you'll take care to do that."

"You see my problem with this Senate race? Shouldn't call it a race, I'm not even a candidate yet, but you know what I mean."

"I don't think Web should be a problem, if you don't let him become one."

"How so?"

"Well, Bobby, let's discuss the scenarios. If you go through with your engagement and marriage to Ginny, the only problem would be your relationship with Web getting public. A smear campaign, but those things mostly never work and just as often backfire. Particularly with the kind of support you can count on from Romeri. Main problem there would be Ginny. But that's not a political difficulty, so we can leave it out of the discussion."

"If you acknowledge your relationship with Web and run with that behind you, my own feeling is that you're electable. This is not the dark ages. It can be done and may even pick you up some votes. So, it seems to me that you can put that issue aside, at least from a political standpoint."

"How come you seem to be able to understand all of this so easily?" Bobby looked directly at his father. "It's burned inside of me most of my adult life. And you and I are sitting here drinking wine and discussing my relationship with Web, as though it were an everyday event."

"I'm *not* all that able to understand, Bobby. I'm as old fashioned and distracted by a lifestyle I don't truly understand as anyone. I have the advantage of loving you and having had six months to sit with this and think it through. I guess I have Web to thank for that. Maybe you do too, although that's your call."

"If you want to know the truth, if I had the opportunity to change that aspect of your life, I would. Not because I disapprove, because that's not relevant, but because I know the pain it causes you to love someone, outside what is too generally thought of as acceptable."

"There's little enough of love in the world today and people are changing. But a hell of a lot of them want to see life played out in their own terms. I'm no different. I wish you didn't have this hurdle in your life, because life already throws us all too many curves. And your statement about this burning inside of you for most of your adult life, just makes me want to weep for all that burning."

"Parents hope their children's lives will be happy and uncomplicated and of course, they never are. No one's are. But we still hope."

"You're really quite a remarkable man to have for a father."

"Yeah, well not so remarkable as you might think, Bobby. I love you and I appreciate your driving up here, with your heart in your mouth, worrying about your father's Senate seat." Bob reached for the menu.

"Let's order some dinner. I'm suddenly very hungry."

FIFTEEN

Dan McCarthy tapped his fingers on the steering wheel of his old blue sedan and glanced over at Bob Fairweather.

"Christ Senator, this smacks of some B-movie, sitting here in a shopping center parking lot, waiting for who knows who to jump into the back seat. I hope he's not wearing phony whiskers."

"I just hope he's got something to say. What time is it?"

"Noon. That may be him, now."

A slightly built man, looking to be in his middle fifties, had parked his car in the adjoining aisle and walked toward them. He knew their car, Dan had described it well and he opened the rear door, tossing in a worn brown leather briefcase, the locks almost falling off. It was scratched and worn with years of hauling papers and lunches. As he slid in, Dan reached over the seat back to shake hands.

"You said your name was John. I'm Dan McCarthy and this is Senator Fairweather."

"John." Nervously confirming his name, he shook hands with Dan and then somewhat tentatively with Bob. "John Wilforth." He laughed anxiously. "No need to be cloak and dagger, I guess. My career's pretty much on the line by coming here, but I guess you probably know that too. Thirty years in Civil Service. I can retire if they don't bring me up on some sort of charges and take it all away. I'm sorry Senator, I know your time is valuable, but all this stuff is on my mind and I'm pretty nervous about being here."

"Why *are* you here, John?" Bob turned halfway in the seat, back against the door, to look this uneasy occupant of the back seat full in the face.

"Senator, I'm Alan Longwell's number two over at Social Security. Have been for the past six or seven years and of course that gives me access to lots of stuff that never comes to open meetings at the Administration." He shifted in the seat and unbuttoned the front of a dark gray tweed topcoat.

"Just like all the major administrations, we do a lot of 'what ifs' at the top. A lot of computer modeling to see what effect various changes in program would have. The stuff we've been doing for the past two years is absolutely outside the mission of our charter. I've watched it go from 'what if' to implementation in several areas that make me lose sleep at night... make me wonder who's running the show. Because I'm pretty sure... no, I'd say *absolutely* sure it's not Alan Longwell. He's pretty much like me, just a few rungs higher on the ladder. A guy who does what he's told and does a good job of it."

"Outside the mission of the charter?" Fairweather's voice was direct. "Don't worry, there are no tape recorders running. Dan will take some hand-written notes as we talk."

"I'm not worried about that, Senator." Wilforth looked back at him, the beginnings of a smile, edging around the corners of his mouth. "I apologize for the secrecy, but I didn't want to be seen with you in a restaurant or walking into your Senate office. What I'm doing isn't very fair to Longwell and I don't feel real good about it. But I've been talking it over with my wife for two months now and she helped me decide to come to you. You'd like her. Her name is June... "

"I'm sure I would, John. You're lucky to have a wife you can confide in."

"Yeah, well she's pretty okay. Been married eighteen years... second wife." John Wilforth was beginning to relax, some of the tenseness easing out of him. Just his fingers showed a lingering concern, running over the loosened locks on the battered case.

"Anyway, what's happening is that we've been loading the dice in the selection of Social Security numbers for *EVOKE* access."

"Loading the dice?" Bob turned sideways in the front seat, one knee up. "How so?"

"Well, it looked like another modeling program at first. But now it's clear to me that *EVOKE* is being given out of all proportion to the unemployed. Mostly black and Hispanic, but whites too."

"Why, John? What do you think Longwell is getting at?" Bob's voice was conversational, showing no unusual concern, putting his informant as much at ease as possible. Yet fascinated by the confirmation of Prentiss Everett's accusation. Dan sat quietly behind the wheel, turned sideways as well, with a legal pad on his knee. He took nearly verbatim shorthand notes.

"Senator, a lot of what I'm about to tell you is conjecture. But it's conjecture filtered out of a couple of years of sitting in meetings, organizing various groups to pull together statistics and picking up bits and pieces from Longwell's attitude. He's become almost fanatical about some things and that's not like him. So, I think it's pretty accurate conjecture. And it points to a certain amount of racism, a certain amount of frustration and a hell of a lot of fear about the times we're going through. Maybe as much, the times we've *been* through."

"Let's take these points one at a time." Bob unbuttoned the front of his own coat. "How racism?"

"Blacks and Hispanics are getting wired to *EVOKE* at twice their proportion of population. Maybe it's semantics, but in my book that's either a strange sort of generosity, or racism. White guys with jobs, don't stand a very good chance of getting access, certainly not as good a chance as black guys without jobs. That seems like a nice thing to do for the underprivileged, until you follow the figures, until you see what happens to people who get hooked up to this system."

"Go on."

"Well, numbers are what we do best. We have numbers on everything. With the crossover work we do with the Bureau of Labor Statistics, we're able to draw some pretty accurate assessments of what's going on out there in the real world." He paused and took a deep breath, but it was evident to Bob that Wilforth had prepared himself well.

"The facts are that when someone gets hooked to *EVOKE*, he stops looking for work. And if he's on drugs, he starts backing off the drug use too, because *EVOKE* takes the place of a lot of the tripping he's been doing. Obviously he stops having babies, 'cause that's part of the access requirements. So, pressure for jobs drops, drug use drops, crime rates drop and, most importantly, the social pressure for relief in all these areas drops. *EVOKE* hookups just stop going out on the street and raising hell, busting up shop windows and attacking each other. They also pretty much stop demanding stuff that the government has no way of providing anymore.

"Go on, John."

"Well, take ADC as an example. Meant to help poor mothers with kids until they could find a job, but all it produced was so many additional kids there's no money to help them. Every time State or Federal Government tries something, it blows up in their face and they're not only frustrated, they're scared to death. It's gotten so that most of us, whether we're elected or appointed or Civil Service, are just trying to make it to the end. Hoping to get there without anyone pointing a finger at us, until we can get our pension and retire to some safe place in the boonies. Safe places in the boonies are getting scarce too."

"So the frustration turns to fear." Bob was fascinated by the scene painted by this upper level civil servant, so closely mirroring his conversation with Bobby. Gripped by the degree to which the philosophy of government was disintegrating at the operative level. Falling apart where people such as John Wilforth struggled with the details of trying to keep flesh and bone on the body politic.

"Absolutely, Senator. Washington is scared shitless, if you'll pardon my using the term. That's why I don't think Longwell is operating on his own. It's not his style, not any of our styles. Those of us who came up through the ranks aren't likely to run off on some independent tangent. That's not how we got where we are and guys like that get weeded out pretty early in the process." This is coming from somewhere up the line and above Longwell, the line is pretty short. Above him is the Commissioner of the Administration, above him a Cabinet Officer. Above him, only the President. Like I said, a pretty short line." He paused, snapped nervously at a briefcase lock.

"I'm just like everyone else, gotten so I hate to read the papers and my doors have too many locks on them. I don't like to feel that way. Maybe what's going on at the Administration is right. The only thing that really makes me crazy, is that it's going on without any sort of Congressional oversight. No one knows and, frankly Senator, I don't trust Representative Baker enough to talk with him. This is too big a load for an ordinary guy like me and I need to share it."

"Ordinary guys have been saving this government, in one way or another John, for centuries. Besides that, for whatever it's worth, I think you're far from ordinary."

"Thanks, Senator, but this is more gutless than brave. I'm not sure I'd be here if it were ten years earlier in my career and I could lose it all."

"Anything else you want me to know, John?"

"Well, this is the most immediate thing that worries me. The rest is the enormous number of modeling programs we're running. But we do that sort of thing all the time and it's what we're supposed to be doing. Guess it's not a problem, unless we just fail to advise Congress and begin to implement some of that stuff as well."

"Such as?"

"We have a subliminal-suggestion program that's in a pilot stage, being tested on a control group. That sort of thing was outlawed decades ago in commercial advertising. It's pretty awesome, when you think of it hooked up to *EVOKE*. People buying something or voting for someone because the idea was put in their mind. A message flashed across their *EVOKE* program at a speed they can't consciously see, but their brain picks up anyway."

"Anything else?"

Bob's voice was casual, as though nothing out of the ordinary had been said, but his heart jumped and he saw Dan raise an eyebrow, as he continued to scribble.

"A bunch of other models. One has research going forward by one of the cereal companies, looking into a sort of combination tofu-vitamin enriched food block, a totally synthetic food. Something that can be produced in farm factories, then consumed in conjunction with an *EVOKE* program that will link the eating experience to the ambience and menu selection of the world's finest restaurants." He looked at Dan and then back at Bob.

"Now what the hell are we doing, over at the Administration, in a program like that? The major food conglomerates would raise holy hell. But the overall idea is to provide acceptable sustenance with a considerable lessening of the degradation of farmland and atmosphere. Another model looks at the effect of an overall reduction in transport, particularly along environmental lines. It presumes, and our early studies confirm this, that *EVOKE* subscribers tend to make far fewer demands on other forms of diversion. They change their residence less often, drive less, vacation less, eat less fast food at point of sale, eat more fast food delivered. Rent fewer video tapes, buy fewer shoes, clothes, cars and refrigerators, take better care of their homes. Have fewer divorces, are more dependable at their job site and are *far* less politically active. Drones is not a fair word, but they are certainly much more docile in their habits. This all contributes to some startling statistics in the early models." Bob nodded for him to continue.

"Automobile use drops by nearly sixty percent, truck traffic by just under fifty percent. Lumbering, mining, farming and other environmentally abusive land uses all take steep drops. And the resulting water and air pollution rates approach equilibrium, perhaps nudging into the realm of natural recovery. So, you can see the news is not all bad."

"Apparently. John, this has all been most interesting and I very much appreciate your coming to me, presumably at some personal risk. Is it too much to hope that you may have some supporting documentation?"

"You understand Senator, that even one of the most minor modeling programs, would fill half a room with paper. I do have some specific introductory material and some out of context sections of studies, to corroborate what I've told you." He grinned for the first time.

"This is an old briefcase. I don't carry anything quite this shabby to work, but I mean to leave it on the floor back here. You and Mr. McCarthy can look it over at your leisure. It's got my fingerprints, literally and figuratively all over it. So you can see that I'm pretty much at your mercy, Senator."

"Quite right, John. No need to worry on that score, but I have to ask you the million dollar question. If it comes to that, would you be willing to testify on these matters in Senate committee?"

"Senator, that was the first thing I thought about when June and I began to discuss this whole thing. You know it comes as no surprise that you'd ask the question." He carefully laid the briefcase on the floor, just behind Dan's seat.

"Yes I will testify if I absolutely have to. You know that I'd rather not and I trust you to try and keep me out of it, although that's probably unrealistic to hope for. At the very least, I would hope you'll give me the protection of a subpoena and perhaps immunity from prosecution. I'm not really worried about being prosecuted but it would help me look more innocent than I am."

"You have my word, John. If we need to talk again, how may we contact you?"

"Mr. McCarthy has a rather elaborate system for phoning people who will in turn get hold of me." He buttoned the overcoat. "Thank you, Senator." He reached for his hat and slid from the car.

A moment later Dan backed out of the parking place and headed back toward the office, biting his tongue with a million questions, waiting for the boss to break the silence. Bob was sitting bolt upright in the seat, looking straight forward, then turned toward him.

"Well?"

"Hell of a lot of things going on up there that we don't know about, Senator. Unless you've been told some of this and haven't let me know."

"No, Dan. It's all pretty much news to me." He sighed and sounded tired, almost resigned. "Shouldn't be news to me, but it is."

They drove the rest of the way without speaking and McCarthy knew enough to leave the thing alone, at least for now.

Julia handed Bob his messages, as they walked into the office, singling one out of the bunch and handing it to him separately. "Representative Baker. Called twice and would appreciate a call as soon as you get a chance."

"Thanks, Julia. Get him on the phone for me, please."

They walked into his office and he tossed his topcoat and scarf on an empty chair, nodding toward another for Dan. "May as well sit in on this, Dan." The phone came to life and Wilson Baker's smiling face came on the screen.

"Thank you for getting back to me, Bob."

"Not at all, Wil. I have you on the speakerphone and Dan McCarthy is here in the office with me. What can I do for you?"

Baker's face went from a broad smile to a broader smile, then turned serious. "Bob, you and I have talked about the commercial access issue. My committee is getting pretty anxious to get a pilot program going. Getting a lot of heat from the lobbyists and I'm not sure how long I can sit on the issue over here on the House side. Frankly, I had a visit from Pres Alberts the other day and he's feeling the pressure in the Senate."

"I'll just bet he is, Wil." Bob glanced over at Dan, keeping a thoughtful expression on his face for Wilson Baker's view. "Go on."

"Well, there isn't much to go on about, Bob. I just think maybe you and I had better get out in front of this thing before our committees run right the hell over us. We're the damned chairmen. I don't know about you, but I don't like to look like I'm behind in that leadership role, like I'm dragging my ass or out of the loop." The euphemism wasn't lost on Bob and he knew who Wil Baker thought was dragging his ass and out of the loop on his committee. Damn, that fool Alberts was lobbying behind his back.

"I understand, Wil."

"Well, Bob, this is really a courtesy call. I appreciate your staying in touch with me and I feel the obligation to let you know which way the wind is blowing over here. There's going to be a bill presented in my committee next week. It will propose a limited, but industry-wide pilot program. That bill is going to have my name on it."

"I see." Bob looked at the phone camera evenly. "How are you proposing to make the initial commercial selections, Wil?"

"One from each industry sector Bob, chosen by lottery for the most part."

"For the most part?"

"Well, there may have to be exceptions, depending upon how well each of the prospective contributors is prepared. Takes a lot of time and a lot of money to get set up on this."

"Might I assume World Star may be one of the exceptions?"

"They probably will, Bob. They're way out in front on this issue and they've done a hell of a lot of independent research. Stuff that they're willing to share with the committee. Seems like they deserve a proprietary shot in the pilot program."

"I'm sure they feel they do, Wil." Bob fingered the papers on his desk and then glanced back at the screen. "I guess we'll have to consider something from the Senate side, Wil. I appreciate your keeping me up to date."

"Not at all, Bob. Glad to keep close to you on this one." The smile was back. "Oh, Bob, one other thing, as long as I have you on the line."

"Yes?"

"Pres Alberts said he was going to sponsor a similar bill and bring it up at the next Senate Committee meeting."

"Thanks, Wil." Representative Baker's smiling face disappeared from the screen.

Bob shoved back in his chair, looked across the room at his great grandfather's portrait, but talked to Dan.

"He's right, you know." He gazed at the portrait, staring resolutely back at him. The old man sat in a different chair, a chair from other times, but at the same desk behind which Bob now sat. "It's either get out in front of this or get run over."

"Or fight." Dan leaned forward in his seat.

"Yes... or fight. But for how long and with what success?"

"What are you going to do?"

"Maybe fight... maybe not... maybe talk to Harwood."

"The President?"

"He and I go back a long way, Dan. He was the Senior Senator from Virginia when I first came over here and he took pretty good care of me. Been out to the farm a lot of times over the years. We used to see a great deal of each other before the world got so complicated and we all got so damned important. Larry Harwood's a good bridge player, a damn fine shot in a duck blind and a good friend. I leave him pretty much alone since he's become President. And the job doesn't leave him very much time for any of his old friends, but I think we need to talk." Bob still looked off across the room, talking almost to himself.

"Shot a lot of ducks together. I think he needs to know what's going on. It may be the only way to fight this fight."

"I like the sound of that. Anything you want me to do?"

"I'm going to sit here and think about it for a while, Dan. Get out of here for the time being and ask Julia to hold my calls for the next hour or so. I'll let her know when I'm ready." Bob slipped his shoes off and propped his stocking feet on the desk, gazing at the glowering old man in the portrait. Dan slipped quietly out the door.

At three-thirty, Bob made his decision and Julia placed a call to the White House. He asked her to continue to hold calls and sat through the failing light of afternoon by the fireplace, re-reading his well-worn Jefferson biography, thumbing his way from one dog-eared page to the next in wonderment at a mind that could look so far into an unknown future with such grace and accuracy.

Julia slipped in at quarter to five, with a message from Alonzo Romeri, who was holding on line two, requesting a meeting for next week. She had penciled him in for Monday afternoon and raised her eyebrows. Bob nodded and she left to confirm the appointment.

Lawrence Harwood personally returned the call at five-thirty, an uncommon courtesy that once again confirmed their friendship.

"Bob, Larry Harwood."

"Mr. President, thank you for getting back to me so quickly."

"What's all this 'Mr. President?' You want me to start calling you 'Senator Fairweather?' I hope you and I are still 'Bob' and 'Larry' and always will be. Sorry it took so long to get back." There was a snort on the other end of the line. "Sometimes I don't think this damn job can be done, Bob. Just flailed-away at. What can I do for you and why haven't I heard from you in so long?"

Bob chuckled. The President had disarmed him as usual with unfailing charm and put him immediately at ease. Just as he had when Bob entered the Senate as a much younger man, carrying the weight and the expectation of his family name. It was why Harwood had been re elected six times by the people of Virginia. And along with a towering intellect, it was probably why he was President.

"Larry, whether you remember or not, we senators do know how busy our presidents are. We meter out our calls, knowing that each of them diminishes the opportunity for another."

"Yeah… I do seem to remember." Another snort from the phone. "Well, what's up? Maggie okay? The kids okay? My spies tell me that son of yours is following your trail at Wayland's office and doing a damn fine job."

"Everyone's fine, Larry. I'm sure Maggie would send her best, but she doesn't know I'm making the call. Something is brewing at *EVOKE* and I need a few minutes of your time. Just the two of us, if that can be managed. Maybe half an hour or so."

"Done. Let me see what Charlie has available." Bob heard the booming voice call his appointment secretary and smiled to know how quickly people jumped at Larry Harwood's voice. He heard muffled conversation, the President's hand over the receiver and then he came back on the line.

"Bob, how does Wednesday afternoon at five-thirty sound? I'm clear until a diplomatic dinner and we can take a half hour… hell, even an hour, if we need it. Have a couple of drinks and chase everyone out."

"That would be wonderful, Larry. I appreciate it. My best to Esther."

"And mine to Maggie. Tell her I miss the bridge games. See you Wednesday."

SIXTEEN

"How am I doing, Dutch?"

Carla Romeri stopped at the overview of the Idaho valley below, the three-mile mark she had started out dreading and come to love.

"Great, Mrs. Romeri." He glanced at the stopwatch. "Twenty one minutes, forty three seconds. You've been running this first stretch for the past ten days, between twenty and twenty five minutes. How do you feel?"

"Terrific."

She did, too. She could feel her heart rate drop, coming easily back to normal. The slight rivulet of sweat, running down her back between the shoulder blades felt natural and welcome.

"It's all your doing, Dutch. You've turned me into one tough little lady." Carla balanced on the log, carrying her weight on her toe, dropping her heels to stretch her calf muscles as he'd taught her. "Let's take the two mile loop back, Dutch. I deserve a light morning today."

She took the left fork, a running-path dropping slightly through a grove of limber pine, then shallowing to skirt the edges of an open grassy meadow just above Wind River Ranch. Cattle dotted the pasture like lumps of coal on a billiard table. Black Angus cattle. Lonny insisted on Angus, for no other reason than he liked the way they looked spread out across pockets of grazing land on his twenty thousand acre spread.

He stopped by Wind River Ranch perhaps twice a year. A few days in the spring to trout fish and again in the late fall when he came to hunt elk or mule deer, but kept a hunting and fishing guide on staff for guests, who were welcomed to come and bring their friends as well. The cattle were a backdrop, part of the stage-setting for his hunting and fishing lodge. But more than that, as everything Lonny touched had an extra dimension, beef prices were up, the ranch showed a healthy profit and most expenses were charged-off against entertaining clients. It was very expensive entertainment, more to the US government than Lonny.

She ran easily, the limber and jack pine slipping by her peripheral vision, like phone-poles seen from a train window. The steady beat of Dutch's running shoes, a half stride behind, focused her mind on the rhythm of her own pace. Legs and arms, heart and lungs slipped into mindless overdrive and her thoughts turned to Tony.

Her son was up for a week between semesters, an obligatory trip she knew he wasn't much looking forward to, but they'd gone riding every day and she'd beaten him twice on the tennis court. Sixteen and full of himself, it was a good week for both of them. By the end of it, they were having honest-to-god conversations and she saw him begin to come out from where he'd hidden all these years, behind those dark eyes. His father's eyes.

Tony was shyly proud of her tennis game and promised to sharpen up and beat her when she came home for good at the end of the month. They shared a couple of glasses of wine their last night at dinner and talked about college and his interest in marine biology. Really talked, like two adults who cared about each other. She hadn't thought she'd ever be able to have just one glass of wine, without a hidden bottle somewhere. But it had finally happened, finally become easy. Hadn't thought she'd ever have a serious conversation with

Tony either, without a fight and that slow retreat behind his eyes. That had been easy too.

Mile and a half to go. The marker flashed by and she drifted to that last scene with Lonny and the burned hole in the carpet. No time to get it sent out before she left for Wind River and now she knew she never would. It would stay there, a treasured reminder of the life she'd left, the life she'd never go back to. Lonny was right. Lonny was always right, but this time for the wrong reason. He'd sent her up here to become what *he* needed and she'd become that. But somewhere along the way, the pupil became the teacher and she realized now that Carla Romeri was indeed a very tough lady. And not only in the legs and wind.

She'd allowed herself to become lost outside Lonny's life. Too big a life, too remote a life and it had damned near swamped her. Seeing her value only as a reflection in his eyes, over the years his disapproval of the neighborhood Italian girl he'd married pulled at her confidence like loose threads. The unraveling was endless as the dark ethnic beauty he'd admired became an embarrassment in the company of the tall, slender trophy-wives of his business associates. Her grammar no longer fit, her taste in clothes, the decor of the house, even hair-style was a cause of constant complaint. So he took them all away from her, a stranger in a home no longer her own and wearing clothes selected for her by top designers. Their home and *their* clothes, not hers and with no place left for Carla. When he finally moved to his own bedroom and turned his eyes away from her, even that wounded reflection of herself was gone and the long slide into isolation and alcohol took over.

She knew she'd have been better off divorced. But a busted marriage wasn't in Lonny's game plan and even that last hope of survival was taken from her. With money and a chance to find herself she might have made it. Maybe not, but there'd have been a chance.

The mile-marker flew by and she smiled. She hated him, but he'd fucked up now and didn't even know it. Carla knew what he expected. Fogged as she was by booze and panic, she never forgot the specifications he laid out that night, like she was a new line of trucks or a fucking corporate jet he planned to develop. Well, she was about to roll off the assembly line and all the conditions had been met. But a few others of her own devising had been added and the thought turned her smile to a broad grin. She'd found the reflection of her own worth where it needed to be. In the bathroom mirror, looking into her own eyes.

God, that first month was agony, an endlessness of withdrawal from pills and booze. A near complete physical and mental breakdown, but Lonny hired the best specialists his limitless money could buy and after a while she felt hopelessness washing out of her. Scattered fragments of that tough Italian broad she'd been began slowly to come together. Jesus, so slowly, but they were there and she began to feel human. Before long she began to feel alert and then finally, she began to feel interested in finding her lost self.

EVOKE was implanted in Boise, under her maiden name. Carla began to travel for the first time in her life, letting it take her to Europe and the Far East and South America, opening an interest in other cultures, making her more sure of her own. The sex wasn't bad either and someone else's or not, it gave her satisfaction she'd never known with Lonny, even in the good days. A sense of self-esteem that she could depend on.

She saw her body tighten and her skin and hair take on a luster that made her smile and run her hands over herself in the shower. Far from being the scary plaything she'd expected, *EVOKE* effortlessly taught her diction, along with a fluency in French and Italian, that made her blush at her mother's rough dialect.

Yes, Lonny would get the package he'd designed, but with an independence he might have a hard time with. She'd be his wife and play the part he needed her to play, she probably owed him that. But someday when he'd finally achieved whatever the hell it was he wanted, she'd make him pay. And the price would be something even Lonny would have a hard time financing.

The half-mile marker slid by Carla's right side and she locked her mind into the cadence. The grin returned, listening to Dutch's breathing from just behind her, coming faster than her own now. The ranch buildings swung into view through the aspen grove and a startled jackrabbit jumped from the edge of the path on her left, darting its way up the slope, zig-zagging, ears laid flat against its back. They slowed and walked the last two hundred yards to the rear door of the training center, her breath returning to normal faster than his.

"What's the watch say, Dutch?"

"Fourteen flat, Mrs. Romeri."

Bob Fairweather rose from his chair and walked around the desk, as Lonny Romeri strode in, reaching out to shake hands and offer a chair by the fire. This probably wasn't going to be as charming a visit as dinner at the farm. May as well be gracious.

"Lonny, good to see you. Julia will bring in coffee."

"Thanks, Bob. I won't be taking a great deal of your time, but I appreciate your seeing me on such short notice." They sat and Julia brought in a tray, setting it on the table and closing the door behind her.

"Julia tells me you wouldn't say what brought you to Washington, Lonny. What can I do for you?"

"Well, I was in town on other business, Bob. But regardless of that, I thought we should have a chat." He leaned forward, pouring a cup of coffee.

"Specifically, to answer your question we need to talk about *EVOKE* and your chairmanship of the committee. I want you to step down, Bob and let Preston Alberts take over as Chairman. Frankly, I don't see any way for you to do that without retiring from the Senate. So that's what I'm here to propose." He looked at Bob squarely, as though he had just suggested a game of bridge.

"I'm fascinated, Lonny, to know a man who seems to think there are no limits to his power." He reached for the coffee pot and took his time pouring, collecting himself. "You come in here and tell me to retire, as though I were an employee of one of your companies. I must remind you, Lonny, that you are not my employer. You're not even one of my constituents. Allowing Pres Alberts into that chair is the same as putting you there."

"I know. That's why I want him in and you out. Because I can deal with him and I can't deal with you, at least not on that issue. I respect you for that, Bob. I even like you and wish you liked me, but that's beside the point." He ignored the coffee in front of him. This was not a time for cream and sugar.

"I need you out and I'm willing to back your son, Bobby, with the kind of backing that will assure his taking over your seat in the Senate.

"I already know about that. Your man Edwards is not very smooth, but he gets his point across. I'm sure you knew it would get directly to me... get me used to the idea before we sat down together."

"Exactly." Romeri's eyes lit with the enthusiasm of a teacher, whose student had just solved a difficult problem. "Your current term will wrap up eighteen years here in the Senate, Bob. Time to move along. Time to give young Bobby his chance, while the Fairweather name is still electable."

"Meaning?"

"Meaning young Bobby's lifestyle, if it were to come out, might not appeal to enough Virginians to get him elected. Another term or two with you in that seat might make it too late for him."

"But you don't see it as an insurmountable problem right now? Not too big for your public relations department, if I just move along."

"I hire some very expensive people, Bob. Their job is to make positives out of negatives. They're very good at it. I will support a campaign, whatever the cost, that will put young Bobby over the top. He's a pretty bright young man, Bob. Once he's there, he can make himself useful enough to the people of the State of Virginia, to stay as long as he likes."

"Suppose I say no."

"How brutal do you want me to be?"

"As brutal as you need to be."

"Well, first of all there would be a leak, concerning Bobby's friend Web Brooking. Enough to cause a scandal and there would be some additional speculation. Rumors, all unsubstantiated that his father, the Senior Senator from Virginia, shared a similar lifestyle."

"Second, we would withdraw our offer of east coast representation to Wayland's law firm, pointing an embarrassed finger at Bobby."

"Third, we would jump in with all our resources, behind the candidacy of a young hell-raising attorney from Roanoke, who came close to taking the nomination away from you the last time. Our confidence in him would be so high that the legal representation for World Star's east coast business would fall to his firm. "

"You make a pretty convincing case. I don't doubt for a moment, that you would do it."

"I mean to have that Chairmanship of *EVOKE*, Bob."

"You expect an answer now?"

"No. I want you to talk this over with Maggie and Bobby if you feel the need. This is Monday. You have a week and I mean just that, Bob. By Tuesday of next week there will be no stopping, no turning back, no second looks. The scenario I've outlined to you this afternoon, will be set in motion."

Alonzo Romeri was finished with what he had to say and stood, his hand held out as though to bind just one more business deal with a handshake. There was even a smile, a not unfriendly smile.

Senator Fairweather shook the hand and stood with one arm on the fireplace mantel, watching Romeri find his own way out.

———

At nine o'clock on the following evening, Frank pulled through the gates of the Romeri mansion, glancing in the rearview mirror to catch the expression on Prentiss Everett's face. Frank gave him a nine for composure. The look was cool and disinterested, the clothes perfect for a meeting with the boss. Dark, conservative, expensive.

The Reverend had been there before, but only twice and he reflected on the first occasion, a year and a half ago at a reception Romeri gave for just about everyone of importance in the industrial and political world. Its purpose was as hazy to him as the collection of tents spanning the property. A diverse collection of power structures that spilled from the inside of the mansion out across the sprawl, to drift in again, rearranged and reconvened. Everett felt very black on that occasion.

The second time, just a year ago, there'd been a dinner for union and management negotiators. A well-orchestrated move away from smoky conference tables, after a long and bitter period of no movement. He'd had plenty of black backup, as everyone looked to him for some sort of healing, a spiritual bringing together. He wasn't interested in bringing together. His power lay in apartness, but he'd enjoyed the spotlight, reveled in the obsequious attention of a power structure that quite clearly feared and hated him.

Now, Romeri asked him to come again, this time to sit down one on one and man to man, to discuss the political future of the country. What a laugh. The political future of the country in Romeri's mind, was a white future. And Everett knew damned well, even though he may be invited to discuss it's direction, Romeri meant to keep it white. Well, so what?

He'd called and asked and been decent enough about it. Sent the corporate jet, allowed Everett to set the time for the meeting. Even allowed him to decline the dinner invitation and opt for this eight-thirty in the evening, all business discussion. Lonny had promised to have the Reverend back in Chicago as quickly as he cared to be there.

That was the way you leveled the table, he mused. You set the rules, you set the time. You said the hell with the fancy dinner.

Romeri met him on the steps, all smiles and warmth and handshakes. The house was even more impressive with just the two of them. A roaring fire, book-lined walls, polished paneling. Christ, he thought as they took their chairs, there were always roaring fires at these meetings, like some sort of pagan ritual. That was all right too. The fire was an offering, just like the twenty year old scotch, an acknowledgement of his importance, an extension of the private plane, private chauffeur and very private meeting.

"I appreciate your coming over." Lonny settled in the chair, still in a business suit. "I know I was a little vague on the reason for our getting together. But politics as you well know, sometimes requires an almost foolish amount of caution."

"You're going to tell me you're about to run for President."

"You're very perceptive."

"I've had to be, it's all part of surviving nowadays in any national political capacity... particularly a minority role." He sipped the scotch. Score one for the Reverend. "So, you want to give me the liberal read on your philosophy and ask for support."

"The black and Hispanic bloc is huge these days. It's possible to win without their endorsement, especially if you have enough money and I have enough money." Lonny sipped his scotch and leaned forward in the chair. "But, it's impossible to lose if that bloc is solidly behind my candidacy. And that's what I'm interested in, the impossibility of losing."

"It's early to bargain, Mr. Romeri."

"Lonny."

"Lonny." So it was to be first names. Well, Prentiss, you've come a long way after all, he thought. Now they're coming to you with the personal planes and first names.

"Minorities have always had to survive by bargaining. That's getting close to changing, but it's still a fact." Prentiss leaned toward Romeri, mirroring his posture, the fire a background to their concentrated profiles.

"We do best for ourselves when we sit back and measure the strong and the weak, throwing our support to the strong if there's something in it for us, concentrating our energies behind the weak if we decide it's best to ride this one out. Sometimes we need to make a statement to the *next* candidate."

"This meeting is to make sure you don't ride it out."

"Like I said, it's early."

"What's the price to come in early? What does the black vote need to bring them solidly behind me? Quietly in the early going, so as not to worry the white power structure and with a roaring support, led by Prentiss Everett at the end?" Romeri sat back in the chair and read the Reverend's eyes, watching him cross his legs and adjust the crease in his trouser leg.

"You're an interesting man, Lonny. You quite clearly believe in laying your cards on the table early and I have a feeling you know you can pull it off." He leaned forward and looked directly at this composed multi-billionaire who meant to be President. "Bottom line, another Supreme Court seat. At least two Cabinet appointments, one of them a major appointment and an end to what's going on at *EVOKE*." It was a tall order, but this was an early meeting.

"Can't do it."

The Reverend shrugged. "You asked, I answered."

"*EVOKE* is a key issue. It's not negotiable, it's where the country's going."

"*EVOKE* is racist, Lonny, blatantly racist. It's aimed at the black and Hispanic population. And, just like the Indians, it's another reservation to which we're being sent." He spread his hands, stretched the fingers.

"We're gaining strength. We're going to have to be dealt with. We won't be put on a reservation."

"So, give me a best-case scenario, Prentiss. Give me the black future as you would see it, in a perfect world."

"We're going to have to take over the power structures, so that we can get access on our own terms. There's just no other way and we're getting damned close to being there. That means the legislatures, the courts, the major corporations." This was comfortable ground, a subject he'd preached and polished over a decade. "We'll never get there bussing dishes, working in fast food restaurants and putting a few brothers through college so they can move to the suburbs and forget."

"You can't get there your way, Prentiss." Lonny rose and walked to the fireplace, leaning an arm on the mantel and fishing in his pocket for a cigarette. "Control of the legislatures and courts only gives you legal equity. For the most part, you've had that for forty years. As for the corporations, they can afford to put a few blacks in key positions, throw them a bone once in a while and still control what they need to control, the money." He pulled a cigarette from the pack and lit it, inhaling deeply and slipping the gold lighter back into his pocket. "Major corporations are not philanthropies. They're money-making machines and they make the money for the investors. You're not an investor yet." Lonny paused and looked reflectively at the tip of the cigarette, letting the words settle.

"As for political control, you already have most of the major cities and they're falling apart under you, as the money moves out and the sewers collapse."

"That's why we need to get control of the big money, the national money." Prentiss smacked his fist into the palm of his hand. "We need to begin to rearrange who has it and who gets it."

"No matter. Listen to me, Prentiss. It just doesn't *matter* anymore, it's too *late* for rearrangement. We're falling apart nationally, the same way we are in the cities. By the time you get there, by the time you get your hands on the national money, there won't be enough to rearrange." He looked into the fire and then back.

"Jesus, Prentiss, for decades we've been sliding into fewer and fewer people working, trying to support more and more people not working. By the time you get there, you'll have your victory parade and all there will be, up and down Pennsylvania Avenue, is outstretched hands." He tossed the cigarette into the fire and reached for another.

"What're you going to give them, Prentiss? The bricks in the Washington Monument? Even that will need tuck-pointing and be in danger of collapse."

"So you have a better way?" Jesus, here he was, getting another lecture on waiting. "You have a white solution and I'm supposed to be the Indian Chief, waiting to hear what the Great White Father will do for me?" This trip had been a waste of time. There was nothing here for him, but the same old bullshit, the same old waiting for things to get better. Romeri would be surprised. The blacks, the Hispanics, the membership of *BURN* was almost there and these people didn't even realize it. The time for waiting was gone. Long gone.

"*No one* has a solution Prentiss. If they did, they'd be Jesus Christ Himself. But *EVOKE* gives us a chance and it may be the last chance we get."

"*EVOKE?*" The reverend snorted the word. "*EVOKE* is the goddamn enemy."

"Prentiss, we need to get a grip on the money, while there still *is* some money."

"The money? You already have goddam control over the money." His voice was rising. "That's what we're goddamn talking about, is control of the money."

"I don't mean that. You're right, the private money is still white-controlled and white-owned. You're also right that minorities will never get their hands on any of it, until they get into the system." Lonny walked back to the seat opposite his guest and sat down, bringing the tone of conversation down with him.

"That's a different matter and I know it's important to you. But this country is turning into an empty shell. And all you're going to inherit is the shell. Society will have already sucked it dry as a bone unless things change. If we don't screw up this last chance, *EVOKE* could be the tool to pull it off."

"How?" He may as well stay for the full show.

"First of all, we've got to stop what you've been trying to promote." The cigarette was still unlit in his hand and he looked at it, staging another pause.

"We've got to get a handle on population and the minorities are breeding at a rate four times that of the more privileged classes." Lonny put up a hand, to stop the Reverend's reply.

"Hear me out. I know that's what you've been striving for, but the facts don't change. The only way we can put a damper on birthrates is to promote the hell out of *EVOKE*. Not that it needs much promoting, everyone seems to want on." Lonny lit the cigarette. "That will give us a breather, slow the momentum of entitlement programs and take some heat off Social Security."

"What're you going to do with your *breather* while we get weak again?"

"Prentiss, the full powers of *EVOKE* haven't even been touched. Education and role-models and the will to succeed in a predominantly white-controlled world have always been the barriers to minorities. Impassable and impossible barriers. This country is at the edge of anarchy because of it." He leaned back, each lean back or forward a stage direction.

"*EVOKE* has the possibility of sidestepping all of those barriers, once we get everyone hooked up. Taking the will to succeed, along with the role-modeling and educational support directly to the brains of all these young, hopeless, undirected minority kids. It also has the potential power to program their parents and grandparents, who are too late to participate on any real and meaningful basis to support these kids." He looked directly at Everett.

"Damn it, Prentiss, your direction can *never* give them that. Your direction just takes what's left in a constantly diminishing world economy and gives it to them. They'll want *more*, Prentiss. They'll always have their hands out and you'll run out of stuff to give."

"Go on."

"*EVOKE* is just a clever mind-game right now. But there are computer models of educational and motivational programs in existence today. Programs that reach into ghettos and prisons and mental institutions with almost unbelievable potential. Rehabilitation programs in medicine, physical and mental therapy are up and working now. On a pilot basis, sure, but showing results that are breathtaking. We need to do that, but we need the *time*. This is a way that we can buy that time and make it work, if we don't screw up." Another pause, another cue from the wings.

"This is a way to reshape a society that hasn't got a shape anymore, that's collapsing around our ears."

"And you want me to buy into this." It wasn't a question, but more of a resigned statement.

"I want you to do more than that. I want you to get behind it and help me with it."

"Bullshit." His voice rose, in spite of the closeness of their chairs. "You want me to wait again. You want me to call off the dogs, because you can hear them snarling at the door. You know they can smell the meat."

"I want you to be my Vice President."

Silence filled the room like an enveloping substance. A taste and smell and physical presence, none of which are the usual attributes of silence. It hung there.

"Vice President. That's not the shiny medal it once was, now that we've had a black *president*"

"And there won't be another for a hundred years. The first one made promises he couldn't keep because of what you and I've just discussed."

"Interesting, Lonny. I must say, you are an interesting man." It was the only thing he could think to say and he was annoyed. The image of himself as the first black Vice President occupied a corner of his brain, even as he spoke. Not the image of a *candidate*, but that of a *Vice President*. He knew Romeri could win. Knew with *exact certainty*, that he and Romeri together could not help but win.

"There's more. There's one other thing."

"What?'

"Five million."

"Five million what?"

"Five million dollars, win or lose. On the front end, in an account anywhere you want it. For any purpose you want to put it and that includes *BURN*. But if you accept, you have to get off the *EVOKE* issue. To quiet down and let your minorities *be* put to sleep for the time being. To buy into what can be done and put the full force of your rhetoric and reputation behind it. There's a price for that. You may see it as a sellout. I see it as the only way left and I want you to see it my way. But I don't have the time to convince, only the time to buy. The price I'm willing to pay is five million. I'll win in any event." He looked at Everett and recognized in his eyes that he'd made the deal. "*You* can win with me.

Bob Fairweather had Wilson stop on the way up the long drive at the kennel and stepped from the car to knock at Jerrold MacCay's door. He saw the curtain draw back, then heard hurried footsteps, the door opening to reveal Jerrold's lank figure. He was still in his worn, everyday corduroy breeches, boots pulled off, revealing heavy gray wool socks. He wore a heavy Irish knit sweater, a newspaper still in his hand.

"Senator, I wasn't expecting … "

"Sorry, Jerrold. No need to fuss, but there was something on my mind and I thought I'd stop for a moment on the way in. Sorry to disturb you and Anne."

"No disturbance to us at all, Senator. Come in. Was it the gray horse on your mind? I think he'll be ready in the morning, he walked-out well enough this afternoon and I've just had a look at that ankle." He closed the door and followed Bob into the small front room. "Right as rain, that ankle."

Bob sat in the offered easy-chair, noticing again the blown-up black and white photo of Jerrold. Centered over the sofa, it was a strangely soft and mystical scene of a much younger Jerrold, standing in front of a cobbled wall. He held the halter rope attached to a big country-bred Irish hunter in his strong young hands. The lush fields fell away behind him, crisscrossed in the distance with similar vine-covered low cobble walls. He'd seldom been in the living room of the kennel-house, but had admired the photo.

"Jerrold, we've talked of Ireland, of your retirement."

"Yes we have. But surely not yet, Master. There's a bit more hunting left in both of us." Jerrold looked at him, a flash of worry in his eyes, instinctively changing from "Senator" to "Master" as the conversation led from everyday events to foxhunting.

"No, I expect we've a few years left to chase foxes. But I was wondering, Jerrold. If I were to buy a place in Ireland, a proper place and not too far from Cork, would you be willing to stay on as my Huntsman over there?"

"Hunting *your* hounds over *there*, Master? That would be a dream come true." His bright blue eyes sparkled.

"Well I don't know, Jerrold." He rose from the chair. "It's been on my mind of late and I wanted to see how you would feel." He shook his Huntsman's hand, walked to the door and opened it to the chill late afternoon, where Wilson waited with the car.

"Let's give the gray a trial on Wednesday."

"He'll be ready, Master."

SEVENTEEN

No matter how well you knew him or know him still, when a friend becomes President there seem to be only two options. Spread the word on how chummy you are and slather the walls of your office with every snapshot you can find, or admit the real fact that for four or eight years the job has come between you. That you value the friendship as well as the office, too much to intrude. Real friends are found among the latter and Bob Fairweather was and remained a real friend to President Lawrence Harwood.

Charlie Devereaux, the President's appointment secretary met him at the west entry. Making small talk along the corridors, Charlie nodded self-importantly toward various opened office doors, their occupants busy at computer screens, telephones or paperwork, no matter the hour. He knocked once, then swung the door to the Oval Office open, stepping aside to follow Bob. Harwood had reading-glasses shoved back on his forehead and was sucking on the cap end of a felt-tip marker. He held a sheaf of stapled papers in one hand, about half of them turned under. Laying them aside, the President came around the desk, wearing his campaign grin.

"Bob, how the hell are you? You're looking great and it's been too long, too goddamn long."

"I'm fine, Mr. President. You don't look all that bad yourself, for a fella in his eighth year behind that desk."

Harwood chuckled. "That's why I look so well, because I'm already thinking about quail hunting when I get out of here." He nodded toward Charlie who, if he'd

JIM FREEMAN

been a pointer, would have held motionlessly, with one paw in the air. "That'll be all for now, Charlie. I don't want to be disturbed for anything short of an invasion." Bob and the President sat down, as Charlie closed the door behind him.

"I apologize for seeing you in here, Bob. Pretty damned stuffy and formal. We'd have been upstairs in the apartment, but Esther's getting ready for tonight and I've learned to keep out of her way when there's a formal dinner coming up."

"I do the same with Maggie, but it's easier for me. I don't move around with an entourage." He grinned at his old friend and thought the earlier compliment didn't miss the mark by far. Larry Harwood did look well and it surprised him a bit.

"Larry, there's never as much time as we'd like and I need to get down to cases. There've been a number of unsettling things coming together lately, all relating to *EVOKE* and frankly I'm worried as hell." Alone together, calling the President by his first name was a natural thing and Bob relaxed into the old ways, the old times.

"Part of it is the same old thing, pressure from the commercial lobbies for access, but we've had that for a number of years now. It's what's going on that I should know, but haven't been informed of that's bothering me. And frankly, it's coming from pretty high. High enough that I feel you need to know, if you don't already."

He went on to give the President an abbreviated, but absolutely accurate appraisal of his meetings with Prentiss Everett, Representative Baker and Alan Longwell. Bob recalled his phone conversation with Emerson Wayland, as well as his recent and unsettling meetings with John Wilforth and Alonzo Romeri. Harwood was attentive.

320

But he asked no questions and took no notes, merely nodding or grunting, from time to time. The further Bob wound into the story, the more he had the eerie feeling that the President knew it all. Perhaps it was a mistake, his coming here. Maybe it was leaning on a friendship that was no longer supportable. Perhaps too many things had changed in eight years. The feeling a stand-up comic must have when no one is laughing and he's losing the house. He willed it to go away, but it wouldn't.

"Bob, what would you think, if I told you that your assumptions are very nearly correct? That the preliminary activity at *EVOKE* is in fact coming from very high up, some of it from this office." Harwood looked at him and the look was that of two old duck hunters, chatting over a thermos of coffee and waiting for the next flight.

"I'd say I was stunned." He wasn't really stunned. It seemed that all the years in Washington had nearly removed that word from his vocabulary. What then? More puzzled perhaps and even offended by the need to come to his President, his friend and ask to be let in to the intrigue that surrounded his own damned committee.

"I'd say, I was not only stunned, but that such an action flies in the face of the Constitution. Jesus, Larry, we have a Senate and a House of Representatives for a reason. I'm embarrassed to remind you that the reason is to keep this very kind of thing from happening." Harwood stirred in his chair, but held his gaze.

"Bob, don't go flying off and waving the Constitution in my face." Larry Harwood flushed a bit, then took a deep breath and felt the flush recede. "Half the people I deal with accuse me of ignoring the Constitution. The other half think I'm running roughshod over it, but don't have the guts to say so.

There are some things that are just too touchy to hang out to dry in the halls of the Congress."

"But Jesus, Larry ... "

"Now hang on a minute." Harwood held up a hand. "This will all come to you, soon enough, in highly constitutional form. All properly presented, so you boys can debate it to death and have your 'advice and consent.' This isn't Princeton and I don't need another lecture, particularly from an old friend like you."

"I grant you it isn't Princeton, Larry. This is the top of the real world, the very top. The place where all those studies of Jefferson are more than just words. Let me back up a minute, before we go on to other things. What did you mean, when you said 'preliminary activity?'"

"Just that. That and nothing more sinister. We're modeling a number of programs that you don't yet know about, things as diverse as you can possibly imagine. Long-range stuff, the complete restructuring of agricultural production and distribution. Studying the impact of a fifty percent reduction in vehicle and air traffic. Looking over the implications of abandoning our educational system as it now exists."

"Through *EVOKE*?"

"Certainly through *EVOKE*. But can you imagine the mayhem in the halls of Congress on a logical discussion of even one of those issues? And there are hundreds, just as broad-brush, just as outrageously volatile."

"Jesus, Larry. What's *EVOKE* got to do with those issues?" It was a stupid question and he regretted how badly he had put it. They were framed constantly in the minds of everyone who had taken *EVOKE* seriously. A question not meant to be answered, but to ferret-out the mind set of his President. Wilforth had given him a damned accurate background assessment.

Everyone who thought through the implications of the power to appeal directly to the intellect, saw the potential of *EVOKE*. More even than direct appeal, the power to *shape* an unshaped intellect, in fact to create it where none may have existed before. To hone the thought process carefully into a form that would be supportive of future social goals. The question was badly put, but he was willing to be lectured, if it meant getting the President's views.

"Bob, let's take just a couple of the things I mentioned." The lecture began. "Education. We've done such a damn poor job of that over the past century, that we're beginning to crack at the top university level. And below that, we're just a disaster. Young job applicants don't know London is in Europe and can't read street-signs well enough to deliver pizza. They hate school and it's hard to blame them, we've made such a hash of it. These kids can be educated Bob, through *EVOKE*. Direct access to the mind. It's not a dream, it's here now and in fact, has been here for a number of years. But there's just no goddamn political forum for such a basic change and the teaching lobby will be all over our ass. We're going to have to slide into these things carefully and the commercial side is probably the route." He paused.

"This is a market-economy we've set up for ourselves and *called* a Republic. Commerce is our god, for better or worse. And commerce needs an educated public for consumer development. They can't sell anything to an illiterate without job hopes. We already have models for a change in public attitude that may well bring a national outcry for *EVOKE* as an educational tool." Another pause and Bob broke in.

"*EVOKE* was never chartered for 'changing public attitude,' Larry."

"Charters can be changed. Stay with me on this. Agriculture, let's take that. We're losing our tillable agricultural land at a rate that will leave us barren in two centuries or so, maybe sooner. We're very nearly back to the dust-bowl days of the middle of the last century. It's blowing away and washing away, being abandoned for lack of productivity at a hell of a rate and has been for two centuries already." He walked over to the liquor cabinet. "You want a scotch?"

"Yeah."

"Anyway, what's left is so intensely fertilized, drenched in insecticide and irrigated, that it's the major source of ground-water pollution, as well as ground water depletion." He was once again the Princeton professor and on a roll. "Everyone has come to expect fresh lettuce in the supermarket in the middle of winter. And they've got it, but at a damned high cost, a cost we can't afford and I don't mean dollars. Our model program shows we can grow enough vegetables and grains and protein to sustain our population on ten percent of the land we now till, without all the abuses. Trouble is, it isn't all that appetizing, all that perfect to look at." He found glasses and seemed uncertain about ice, rummaging around. There was supposed to be an ice bucket in there somewhere.

"But it'll do the trick and be a hell of a lot more healthy in the bargain. If it can be ingested... now there's a hell of a word. Eaten anyway, as part of an *EVOKE* meal program, the user will *feel* just as though he's had dinner at the finest restaurant in the country." The ice rattled into glasses. "That's something we need to look into. That's something we're *going* to goddamn well look into and I'm not about to have the California farm lobby in my hair in the meantime."

"Larry, this is a country of choice. We're not some banana republic."

"Well shit, we're running *out* of choices." He poured and brought the glasses back, handing one to Bob, still standing beside the chair.

"What do I say, or what does the next poor bastard who sits in my chair say, when it happens? Sorry there's no more water? Sorry there's no farmland, but this is a country of choices and your *choice* was to use it all up?" He settled into his chair and the campaign smile was gone.

"The citizens don't run this country Bob and they never have and you and I both know it. Power runs this country and these days, power is in the special interest groups, the lobbies. We just let the voters loose every four years, so they can pick out the man or woman, who has to answer to the power." He sipped. "That means me, too. I answer to the same damned people you do. The special-interest groups are just that, 'special interest' and *their* interest is making money." He snorted and Bob smiled. Snorts were part of Larry's punctuation.

"Do you really think the money guys care if the water and land run out? Not unless it effects this quarter's earnings. And if we don't do something now, it will damn soon be too late to computer-model anything but the rate of starvation."

"Jefferson said much the same thing," Bob replied, "two hundred fifty years ago. I was just reading it again the other day and I'm still amazed at what he saw coming, even then."

"Jefferson be damned." Another snort, followed by a sip of scotch. "He may have known human nature, but he didn't realize we'd have a country with three hundred million people in it *and doubling every fifty years*. Not by a long shot. Much less, fifty million of them without jobs. A hundred million of them retired, another fifty million on the public payrolls. The remaining productive hundred million are scared to death and trying to support the whole ball-game. All of that under a fifty trillion dollar debt-load, the legacy we left ourselves by winning the Second World War, losing

Vietnam and Iraq and running Congress without any long-range responsibility." He sat back and half the grin returned.

"Every four years, they elect some poor bastard like me, to solve it. Of course we can't *do* it, because the Presidency has become just as short-term responsive as the business world. We spend the first two years trying to get a grip on things and then waste the next two trying to get re-elected. It's only in the second term we get a chance to do anything. The last year of that, we're lame ducks and can't get any legislation passed. Three years out of eight isn't enough time, Bob. The Presidency's become an impossible, downward-spiraling, self-fulfilling prophesy of ineptitude. And that's just not good enough, not any more."

"But the answer can't be to go behind the backs of the electorate?"

"Well, I guess you have to define 'behind their backs.' Do you think you're going 'behind their backs,' when you have a closed-door hearing? When you guys discuss an issue in the Senate that's just too volatile for newsmen and television?"

"The law provides for that."

"Shit Bob, you're getting semantic on me and lecturing me on *law*. We haven't broken any laws in the computer modeling we're not telling you about. And we won't. When we've got it all together, we'll bring it before you."

"What about skewing *EVOKE* access to minorities?"

"That's a little gray, I admit it."

"That's more than gray, Larry. It's absolutely and fundamentally against the laws that were enacted for access."

"All right, let's talk about that." He got up, walked over to the cabinet and came back with the bottle of scotch, setting it on the table. "You're right and you know you're right. But the birthrate among the educated is declining, has been for decades. Lots of reasons for that, but mostly it's because the more educated a couple is, the better they understand the cost and responsibility of having children. Thank God, they weigh just how much of that burden they're willing to take on." He poured and shoved his reading glasses back.

"The minorities are exploding, just out of all control. For one thing, it's become a profit-center to have children because we got way off base in the sixties with our well-meaning and much needed entitlement programs. For another, the smart politicians like this guy Everett didn't take long to find the magic in numbers. They've decided to take over this country, for the most part with minority-bloc votes. So it's in their interests to encourage big families and they're meeting those goals. Taking political control of the poorest parts of our country, mainly the big cities. Minority isn't even a correct *term* anymore. Where they rule, they are the majority and they rule a great deal nowadays. More power to them if they were self-sustaining, but they're not. They have a minority of jobs, minority of income, minority of education. And damned little hope for gaining any of those things. Everett and his kind have sold them down the river for power." He topped Bob's glass.

"Their health care is the worst, their death rate is the highest, including babies and a hugely disproportionate share of their support comes from the public sector. We've simply got to get a handle on this and stop the explosion. We absolutely have to get the decade or two that it will take to get some of these models functioning."

"That's terribly close to racism, Larry." Bob paused and turned the glass in his hand. "It probably is racism, by any normal standard"

"I know." Harwood sighed and sat back. "It doesn't make me happy, but it's why we got the whole sterilization business out front, at the inception of *EVOKE*. It raised a hell of a ruckus, but we got it done."

"I was solidly against that, as you well know."

"It's why you became the first and only Chairman. You were the quid pro quo. Your chairmanship was the final chip shoved across the table."

"I didn't know that." He didn't, and it stung him a bit to learn it from the President.

"Well, you were the junior Senator from Virginia and I was senior. There were a few things you didn't know then and that was one of them." Harwood grinned. "I sold you to the other objectors for their votes. I think they knew we were going to win this one eventually and I sold them you. You and the sperm-bank, to get it done. Told them you were the only one with courage enough to be a moralist in that chair and they bought it." He looked directly at his friend.

"They were *right* to buy it and I was right to sell them on it. You have been a moralist in that chair and a damn fine one. You should be proud of that."

"I guess I am, Larry." Bob sighed. "But the Indians are circling and I came to you with some hope of reinforcements. Now, I find that most of the arrows, particularly the flaming ones are yours. I thought I had this town figured out, but maybe no one ever really figures it out."

"Don't be too hard on yourself or me either, Bob." He reached for the scotch. "Why don't you retire?"

"You too, huh? I guess I should have expected it. Seems everyone is asking me that, these days."

"Well?"

"Because I still believe in the people and their right to some reasonable sort of self determination. *EVOKE* has the power to change all that and it scares the hell out of me."

"It can just as easily be seen as the last best hope, Bob. But it needs someone fully behind it, someone who sees it from that perspective."

"And that's not me. Way past time for a moralist, no matter what you sold the opposition. Preston Alberts? You don't really think he has a perspective, do you?"

"No. But he does what he's told and he has a marvelous speaking voice and all that lush, wavy gray hair." The campaign grin reappeared.

"What if I fight you on this, Larry?"

"You won't win. You can't win, not this one, Bob."

"What if I disclose our conversation, or at least the general scope of it?"

"Well, for one thing Bob, you won't do that because it's too far out of character for you. And, even if it wasn't, you know better." He grinned again.

"I'd deny it and we'd set out to make you look a fool. Then drive you out of office and systematically wreck a very fine reputation. You'd look like a frantic old man and end up a laughingstock. Bobby would get buried in the elections and that would be the end of every political aspect of the Fairweather dynasty."

"Pretty stern words, from my old bridge partner."

"This isn't like making seven no-trump, doubled and vulnerable, Bob. This is a real game and I'm not sure even you know how high the stakes have become."

"Maybe not. Where does Romeri fit in? Your scenario is nearly the same as his. I feel like he's been standing in all the alleys I've looked down."

"He's going to be the next guy in my chair."

"He hasn't even put his name in the Primaries."

"I know." Larry sipped his drink. "That's not his style, to get out there and slug with all the little guys on issues. He thinks early issues kill a candidacy and he's right. He'll come in late, with a lot of money and media attention and whatever he needs for television time."

The President wasn't about to get into the issue of Romeri's use of *EVOKE* as a campaign tool. He'd leveled with Bob enough, almost too much and pushed him, nearly pushed him too hard. Subliminal advertising was a delicate issue in the best of circumstances. Something that would require a great deal of discretion and subtlety in the coming year.

"Everyone learned from Perot." He snorted. "He'd have won, if he'd kept his head and stayed in. Or come in later. Lonny won't make that mistake."

"Jesus Larry, what are we coming to when someone can just buy your seat?"

"Jefferson's ruling aristocracy, Bob. You've read him as well as any man I know. He always believed that. It was just not a popular point of view at the time, having just driven the British aristocracy off the continent. The Presidency has *always* been bought, one way or another." He looked at Bob and pointed a finger. "Don't you raise your eyebrows at me. It's just semantics again. You've had your head in the same trough from time to time. We all have, from dog-catcher to President. If it's an electable office there are deals being made and favors being passed. Let's at least hope we elect someone with the skills to do that on a somewhat equitable basis."

"I'm tired, Larry." Bob drained the scotch from his glass and stood.

The President stood and held out his hand. "We still friends?"

"You know we are. But I don't know where I'm going on this." They walked to the door. "We still friends, if I come down on the other side of the issue?"

"Always personal friends Bob, but it's going to get bloody."

"Fair enough. My best to Esther."

Bob walked down the corridor and a Secret Service agent dropped in next to him, making easy conversation on the way to the west portico.

———————————

"Ginny, all we seem to do lately is bicker."

They were driving up Route 64 toward Charlottesville to have dinner with Ginny's old Foxcroft roommate and her new husband. A man Bobby hardly knew, older than her by twenty years, a big player in the small tobacco-markets. Maybe the roommate thought it was the best she could do. Who the hell knew, maybe she loved him, plump and slightly balding, always hovering, lingering on her words.

Bobby was disinterested, another obligatory squiring along Ginny's perpetual trail of social engagement. He gripped the wheel too tightly and drove a little too fast. Not from the joy of the Porsche, but from mean spiritedness. Bobby disliked the feeling, but it kept returning, washing over him in recent weeks.

"Now, darlin', you're just gettin' all out of sorts, because you don't care much for Randall."

She'd been sunk against the passenger door for twenty miles now, baiting him about his driving. Sulking at his choice of tweed jacket and slacks over the dark suit she had suggested, making him know she felt over-dressed by comparison.

"It's just the jitters, darlin'. All engaged couples get the jitters and that's all that's goin' on. You're just jittery. Mary Ellen told me that she and Randall nearly fell apart with the jitters, but they're just fine now."

"I don't blame her. She must have had a lot of second thoughts about good old pudgy Randall."

"Now, darlin', it doesn't become you to snipe."

The off-ramp to Zion Crossroads rose in the headlights and on impulse, he jerked the Porsche to the right at the last moment and headed down the ramp.

"Where are you *goin*? Do we need gas or somethin'?"

"We need to talk." Without the driving gloves, his knuckles would have shown white on the wheel.

"*Talk*? Darlin', we're going to be late as it is. What do we need to talk about, that won't wait 'till later?"

He wheeled across the tarmac apron of the *Trucker's Home Gas and Eats,*' cutting the tires against the gravel of the parking lot, headed for the far corner. Bobby spun the car to a stop, shutting off the engine and lights. He turned in the seat to face her. Ginny's jaw was set, the mouth a straight red line, arms folded across her chest. No, not folded. Clenched with anger was more accurate. This wasn't a great place or a great time for conversation, but he knew there were no proper places, no proper times for what he had to say.

"Ginny, it's not working." He dropped his hands in his lap. "I just can't do this."

"Bobby, get hold of yourself." She glared at him. "It's just a foolish dinner, with an old friend of mine and we're goin' to be damned late."

"Jesus Ginny, I'm not talking about the goddamn dinner. I'm talking about us, you and me. It's you and me that aren't working and this goddamn dinner is just a stupid example." His words felt like a rush, the first moments of some drug and he watched her arms relax, watched her make a recovery from anger to conciliation, as she so often did when his anger flared.

"We want different things from life Ginny, we just don't have any common ground."

"Now, darlin', let's just have this little old conversation later." She put a hand on his leg and he wished he could jump out of the car and walk away.

"Let's just put this little old car in gear and get back on the road and we'll talk on the way home. I know you don't like all the parties, but we'll feel better on the way home, with a little wine in us."

God, he realized, she doesn't even know what I'm talking about.

"We might even pull off to the back of one of those rest stops on the way home and I'll do you, like I like to sometimes when I'm feelin' hot. It'll be better later, darlin'."

"Won't work, Gin. We're going to talk this all the way through and I don't give a shit about Mary Ellen or lard-ass Randall or their goddamn dinner. We're not going. We can call later and tell them the car broke down or we had a wreck or whatever. But we're not going. We're going to talk this through."

"Bobby, sometimes you just make me so *angry.*" Her face reddened and she turned to the window, arms clenched across her chest again.

"I know. That's why I want to break the engagement."

"*What?*" The word was a rifle-shot. "*Break the engagement?*" She wheeled on him, glaring like a cat. "Because sometimes I get angry, you want to *break our engagement?*"

"I guess that would be reason enough, the constant bickering. If we're like this now, what the hell will we be like when we're married, ten years, twenty years down the road?" He knew he had to tell her the other reason, the reason that went beyond reason enough. Knew he was going to have to tell the world and right now, the world began with Ginny.

"There's more. There's someone else. Someone else I love."

"Why you slimy, worthless, creepy son of a bitch."

The words were slow and murderous. Her eyes burned at him from the place she had wedged herself against the window, facing him. Backed up as far as she could ram herself against the door, her voice low and without the slightest southern accent.

"You miserable cock-sucker. All the time I've been planning a wedding and sitting down in your goddamn home, with your goddamn mother to plan it, you've been creeping around behind my back, finding some slut to screw." No hysterics, no tears or recriminations, she was venomous and striking out with gutter words.

"*Who is she?* Who is this worthless, scheming piece of pussy you plan to replace me with?"

"It's not a woman." No turning back.

"What? What the hell does that mean, *not a woman?*"

"It's a man, Ginny. I'm gay and have been my whole life."

Bobby didn't know what to expect and didn't really care anymore. He felt like something he'd held inside him for so long it was part of him, was gone. Not relief. Not the kind of thing you feel when you're a child and some terrible childlike secret has been found out. Just an undefined lifting of weight. That was it, he felt weightless and it made him want to laugh, this fact of this weightlessness, this floating. Maybe she would shut up. He didn't really care. She didn't shut up.

"A *man?*" Ginny's voice was rising, losing control, edging toward hysteria. "*Gay?* What is this, some joke? Is that it, Bobby? Is this some kind of joke, because if it is, I'm not amused."

Her arms were at her side and all the careful pretensions of body position, all the choreography of her anger were gone. For probably the first time, Bobby saw in her eyes the actual emotion of the moment. Absolute, flat-out Ginny, without pretext or coloring or disguise. She was startled, but there was questioning and fear, amazement and disbelief in her eyes.

"You've been fucking me for months and loving it."

"Being gay doesn't mean I can't fuck a woman and enjoy it."

"I *hate* that word gay."

"I don't care much for it myself. There seems to be so little gaiety in being gay."

"I suppose you know, you've thrown me just about the only argument I can't fight."

She was a little slumped now in the seat and he suddenly felt sorry for her. Almost wanted to reach out and touch her hand or her arm. She was such a shell of a woman and now, in the back of a gravel parking lot in Zion Crossroads, Virginia, it seemed the shell was gone and somehow she needed protection.

"Why did you do this to me, Bobby? Why did you do this to us?"

"I guess I thought it would work. I know now that was foolish and terribly unfair to you. But I somehow thought that a wife and family, a life here in Virginia like the life my parents led, would in some way make me well, make me all right." He rolled the window down, suddenly needing air.

"I know now I *am* all right, I *am* well. That I live a life many men and women live." He took a deep breath of spring air and watched her stare vacantly out the other window.

"I'm sorry, Gin, I really am sorry that you're paying the price for my self-knowledge. When engagements break up, it should be both people's responsibility. At least a little. This isn't your fault and I guess I'm sorry it isn't. That would be easier." She continued her gaze and he wondered if she was listening.

"It isn't my fault either, except for letting it go this far. For not having faced my life and what it means, a long time ago."

She stirred and looked at him as though he were a stranger, as if he were someone from whom she'd just asked the time. "So, what do we do now?"

"Do?"

"Yes, Bobby, *do*." The edge came back into her voice. "What do we *do*, Bobby? Just put an announcement in the papers, in the 'corrections' column? Say we're sorry, but due to circumstances beyond our control, you're in love with a man and we're calling everything off? Sorry to put all you mothers and fathers and cousins and brothers and friends and aunts and uncles and stray dogs and cats through all of this?" She looked at him blankly and he realized that he was no longer a love lost, but a social embarrassment she must face.

"What do we fucking *do*?"

"Well, I suppose you announce that you've broken off the engagement, Gin. Use any excuse you care to or none at all, for that matter." He felt the flood of fresh air sweep across the parking lot and watched a trucker climb into the cab of his tractor. "Engagements have been broken before and I guess they'll be broken again and the real reasons are almost never given. If you want to tell the world I'm gay and you're shocked, I guess that's all right too. I would rather have it come from me."

"You're going to *announce* it? You're going to fucking *announce* it and make me look like the laughing-stock of Richmond, of all fucking Virginia?" First disbelief and hopelessness had been sucked from her, like an ebb-tide. Now the rip-tide of anger was flooding back.

"Ginny, I am a public man and I expect to have a public career. I have no timetable for this. But I won't have my sexuality sniffed out and speculated upon by sniggering gossips, glancing at me in restaurants and whispering behind their hands. This has got to come out. Not dragged out, but explained publicly. And explained by me, not some press-agent or campaign handler."

"*Whispering* about you! *Whispering* about *you?*" Her voice was low again, the venom was back, a snakelike hissing of the words.

"What about the whispering about *me?* How do you think I'm going to feel, seeing people duck behind their hands and snigger about *me?* I don't even have a fucking choice! This is your little announcement, that you drop on me on the way to a dinner party. In the middle of some fucking parking lot, for chrissakes and I don't even have a fucking *choice.*"

"I know. I'm sorry."

"You're sorry. You're fucking *sorry.* Well, thank you very much for that. I'm sorry too."

Maggie and Bob had talked for the past four hours. Dismissing the lingering servants shortly before ten, as soon as the last dinner dishes were removed, they talked. Through an unusual second bottle of wine, they talked.

He told her in detail about the meeting with Larry Harwood. They drifted to the kitchen for cold pie from the refrigerator and Maggie made a pot of coffee. The two of them sat at the kitchen table and he filled in the details of the sketchy conversations they'd had over the past few months. Particulars of his meeting with Prentiss Everett, a meeting that had shocked him and made him begin to understand just how far out of the loop he had drifted. A United States Senator getting inside information, knowledge he had no access to, from a private citizen.

Romeri hadn't shocked him. There were always Romeri's around and always would be. Men with power and money, who lusted after more power and more money, looking at the Congress as their private hunting ground. Business as usual, to be expected. Romeri had Wilson Baker in his pocket and Wilson had tried to soften Bob. That was business too and when it wasn't working, Pres Alberts was dragged out, polished up and sent around to find out what kind of deal had to be made to get control of the Chairmanship.

It could be done and Bob had seen it done. Seen un-shakable seniority shaken. Men higher and lower than himself, pulled out of positions of power when the stakes were high enough. Forced out with hastily contrived references to the pull of personal affairs. Press conferences, attended by the smiling executioner who regretted the call to personal life for the benefit of cameras. Listing achievements, nodding thoughtfully through the sad announcement, shaking the tired hand, gripping the slumped shoulder. When the money brokers and power brokers were hungry enough, even the immovable moved.

Romeri was both hungry and rich, his power running all the way to the Oval Office. Maggie refilled the coffee cup and put a hand on his shoulder.

"Maybe Larry Harwood's right."

She stood there, coffee pot in one hand and the other on the back of his neck. She set the pot down and rubbed his shoulders, strong fingers working on the spot on the right side that always knotted up when he was worried.

"Maybe it's time to buy the place in Ireland and let Bobby have this place. It's what we've always talked about."

"Maybe."

Her fingers felt good and the muscle began to relax. He ran his hand up to hers and covered her fingers.

"I even broached Jerrold about it the other day, in a weak moment. He'd love it. Love to put in some years hunting before he retires and I get too goddamn old to sit a horse."

"You're twenty years away from that."

"Yeah."

She picked up the pot and returned it to the stove and he watched her standing there and felt tears in his eyes.

"Maggie, how is a man supposed to know when to fight and when to cut and run?"

She came back to the table and sat down, stirring her coffee. "Sometimes it's not cutting and running." A long time since they'd had this conversation about 'duty.' They'd talked about such things a lot, when he was a freshman Senator. But somehow over the years, he'd come to know his duty and neither of them felt the need to pull it apart anymore. "Sometimes its knowing which battles can be won and which ones can't. You think you can win this one, Bob?"

"No."

"Neither do I."

"What then, just quit? Just quietly retire and drift off to Ireland and try to feel that I haven't let anybody down?" He got up, walked into the butler's pantry and found a bottle of brandy, pouring a little into the coffee. He looked at her and she nodded and he poured a shot in her cup.

"What say you, my muse?"

"Doesn't even a small part of you wonder if they're right? Don't you wonder too, where the country is headed? How we're going to solve all the unsolvable problems, that just seem to be getting worse, while the time and the money and the ability to solve them runs out?"

"Sure I do. What else could a thinking man wonder in Washington?"

"Well?"

"Ah, Maggie, it's the same old question. Does the end really justify the means? God, we've gotten so that no one wants to work anything *out* anymore." He drained the last of the coffee and poured a quarter cup of brandy.

"The problems are all solvable, we just don't seem to have the will to solve them anymore. It's awfully hard for me to give up on the system, bent and battered and sometimes as broken as it is. Awfully hard to give up on what we call democracy. To trust someone to jam stainless steel chips in our heads and re-create society from their point of view. What if they're wrong? What if they're evil? We're on the threshold of a whole new humanity and no one's really asking the ultimate participants if they want to *try* a whole new humanity."

"Someone had to do it," she said. "To start this unknown experiment called the United States. Is it all that different?"

"Oh, I know Mag, but there were controls back then. All kinds of controls that have served us well up to now. And I'm afraid we're going to throw them out, because we're spoiled children. Unwilling to find compromises, stamping our foot, bursting into tears and taking our toys home in a moment of anger."

"No one's talking about getting rid of the controls, Bob. No one's talking about disbanding the Constitution, at least so far as you've told me." She went into the pantry again and rummaged around in the cupboards, until she found the cigarettes, came back and tossed them on the table, then began to open the pack. "Didn't Larry say that it would all come by the Committee?"

"Yes… and it will, I'm sure. Come in front of Pres Alberts and get debated and passed."

"That's the system, Bob."

"I know, Maggie. I know the system." He reached for the cigarettes and joined her, leaning back and inhaling, feeling lightheaded.

"*EVOKE* started out as a unique little piece of computer technology and no one took it seriously. But we were struggling for some kind, any kind, of control over population growth and the sterility amendment got tacked on because the administration thought it could be sold as part of the package. Almost like selling automobiles… frighteningly like selling automobiles. If you want the car, take the high-end audio system as well." He flicked the ash from his cigarette in the saucer. "They were right. The public bought it, in spite of the rage of the Catholic Church, the ACLU and a few other groups. Now, twenty million people have virtually given up their right to raise families, for the pleasures *EVOKE* offers. There's not even a debate anymore."

"Raising a family is still an option."

"Yeah well, sure it is, but the government now has their finger in that too. You need to qualify for access to the sperm-bank. Yeah, sure… I guess, still an option. Christ, Maggie, it just wasn't *meant* to be this way."

"I know, Bob, and I'm not taking the other side, because I don't know if I'm *on* the other side. But we were never meant to explode onto this earth and wreck it so quickly, either." She lit her cigarette.

" You and I," she said, "talk about going to Ireland to spend the end of our lives in all that green simplicity. But look at us. We're able to do that, because we have more money and opportunity than all but the tiniest fraction of the world's people. The ones we're leaving behind are piling up in the cities, without enough jobs and no place to send their kids for a decent education."

"I know."

"What happens, if someone like Larry Harwood doesn't come along and try to get a grip on it? Can we depend on the people, who just keep getting poorer and poorer, more and more desperate, to come up with a better way? Where does it end, Bob? In some sort of horrible plague, that sweeps the world? Something out of the Middle Ages? Something that pares us back to a supportable size? You tell me our technological growth is the only hope you see for a way back from all this mindless destruction of resources. What happens to that technology if we tip over in the meantime? Do we just kick it all back ten centuries and start over?"

"But we're talking about people's *minds*, Maggie. We're talking about direct access, from the very top of the pyramid, to the way people *think*... the way they perceive the world."

"Is that really any different than it's always been?"

"It'll be all inclusive, Mag. Pretty damned soon, it'll be all inclusive and it's never been that way before."

"There will be people who will never hook up, Bob. There will always be a certain number of people, who will stand outside the system and shout. They've always been there, too."

"Yes, and I know it's a pretty pessimistic view. But it may just be that the ones at the top, the few in control, will use *EVOKE* to inspire the hatred and distrust of those on the outside. Perhaps they'll be hunted down and destroyed. Then, where's the voice of opposition?"

"That's pretty gruesome, Bob." She stubbed out the cigarette. "We've gotten down to choices between the anarchy of hopeless starving people and some small group acting as an avenging god. Maybe it's time for us to go to bed and see if we're a bit more hopeful in the morning."

"Ah, Maggie, my darling Maggie." He stretched his legs and sat back in the chair, reaching for another cigarette.

"I need you, as I've always needed you, to help me think this one through. There's no putting it off, no sleeping on it. Help me, Mag. Sit here and talk to me a while longer."

"You want my advice?"

"You know I do. I always have and you've always given it when I've asked." He chuckled. "Sometimes, when I didn't ask, but needed it and didn't know."

"I think it's time for us to go to Ireland."

"You think I'm wrong?"

"Not wrong, Bob. Not right either, maybe. Perhaps it's just a time in the history of civilization when there's a crack in the fault line. The continents are shifting again, a rattling of human confidence coming from that. Lot's of shaking and rolling and falling down of people's ideals and faith in the future. Clouds of dust around their ability to cope and a general running out into the streets, trying to cope in panic, waving their arms and screaming."

"And you think I'm part of that? Part of the running and screaming and panic?"

"Of course not. You're the voice of reason in the middle of all that chaos. But earthquakes are not a time for reason and maybe you're standing on the wrong side of the crack."

"Do *you* think I'm on the wrong side of the crack?"

"Yes, my dear, sweet loving husband, I do. All of this will settle out and the rebuilding will begin and mankind will probably survive, but I think it's time for us to go to Ireland."

EIGHTEEN

Spring came to Fairacres in a rush, as it often does in Virginia. Magnolia and azalea exploded against a backdrop of budding trees, the woods a green haze of promised leafy tangle that would darken and intensify as the days marched toward summer.

The last hunt of the season was some weeks gone by, vixen heavy with pups and whelping not far off. New life in these old woods. Young foxes to hunt, once they'd been weaned and learned to hunt, marking territories and staking out their own small part of the rolling Virginia countryside. New leaves, tightly wrapped at branch tips, unfurled themselves all according to species, locked in genetic timelessness, showing themselves shyly or with boldness at the break of season. Insects, frogs and other woodland creatures cracked eggs, wriggled out of cocoons, dried wings, rested from the breathlessness of birth.

A reawakening, new and hopeful and yet nothing changed, merely the seasonal shift that signaled starting over. Horses welcomed the leisure and freedom of spring pastures after a hard season, free from their confining stables. Saddles and bridles were soaped, oiled, polished and gleaming in the tack room, put by for the time being as interest shifted from riding to the spring race season. The extra stable hand had been let go to find summer work and the remainder idled away their hours, a time when minor repairs gave way to cigarettes and stories.

The house was open front to back and a red, white and blue-striped tent had been set up in the forecourt. From this patriotic canvas, at about two in the afternoon, Bobby Fairweather would announce his candidacy, declaring for his father's seat in the United States Senate.

Television crews worked among catering trucks, everyone carrying something, stepping over cables with the busyness of business. A sort of measured liveliness, professional to be sure, but with that indefinable sense of expectation that accompanies an opening-night. This show had run for generations, the youngest in a family of actors about to take the stage, the audience expected in about an hour.

Though it hadn't been announced, the President would be among that audience and an area for his arriving helicopter had been fenced off in the kennel courtyard, out of general view. The Presidential limousine was parked innocuously in an aisle of the kennels horse-barn. The Secret Service had been there since yesterday afternoon, trying to look as if they belonged in the country.

Jerrold was somewhat awed by the whole event in his front yard, helpful as always and fascinated by the limousine. The President's chauffeur lounged and smoked and chatted with him, letting him sit where the President sat, letting him slide behind the wheel, to peer down the long hood and admire the fender flags. His wife, Anne kept a fresh pot of coffee going and the screen door to the kitchen was in constant motion.

The back lawn was the very definition of understated elegance, freshly cut and manicured, showing great sweeps of yellow daffodils along the edges of the woods. For that was where most everything would happen after the announcement. Seven small tents, each midnight blue with narrow white piping at the entries, were arranged to provide ample access to the wines and hors d'oeuvres that would accompany a small band.

Those invited, would enjoy a chat about early golf and the latest busted marriage, as well as the opportunity to savor the probability of a fourth Fairweather in the Senate.

Bobby was nervous. The caterers and television crews were not nervous. The Secret Service fell somewhere in the middle, as they always did at public showings of their President. Publicly confident and privately edgy.

Bob looked down from the window of the upstairs study. "Looks like they know what they're doing down there, Maggie." She came in from their dressing room, wearing a stunning silver silk dress of medium length, fitted at the top and waist and running to a river of pleats. "You look very young and very attractive in that dress."

"And you look very relaxed and retired. How do you feel, now that it's here?"

"I announced a month ago, Mag. And I feel a damn-site better than I thought I would, so what's so special about today?" He chuckled and sat down across from her.

"Today's the 'Changing of the Guard,' no matter when you announced.

"Yeah... feels fine."

At about one thirty, the first guests began to arrive. By three the front doors of the mansion were closed and locked, corralling everyone temporarily in the front court, to mill about until the announcement was made. Afterward they could do what they had really come to do, watch the powerful show off their power and have a good time.

Twenty-five car-hikers were there in uniform, to open doors and hustle the arriving cars out a side gate to the east pasture. Rain had been a worry. The pasture would be a mire in the rain, but there was none, the sky agreeably clear and sunny. By two-thirty, the fifteen hundred seats under the tent were filled and an overflow crowd stood around the outside edges. There were murmurings of thirst and more than one pocket-flask caught the sun.

Bob and Maggie and Bobby came out the front door, smiling and shaking hands and acknowledging friends with a wave or a wink, on their way to the tent. Bobby and his mother sat in the first row, as Bob climbed the several steps to the lectern and waited for quiet.

"Friends, neighbors, a few of you from the press who've known me over the years, thank you for coming." The smile was relaxed and he waited for the murmurings to quiet.

"About an hour ago, Maggie asked me how it felt to be stepping back into private life and likened today to a changing of the guard. Well, it feels just fine. But this is not an aristocracy and the so-called guard will only change if you good people and the rest of the voters of Virginia feel that Robert Billings Fairweather the third, is qualified for that guard and has your best interests at heart. I'm satisfied that he does, but I'm his father and have only known him all his life. This is his day and not mine, so I'm proud to introduce to you, my personal choice for the next United States Senator from Virginia, Bobby Fairweather."

The crowd cheered and the band played the first few bars of "Old Virginia," as Bob waved at them and stepped down to shake hands with his son and give him a hug. Bobby was still nervous, but it ebbed away in his father's embrace and he mounted the steps, eager to get on with it. The cheering continued and he waited for it to quiet, knowing it was more for his father than himself. An eager tribute to Bob, for eighteen distinguished years in the Senate. They finally quieted and he stepped to the microphones.

"Thanks Dad. You and your father and his father's father, have set a standard of service and foresightedness, in a combined sixty years of dedication to the government of this country and this state that I expect to live by." There was polite applause, perhaps a little holding back to see how the younger Fairweather handled himself. "You're right, there are no family legacies, no rights of passage in the Senate. A seat in government is earned, not given. Just as the trust of the people of Virginia is earned, not given. Let me tell you my plans. Let me share my hopes for that trust and my hopes and aspirations for the people of my state... my home... my Virginia... "

He went on to outline a broad, yet focused and well-defined platform for the conduct of his office. He spoke sincerely and well, because he was sincere. As the words flowed, extemporaneously, with nothing more than the five by seven note cards for guidance, he knew the goals could not be achieved, not in their entirety. Bobby told them that and they looked at him a little more intently.

The things he could not and would not tell them, flashed across Bobby's mind even as he made this speech. No one grows up in the house of a Senator, he thought to himself, without knowing the agony as well as the constant energy of compromise. *The art of the possible* and his father excelled at that art. But the dedication to brush and stroke, the ability to take the art of the possible to another level, a level of integrity as he defined integrity, had finally brought him down. That was why Bobby stood in front of the microphones, ten years at least before he had expected to be there. He was proud of his father's failure. In that sixty years of family service, he was most proud of his father's willingness to step down rather than make this ethical concession. But he wouldn't tell them that and the thoughts flew across his mind in a separate channel as he told them his plans and measured their applause. He watched himself, somehow from a distance, as he held the stage in a first starring role.

"Ladies and gentlemen, I would like to introduce my staff. The people who will be working with me, not only until the election, but well after that if we win… and we *expect* to win." The anticipated applause washed back over him and he watched his father smiling and nodding at his mother.

"Some of these people you know. They've agreed to continue from my father's staff. And I feel that's an important endorsement of their faith in our shared political philosophy. As I've outlined, much will change and these people will be there to help me make changes."

"First of all, Sally Brentwood, Dad's appointment secretary and my new Director of Women's Issues." Applause, as Sally stood and waved.

"Next, Dan McCarthy, who will continue as my Senior Aide in Government Affairs." Applause again, as Dan stood.

"And, finally, my Campaign Manager, Webster Brooking." Polite applause and exchanges of 'who's Web Brooking?' glances. Bobby settled in and gripped the lectern.

"I'd like to say a few words about Web, because not many of you know him. Web is a freelance writer in Richmond, writing mostly about sporting and political events in Virginia and, as all freelance writers are, halfway through a novel." Polite laughter. "He wrote an expose' several years ago on the then current conditions in Virginia's mental hospitals, a piece that took a year to research and write, resulting in a restructuring of that system. A building program, very long overdue that brought a new Director and a number of new facilities that are now under construction. Web Brooking is a very fine writer, with a fine mind and an impatience with bureaucracy." He paused and gripped the edge of the lectern, taking a deep breath.

"Web Brooking is also my lover and has been for nearly two years."

There was an ear shattering moment of silence and then a gabbling noise, as over fifteen hundred people turned to one another and put their own interpretation on what they thought they had heard.

Two-dozen flashbulbs went off in Bobby's face and the television cameras zoomed in, some of them swinging to crowd reaction. Cameramen and directors, suddenly jolted, spoke softly into mobile phones, to hold time on the evening news. Bobby waited for quiet, ignoring shouted questions from reporters, feeling suddenly very calm. The crowd finally quieted, when they saw him waiting for their attention. There was evidently more. What more could there be?

"Thank you for your attention. I know that statement may shock a good many of you. Fewer perhaps today than twenty or fifty or a hundred years ago. Today will be my only statement on this issue and Web and I will make no further comment, answer no questions, today or any other day." There was a murmur and a few more shouted inquiries from reporters. Bobby looked directly at them. "Today or *any other day*. I would, however, like to quote Thomas Jefferson. It's a popular thing here in Virginia, to quote Jefferson. And I guess it's hard to listen to any politician, without Jefferson creeping in."

"In any event, he was writing about his authorship of the Statute of Virginia for Religious Freedom, at the time. And I think it's not unfair to equate gay-rights and religious-rights. It was 1777 and he wrote, *The legitimate powers of government extend to such acts only as are injurious to others. But it does me no injury for my neighbor to say there are twenty gods, or no god. It neither picks my pocket, nor breaks my leg.'* Flashbulbs flashed and cameras swung.

"I would suggest, that the relationship between myself and Web Brooking, neither picks your pocket, nor breaks your leg. Ladies and gentlemen, Web and I will have a great deal upon which to comment as this campaign goes forward. Virginia and the Country face challenges that are very nearly unprecedented and there is much to say, much to ask. On this issue, we have no further comment." He paused and, miraculously, they paused with him.

"Thank you very much for coming. There are refreshments on the back lawn. We look forward to your support in a very vigorous campaign."

With that, he stood down, shook hands with Dan McCarthy, who threw an arm around his shoulder. He hugged Bob, Maggie, Web and Sally, skillfully ignoring microphones shoved in his face. Twenty flashbulbs went off as he hugged Web. They made their way to the now opened front door, through the house and onto the terrace and lawn. Bobby thought, momentarily, of the time the Governor had made him wet his pants and knew he'd never have that feeling again. As a waiter offered champagne, the chop of the Presidential helicopter could be heard over the edge of the woods.

There was a general excitement at this recognized sound, a shading of eyes and looking toward the sky, knowing someone important was about to arrive. The wondering, the cautious inquiry, the electric anticipation that it *might* be the President.

He was after all, a Virginian. He was after all, an ex-Senator of this state and long-time good friend of Fairweather's. Conversations quickly turned from Bobby's announcement. Some would always refer to it as a 'confession.'

Then, very suddenly the President arrived, just walked out of the back of the mansion with Bob and

Maggie, as though they'd come from a conversation in the library. The three of them stood and chatted and smiled, obviously at ease with one another. But it didn't take long for the hushed circle to form around them and of course that made any easiness impossible. The three began to drift through the crowd, pausing with friends, political allies and political enemies. The circle grew smaller and uncomfortably tight, following the three like a spotlight across a darkened stage.

A few words were expected, needed. Lawrence Harwood knew that, he always knew that, it was part of the drill and of course he had carefully prepared a few off the cuff remarks. Remarks hardly anyone would remember, but in whose glow fifteen hundred people would bask for days to come. Each with a faulty recollection tailored to fit their own perspective.

A microphone and PA system appeared, not accidentally nor by chance. The lectern from the tent out front also appeared. The President stood above the crowd by the height of the platform, smiling and waving, savoring the applause. Finally holding both hands up, palms out, he asked for quiet with a mock plead of eyes.

"Friends and neighbors, Bob, Maggie, Bobby ... " He smiled benevolently down on his hosts and the beaming candidate.

"I called off any international incidents for the day, because it's important for me to be here to add my complete and enthusiastic support for the candidacy of Bobby Fairweather." Applause, laughter, mixtures of both and a few zealous whistles, amid much craning of necks, cell-phones held high for pictures and general jostling for more advantageous position.

Reporters, caught off guard, remembering now that they were reporters, scribbled questions, all of them the *same* question. The nervous young men with crew cuts and jackets conveniently unbuttoned, scanned those outstretched hands, studying eyes across a sea of eyes.

"I've known Bobby all his life. Know his father and knew his grandfather. Known the family dedication for the welfare of the State of Virginia and the personal sacrifices that have been made by the Fairweather family in the service of this state." He paused, owning this moment as few politicians ever own their moments before the public.

"They are many. They are meaningful… to the rich and the not so rich. To the miners and shopkeepers, the working men and women. To the young and unprotected, the old and infirm. They have a great new young champion in Bobby Fairweather." Sustained and enthusiastic applause broke once more, amid the heads turned to one another. The whispered question in different forms of the same question, '*does he know, do you suppose he has heard?*' Anything handy to wave was waved. Harwood let it run, judging the strength of the support, knowing when to hold his hands up for quiet, before it came of its own accord.

"And I don't want to take anything away from this well-deserved focus on Bobby. But I'd be greatly remiss, if I didn't take a few moments to thank his father. Ladies and gentlemen, please help me thank my friend, the Honorable Robert Billings Fairweather, for his dedication and service to the Sovereign State of Virginia." Huge applause roared back from his appeal, sustained and rolling. Everything not nailed down was now waving. Bob Fairweather was popular, but a great share of the clamor was born of pride for their Virginian President and his unexpected arrival in their midst. The President reached down and pulled Bob Fairweather up the steps to stand with him.

"Bob, we're going to miss you in the Senate." He beamed the beam of Presidential light in Bob's direction, pausing as if searching for words.

"Ladies and gentlemen, I asked him not to go. Matter of fact, I pleaded with him. We need him badly in the Senate, chairing the important committees he chairs. Giving counsel to his fellow Senators, giving counsel to his President. But he's a man among men and I respect his need to move on as much as I regret and tried to prevent it. Bob, I thank you as your friend and I thank you as your President." They shook hands and the President hugged an obviously embarrassed Senator.

The crowd went wild again and took its own time to settle down. Harwood reached his hand down to Bobby. Pulling him up the steps, the three of them stood together, holding upraised hands as cameras clicked and video-cams whirred to catch the moment.

Reporters shouted questions to the President, the same question in varied forms and at varied volumes. He could easily have ignored them. This was, after all, no press conference, but he stood and waited for the crowd to quiet. Waited because he wanted this question. Wanted it from the raised stage and microphone and *had come to answer it*. The crowd sensed the question, in the closer rows first, but then the hush rolled back like a wave.

"Gentlemen, gentlemen, this is not a press conference. But I'll entertain just one or two questions, as long as they relate to this wonderful event."

They did. They did, indeed and there was a flurry of shouts.

"You there." Harwood pointed to one of the old pros, whom he could have called by name, a man he knew could get the question right.

"Mr. President, are you aware of the announcement, made by the candidate an hour ago?"

"That, I believe, is why we are all here." A chuckle from the President and some scattered laughter from the crowd, but they were straining to hear, eager for the follow up.

"Mr. President, the candidate also announced that he is a homosexual. Engaged in a long-term gay relationship with his campaign manager, Webster Brooking. Would you comment, please."

Harwood paused and looked at the reporter, as though the question was new to him, as though he was caught a bit off guard.

"Mr. Edwards … " He paused a half heartbeat longer, knowing the timing. "I am not acquainted with Mr. Brooking. But I've known Bobby Fairweather his whole life and I have the greatest respect and admiration for his integrity. Respect for his honesty in all matters, including whatever lifestyle he chooses to pursue." He paused again, waiting for the murmur to subside.

"You have stood, Mr. Edwards, pad and pencil in hand for many years in Washington and I know you to be a man who is careful with his judgment. I believe you know, as I know, that if all of the dedicated men of honor who have served their country in an alternative or so called *gay* lifestyle had not been willing to serve, this country would be much the poorer." A two-heartbeat pause and polite quiet. "*Much the poorer.*" Half heartbeat pause. "Most of those fine men and women too, I would add, have served and served outstandingly well with the added burden of a hidden lifestyle." Single heartbeat pause.

"If Bobby Fairweather feels the need to serve without this burden, I applaud him for it. More than that, I resoundingly support and urge all others, who value honesty and candor, to vigorously support his candidacy for the United States Senate. I will take no other questions."

The applause was instant but hesitant, as though a huge breath had been exhaled from everyone at the same time. It gained ground, as Harwood turned to shake Bob's hand. Gained still further as he turned the other direction to shake Bobby's hand and gave him a Presidential bear hug. Regained its roar, as the three of them stood, beaming and holding each other's raised hands in the traditional victory gesture.

In the quiet woods behind this cheering, other new wings were spread tentatively. They trembled and dried in the soft spring air, readying themselves for flight.

Bob sat on the big bay gelding, looking down across the rolling Irish meadow. Listening for his hounds, alert for any short-calls from Jerrold's old bent horn and thought to himself, he was much like a forest ranger watching for smoke. Intent on a patch of woods, yet the intensity satisfied him totally.

It had been a bit of a rag-tag start to hunting in Ireland, perhaps. But they'd bought the rambling old seventeenth-century property in mid-June and Maggie had her hands full just trying to put the living areas in order. Harrowleigh, six thousand acres not too unlike the size of Fairacres. A third of a world away, in a corner that remained partly medieval, partly the 'miracle of Europe,' due to computer-literacy and tax laws. That miracle had had its ups and downs in recent decades, but the land remained. Good times, bad times, through wars and famines the land always remained.

A portion of the southwest corner of the mansion's foundation dated to the sixth century, a mere remnant of an early castle that sent Maggie to the archives in Cork, tracing the history of the place. That corner of his home was seven-times the age of his native country and it brought him a sense of perspective. Bob pondered the fact that this corner of

Ireland was so much unchanged from those ancient times, while the balance seemed hell-bent to travel at the speed of light. Maggie's research dedicated them to a good deal of additional care in the remodeling and restoration. Unrushed work, badly needed after a century's slide into disrepair.

Jerrold seemed a young man again. Leaping about the stables, supervising construction of a new kennel, walking-out hounds on summer mornings and tending to a hundred details with the light in his eyes of being home again in this green country.

November now and foxhunting season had finally arrived, ready or not. Jerrold insisted on hunting a full pack, a matter of pride for him that Bob allowed against his better judgment. It had gone well and badly, as hunting does.

Two young Whippers-In were hired locally under Jerrold's practiced eye, along with a stable man, kennel man and two grooms. Amidst all this furor, they were hunting regularly three days a week and Bob was pleased that Maggie joined him nearly half the time. She was glad to be riding alongside him, learning the lay of this green land, revisiting the thrill of hounds in tongue. She thoroughly enjoyed the solitude and promised more when the house and staff was better settled.

One morning when they'd been particularly embarrassed by a wise old dog-fox, Jerrold turned to Bob in exasperation.

"Seems Master, that when I was a younger man, they ran a straighter line. Now, I'm getting older and all the foxes seem to double-back."

Bob had chuckled and remembered the line... a fitting metaphor for life in general and particularly his life in the Senate.

Then was then and now is now. He scanned the woods as first hounds, led by Ravage began to leak tentatively from the edges, heads down and working their way along the dry creek towards the next big patch of timber, Jerrold drifting well behind and letting them work. There were a few small private packs nearby and neighbors who understood the hunting of foxes. Harrowleigh seemed a comfortable choice for their Irish home and Jerrold was the linchpin that made it practical to be away a half-year at a time. The Virginia staff had mostly stayed on when Bobby and Web moved to Fairacres, so Maggie spent a considerable part of her time interviewing for local staff, looking as far as Dublin for a butler to run it all and wishing he were in place to handle housekeeping choices.

Bob nudged the bay, walking quietly along the ridge, watching hounds and reflecting on the past seven months. The Romeri-Everett ticket had pretty much walked away with the election, another of Lonny's well-oiled acquisitions, everything according to plan.

He and Everett hadn't announced until July, coming in 'reluctantly' after the two national conventions. Romeri positioned himself as no more than responding to his sense of 'public duty,' brutally assaulting the Republican and Democratic candidates as ineffective clones of one another. Not a workable program in the lot, which was pretty much true. There wasn't much clear leadership in an atmosphere of vicious partisanship and Larry Harwood had done his best behind the scenes to make sure there wouldn't be. At least on the Republican side.

It had been a blitz third-party move on Romeri's part, totally under his personal control and without any need for compromise. He'd made a simple and clear statement of his platform, including the unprecedented announcement of his full Cabinet, should he be elected. There were no deals to make, no need to respond to the shifting power structures that tied the hands and mouths of party candidates. He *was* the power structure. He knew it, depended on it, operated from it.

The full force of World Star's resources engineered and advertised a sixteen-week campaign that was as well programmed and way more expensive than the introduction of a new line of cars and guaranteed excellent political mileage thrown in. A beautifully crafted and gold-plated media crusade, building slowly to a thundering finish. Lonny made carefully orchestrated appearances, his 'Cabinet' criss-crossing the country in a fleet of corporate aircraft. It was all well-staffed and financed, well-rehearsed in varied shadings of the same clear message: *the country was a corporation and it was time to run it like one. The voters, like stockholders, had the opportunity to elect a board of directors and Alonzo Romeri was the best candidate for its chairman.*

In many ways it made the party candidates look like amateurs, incapable of efficiently running their own campaigns, much less the country. Which was of course, exactly what they were, underfunded and over committed to their party's intravenous-drip of campaign cash. Constantly on the defensive, they lost momentum to a media that smelled blood, trying to hold on by their fingernails. The pundits and talk-shows literally had a field-day comparing the casual confidence of Romeri and fervor of his running-mate with the hesitant and poll-driven blather coming from the Republicans and Democrats. Senatorial and congressional candidates fell all over themselves ingratiating themselves with Lonny and his explosive new brand of politics, feeling in their well-padded bones that life in Washington was no longer predictable. A seat on his band-wagon was available, but Lonny set the terms. Bill Wearley had never had such fun.

There were a couple of dicey weeks when an exposé tried to link Prentiss Everett to drug activity and a purported gangland murder in Chicago. But it seemed to blow over and other papers outside Chicago lost interest.

President Harwood publicly supported his party's candidate, but when questioned by the press, admitted that he 'saw much good' in Romeri's programs. It was enough. It was a runaway and Presidential races would never be the same. The two major parties, their machinery in shambles, licked their wounds and, like the Sicilian mob in Chicago, tried to think of a way back to the good old days.

Bob heard Ravage's deep voice and watched the old hound break from the woods. Head down, he worked his way fifty-yards into the meadow, before deciding it was a cold trail and returning to the pack.

Bobby had come through in pretty good shape, he mused. Even so, it was a close enough race to keep everyone's interest. Bob and Maggie got no sleep at all, watching the satellite broadcast of election returns, five time zones east. Bobby's candor, along with the President's 'off the cuff' remarks had effectively put the cork in the bottle of any whispering campaign.

Ginny had taken the brunt and deserved not a moment of it. Mercilessly pursued by the press. hounded to the point of tears on national TV, she held to her story of a continuing friendship with Bobby and faith in his ability to follow his father into the Senate. The media finally tired, as the story lost any relevance and left her alone. She announced her engagement in October to Robert Wilson Pennant of Baltimore, the old-beau Bobby had saved her from on the dance floor. Heir to a manufacturing fortune in decline, his old family name was a perfect match for Fentress money. This one would last, tickled to death to be called darlin'.

The firebrand attorney from Roanoake, trying to ride a tired horse to the finish, announced as an independent candidate. He jumped too soon and alluded, throughout the campaign to Bobby's 'queer' notions of economics and anticipation of a 'gay lifestyle' in the Capitol. Learning how painful it can be to misunderstand an electorate, he was swept away in a backlash of Virginian independence and his political career was probably finished. The end result was to pull some of the more radical voters away from Bobby's Democratic opponent and angrily swing a good many of the undecided to Bobby's side.

It wasn't all that close, but it was interesting and the national attention on a statewide race gave Bobby instant name recognition across the country, as well as a news-magazine cover.

Romeri was pulling strings for several top committee memberships and it looked as though Bobby would have a running start as a freshman Senator. Bob and Maggie would be home for a month at Christmas, staying for the Inauguration and Bobby's installation in the Senate, then a string of European Cup ski races before a return to Harrowleigh.

The faint notes of Jerrold's horn carried up the ridge from deep in the woods and Bob steadied the bay horse. He listened for hounds, hearing them open, the babble taking on form, shaping itself to the rhythm of a pack in full cry. This fox might not turn back.

The bay's ears were pricked and Bob felt the slight tremble of the horse's anticipation, nudging into a slow gallop, standing in the irons and making his bet where hounds would break from the woods. Jerrold broke cover, looking over his shoulder for the Master. His pink coat caught the early morning sun, as he pointed with his whip-hand to the west, where hounds rippled from the woods in full cry.

Maybe Romeri and Harwood were right, Bob thought. Maybe man would find a way to manage himself on this earth and perhaps they had a new key to that old lock. He hoped so. At any rate, he wished them well, wished them every piece of luck.

Bob Fairweather spurred the big bay horse and galloped after his Huntsman, to the wavering call of *'gone away.'*

ABOUT THE AUTHOR

NOVELS

- *EVOKE* – exploring the societal effects of technology in a fictional context of the near future
- *Letters from Ceilia* – an intimate story of a career woman's struggle in a world run largely by men
- *The Island* – situated in duck-hunting country where two strong men clash in a conflict over land

NON-FICTION

- *The Dark Side of the Moon* – five books of political and social commentary on America's recent history
- *Dick Cheney's Fingerprints* – a collection of observations focusing on the Iraq war and its origins

POETRY COLLECTIONS

- *The Smell of Tweed and Tobacco* – poems spanning relationships and life in Prague
- *Corner of My Mind* – a more introspective collection also discussing the writing process
- *Broken Pieces* – a mosaic of reflections about nature, hunting, travel, politics and life

DRAMA

- *The Island* – a screenplay based on the novel
- *Colors* – a one-act stage play, winner of 1999 Pennsylvania Playhouse competition

Jim Freeman was born in Evanston, Illinois and now lives and writes in Prague. His work has been published in a number of newspapers, magazines and anthologies. His current political and social commentary is available at **www.dark-side-of-the-moon.com**

For print or Kindle editions please visit Amazon.com. For other available formats and to contact Jim, see the author's website at **www.jim-freeman.com**